PEACH

Also by Elizabeth Adler

Léonie

PEACH

Elizabeth Adler

DELACORTE PRESS/NEW YORK

Fiction
Adl

Published by
Delacorte Press
1 Dag Hammarskjold Plaza
New York, New York 10017

Cole Porter's song "I Get a Kick out of You," © 1934 Harms Inc., is reproduced by permission of Chappell Music Limited, London.

I would like to thank M. Arnaud de Mareuil of Champagne Moët et Chandon, Épernay, whose memories of his father Camille de Mareuil's and the Comte de Vogüé's work with the Resistance during World War II, along with M. Jean-Paul Médard's wealth of anecdotes, provided an authentic background for a chapter of this work of fiction.

Thanks too, to Wang UK Ltd, whose splendid word processor saved hours of valuable time.

And, most of all, thanks to my wonderful editor, Maureen Waller, who gave of her time and talents most generously.

This work was first published in Great Britain by Hodder & Stoughton Limited.

Manufactured in the United States of America

First U.S.A. Printing

Library of Congress Cataloging in Publication Data

Adler, Elizabeth.
Peach.

I. Title.
PR6051.D56P4   1986   823'.914   86-24289
ISBN 0-385-29535-9

For my daughter Anabelle, with love

FAMILY TREE

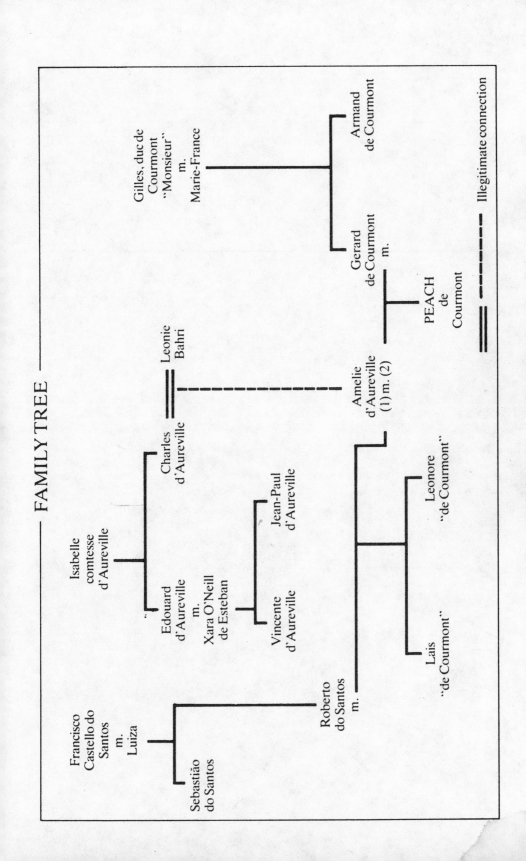

Francisco Castello do Santos m. Luiza

Sebastião do Santos

Roberto do Santos

Isabelle comtesse d'Aureville

Edouard d'Aureville m. Xara O'Neill de Esteban

Vincente d'Aureville

Jean-Paul d'Aureville

Charles d'Aureville

Leonie Bahri

Amelie d'Aureville (1) m. (2)

Lais "de Courmont"

Leonore "de Courmont"

Gilles, duc de Courmont "Monsieur" m. Marie-France

Gerard de Courmont m.

Armand de Courmont

PEACH de Courmont

Illegitimate connection

Part I

Part 1

1

Iowa, USA, 1932

The night was black, without a glimmer of moon or even a single star, and a chill wind searched across the plains, rustling the endless stretches of grain in a sad, rippling lullaby.

The girl was young. Her cheap, brashly patterned summer dress clung to her too-thin body, inching its way up her pale thighs as she struggled from the car with her burden. Standing in the road she gazed doubtfully at the gravel driveway. She could just make out the outline of a large building lit by the flickering gleam of a single lamp.

"Go on. Hurry up, will ya," a man's voice commanded her from the car. "Get it done and let's get out of here."

Stumbling in her high heels, the girl walked down the dark driveway, breathing quickly, clutching the bundle close to her, gasping with pain as she turned her ankle on the treacherous gravel. The walk seemed endless, dark with nameless fears. A walk that would cut her off from her future.

Steps, worn by the frequent scrubbing of unwilling hands, gleamed in the sudden lamplight. Trembling, she lay down her burden, wrapping its blue blanket firmly and checking the pin that held it closed. Lifting her eyes she read the sign inscribed in letters wrought from steel, MADDOX CHARITY ORPHANAGE. Est. 1885. Her eyes fell to the motionless blue bundle. "No message," the man had said, "no notes or they will be able to trace you." The wind soughed down the drive chilling her, and she glanced hesitantly at the polished brass doorbell. She could ring it and then run, she'd be gone before anyone answered. But what if she weren't?

The lamplight caught the pale gleam of her legs and the flimsy scarlet stiletto-heeled shoes as she turned and ran, tripping on the gravel, back down the driveway to the waiting car and her lover. She was free.

The sudden sound of the engine and the roar of its loose exhaust pipe startled the child from his sleep. Struggling in his cocoon of blankets he began to cry, a tiny sound at first, growing louder and then louder until it became a roar. A great shout of anger.

Two women in flannel dressing-gowns and curlers pulled back the massive bolts and threw open the door. "Another baby," said one to the other. "It's the third this month; whatever shall we do with them all?"

"Folks shouldn't go getting themselves kids they don't want," grumbled the other, bending to pick up the screaming bundle. "My God, this one's gonna give us trouble, listen to him yell."

"I'll call the police," said the first, "she can't have gotten far."

"Far enough. I heard the car. We're too close to the county line here – they should've thought of that when they built this place. We get the illegitimate brats from four counties and no chance of finding the mothers. Well, what is it, a boy or a girl?"

The woman unpinned the blanket and lifted the baby, red-faced and still yelling. "A boy," she said, "no more than a couple of days old."

"We'd better take him upstairs and give him a bottle. Maybe it'll stop him yelling before he wakes up the entire place."

Wrapping the blue blanket around him they moved across the cold, darkened hallway.

"What shall we call him?" asked one of the other as they mounted the uncarpeted stairs.

"Noel," she replied firmly.

"But it's April," protested the other. "Noel's a name given to children born on Christmas Day."

The woman's laugh rang harshly in the dark. "Let him have a Christmas name then. It's the closest he'll get to Christmas in here."

2

Amelie de Courmont's room was lit with the glow of a perfect Florida dawn promising another golden day. Closing the door softly behind him, Gerard paused, identifying the tangle of scents that hung in the air. Amelie's favourite perfume, carelessly unstoppered in the big crystal *flacon* that he'd bought her on their last trip to Paris, the butter-yellow jug of fading blossoms whose weightless petals drifted like confetti across the soft silk of the Persian rug, and the green garden scents on the early morning breeze from the open windows.

The baby's elaborate crib, ruffled in white lace, stood by the side of Amelie's bed. Walking softly so as not to disturb his wife and child, he peered at the little pink bundle that was his daughter. Her flawless lids with the ridiculously long curve of blond-tipped lashes fluttered for a moment, as if she knew he were watching her, then her gaze locked with his. His daughter had deep, dark blue eyes, definitely her grandfather's but, unlike Monsieur's, hers were full of innocence. Her hair was neither brown nor blonde, but a sleek bronze shade, somewhere in between. And, miraculously, her skin was not the usual blotched pink and white of the newborn, but a pale golden colour as though from a summer spent beneath some gentle sun. The curve of her cheek, the slender arms and dimpled wrists, the fragile bumps of her spine were dusted with a golden down too fine even for the silkiest velvet. It was exactly, thought Gerard with a smile, like the tender bloom of a fresh peach.

Half-asleep against her pillows Amelie watched as Gerard ran a gentle finger over the baby's soft cheek. After fourteen years of happy marriage she had almost given up hope of giving Gerard a child and when she knew she was pregnant she had hoped for a boy. Gerard would have a son to succeed him and to inherit the business empire created by his father. But Gerard hadn't cared about the sex of the child – he'd been too worried about *her*. Having a baby at forty wasn't the easy business it had been when she was nineteen and married to her first husband, Roberto do Santos. The birth of their twin girls, Lais and Leonore, had been effortless. This time the pregnancy had been tiring and fraught with risk – but it had been worth it even if just to see Gerard's face now, as he looked at their daughter.

"It seems I woke you both," said Gerard ruefully.

Amelie took his hand as he sat beside her on the bed. "I was half-awake, remembering when Lais and Leonore were born. Gerard, I hope they will be pleased with their new half-sister."

"They'll be as thrilled as I am," he replied firmly. "How could they resist her?" Lifting the baby he placed her in her mother's arms. "Just look at our daughter, Amelie. She's a beauty. A perfect little peach."

Amelie laughed delightedly, folding their baby close to her breast. "Of course she is, and she will be named Marie-Isabelle Leonie de Courmont. But from now on, Gerard, she'll be just Peach."

Paris, 1934

At the de Courmont mansion on the Ile St Louis the butler waited, a silver tray in his hand.

"A telegram for you, Mademoiselle, from America."

Lais snatched the flimsy envelope, tearing at it impatiently. It must be the baby. Oh God, she begged, suddenly afraid, let Maman be all right, forty is too told to be having babies. Damn! *It was a girl*. All she needed was *another* sister! *Peach!* My God, what a name. She only hoped the creature could live up to it. Lais stared at the telegram uneasily, unable to shake off the feeling that this new half-sister would cause ripples on her smooth personal pond. Or maybe even a tidal wave.

"It's a girl, Bennet," she called, heading for the door. There was just time to make Cartier's before they closed. She would buy the baby a christening gift, squander her monthly allowance on something wildly extravagant to make up for the guilt at her lack of joy in having a new sister, and something totally unsuitable, damn her, because she didn't really want to give her anything at all. She didn't want to share any part of her life with Peach.

* * *

14

Tossing the expensively wrapped gift into the back of the big, dark blue de Courmont convertible, Lais pulled into the Paris traffic, checking her appearance in the mirror as she drove.

Lais patted her tawny blonde hair doubtfully. Perhaps the short haircut was a mistake? But it *was* fashionable and if you didn't have the latest look, if you weren't wearing the latest style, weren't seen in the smartest places, then you simply didn't exist! She was in Paris supposedly studying at the Sorbonne but, in truth, the number of lectures she attended were few. Her blue eyes looked back at her from the mirror with disarming innocence and Lais turned away impatiently. Maybe she was a bit selfish, but she only wanted to enjoy herself. And the truth was she had a short fuse on boredom.

Lais double-parked the car on the corner of rue St Germain and rue Bonaparte in front of the Café Deux Magots and sauntered towards the young man waiting for her at a table on the terrace.

He had been waiting for her over an hour and empty coffee cups and small glasses marked the passing of time that for him had been an eternity. "Here you are at last," he cried, relieved. "I thought you weren't coming."

Why was it, wondered Lais frowning, that he had seemed so attractive last night? For that matter, why did all the men she met seem more attractive by night than in the cold light of day?

The young man smiled anxiously as the waiter placed a Pernod in front of her. "Your drink, Lais," he said, touching her hand.

"I can't stay," she rose almost immediately. "I'm already late for an appointment."

He knocked over the glass as he pushed past the table after her. "Lais, Lais . . . wait . . ."

Lais pressed a firm white-shod foot on the accelerator. She flung back her head relieved at her escape, taking deep breaths of the special Paris smells of chestnut trees in blossom, of petrol fumes and fresh baked breads and rich coffee and wonderfully scented women. Dusk was closing in, lights sparkled from shops and in cafés, threading jewelled necklaces along the River Seine. The passion she'd felt for him the previous night was gone, withered by his very eagerness to see her and his anxiety to please. What Lais liked was the anonymity of a hotel room, the secret rendezvous in some afternoon apartment, or the shuttered heat of a summer boathouse . . . sometimes she wondered if the intrigue weren't more exciting than the sex. And sometimes it was.

There was that man she'd met the other night, the Russian exile

– Nikolai. He was different, intriguing. His harrowed dark eyes had stared at her with such calculating appraisal that she'd trembled inside. Nikolai was older than her crowd, and maybe a little bit dangerous. She'd waited for him to come over to her, but he hadn't and she'd circled the crowded room, ignoring the rest of the party, lured by his gaze. But when she'd finally approached him, he'd dismissed her with a disdainful smile as though she were a tiresome child and departed, a glamorous woman in large diamonds and ink-blue velvet on his arm. Lais knew Nikolai had been invited to the Villiers' party tonight. And that's where she was heading.

Lais laughed out loud. She was free again and just twenty years old. And life was a marvellous game – to be played on her terms.

3

St Jean Cap Ferrat, France, 1934

Leonore de Courmont hurried across the pink marble hall of the hotel on her way to the restaurant where she had been warned there was a problem of overbooking. Distinguished guests were being kept waiting and were not at all happy about it. It was just one of a dozen problems that had confronted her that day and which only she was able to sort out because, as general manager of the Hostellerie la Rose du Cap she was responsible for the mistakes, as well as the triumphs, that made up its daily life.

Leonore had served her apprenticeship well, beginning at the Palaçio d'Aureville, her mother's family's hotel in Florida. As a child she had lurked wide-eyed in the hotel's great kitchens, marvelling at the flurry of lunchtime activity that seemed to her like a ballet choreographed to split-second timing. The head chef called out the orders to his under-chefs who were cooking meats or preparing vegetables, or whisking delicate sauces, while pâtisserie chefs created elaborate sweet delights, and waiters hurried in and out through the swinging double doors submitting each dish for a quick inspection by the head chef before departing for the restaurant tables. Leonore had got under their feet, earning their temporary wrath as she peered into pots or stole the little pastries. She'd followed the housekeeper, checking the huge piles of linen sheets and fluffy towels that lived in vast closets, loving their fresh crisp smell. She had helped the chambermaids make beds and she'd hovered around the reception desk investigating the miracles of the switchboard. She had chatted with the concierge and with the porters, smiling shyly at the people on whom all this activity centred. *The guests*. It had been a natural progression to the hotel school in Lausanne, and then six months ago, when she was only twenty, Amelie, her mother, had surprised her by giving her the entire responsibility for this new hotel in its jewelled setting – the green wooded headland of Cap Ferrat jutting into the blueness of the Mediterranean that gave the coast its name, the Côte d'Azur.

Leonore could still remember the feeling of terror as her mother, smiling in anticipation of Leonore's delight, had broken the news. How ever would she live up to the task? How could she possibly *cope* when most of the guests would be *older* than she?

"Nonsense," Amelie had dismissed her plea that her inexperience would be disastrous for the new hotel. "I was only a little older than you when I took over the Palaçio in Miami. Your Uncle Edouard simply handed me the keys and said, 'It's all yours – if you don't do it then nobody will. The Palaçio will close before it even opens.' I worked eighteen hours a day then – and I had you and your sister to look after. You must plunge right in at the deep end, Leonore, it's the only way."

Leonore had felt closer to the schoolgirl that she had so recently been than the manager of the Riviera's newest and most exclusive hotel. And she had this awful stammer – true it wasn't so bad now, but when she was upset it resurfaced to embarrass her.

"It's your chance, Leonore," Amelie had said, trying to impart some of her own confidence to her shy daughter. "Take it and win."

It seemed to Leonore that she'd always had to try harder, that she'd always been in the shadow of her outgoing, extrovert sister, Lais. Yet *she* had been cleverer than Lais – it was *her* school reports that Maman and Gerard had been so proud of. But it was Lais who had been the star of the school plays, and Lais who on sports day had collected the little silver cups for hurdles and high jumps and swallow dives. It wouldn't have been like her sister to go in for something long and tedious like the cross-country run or the marathon.

When they were children Lais had discovered that having an almost identical sister could be a distinct advantage when she was in trouble – though Maman and Gerard had soon put a stop to that! And, of course, they weren't *exactly* alike. Lais had blue eyes, like their real father who had died when they were only two years old, and Leonore had the odd tawny-colour eyes of their grandmother, Leonie. "Cat's eyes," Lais had taunted her when they were small, but Leonore had always suspected that they were the one thing that Lais envied about her.

Pausing for a second in front of the large Florentine gilt mirror in the corridor, she smoothed back an escaped strand of fine blonde hair, tightening the velvet ribbon that secured it. Her dark blue silk suit was cool and businesslike and she wore tear-shaped canary diamonds in her ears – a touch of vanity for they complimented her golden eyes. The Cartier watch had been a present from her stepfather Gerard when she had taken over the hotel and she had worn it every day since – like a lucky charm. And so far her luck was holding. No one could mistake Leonore for a carefree holidaymaker; she looked what she was, a young businesswoman with things on her mind that placed a permanent small furrow between her brows. And one of those worries was still her sister, Lais. Stories of Lais's antics in Paris were filtering back to her – and they weren't the sort of stories she'd want Grand-mère Leonie – nor Maman and Gerard – to hear.

With a sigh Leonore placed the gold-rimmed spectacles on her small straight nose, hoping they added a touch of authority a twenty-year-old girl might lack. She would soothe the ruffled egos of her guests with complimentary champagne – the best, naturally – and arrange for an extra table to be squeezed in so that they might be served immediately. Then she must reprimand the receptionist who had taken the booking and warn her to be more careful. The Hostellerie couldn't afford to upset its customers when its reputation was based on exactly the opposite principle. She would make time to scan the bookings for next week to see who needed to be VIP'd – and then she'd dash down the path from the hotel to the villa to dine with her grandmother and Jim. And of course, she'd be late, as usual!

Jim Jamieson watched Leonie making her way along the chalky path that curved around the headland, her step quickening as she drew nearer, heading like a homing pigeon for her beloved villa.

18

From a distance she looked no more than a girl, tall and slender with that long, smooth, cat-like stride that had marked her progress across the starry stages of the world. Even close-up it seemed as though time were reluctant to mar the surface of her smooth skin; there were just the lines of laughter around her eyes when she smiled, or a sad haunted look to her face. He had observed her occasionally, searching in the mirror for some sign of events in her life that Leonie told him she felt sure should be written there, wondering that its tragedies and joys should have left her so unscarred.

Leonie was fifty-six years old and they had been married for seventeen years. Jim still treasured the memory of her as the young midnight-hours poker player, sleeves rolled to elbows, scooping up her winnings with a laugh and leaving the half-dozen passengers who had been able to survive the transatlantic liner's stormy crossing, admiring but broke. Leonie had been the only woman on the voyage to New York to leave her cabin – but only at night when she joined the men in their game. Later she'd confessed that she had been afraid to go to sleep in case the ship went down, but at the time he'd been dazzled by her bravery, her poker playing – and her beauty. It had seemed a simple sort of beauty as she'd walked towards him across the darkened saloon that first night, and only later had he learned that she had the ability to be two people – *his* Leonie Bahri, the half-French, half-Egyptian girl and "Leonie", the great star of the stage who, in bizarre and wonderful make-up and her clinging gold Fortuny gowns, a black panther docile at her feet on its chain, had prowled the stages of Paris and London and New York mesmerizing her audiences with songs of passion. And Leonie still had the same mystery and the same allure for him that he had always felt.

The little brown cat frisked around Leonie's feet and then dashed on ahead to the gate, waiting imperiously for it to be opened. There was always a little brown cat with Leonie – the ancient Egyptians had believed in their immortality, she'd told him with a smile. Despite his attempts to disprove it, Leonie clung to the belief in the Egyptian goddess Sekhmet's mysterious powers. Hadn't the goddess proved her power? Monsieur was dead. She still kept Sekhmet's statue, on its tall marble plinth, in their room, lit softly so that it seemed to glow in the dark. Of course she agreed when he said that surely she could no longer believe that Sekhmet ruled her life, but her eyes avoided his and her expression would grow remote.

Shrugging aside the past, Jim walked down the path to meet her. There were enough family problems without bringing up the dead. Should he, or should he not, tell Leonie about her granddaughter? Leonie's great friend, Caro Montalva had telephoned from Paris only an hour ago to say that something had better be done before Lais caused as big a scandal in the de Courmont family as Leonie had done forty years ago.

Leonie's garden never failed to give her pleasure, it was so full of memories. The reflecting pool with its fountains shimmered in the twilight and beside it was the bench placed so that she could watch the sunset over the sea. And there was the flowering oleander that she had planted in remembrance of Bébé, her very first and most beloved cat. Terraced steps led to the curve of beach, tucked between the tangled green headlands that framed the blue and jade and aquamarine bay.

The villa itself had been just a small foursquare white building when it first became hers, but now it had sprawled and expanded with arches and terraces and terracotta tiled floors, cool and white and green-shuttered. Her home and her refuge. The place she loved most in the world. *Her life had begun here.* And it was here she had finally come to terms with who she was.

Old Madame Frénard was pottering around the dining room setting out Leonie's favourite blue plates and the big blue lustre jug full of bright summer flowers. Madame Frénard had been with her grandmother ever since Leonore could remember. "Bonsoir, Madame," she called loudly to combat the old lady's increasing deafness.

"Bonsoir, Mademoiselle Leonore. What news of your little sister Peach?"

Leonore laughed. Three-month-old Peach was the centre of all interest at the villa. "I have some photographs to show you later, Madame Frénard," she called.

On the long terrace with its view of the bay a silver ice-bucket beaded with chilly drops held a bottle of champagne. Leonore waved as Jim and her grandmother walked up the steps to the terrace. They made a handsome couple, Jim tall, clean-cut and all-American, and Grand-mère, who managed to look French and glamorous even in a simple shirt and skirt. She wondered nervously whether she should tell them the rumours about Lais.

Leonie regarded her granddaughter with a critical eye as she

kissed her. "I do wish you would wear something less severe," she
said. "You're too young to look so . . . buttoned up!"

They laughed at her description but it fitted. Leonore did give the
impression that she was buttoning away her youth and femininity
behind her business façade.

"You may feel glad about that," Jim said, pouring the champagne, "when you hear what Caro had to say about your other
granddaughter."

"Lais? Why, what is it this time?"

"I'm afraid I heard the rumours too," admitted Leonore.

"All right," said Leonie with a sigh, "you'd better tell me the
worst."

"The worst," said Jim, "is twenty years older than Lais and was
disowned by his family for his bad ways. He claims to be a Russian
aristocrat who is the only member of his family to survive the
Revolution. He also claims their money and possessions went with
them, confiscated by the Bolsheviks. Over the years he's been a
cab-driver, a singer in various nightclubs and, Caro says, a procurer.
Currently he's living with – and off – your granddaughter – apparently with various little sidelines that Lais may, or may not, be
aware of."

Leonie sighed. "Such as?"

"Supplying drugs, women – anything he can put a price on – to
those who need them."

Leonie's face looked set with anger. "And what did you hear,
Leonore?"

Leonore stared at the terracotta tiles at her feet. "Must I tell you,
Grand-mère?"

"You must."

"There are wild parties. The police are called often because of
the noise, it's causing quite a scandal." She stared at the floor,
reluctant to say any more.

"There have been enough scandals in the de Courmont family,"
said Leonie abruptly, "I shall go to Paris tomorrow and see
Lais."

Jim noticed that her hand shook a little as she held her champagne
glass and he wondered whether it was anger she felt for Lais, or
shame.

Leonie could never enter Monsieur's house without a flicker of fear,
though she had never set foot in it when Gilles de Courmont was

alive. In the years they were together, they had lived on his great yacht or at their house on the Place St Georges, or her little villa at St Jean Cap Ferrat. It was only after her daughter Amelie had married Monsieur's son Gerard that she had been invited here. But she felt his presence all the time, his dark, sternly handsome face looked at her from generations of de Courmont family portraits, and the lofty rooms still held his secrets.

The maid who had answered the door led her to the drawing room and Leonie looked around in dismay. Dust bloomed thickly on tables and mirrors and long-dead flowers drooped in crystal containers half-full of greenish water. Glasses and plates littered every surface and there were ominous dark stains upon the beautiful old carpets. Broken glass crunched under her feet as she walked towards the windows and, as she bent to pick up the remains of a once-beautiful Lalique wine glass, she gazed angrily at the sluttish-looking little maid, waiting indifferently by the door.

"And *where* is Bennet?" demanded Leonie. The English butler had been with the de Courmont family for decades and ran the house like clockwork. He must be getting senile to let the place get into this state.

"Bennet's gone, Madame." The girl's head drooped tiredly and Leonie noticed that her apron, like the carpet, was stained.

"You mean Bennet has left?"

"Two weeks ago. He said he wasn't coming back neither. They've all left, except me and Jeanne. And we're off at the end of this week – when she pays us our wages, that is. Or *if* she pays our wages, more like."

Leonie's jaw tightened angrily. "Exactly where is my grand-daughter?"

The little maid avoided her glance. "I think she's still sleeping, Madame."

The gilt hands of the pretty porcelain clock on the marble mantel pointed to two o'clock. "Which is her room?" Leonie made purposefully for the door.

"Wait, wait Madame, please." The girl made an attempt to bar the door, "Madame, she's sleeping. I don't think you should. Oh dear," she wailed as Leonie mounted the stairs determinedly.

Leonie took in at a glance Lais's littered sitting room. The silk curtains were half-drawn and trailing from their hooks. A brandy decanter, one-third full, sat on an inlaid satinwood table stained with sticky circles where glasses had been carelessly spilt. The room smelled of cigarettes and brandy and wrinkling her nose Leonie flung open the windows, letting in the fresh breeze.

"Jeanne is that you?" Lais's voice came sleepily from the darkened bedroom. "Bring some coffee, will you. Lots of it. And make sure it's hot this time."

"Lais. Kindly put on some clothes and come out here at once."

A muffled shriek emerged from the bedroom. "*Grand-mère!* Go away. Oh go away, *please.*"

Removing a pile of flimsy undergarments from the chair, Leonie took a seat. "I'm waiting until you come out, Lais. And please hurry yourself."

"Grand-mère, *please*, I'll meet you in half an hour – wherever you say."

"I'm *waiting here*, Lais."

"What's going on?" The heavily accented voice was deep and booming. "Keep quiet for once, you stupid girl."

Lais shushed the masculine voice. "Don't *whisper* to me for God's sake when you've been *shouting* for the last ten minutes. I told you I wanted to sleep ... *Your grandmother?* What's she doing here? Interfering, I've no doubt. Let me take care of her!"

Lais's whispered voice was imploring. "No, no, please Nikolai, please. Wait here. I'll speak with her. Just wait."

Leonie stood, her back straight, chin up, the way she always reacted when she was a little afraid, as Nikolai swaggered into the room, wrapping a paisley silk robe around his nakedness. He stood well over six feet with massive shoulders and chest and his dark eyes glowered at Leonie from beneath bushy eyebrows.

"And to what do we owe this sudden visit?" he demanded, thrusting his hands into the pockets of his robe, looming over her threateningly.

"I am here to speak to my granddaughter," answered Leonie stiffly. "Be so kind as to tell her that."

"We want you to leave. *Now!*" Nikolai's finger pointed towards the open door where the little maid lurked outside, listening agog to what was being said.

"And exactly *who* are *you?*" Leonie's back was even straighter as she held her ground.

"I am Count Nikolai Oblakoff, former officer in the Tsar's army, and a son of one of Russia's noblest families." He pulled himself to his full, impressive height.

"In that case there is no need for you to be living off my granddaughter!"

"Oh Grand-mère!" Lais pushed in front of Nikolai. Her blonde hair was dishevelled and there were the remains of the previous night's make-up on her pale face. Her pink silk nightdress barely concealed her slender body and with a pang Leonie noticed the puffy eyelids and the pink-violet shadows beneath her eyes. Excess never aided the cause of beauty.

"Please, Grand-mère. Wait downstairs for me," begged Lais. "We can talk then. Alone."

"This isn't your grandmother's house," stormed Nikolai. "You are not spending her money. And who cares about her anyway?"

"Nikolai, wait, please, just let me talk to Grand'mère alone. Everything will be all right, I promise you."

"This has gone far enough," cried Leonie angrily. "*Just look at you, Lais. Look at this house!* Have you no *shame?* This is your father's home – it's *his* roof you are sleeping under with this – this impostor!"

With a bellow of rage Nikolai shook Leonie by the shoulders. Lais leapt at him, screaming, clawing his face with her long scarlet nails. "You bastard. Don't you dare touch her."

Nikolai put his hands to his face, then gazed at the blood on his fingers. Raising his arm he struck Lais a stinging blow, sending her reeling to the floor. "That is the way we treat whores in my country," he said to Leonie, straightening his robe.

"I hear that there are certain things about your life that would be of great interest to the police," said Leonie, picking up the telephone. "I'm calling them to have you evicted from this house, and if necessary I will obtain a court order to prevent you from ever seeing Lais again. If you should dare to come near her or this house ever again, *Count* Nikolai, you will find yourself behind bars."

"I have, no intention of staying here a moment longer than necessary," said Nikolai, recognising defeat when it stared him in the face. "This place is a pigsty." Kicking an empty bottle from his path, he walked towards the bedroom. "She's not only a whore – but a slut too."

"Nikolai," wailed Lais, "wait, please . . . wait."

"Lais!" Leonie's voice had an edge of ice. "Come with me. I want you to take a look at yourself in the mirror."

They walked together towards the great carved overmantel. "Now tell me what you see."

Lais peered through her swollen and bruised eye at her reflected image. Blood trickled from the corner of her mouth mingling with the smudges of red lipstick, and the left side of her face looked puffed and angry. Her blonde hair was tangled and her crumpled nightdress stained with blood.

"Well?" demanded Leonie. "Do you see a slut, Lais? Or maybe a whore? Is Nikolai right then?"

Lais flinched. "No. No Grand-mère, it wasn't like that . . ."

"Then why do you look the role? Is this just a game you're playing?"

"I loved Nikolai, Grand-mère," she murmured.

Leonie stared at her granddaughter aghast. "Is that the truth?" she whispered.

"You see?" Nikolai, dressed in an immaculate dark suit, was knotting a silk tie over a crisply laundered shirt. "She's in love with me. I told you so. *She* chased after *me*! She couldn't live without me. She couldn't live without what she says only I can do for her . . ."

Lais stared at Nikolai's reflection in the mirror and then back at herself. Could it be only three months ago that she had imagined that she held all the cards in the game of life, that she could take any man and discard him at will when he bored her with his possessiveness? And look at her now!

"Please let the maid know where to send your possessions, Nikolai," she said coldly. "And please never come to this house again."

The little maid dodged quickly back along the corridor as Nikolai pushed open the door. "My dear Lais," he said, his glance raking her from head to foot, "there is nothing more I need to see you for."

Leonie and Lais waited in silence until they heard the great double doors slam and Lais sank trembling on to the chaise-longue.

"Oh Grand-mère, Grand-mère," she wailed, "what have I done? I'm so sorry. I didn't mean it to get like this . . . somehow it just got crazier and crazier . . ."

Putting her arms around her granddaughter, Leonie stroked back her straggling blonde hair with gentle fingers, the way she had when Lais was a child.

"It was a mistake, just a foolish mistake," she murmured soothingly.

"But what will I do now, Grand-mère?" whispered Lais, like a biddable child.

"I'm taking you home to Florida, darling, to your mother and father," said Leonie firmly. "And to Peach. Perhaps your little sister will be just what you need to bring you back to reality."

4

Noel Maddox was small for a seven-year-old – much smaller than his best friend, Luke Robinson. Of course Luke was quite old – he was ten. Luke had a shock of red hair and round blue eyes whose innocent expression never failed to bring a smile to anyone's face. Luke could get away with *anything*. He could get an extra slice of bread when he was hungry and once, by looking extra wistful at the governors when they came to visit, even a large piece of angel cake – pink, white and yellow with creamy bits in between. Of course Luke had shared it with him – not exactly half-and-half, but Noel didn't expect that. It had tasted better than all the cake in the world, partly because the children in the Maddox Charity Orphanage didn't get much cake but mostly because *Luke* had given it to him.

Noel sat on the hard wooden bench outside Mrs Grenfell's office, waiting for Luke. His thick black hair had been cropped close to his skull, Matron's answer to the ever-present threat of head-lice, and it emphasised his jutting raw-boned face, making his ears seem unusually prominent. Somehow there was nothing remotely childish about Noel's seven-year-old face. His deeply set grey eyes appeared colourless and his lips were chapped and cracked from the wind that gathered force across the endless flat plains, whistling around the squat, square buildings of the Orphanage. Noel's underfleshed little body appeared shrunken under the faded blue overalls and as he sat on the bench, his feet swung above the glossy linoleum floor. Of course, *Luke's* feet would touch the floor. And *Luke's* hair hadn't been cut because Matron said that Luke had never, ever, had lice. She didn't know how he'd managed it, but she just guessed the angels were on his side! Noel guessed so, too.

He shifted impatiently on the bench. He'd been there almost half an hour and if Matron caught him he'd be in trouble. But he'd promised Luke he'd wait. Luke hadn't told him why he was going to Mrs Grenfell's office, but it surely must be important to take so long.

The door opened suddenly and the sound of voices and the high, amused laugh of a woman came from inside. Noel stiffened. *That wasn't Mrs Grenfell's laugh.* Slipping from the bench, he half-ran, half-slid along the corridor and around the corner, peering cautiously at the door. As he watched, Luke backed out calling goodbye to someone inside, giving them a cheery wave of the hand. He wore his widest grin as he turned and sauntered down the corridor towards Noel.

"Luke." Noel caught his arm as he went by.

"Oh. Hi." Luke continued on his way as if not remembering that he'd asked Noel to wait.

"What happened?" demanded Noel. "Did you get into trouble?"

"For what? I haven't done anything bad."

Before Luke had answered Mrs Grenfell's sudden summons the two of them had run hastily through Luke's possible crimes, and now he had forgotten. Noel hurried alongside his friend, trying to match his easy, loping stride. "Then what?" he asked. "Why did she want to see you?"

Luke shrugged. "Just visitors, wanting to see some of the kids I guess."

Noel frowned. Visitors were few and far between. Occasionally an older couple would come and they might take away a girl baby, wrapped in soft, new pink blankets. But folks rarely asked to see growing boys like them. They were just charity orphans. Noel's steps slowed as he thought about it. He ran to catch Luke's jaunty figure as he leapt down the worn stone steps.

In the backyard of flattened, grassless earth a score of small boys in rough denim shorts and white vests were playing basketball, watched desultorily by Mr Hill who came in twice a week and on Saturdays to teach them physical training and sports. Noel hated physical exercise. The running on the spot knees bend routines exhausted him and in his shorts and vest he knew he looked bony – all elbows and knees. He was no good at baseball or football either. Instead of giving him a break because he was the youngest, Mr Hill would exhort him to try harder, telling him he should keep up with the others. It was Luke who had protected him from Mr Hill's vicious pushes into the mêlée around the basketball net and Luke who had run alongside him to come in last – way behind all the others – in the cross-country run. Without Luke, Noel thought he might have just lain down and died after the first half mile. He'd slumped by the side of the stony road, with red shadows fluttering ominously behind his closed lids, his dry throat burning and his heart thudding so hard he could hear it. Luke had spotted him and run back, putting a friendly arm around his shoulders. "Come on, kid," he'd said kindly, "the first bit's always the worst and you ran too hard trying to keep up. You'll be okay now. We'll just take it easy and get there in our own time."

Gratitude and admiration had mingled in Noel's gaze. Because of his youth, Noel had always been lonely. The children entering the orphanage at the same time as Noel had, by chance, all been girls and therefore quickly adopted, depriving him of the companionship of his contemporaries. The other boys were older – many older than Luke – or were the real young ones, still in the infants department. No one wanted to wait for the youngest, or to choose him for their team or to take him as their friend. With those words Luke cut through the isolation that surrounded Noel. And in return Noel loved him. He went out of his way to be near Luke, he made Luke's bed for him, he put Luke's grey flannel trousers under his own thin mattress to press Sunday creases in them, and he shined Luke's shoes to glittering blackness for Sabbath chapel. His devotion to his friend was complete and Luke, who, although only ten himself, was popular with the older boys because of his size as well as his personality, tolerated Noel with a wide, kind grin, calling him "the kid" when the other boys were around. But when they were alone Luke talked to him. He told Noel what he was going to have when he was a man. Never what he was going *to be*. Just what he would *have*. A house, he would say, as Noel listened wide-eyed, with a big warm kitchen where you could sit and have as much cake as you liked and big cold glasses of milk, and nice bedrooms upstairs with real big beds, soft – not like the orphanage's narrow, straw mattresses. And the stairs would have thick white carpets and (Noel liked this best of all) in the garage there'd be a big red automobile, shiny, fast and expensive. At this point Luke would grin and nudge Noel. "Course," he'd say with a wink, "I'd have a good-looking girl next to me in that fancy car."

Noel's heart would skip a beat. He'd wait every time for Luke to say that of course *he* would be beside him in the front seat of that fancy red car – that it would be the two of them together. Why Luke could possibly want some dumb girl with him was a mystery that worried him in the middle of the night, undermining his new security. Why didn't Luke want *him*? Why some silly girl! It was unfathomable.

Noel watched as Luke ran the length of the yard and hurled himself at the topmost bar of the climbing frame, swinging for a moment and then levering himself up until he was parallel with the bar. Murmurs of admiration came from the watching boys as Luke, in perfect control, swung his muscular body over the bar in a deft loop, landing neatly. Dusting his hands on his overalls he ran across the basketball court, flicked the ball from beneath the nose of the waiting boys and tossed it in a perfect arc through the net.

Noel's grey eyes widened with admiration. He forgot Luke's visit to Mrs Grenfell's office, the mysterious feminine laughter, Luke's dismissal of his questions and the fact that Luke had not remembered that he'd asked him to wait. Noel felt proud to be Luke's friend.

The girls of the Maddox Charity Orphanage were kept apart as much as possible from the boys. Wearing blue print dresses that were droopy and too long in the summer, and harsh dark blue wool that scratched their tender skin in the winter, they learned to read and to write with round uniform letters looped together, and they learned arithmetic so that they might shop and deal with housekeeping money, and they learned American history so that they knew to which flag they were pledging allegiance and why. These activities were secondary to those considered necessary for the life that lay ahead of them as young women. Cooking, homecraft, sewing. Maddox girls were snapped up by domestic agencies as good, reliable girls who with training might make good maids, cooks or housekeepers. Of course they were of neat appearance, always modestly dressed, and Maddox insisted on Sundays off for its girls so that they might attend chapel. The Maddox had its standards.

For most of the older boys at the orphanage arithmetic and English were made bearable only by the presence of the girls. Breathless glances locked across stained wooden desks, twisted paper notes skittered dangerously along narrow benches beneath the bewildered myopic gaze of the teacher, and daring assignations were kept behind the chicken huts in the evening. Things went on at the chicken huts that Noel didn't understand, though he suspected dimly that they were things that would not be considered "Maddox standards". Sent to collect eggs, he'd stumbled over a couple clasped in a passionate embrace. The girl had turned her face away so that he didn't see who she was and the boy, fourteen-year-old Matt Brown, had glared at him and told him to shove off. But not before he'd noticed that the girl's print dress was unbuttoned down to the waist and that Matt's hands had been inside. It had made Noel feel odd then, sort of fluttery and excited, but he'd dashed off to get the eggs, whistling loudly to cover his sudden nervousness and scattering the hens. He'd told Luke about it later and Luke had laughed. "Lucky Matt," was all he'd said, and in answer to Noel's enquiring stare, "You're not old enough yet, you'll understand what it's all about one day." Sometimes, Noel had thought admiringly, you'd think Luke was at least twelve.

It was two weeks after Luke's mysterious visit to Mrs Grenfell's office that it happened. Luke had been taken from class, watched with a mixture of envy because he was missing maths, and sympathy because he was being summoned to the office for who knew what reason. Luke had returned an hour later, red-faced and smiling. Afterwards the older boys had crowded round, asking questions, laughing and talking loudly. Noel had lingered on the outside of the magic circle, catching snatches of the excited talk. "What're they like? Are they rich? Where'd they live? What kinda car? Where? When? How soon are you leaving? . . ."

Noel waited, white-faced, leaning against the wall. He thrust his clenched fists deeper into his pockets, biting his chapped lips to stop them trembling, tasting the saltiness of blood in his mouth.

"Not only that," Luke's voice came clearly from the ring of boys, "they said that it would be unfair to have me leave all my friends. They've decided they'd like a ready-made family." He paused to give weight to what he was going to say next. "And I am to choose who I want to come with me."

Noel stopped breathing. He waited, listening to the blood pounding in his ears.

"You! Nah!" There were jeers of disbelief.

"Well, sure they have to approve – I mean they have to *like* them . . . but I can say *who* . . ."

Noel breathed again. Straightening up, he walked to the edge of the excited crowd. Standing on tip-toe he could see Luke's excited face. "When?" he called. "When, Luke?"

Luke's eyes met his. "On Saturday," he called, giving Noel the thumbs-up signal.

Noel walked slowly away from the crowd, down the long brown linoleum-covered corridor, past the dining room with its rows of wooden chairs and undraped tables and the institutional smells of polish and strong disinfectant with lurking undertones of vegetables and brown gravy from many meals past, into the hall where they were forbidden to go. Flinging open the front door, he gazed down at the worn stone steps, at the long gravel driveway and the big metal gates beyond which lay freedom. Noel took great breaths of the cold air, it felt fresh to him, new and clean. Luke would free him.

The Maddox Orphanage had a system with names. In the case of abandoned *children*, surnames were modest, common ones that could be found anywhere in America – Smith, Jones, Brown, Robinson. First names were after the apostles or the saints, Matthew, Mark, Luke, John, Paul, Peter ... or Cecilia, Mary, Joan for the girls. But abandoned babies were always given the surname "Maddox", after the orphanage itself. Mrs Grenfell told the Maddox children that they should consider it a privilege to be named after such a wonderful, well-thought of institution. Noel was one of a dozen Maddoxes at the Orphanage, though there were, he knew, hundreds more who had gone before him and were now out in the world. "Wherever you go," Mrs Grenfell said proudly, "they'll know you were a Maddox boy."

"What are the family called?" he asked later that evening as he polished Luke's shoes, spitting on the leather and brushing briskly.

"Malone." Luke grinned. "Irish. That's why they liked me – the red hair and all."

"Malone." Noel savoured the name. It felt solid. A real name, passed on from father to son. He brushed again, harder, until he could see his face reflected in the gleaming leather.

"What happens on Saturday?" he asked, putting away his brushes.

"They're coming at four o'clock. For coffee and cake. We all meet and get to know each other a bit better. Then we go. 'Course, if they don't like the other person then it'll be no good, they'll just have to come back. But I guess they will all right." He grinned at Noel.

They had been told to wear their Sunday clothes and be on their best behaviour to meet Mr and Mrs Malone and say goodbye to Luke. And then the announcement was to be made as to whom Luke had chosen to go with him. More than to go with him, thought Noel. *To be Luke's brother.*

The platform at the end of the small assembly hall held a table with a vase of subdued flowers and six wooden chairs arranged in a straight line. Mrs Grenfell mounted the dais, sweeping her visitors along with her and Matron hastily held chairs for the smiling new parents. Luke, flushed and excited, took a seat next to Mrs Malone. She reached over and patted his hand. She was small and slender and not at all old. Noel thought she looked quite beautiful. And Mr Malone was tall, upright, comfortable in tweeds. Noel could see the tip of a pipe peeking from the top of his jacket pocket. He looked calm and jovial. The way a proper father should.

"We are very lucky," began Mrs Grenfell in that high-pitched voice she used when she thought she should talk louder, "to have Mr and Mrs Malone come to us to offer a home to two of our children. Of course," she glanced over the top of her glasses at the assembled rows of clean young faces, chapped hands neatly folded in their laps, "we shall miss them. But they are two of our finest children and I am sure they will work hard to make their new family happy."

Mr Malone shifted uncomfortably on his hard chair and his eyes met his wife's behind Mrs Grenfell's back. Mrs Malone raised her eyebrows slightly and then looked away. Noel waited for what Mrs Grenfell would say next. It wouldn't matter if they thought he was ugly or anything, he'd prove to them that he was clever and quick, soon he'd grow bigger and Luke would help him with sports so that he wouldn't let them down . . . Lost in his dreams he didn't hear Mrs Grenfell's next words. He watched Cecilia Brown rise from her seat two rows in front of him and walk to the platform. She mounted the steps and walked towards Luke as applause swelled around the hall. Cecilia Brown was the prettiest girl at Maddox. She was twelve years old and had been at Maddox for eight years, since her parents had been killed in an automobile accident in St Louis. Her aunt, her father's sister, had refused to take her; having enjoyed a spinster life for forty years she had no mind to take on her brother's child. She had never visited, never written. Cecilia Brown deserved a break. Sweet Mrs Malone put her arms around her new daughter and Cecilia smiled tremulously and took hold of Luke's hand.

Ice crept into Noel's veins, inching its way around his heart, chilling its way through his brain. "Come on," hissed his neighbour, "move along. We're supposed to go outside and wave goodbye."

Noel walked carefully down the forbidden front steps, standing quietly at the back of the crowd. Mr and Mrs Malone climbed into the bright, shiny red car. Cecilia hugged her friends and with a sweet smile took her place in the seat behind them. Two small new suitcases were hefted into the trunk and it snapped shut with a solid thunk. It was a very beautiful car.

"Noel! Noel." Luke pushed his way through the crowd of envious well-wishers. He grasped Noel's hand in his.

"Good luck, kid. I'll write. When I can. I guess I'm gonna be awful busy from now on." He turned and strode towards the car, tall, red-haired, confident. "By the way," he called, "I left something on your bed. A present." With a final wave he stepped into the car and took his place beside Cecilia. Her smile seemed to light up the landscape like the setting sun as the car took off in a spurt of gravel, to freedom.

Noel lay on the bed, the unwrapped present beside him. Its pink paper napkin was stained with grease from the buttercream that sandwiched together the pastel pieces of angel cake. Cecilia's smile floated hazily in his memory. And Luke, so strong, so tall, so free – sitting confidently beside her. Noel had no doubt the Malones' house would have a huge, warm kitchen with milk and cake, there would be soft beds and deep carpets, to go with the shining red car and the beautiful girl on the seat beside Luke. Luke Robinson – no – Luke Malone was a winner! Noel picked up the piece of cake and crunched it in his hands, feeling it squelch creamily in his fingers. Then, tearless and stern and desperately alone, he walked to the toilet and flushed away Luke's parting gift.

5

Five-year-old Peach could remember, when she was *very* small, looking up to Lais's great height, trying to catch her sister's impatient glance and sliding her small hand into Lais's cool one, always wanting to be with her, to go where Lais was. Now that she was older she was allowed to sit on the white carpet in Lais's room,

33

waiting while her sister prepared for some evening out. She would hold the beautiful earrings for her or slide sparkling rings on to Lais's white fingers, touching the long lacquered nails wonderingly, her mouth copying Lais's pout as she applied the lovely shiny red lipstick.

Amelie fell and broke her hip just two days before they were due to sail on the liner for France. Lais was furious at the thought of forfeiting the trip; it was to be her first visit to Paris since she had been brought home by Leonie five years ago – "in disgrace", Peach had heard whispered, though she didn't understand why. But it was not Lais's anger that caused their parents to relent and allow them to go alone, it was Leonie's disappointment.

"Very well," Gerard said sternly to Lais while Peach hovered anxiously in the background. "But *you* will be in charge of your little sister. We are trusting Peach to your care on this trip."

"Don't worry, Gerard," Lais called, dancing her way from the room, "Peach will be just fine. I'll take good care of her."

Peach dashed excitedly along to the nursery, flinging aside the stuffed animals, her teddy, the Raggedy Ann doll and the friendly little dog on wheels, desperately trying to find it. At last! There it was – banished to the back of the toy cupboard by Amelie, angry with Lais for buying something so totally unsuitable. It was still in its elegant burgundy box and Peach ran an admiring finger over the raised gold letters, Cartier. Lifting the lid she flung aside the protective layers of tissue-paper. It was a beautiful grown-up dressing case, fashioned from smooth burgundy leather with a tiny little gold lock and key at the front and on top, her initials. "M.I.L. de C." and then beneath that in gold, "Peach".

Smiling, she turned the tiny key and peered inside. The deep claret suede felt soft to her small exploring fingers. There were little compartments meant for trinkets and jewels, crystal jars with enamelled lids for potions and powders and the prettiest gold and enamel hairbrush and comb. It was Lais's christening gift to her and Peach sat back on her heels, with a sigh of satisfaction. The little case was *exactly* what she would need for travelling with Lais.

Papa took them to New York. The pier was abustle with voyagers and well-wishers and friends. A band played merrily and to Peach the waiting liner looked as big as their hotel in Florida.

Papa carried Peach up the gangplank and Peach carried her precious case. Their staterooms were filled with flowers and she ran around excitedly, wondering how this could possibly be a boat when it looked just like a proper room, while Gerard talked quietly with Lais, looking very serious. And then there was a flurry of kisses and goodbyes and they were waving to Papa on the pier and throwing coloured streamers while the band played far too loudly and quite suddenly she wanted to cry.

"Oh no you don't," Lais said firmly, "no crying when you're with me." So Peach swallowed hard and licked away the solitary tear that had crept to the corner of her mouth.

The first night at sea Lais dressed her in her prettiest dress – white organdy with a red satin sash and little red slippers – and then she had to sit still so as not to get creased while Lais designed her face for the evening. Lais's dress was as scarlet as Peach's sash, a slender column that foamed around her ankles like the wake left by the liner. At dinner they sat at a table with other people and a big man with a lot of gold braid on his smart jacket who smiled at Peach a lot and told her how pretty she looked. Afterwards they went dancing and Peach sat on a big gilt chair clutching Lais's tiny satin purse to her chest so that it wouldn't get lost because Lais had told her to look after it. After a while she began to yawn. Her eyelids drooped from the smoke and fatigue. It was so noisy and she couldn't see Lais anywhere. Fatherly men patted her head admiringly and older ladies frowned at the sight of her.

"Surely the child should be in bed," they murmured. "Whoever is her mother?"

"She's not my mother," Peach replied sleepily, "she's my sister. Lais."

"Disgraceful," they complained, "keeping a child up like that."

Lais returned and hauled her off to bed angrily. "Stupid busy-bodies," she muttered as she dragged Peach along endless corridors, lurching as the boat swung under their feet, "you didn't want to go to bed, did you?"

"No. Oh no," replied Peach, trying to keep up with Lais's long stride. All she wanted was to be with Lais.

Lais unlocked the cabin door and pushed her inside. "Come on then, into bed with you." She pulled off Peach's pretty white dress hurriedly.

Peach sat on the edge of her bed sliding off the little red slippers. "What about my teeth?" she asked, thinking of her mother.

"In the morning," called Lais, already at the door.

"But Lais. Where are you going?" Peach sat up in bed anxiously. She still wore her vest and knickers and her socks. There was no

35

sign of her nightie, or a drink of milk or anything. And where was Teddy?

Lais hesitated then hurried back across the room and hauled the teddy bear from beneath a pile of clothes. "There," she said. "Now go to sleep."

Peach relaxed under the covers. "Yes," she murmured, yawning. "But Lais. Where *are* you going?"

"Dancing," said Lais, closing the door.

Lais danced her way across the Atlantic Ocean, sleeping during the day. Peach was placed in the nursery with other children and had a lot of fun there with the nannies and the toys and games. But she was lonely and she missed her mother and Lais. Each night she sat and watched Lais prepare for her evening, but now she had early supper with other children and was tucked up in bed before Lais left for dinner. The rhythm of the boat was soothing, a sort of low wallow and roll that lulled her to sleep like a rocking chair, and only occasionally did she wake when Lais came in, sometimes thinking she heard laughter and voices from the next room.

In Paris they went straight to the de Courmont town house on the Ile St Louis. Peach felt a little awed by its grand rooms and suspicious of those fat babies that Lais called cherubs peeking down at her from the ceilings. She was allowed into the kitchens to have milk and a chunk of bread with chocolate – "pain chocolat" – something Maman would never have permitted had she been there.

One night she awoke with a pain in her stomach. She didn't know how late it was but she climbed out of bed and went in search of Lais. She hurried along the corridor relieved to see that there was a chink of light beneath Lais's door. Opening it she gazed puzzled at the two people there. She didn't recognize Lais at first because she was sort of buried beneath the man. They looked so cosy, she thought enviously, with their arms around each other, but she still wondered why didn't they have their night clothes on?

"My God. Peach!" Lais leapt from the bed wrapping the sheet around her. "What the hell are you doing here?"

"You shouldn't say that word," said Peach disapprovingly.

The man started to laugh and Lais glared at him angrily, grabbing Peach's hand and marching her from the room. She gave Peach a glass of water with a hand that shook. "Promise," she said, "that

you'll never tell *anyone*. *Anyone at all*. Especially Maman and Gerard."
Peach promised, though she did wonder why it should be such a
secret.

The very next day they travelled down to St Jean Cap Ferrat and
it was wonderful to see Grand-mère. She looked so much like
Maman, and that was comforting because she did miss Maman so.
And there was Jim who made her laugh and played games of
hide-and-seek with her and helped her with her swimming and took
her fishing. And Leonore, her other sister, who looked like Lais but
was different. Of course she loved Leonore too – but not quite like
Lais.

After a while Peach began to notice strange things. People would
break off their conversations when she came into the room, they'd
put on that special sort of bright face that grown-ups use when they
want to "amuse the children", but their eyes weren't smiling the
way they used to. And when they thought she wasn't around their
faces were long and serious. "War," they said, "it's war after all."
Peach stared at the disbelief mirrored in their faces, sensing the fear
that lay behind the unknown word.

Suddenly there was a flurry of activity, their bags were packed
hurriedly and they were to leave that very day. Jim had managed
to get them berths on a ship. "One of the last," Peach heard him
telling Lais, "there's no time left. You must leave *now*."

Peach rubbed her aching head tiredly. "Please can't I stay?" she
begged, clinging to Jim's hand. "Don't you and Grand-mère want
me any more?"

Jim swung her up in his arms. "We want you," he smiled, "but
so do your maman and papa. We'll see you again soon, little Peach
– and anyway, I'm driving you to Marseilles so it's not quite
goodbye yet."

On the journey Peach slept at first, but they seemed to be stopping
and starting all the time and the car was stuffy. She peered out of
the windows and noticed that everyone else seemed to be driving
the same way – west towards Spain. "Please," she begged, "can't
we go back? My eyes hurt and my head."

"Stretch out on the seat and try to sleep, darling," commanded
Lais, sitting in the front with Jim, "this looks like being a long
drive."

"But Lais, my head really hurts." Peach leaned forward, threading her arms around her sister's neck and resting her aching head
against Lais's cool cheek.

37

Lais took Peach's hand in hers. "Jim," she said in a small voice, "I think we're in trouble."

Jim tore his anxious gaze from the road and their glances met. "She's burning with fever," Lais said quietly.

Lais held her in her arms all the way back to the villa. Leonie hurried to greet them, surprised and dismayed by their return. She swept Peach off and plunged her into a bath of cool water, gradually adding ice until the coolness penetrated Peach's very bones. Then the doctor arrived and examined her gravely. Lais laughed when he said it was measles – a severe case. "I always thought measles were simple," she said. "Trust Peach to exaggerate them."

"We'll get the next boat," Jim said wearily.

Peach grew worse. Her head felt as though it would burst and her legs hurt. Then her chest began to feel as though it were crushing her. "Papa," she cried, twisting her head from side to side to try to rid herself of the pain, searching in vain for a cool spot on the pillows that were soon soaked with her sweat. "Papa."

"It's not measles, its poliomyelitis," said Doctor Marnaux at the hospital in Nice, "a rare disease that affects mainly children and young people. She will be put on a respirator to help her breathe, but Madame and Monsieur," his large brown eyes faced them sadly, "I'm afraid I cannot offer much hope."

Lais hurled herself at the doctor. "What do you mean?" she cried. "Are you saying my sister is going to die?" Gripping the lapels of his starched white coat fiercely, she looked ready to kill him.

"Mademoiselle, Mademoiselle – please," he tried futilely to remove her. "I cannot say. It is a disease of which we have little knowledge. We can only hope."

Lais's hands dropped limply to her sides and the doctor smoothed his ruffled coat nervously. "I will do my best for her, of course. We all will."

"Doctor Marnaux," said Leonie in a high clear voice. *"My granddaughter will not die.* You understand, Monsieur. *She will not die."*

Doctor Marnaux eyed the frantic young woman and the quietly desperate older one nervously. "Of course not, Madame," he replied soothingly, "of course not."

"I will stay with her," said Leonie, walking to the severe white door behind which her granddaughter lay.

The doctor glanced at Jim and shrugged helplessly. "As she

38

wishes, Monsieur," he murmured. "We have done all we can."

All transatlantic telephone lines were occupied and calls were already being censored or curtailed. It took Jim two days and considerable influence to reach Gerard in Miami.

"I'm leaving right away," said Gerard, his voice tense across the crackle and woosh of the line.

"Things are already difficult here," warned Jim. "Remember, once you are here as a French citizen you may find it impossible to leave."

"Even if Peach were not so ill," replied Gerard, "I would return to do what I can for my country."

Gerard had only ever taken a nominal interest in the de Courmont business empire built by his father, preferring to leave the running of Monsieur's vast automobile plants and their peripheral companies, the monumental iron and steel works, the rolling mills and the factories at Valenciennes that had produced guns and weapons for other wars, to the capable management of governing boards. And even the fact that the empire was now in jeopardy with the country at war, came a far second in his priorities to the fact that his beloved little Peach was desperately ill.

By pulling strings he was able to get a plane from New York to Lisbon. After two days spent waiting for a flight to Paris that never took off, he wangled his way on to a plane to Madrid and from there took a crowded, slow-moving train to Barcelona, where he persuaded a reluctant taxi-driver to drive him as far as Gerona. He scoured the town for a car but, ironically for a man who owned one of the oldest automobile companies in Europe, there was not a vehicle to be found anywhere. Desperate with worry he stormed the steps of the American consulate, elbowing his way past the line of sullen, anxious people awaiting visas, that stretched down the stairs and around the block and never seemed to move. His business card, sent in via a supercilious lackey who was wielding his petty bureaucratic power with relish, brought an instant response. De Courmont was not a name to be ignored. The consul's own car and driver were placed at his disposal immediately and Gerard crossed the border, covering the endless kilometres between Gerona and Nice in a vast Chrysler flying the American flag that turned heads in the queue of traffic heading the other way towards the border.

Even unshaven and weary after almost six days of travel and with very little sleep, Leonie thought that Gerard was still a very handsome man – like Monsieur. But Gerard's strong face and steady blue eyes held none of the cynicism of his father's. Though he had Monsieur's powerful shoulders and forceful stride, Gerard was a gentle man whose consuming interests were in his chosen career of architecture, and in his family. He had none of the lust for power both personally and in business that had motivated Monsieur.

Leonie held his hands tightly in hers. "Peach is still gravely ill, Gerard," she said quietly, "but she's been the same for over a week now. It's a sign of hope."

Peach knew as soon as he took her hand that it was Papa, even though she couldn't open her eyes. When he bent over to kiss her she could smell his cologne and feel the slight roughness of his face against hers. It would be all right now. Papa was here.

Doctor Marnaux seemed surprised by the improvement in Peach's breathing. He had been confident she would not last the night – but then, he'd thought that every night for nine days as he'd watched the grandmother sitting there, holding the child's hand in hers, talking to her in a low murmur, sometimes even singing to her, as though she were well and quite normal. And the improvement didn't stop there. The next day Peach opened her eyes. The following day she was pronounced out of danger.

"The only thing left," said Dr Marnaux at a conference in his efficient book-lined office, "is to assess the damage."

They gazed at him enquiringly.

"To the limbs, you see," he added apologetically. "The disease has attacked the muscles and now we must see what is affected."

"You mean Peach may be *crippled?*" Lais's voice was filled with horror. "But that can't be. *She's only five years old.*"

Dr Marnaux shrugged. "We must hope for the best."

Leonie was beside Peach's bed that night when she awoke, just as she had been every night of her illness. Her own face looked tired and worn but she managed to smile for the child. "Hold out your hands to me, Peach," she murmured, "let me catch them."

The child smiled and lifted her arms, feeling Leonie's secure grasp on her small hands.

"Now," murmured Leonie, "you've been in bed so long, your muscles have become tired. Let's give them a little test, Peach. Wiggle your toes for me."

Peach tried and tried, but the toes wouldn't wiggle. Her high, childish laugh cut through the silent room, a sound that gladdened

Leonie's heart, only to turn to stone again. "I think they're too tired, Grand-mère Leonie," whispered Peach, "I expect tomorrow they'll be all right."

The day they clamped the steel braces with the ugly black leather straps around Peach's small wasted legs was the day that Gerard was summoned to Paris by the wartime government of France. "It'll just be a few days, sweetheart," he promised her, "and then I'll be back with you."

"But what will I do without you, Papa?" Peach's eyes brimmed with tears. "Why have they put these things on my legs? Why can't I run and skip any more?"

"You will, Peach, you will," cried Leonie, throwing her arms around her. "We just have to teach those muscles how to work again. They are still there, you know, but they're just being lazy."

"Promise me, Grand-mère," begged Peach. "I want to chase the little brown cat so badly."

Leonie managed a laugh. "I promise," she vowed.

Gerard's few days stretched to a week, and then two. He managed to call them to say he was being sent to Valenciennes to meet with the management, that things were chaotic and he would call as soon as he could. Then for a month there was silence.

Leonie worked every morning with Peach. And every afternoon and again in the evening. She fastened small weights to the child's legs and lifted them up and down, she massaged them, she hauled Peach to her feet and forced the legs out in front of her until Peach was close to tears. And then one day Leonie carried her into the warm, blissful sea and Peach felt her legs floating with her like they used to, freed from their cruel steel braces.

Gerard returned in the uniform of a major in the French army with the news that he must go back to Paris in two days' time. He had spoken with Amelie who, though still incapacitated with her broken hip, was desperate to see Peach. What few sailings there were, were overcrowded and dangerous. One ship loaded with women and children had already been sunk. Peach and Lais must stay with Leonie, and Gerard would come to them whenever he could. They all prayed that the war wouldn't last long. He left almost immediately without telling them his mission and Peach's eyes followed him anxiously as the grey army car with a uniformed driver at the wheel disappeared down the road in a cloud of white dust. She'd promised her father that she would be walking by herself the next time she saw him and she would try to keep that promise.

The months drifted into winter and still Peach and Leonie swam every day in the now deserted hotel pool, braving its cool depths together as Peach slowly gained strength.

Six months later, in February, Dr Marnaux was able to remove the calliper from her left leg. But the right, where the muscles had suffered more severe damage, was weaker and still needed the support of the hated steel frame. Sometimes Leonie would observe Peach with her right leg stuck out in front of her, just staring at it with such an unchildish look of loathing on her face that it shocked her. "I hate it, Grand-mère, I hate it," whispered Peach. "One day I shall throw it into the sea for ever."

"In a way," said Jim on a chill March morning as they drank their coffee and tucked into a fresh batch of Madame Frenard's brioches, "it's a good thing you've got Peach here. And Lais and Leonore."

Leonie paused in mid-bite and looked at him in surprise. "Why now, especially?"

"I'm off to Paris tomorrow, my darling," Jim set down his cup and took her hand in his. "They may consider me too old to fight but at least they can use my organising and administration experience."

She might have guessed he would do something like this. Jim wasn't the sort to sit around and let someone else fight his war. Gerard was already involved, she didn't know exactly how but they heard from him intermittently, when he told them about Amelie, alone in Florida, worried about her family – and especially Peach. "Amelie will be all right," Gerard had said on the telephone, "just look after her girls for her."

They told Leonore and Lais later that afternoon. "Let me come with you, Jim," begged Lais, bored with the lack of activity at the Cap. The hotel was almost empty and all the young men had been drafted into the army. At least Paris would be *alive*. "Someone had better pack up the silver and the paintings at the Ile St Louis, and get them into a safer place," she said. "I'll take care of it, I promise."

But listening to her sister's easy promises, Leonore knew why Lais wanted to be in Paris.

6

Lais prowled the big house on the Ile St Louis like a caged animal, pausing now and then to peer from the long windows of the great first-floor drawing room. The bridges were empty and the streets silent. Even the Seine was quiet without its usual bustle of barges and river traffic.

Switching back the heavy yellow silk curtains, she peered out yet again. There was nothing. Just the noise in the distance. The heavy roar and rumble of the traffic of an advancing victorious army.

The staff had departed and the house was deathly quiet. There was just the concierge left in his apartment by the gate. Faithful old Bennet, who had returned after the incident with Nikolai years ago that had precipitated her own departure from Paris, had left last week for the south where he was to stay at the hotel for the duration of the war, though the butler was now so aged that Lais had privately doubted whether he would survive the terrifying journey. All the roads south of Paris were jammed with families fleeing the city, their possessions strapped to the roofs of their cars, and they were sitting targets for the German planes raking them with machine guns.

She'd done her best to persuade Bennet to stay, assuring him that he would be safer here than on the roads of France, but Bennet had made it clear that not only was he not prepared to stay in Paris and be polite to the Germans, but that he would not be prepared either to stay there with *her*.

Lais shrugged away her discomfort at the remembrance of what Bennet thought of her. She could bear it here alone no longer, *she had to see what was happening.*

Driving too fast, Lais crossed the Pont Marie and sped along the Quai de l'Hôtel de Ville, making for the Place de la Concorde. France was defeated. To avoid the destruction that had already devastated cities like Reims, Paris had been declared an open city and was to be handed over to the Germans at the American Embassy that day. Tears flowed suddenly down Lais's face as she saw the ugly swastika flag already flying over the German HQ at the Hôtel Crillon. The streets were empty and shuttered; no one wanted to give the enemy the satisfaction of watching them take their city. Lais felt as if she were abandoned in a lonely nightmare. Tearfully she pulled the car into a side street. The rumble of tanks and armoured vehicles drummed through the silent city as she ran the last few blocks, along the rue de Rivoli. A few people, their faces grey and bitter, stood on the pavement behind rows of immaculate French gendarmes, as their enemies – young and blond and strong – marched through the Paris they now claimed as their own.

With a roar a fleet of powerful motor cycles revved down the rue Boissy d'Anglais. Their riders were helmeted and sinister behind dark goggles and black leather. A long, black, shiny Mercedes followed, its swastika flying, its chauffeur stiff and proud with the importance of his task and his passenger.

Lais's thin flowered silk dress whipped against her as she stood on the kerb shivering, not from the wind, but with fear. The eyes of the man in the back of the car flickered her way for an instant, his monocle glinting as it caught the sun. Gold braid gleamed on his immaculate grey-green uniform, and a rainbow of medals decorated his chest.

Tears burned Lais's eyes. Paris would never, ever be the same. Turning suddenly, she ran for the safety of the car and, curling up on the soft cream leather of the back seat, she cried for Paris, and for herself.

When the tears were over, she sat up and peered at her swollen face in the mirror. Pulling out the oval gold Cartier compact she dabbed on a layer of powder and dashed the scarlet lipstick across her trembling mouth. With her hair pulled back and secured severely by two tortoise-shell combs and the dark glasses to cover her swollen eyes, she didn't look too bad. What she needed now was company. Company – and a drink!

She toured the streets in the car searching for a bar that was open, but everywhere was locked and shuttered. No Paris café was prepared that day to offer its hospitality to the conquerer. Lais drove aimlessly, avoiding the northern roads where the Germans were still pouring in, until she found herself near Les Halles. Paris still needed to be supplied with food and such fruit and vegetables as were available were being sorted and crated. A couple of bars were open to service the porters and working men and Lais sank thankfully on to a stool at the zinc counter. "Brandy," she ordered, her throat raspy from the storm of tears. Shifting his Gauloise from one side of his mouth to the other in a cloud of pungent smoke, the barman placed the drink on the counter. Lais's hand shook as she downed the dense amber liquid. She pushed the glass back across the counter. "Another," she said.

Her eye caught that of the man sitting next to her. He was of middle height, with the olive skin of a southerner and dark hair that sprang in thick waves from an intelligent forehead. He was maybe thirty-four or thirty-five and his hand, clamped firmly around the neck of a bottle of brandy as he topped up his glass, was large and square with a sprinkling of crisp black hair. Lais turned back to her brandy, sipping it this time.

"So," he said quietly, "the Germans are sticking in your throat too." His voice was low with a faint regional intonation.

Lais nodded, sipping her drink without looking at him.

"You are a foreigner?"

She frowned. He was persistent. But then she needed company – all her friends had flown. "American," she replied, "and French too."

Leaning forward he topped up her glass from his personal bottle. "I am from Spain," he said, "a Basque from Barcelona. Enrique García," he bowed with a slightly mocking smile, "at your service."

Lais stared at her drink. Was she ready for this kind of encounter on a day like today? A pick-up in a bar? She wondered how many men she had gone home with after some mad gay night that had ended here in Les Halles, in just such a bar as this? The brandy tasted bitter as it flowed down her aching throat and tears stung her eyes. Damn it, oh damn it, why did this war have to *spoil everything? Why did it have to spoil her life!* Her eyes met Enrique García's knowing glance. Suddenly she recalled overhearing a snatch of conversation between her mother and Uncle Sebastião do Santos, her real father's brother.

"She's like *him,* Amelie," he'd been saying to her. "You *know* that Roberto was two people – but you don't know the whole story and you never will. Roberto loved you, but he kept his other life away from you. There were the temptations that Roberto never could resist – not with Diego leading him on."

The door had slammed, leaving Lais still standing in the hall, her mouth open in shock and her heart pounding. The picture of her father that she had carried in her mind, cribbed from the old sepia photographs that curled at the edges, of Roberto, blond and open-faced, his blue eyes meeting the camera's stare head-on, was shattered. *And she was like him.* What did it mean? *What was she?*

What did it matter any more? They were probably all doomed now anyway. She pushed her empty glass towards Enrique García's. "I'm Lais," she said to him, "at your service."

They finished his brandy while he talked. He was a lecturer in Economics at the Sorbonne, and a stringer for a Spanish newspaper contributing a weekly Paris column. He should have left weeks ago, but for some reason he'd hung on. There was a good story to be had and his paper – as well as others – would pay him well for it.

"So," said Lais flatly, "you're profiting from Paris's downfall."

He shrugged. "Maybe. But the world needs to know what's going on, what Paris really feels like in the throes of a defeat. People like me can fill that gap."

The night was blue-black and filled with the strong odours of over-ripe fruit and rotting vegetables as they made their way back through the streets around the market to where she had left her car.

"A de Courmont," Enrique said admiringly. "A wonderful car."

Lais drove in silence back to the Ile St Louis, avoiding the main boulevards and ignoring the curfew, daring any German to stop her, but the streets were empty and none did.

Enrique's low whistle took in the immaculate courtyard and the grey stone mansion admiringly. "You live here?" he asked, surprised.

"Like the car," said Lais, slamming shut the door, "I'm a de Courmont."

"Well, well," said Enrique as he followed her up the steps, "how very useful."

7

The bulky figure of the German commandant strode up the steps of the Hostellerie la Rose du Cap, pausing for a moment, silhouetted against the blue and gold of a calm Mediterranean evening. Leonie clutched Peach's hand tighter in hers, her eyes meeting Leonore's apprehensively. "I will deal with this," she murmured, "you are not to speak to them unless addressed directly."

"But Grand-mère . . ."

"It's better this way," whispered Leonie, "they'll not dare to try to bully an old woman."

Despite herself, Leonore smiled. Leonie was sixty-six years old and looked fifty. She was wearing her favourite yellow linen dress and pretty cream high-heeled shoes with Jim's pearls gleaming against her elegant neck. Her blonde hair was pulled back into a smooth chignon and tied with a yellow silk bow. She looked every inch the chic Frenchwoman and any man – even the enemy – would surely find her desirable. "I warn you," whispered Leonore, "if it's rape the enemy is after it'll be you, Grand-mère, not me."

"Sshh." Leonie pulled herself taller, head up, shoulders back, praying the pounding of her heart couldn't be heard.

"Kommandant Gerhard von Steinholz." The burly man removed his gold-braided cap and clicked his heels, bowing. "May I say, Madame Leonie, that I saw you many times in my youth, at theatres in Munich and Paris. It is a great honour for me to meet my idol in person."

"I am always pleased to make the acquaintance of an admirer of my work," said Leonie coldly, "but I am afraid I cannot say the same for my country's enemy."

Herr Kommandant von Steinholz shrugged away her comment with a genial smile. "It is the misfortune of war, Madame, that places us in this position. But our personal views are our own." He turned to Leonore, clicking his heels smartly. "Mademoiselle." His pale blue glance took her in from head to toe.

"My granddaughter, Mademoiselle Leonore de Courmont."

Leonore nodded coldly, ignoring his outstretched hand.

"Ah yes. Of course, a de Courmont. Though by adoption only, I understand?"

Leonore flushed angrily. "Gerard de Courmont is my stepfather," she said, then biting her lip she fell silent. Damn, he'd already provoked her into speaking to him!

"And this?" Kommandant von Steinholz smiled at Peach and she gazed up at him in awe, dazzled by the glitter of gold braid and the glint of medals.

"Peach de Courmont," said Leonie. "My youngest grand-daughter."

47

Von Steinholz patted Peach's head with a large heavy hand, and Peach wriggled uncomfortably. "I understand this one is a true de Courmont." He frowned as he caught sight of the steel calliper on her leg. "But what happened here?"

"An illness," replied Leonie, "she is almost better now."

"We have very good doctors, Madame Leonie. If there is anything we can do to help I can place them at your disposal."

Her eyes met von Steinholz's round pale blue ones. "I am very fond of children, Madame," he said quietly. "I have three of my own."

"Thank you, but Peach has had the best of attention."

"And Grand-mère makes me better than any doctor." Peach rubbed her hair where he had touched it. His hand had been warm and sweaty. She didn't like this man. Gripping Leonie's hand tighter she slid out of sight behind her grandmother.

Steinholz summoned the young officer waiting at attention behind him. "Kruger!"

"Sir." The officer stepped forward smartly and waited at attention, eyes raised to some point above their heads, and Peach peeked at him wonderingly.

"This is Captain Volker Kruger. He will be in charge of this hotel from now on. Of course it is our wish that you run the hotel as usual, but Captain Kruger will be in charge of allocating accommodations and supplies. Only our senior officers will be coming here to enjoy a much needed rest from their endeavours at the front. And perhaps, occasionally, you may be asked to accommodate some very *special* guests. This hotel and its facilities will make an ideal location for top-level conferences between ourselves and our Italian allies. You may rest assured, Madame, that the hotel will be kept in tip-top condition and Kruger will see that you have a full staff. All we ask is that you continue to do your job – with a little extra help from us."

"But I . . ."

"Leonore." Leonie shot her a warning glance and Leonore flushed, staring down angrily at her feet. "Herr von Steinholz," said Leonie, "I must demand complete control. Captain Kruger will answer to myself or my granddaughter. No one, Herr von Steinholz, runs this hotel except Mademoiselle de Courmont."

Von Steinholz pursed his lips angrily. "You realise, of course, that we could simply requisition the hotel?"

Von Steinholz wanted the prestige of having Leonie Bahri and a

48

de Courmont granddaughter running *his* hotel . . . and Leonie knew it. She stared back at him calmly.

"Oh, very well," agreed von Steinholz. "Kruger, you hear that?" The young man's eyes dropped from the ceiling to their level.

"Herr Kommandant," he replied.

"You will work with these ladies, Kruger. They know more than you about running a hotel anyway. Standards must be kept up."

Leonie noticed a glint of anger flash through the Captain's eyes. The man was a small bureaucrat jumped up to a position of "assistant to power" – and longing for that power himself. Captain Kruger was a dangerous man.

"It's understandable," von Steinholz turned to Leonore with a superior smile, "that with Germans now running the de Courmont factories you might want to keep some small part of the family's properties under your own control."

It had been six months since they had heard from Gerard, though they knew about the take-over of the steel works and that the factories now produced vehicles and armaments for the Third Reich.

"My men will be here first thing in the morning. I bid you goodnight. It has been a pleasure meeting you both." Von Steinholz strode towards the door, his footsteps ringing hollowly on the marble.

He paused by the great glass door, held open for him by the watchful Kruger. "Oh, and tell the little one – Peach – hiding behind her grandmother, that she has my permission to swim in the hotel pool at any time."

"Grand-mère," said Peach as Leonie unbuckled the brace from her leg that night as she prepared for bed. "Can we throw it into the sea now?"

Peach's face was rosy with health, her soft, springy russet hair was held back with a scrap of ribbon and her dark blue eyes were round and serious.

Leonie paused, the ugly leather straps half-unbuckled. "The calliper you mean?"

Peach nodded.

"I know you hate it," said Leonie, "but you need its support." The right leg, unbuckled from its cage, was visibly thinner than its twin.

"No I don't. I can walk on it."

"Not properly, darling . . ."

"*I will*," said Peach fiercely, "*Grand-mère, I will*. And I don't want to swim in the pool with those men. I'll never swim there again!"

Leonie had thought they'd come through this afternoon's ordeal unscathed, but it was little six-year-old Peach who had been damaged by their first encounter with the enemy.

Peach gazed at Leonie earnestly. "We'll swim in the sea, Grand-mère," she promised, putting a small consoling hand on Leonie's shoulder. "They can't stop us doing that, can they?"

How did she know, marvelled Leonie? How could she possibly understand the situation? But Peach had sensed the display of power in the clicking heels, the gleaming braid, the silent watching soldiers. Out of the mouths of babes . . . "Well," she said briskly, "let's get you tucked up in that nice comfy bed, and we'll talk about this again in the morning."

"*They'll* be here in the morning," said Peach, lying back against the pillows. "*It'll never be the same here again.*"

8

Lais strolled down the rue Cambon dressed in a fashionable little spring suit. The navy wool skirt showed a split of silk piping to match the cream silk shirt with its jaunty bow, and the jacket, edged with a military glitter of braid and buttons, swung pertly as she walked. It was mere steps to the Ritz bar where her new love was waiting for her.

"Lais." He waved from his seat at a crowded table at the far end of the bar as she threaded her way through the tables towards him.

"You're late," he said reprovingly as she took a seat.

"A woman's privilege," Lais patted her blonde hair into place beneath her pretty little hat, glancing round at the assembled company. "My, my," she commented as her usual champagne cocktail was placed on the table in front of her, "I thought Chanel had cornered the market on gold braid."

Ignoring their guffaws of laughter, she sipped her drink. "Mmm. Heaven," she said, sinking back into her chair. "Sheer heaven." Crossing her long silk-clad legs, she eyed her audience of admiring men levelly. "So, gentlemen. Who is fighting the war if you are all here?"

They laughed again, delighted with her. "*Liebchen*," the tall one placed a proprietory hand on her knee, "I'm afraid I have an important meeting this afternoon, so we won't be able to have lunch."

Lais pouted over her drink.

"But don't worry. I've invited them all for dinner. Call up some friends, my darling. Tell Johann to put the champagne on ice. And say that we'd like the caviare and the dish Albert at Maxim's always orders for us – you know the one – with the veal. And a *Norvegienne* – with *fraises des bois*."

"All your favourites," commented Lais drily.

He beamed at her, and then at his colleagues. "Let me introduce you," he said. "Mademoiselle Lais de Courmont – General von Rausch, of Oberkommand, his aides, Captain Albers, Major Dorsch of the Waffen SS. And this is Herr Otto Klebbich who has just been appointed director of affairs for champagne." Her lover's laugh echoed around the still elegant Ritz bar. "You know who Otto is? He's the *Führer of Champagne*."

It had been just another boring evening, thought Lais irritably as she prepared for bed. There was no doubt that Hitler's preference for promoting men of the same intellectual background as himself made for dull parties. Tonight there'd been a couple of "Gauleiters" on their first ever trip outside Germany, small-minded provincial men bumped-up to party officials, though they must be in line for higher power or Karl would never have tolerated them. The others had been marginally more interesting – an architect, involved with building Goering's new home and whom Karl had commissioned to design his chalet in the mountains, and a couple of his assistants – and Otto Klebbich. But no one really worth her trouble.

As Karl had commanded, she had seen that the table looked exquisite. The elaborate silver candelabra had thrown soft light on to the bowls of trailing tawny orchids and the crested de Courmont dinner service, sparkling off the thinnest Lalique champagne flutes that brimmed with an endless supply of the sweet champagne the Nazis preferred. But the delicious food had been too delicate for their hearty taste.

There was one young officer, though – Ferdi von Schönberg, an aide to Otto Klebbich – who'd known his wines. He'd known about music too. He had come to stand beside her as Lais leaned over the piano, while the old man who always entertained at her parties played Mozart and Chopin as well as Cole Porter – with equal tenderness. The other officers had remained at the table with Karl, discussing the latest developments in the war. Maps had been brought out and were pored over and their talk and laughter grew louder as the excellent brandy flowed. Several bored girls in pretty evening dresses were waiting disconsolately in the drawing room, ignored by the Germans and by their hostess.

> "I get no kick from champagne,
> Mere alcohol doesn't thrill me at all,
> So tell me why should it be true,
> That I get a kick – out of you . . ."

Lais sang along with the piano.

"You like Cole Porter?" Ferdi von Schönberg had asked with a smile.

He was tall and blond with a nice hard young body. "Cole Porter – and *good* champagne," she'd said, lifting her glass filled with a delicate golden liquid whose tiny bubbles fizzed gently and steadily upwards. "None of that sweet wine served in there." She'd grimaced towards the open dining room door and he'd laughed.

"To each his own," he'd said, toasting her with his brandy glass.

"Yes," she had replied, eyeing him steadily. Just then the door opened and the others began to emerge from the dining room so she had no further opportunity to talk to him.

With a sigh Lais pulled the soft green silk nightdress over her nakedness. Karl liked her in green. And in silk.

He was already in bed, waiting for her, as she walked from her dressing room. The smell of the roses she had piled into enormous crystal vases drenched the room and she flung open the window, gazing out across the courtyard to the Seine. Moonlight glinted off the rifles of the sentries as they patrolled the area in front of the house, lighting up the long black Mercedes that waited, chauffeur

52

at the ready in case of emergency. Her lover was a very important man. Leaning against the window she lit a cigarette and stared out into the night.

"*Liebchen,*" General Karl von Bruhel lifted his eyes from the papers he was reading and smiled at her. "Time for bed, my angel." He placed the documents with their important looking seals and stamps to one side. "Come to me."

Karl von Bruhel was forty years old. He had harsh grey hair and very blue eyes that looked even bluer because of the clean pinkness of his complexion. His skin was smooth, his body spare. He had been married for eighteen years to a quiet woman of a good Munich family and he had a daughter Peach's age.

Lais tossed her cigarette from the window. Sliding the straps of the nightdress from her shoulders, she walked slowly towards him, easing the silk over her breasts, letting it slide in a soft rustle to her feet.

Karl's eyes devoured her nakedness, his hands waited for her, hard, predatory, exploring. Lais hesitated by the side of the bed, she was always a little afraid of him, a little wary as he approached her. His hand slid ruthlessly between her legs, gripping her until she cried out, only partly from pain. "Tell me you like it, Mademoiselle de Courmont," he commanded, with a disdainful smile, "tell me what it is you want. Come on. *Tell me!*"

"Please, please, Karl," she gasped as his hand gripped tighter, crushing her softness. Even as she spoke a tremor shook her. Oh God, oh God! His hard fingers caressed her ruthlessly and she moaned with pleasure. Abruptly he removed his hand, leaving her gasping, desperate.

"Now," he whispered, lying back against the pillows, hands clasped behind his head. "*What* is it you want, Mademoiselle de Courmont?"

"Please Karl," she begged. "Please Karl, oh please, *fuck me.*"

With a great roar of laughter he lifted her from her feet and swung her on top of him, forcing her down on his hardness, enjoying her moans of pleasure.

"Now," he said, "wait. Wait one moment, Lais. Take a look in the mirror over the bed."

Obediently Lais stared into the mirror at their reflected image. Roughly he lifted her from him so that she could watch them. Her eyes were dark with excitement, she would do anything he asked, he knew it. "Now," he said, "lift your eyes higher, Lais, away from us. What else do you see, reflected in the mirror?"

53

Lais raised her eyes reluctantly. The portrait that Karl had insisted on hanging there stared back at her. His face was lean, with a full sensual mouth – a darkly handsome, slightly cruel-looking man with Peach's deep dark blue eyes.

"Monsieur," she whispered, trembling. "I see Monsieur."

Karl roared with laughter again, letting her sink back on to him, feeling her juices flow. "So what do you think of this, Monsieur le Duc de Courmont?" he called to the portrait. "First we took your country, then we took your factories and your estates. And now I'm going to take your granddaughter. Again!"

Lais cried out with pain as, still inside her, he rolled on top of her. She gasped as he began to thrust harder. "More, more," she begged. God, he was such a fantastic lover, oh my God . . . "More, more. Don't stop now. Oh please . . . Karl, don't stop." It seemed the night would never end.

9

Caroline Montalva had always been considered one of the smartest of Parisians and like most of them she was also thrifty. Caro never threw anything away. From the moment she was seventeen and had bought her first couture dress, she had saved every single garment. "After all," she'd said to her lover Alphonse, when he'd protested as the closets and armoires grew in size and quantity until whole rooms had to be converted to hold her expanding wardrobe, "anything that costs this much can't possibly be thrown away. You wouldn't discard a chair or a painting simply because it had been purchased last year." And dear Alphonse, round, bespectacled and adoring, had agreed, adding with a laugh, "And when we run out of rooms, your economy will force me to buy a larger house!"

What a pity, thought Caro as she hurried down the rue de Rivoli, that Alphonse was no longer here to see her thrift put to such good use. Despite the war she able to clothe herself decently from the depths of her closet – and some of those garments dated back to the days of Worth at the turn of the century – and, with the aid of a little sewing woman, she saw to it that her friends, too, were supplied with her newly converted "old" clothes. She felt quite chic in this soft blue wool suit, despite the wartime restrictions. And, of course, the hat added just the right finishing touch – a wonderful fine woven straw bought from Madame Reboux ten years ago; she'd simply added a length of spotted veil from another hat and a clutch of purple-blue flowers that had decorated the bosom of some twenties evening dress. Growing older, she decided with a wry smile, had its advantages. But it was *feeling* old she didn't like, and she had to admit that there were days when she felt every one of her seventy-three years.

A glance at her reflection in a shop window showed that her back was still straight and that the new shorter skirts quite suited her – thank God her legs were still good. "Like a thoroughbred filly," Alphonse used to say, "high-stepping with slender ankles and a skittish rear end!" She still missed him even though he'd died twenty years ago – in the *last* war.

Caro stepped smartly aside to avoid being jostled by a band of laughing noisy young German soldiers, back from the front for a few days' leave in Gay Paree. God, how she hated the very *sound* of that language! Was it different now than it used to be in the old days when she'd enjoyed herself at Baden-Baden in the company of those civilised men and women of Germany? She'd never noticed *then* that her companions were any different. They were cultured, charming, softly spoken. Then who were these new people? All she knew was that they were the enemy and they had driven through her beloved Paris as conquerors. Their ugly swastika flag flew from the city's most beautiful buildings and so-called "officers", who were merely underlings inflated with a sense of their own power, could command tables at the Ritz. Rumours of mass exterminations were filtering through the city, though the stories were too hard to believe. Yet people disappeared every day and the Jewish family who owned the elegant apartment on the next floor – a well-known banker with whom she'd been friendly for years – had been escorted away late one night. She had watched from her window, tears streaming down her face, as silently the small family – the banker, his wife and two young daughters – had climbed into the black van with the wire mesh on the windows and the flash of yellow on the hub caps. She knew what that meant. Gestapo. The very word filled the nation with fear.

She had had a visit from them too – a tall young officer in that black uniform with the gleaming high boots they all wore. Did they, as a nation, she'd wondered naughtily, perhaps have a boot fetish? All that polish and heel-clicking?

"Madame Montalva," he'd said. It was a statement, not a question and therefore she hadn't deigned to reply. "Lieutenant Ernst Müller. I'm here to check your accommodation, Madame, with a view to billeting some of my men here." His unsmiling gaze had taken in her elegant salon filled with memorabilia and possessions collected over a lifetime, but the tall windows flooding the room with light had revealed little of value other than her beautiful antique furniture. Thank God, she'd had the sense to follow Jim's advice and get the paintings and silver out of Paris, though whether they were still there, beneath the flagstones of the kitchen of her country house at Rambouillet, she didn't know. Of course she realised that the officer didn't want it for his men – he fancied a grand apartment for himself. Well, she wasn't about to let this little upstart have *her* home. But you had to be careful with this type – a *petit bourgeois* feeling his power. In her day an officer was also a gentleman. Now you couldn't be sure. She considered telling him she was an old woman and he should be ashamed of himself for thinking of evicting her from her home, but she was damned if she would admit to *him* that she was old. "In that case," she'd replied smartly instead, "I'll have a word with your commandant. We'll see how pleased he'd be about billeting non-commissioned men here."

"Marie-Luce," she summoned her sole remaining maid. The old woman, more aged than her mistress, trembled with fear at the sight of the uniform, twisting her hands together nervously, unable to speak.

"Marie-Luce, get me my coat, please." Caro hauled herself to her feet with an effort – it was one of the bad days for her arthritis. "I shall leave with this person for the Gestapo headquarters."

Marie-Luce gasped. "Oh Madame, Madame. No ..." she wailed.

Caro glared at her. "For God's sake be quiet, Marie-Luce. I need to speak to this officer's commandant."

"No. No. You can't do that," he protested, stepping back a pace.

"Oh. And why not?" Caro challenged him.

56

"No one can just see the Commandant. He's a very busy man . . ."

"Then I shall return with you and make an appointment." Caro knew she had him. His face was flushed and his accent was becoming more pronounced – he was just a country boy who had suddenly hit the big time. He was no game for a wily old woman of the world like her: she'd matched wits with better than he for more than half a century.

Clicking the heels of his glossy boots once more, he crammed the cap with its oversized peak hastily on his head and made for the door. "I will ask the Commandant's office to be in touch with you to discuss the matter," he called.

Caro smiled as the door closed behind him. "Greed," she said to Marie-Luce, sinking back into her chair. "The enemy is greedy, Marie-Luce. He calls himself an officer but he is little better than the common soldier looting in the streets." She knew she wouldn't hear from him again.

It had been a long time since she'd lunched at Maxim's, but of course Albert remembered her. Kissing her emotionally on both cheeks, his plump face was torn between smiles and tears. "I hear you are collaborating with the enemy, Albert," she commented loudly, taking in the mass of Germans at the closely packed tables.

"Ssh, please, Madame Caro!" Albert shrugged, rolling his eyes expressively heavenwards, his jowled face looking even more lugubrious than usual. "It's a necessary evil, Madame – Maxim's must be kept open, it cannot be allowed to die. Maxim's will be here when our men return in victory. But *collaborate*," he pulled himself to his full short height, "never, Madame. Never!"

"Albert, you are a true bourgeois – business will always come first. And today, I for one am glad. It's been a long time since I tasted Maxim's food. And the champagne . . ."

"Ah, the champagne. For you, Madame, we have the best – and on the house." Escorting her personally to her table, Albert summoned the sommelier. "The Dom Perignon '34 please, for Madame, and her companion." He looked enquiringly at Caro.

"I'm expecting Señor Goncalvez-Herrera from the Spanish Embassy," she explained. Caro's Spanish citizenship enabled her a degree of freedom denied the French, and now she was glad she had never succumbed to the temptation to change it, even though she had lived most of her life in France.

Caro sipped the delicate champagne, closing her eyes as it slid deliciously down her throat, bringing back memories of magical nights when, in silks and jewels, she had been considered the toast of Paris. She and Leonie. Old friends, old companions in troubles and triumphs. Thank God Leonie had found a lasting happiness in her relationship with Jim. Good, all-American Jim, tall and handsome and ten years younger than Leonie, who had taken over her life and brought order from its chaos, ridding her of the Sekhmet legend . . . almost. God, how he loved her! Lucky, lucky Leonie to be so loved still.

Enough of the past with all its regrets! She might as well see how the enemy behaved themselves in a place like this. She certainly hoped Albert didn't let in any little upstarts like the officer who'd wanted her apartment! Her alert dark eyes roamed the familiar room. It was the same and yet it was different – the huge Art Nouveau mirrors reflected too many uniforms with only here and there the brightly coloured dress of a woman to relieve the monotony. Ah, it used to be a peacock's paradise here at Maxim's, and now, in her modest little blue suit and bravely flowered hat, she looked quite exotic!

"Madame Montalva. Do forgive me for being late. I'm afraid I was delayed at the embassy." Her lunch companion took his seat with a smile. Carolina Montalva had never married but the "Madame" was a courtesy everyone afforded her these days.

Caro smiled at him. He was quite young – well, to her he was young – forty-five or so! And he was charming and civilised – and he wasn't wearing that *damned uniform*! "We look quite normal, you and I," she said as the waiter filled their glasses, "and I feel quite gay, drinking champagne at Maxim's. Like old times."

"Almost," he said quietly. "And it's as good a place as any to talk over your problems."

Caro shrugged. "They are not very bad problems," she admitted, "when I think of some."

A burst of laughter came from the entrance cutting across their conversation, distracting her, and Caro glanced up irritably.

The German officer must be of a very high rank for Albert to be quite so obsequious. Even from here she could see the glint of gold braid. And the man was loud, calling attention to his presence. Several officers near the entrance scrambled to their feet, saluting, and he waved them back genially. He was a good-looking man, if a little florid, and an officer of the old school. Aristocratic with the ridiculous monocle they all affected, and a coldness behind the smile that could chill your heart. Putting an arm around his companion he drew her forward into the restaurant. Albert bowed over the girl's hand – Caro would bet it wasn't his wife. Who then? Some little French tart selling out for a taste of the good life? Poor silly creature. These girls did it all for the wrong reasons. She looked attractive and beautifully dressed – in this year's clothes, not 1920s made over! Her eyes must be getting worse, though, because she could swear the girl looked like Lais, but no – it couldn't be. *It simply couldn't be her!*

Lais paused beside Caro's table. "Why, Caro," she said with a surprised smile, "I didn't expect to see you here."

"Nor I you, Lais."

"A friend of yours, my angel?" The officer's hand lingered possessively on Lais's arm.

"An old friend of my grandmother's," replied Lais, "Carolina Montalva – may I introduce General Karl von Bruhel."

"Well of course any friend of the famous Leonie is welcome at our house, isn't that so, *Liebchen?*" General von Bruhel bowed. "I am at your service, Madame Montalva. We should be honoured to see you at dinner one evening soon. Lais will arrange it."

"And which house is that then, Lais?" Caro's gaze fixed her unmercifully and Lais flushed a little.

"Why," she tilted her chin defiantly, "the de Courmont house on the Ile St Louis, of course." She gathered the soft sable stole around her shoulders nervously. "We shall expect you then, Aunt Caro."

Señor Goncalvez-Herrera had been standing politely by his chair, waiting, and Caro felt sorry for him, caught up in undercurrents that didn't concern him. He looked desperately uncomfortable as he took his seat again. Caro watched as Lais and her escort were given the best table in the crowded room.

"Don't ask me, Señor Herrera," she said, "because I can't even speak about it right now."

"I won't ask," Goncalvez-Herrera replied, "but I can *tell* you, if you wish."

Caro took a sip of her champagne wishing it would obliterate what she had just seen so that she needn't ever think of it again. "Go ahead," she said quietly, "tell me the worst."

"The de Courmont mansion is the centre of high-level social activity in Paris. The parties there are not necessarily the biggest, but they are the best – the most *exclusive*. Von Bruhel took over the

mansion as his headquarters and the de Courmont girl stayed on –
supposedly in her own section of the house. But," he shrugged
expressively, "what happens between a man and a woman happened. Now she lives with him quite openly as his mistress. She
shops at the couturiers and her car has a German chauffeur. Von
Bruhel loads her with jewels – and humiliates her in small ways in
front of their guests."

Caro raised her eyebrows. "For instance?"

"For one thing, she is never allowed to call him Karl in public. She
must always address him formally." Goncalvez-Herrera hesitated.

"Continue," Caro prompted.

"Well – I've only *heard* this, you understand – but von Bruhel
caresses her – intimately – in public . . ."

Caro drew a shocked breath. "And she permits that?"

"I'm afraid, Caro, that the word is that not only does she permit
it, she enjoys it."

"Oh my God," said Caro quietly, her eyes resting on Lais. Von
Bruhel had his arm around her and was whispering something in
her ear. Caro's appetite for Maxim's good food suddenly disappeared. She must get in touch with Leonie at once.

10

The train from Nice jolted slowly towards Paris, crammed with
German and Italian soldiers. There were a few civilian agricultural
workers with permission to move to another work area and a scatter
of women and children. The train stopped at every small station
and occasionally broke down; it re-started only to be halted in the
middle of nowhere – just endless brown fields and the now distant
snow-capped mountains of the Alpes Maritimes – while a search
party of officious young German soldiers inspected their papers.

Leonie had asked Commandant von Steinholz to grant her special
permission to travel.

"To Paris?" he'd commented lazily, tossing down his pen. "And what takes you there, Madame Leonie?"

"Family business," she'd replied firmly. "I must see my lawyers regarding my will. In these uncertain times," she added drily, "one never knows when one's will might be needed."

"Is that the only reason?" His amused gaze bored into her. He knew about Lais, she felt sure.

"I intend to see my granddaughter and to inspect my son-in-law's property on the Ile St Louis. The de Courmont house is a national monument. It's my duty to see that it is kept up to standard."

"You'll find the house a little changed," said von Steinholz, pushing a button to summon his aide. "Though from what I hear, your granddaughter has not."

"All I need from you, Herr von Steinholz, are the necessary travel papers," said Leonie icily. "I do not need your opinions."

His eyes glinted angrily behind the gold spectacles, as he spoke to his assistant.

"Kruger, Madame is to leave for Paris. Please provide her with the necessary documents." Turning to Leonie he said, "I will sign them personally to ensure that you will have no trouble on your journey. The papers will be delivered to you tomorrow." Picking up the telephone he made it clear that she was dismissed.

As she left von Steinholz's office Leonie had never wished more fervently for Jim. *He* would have known how to deal with this slimy man. But Jim was in England with the US Air Force Bomber Command. She had received this information from Gaston Lafarge, the baker in St Jean, the leader of the local Resistance and the source of all her information. It was Gaston who had also told her about Gerard. Handing her a long baguette loaf fresh from the ovens, he'd said, "I'm sorry it's not such good news for Monsieur Gerard. He's safe at the moment," he added as Leonie's eyes widened in alarm, "but we've heard he is interned at a forced labour camp near the Belgian border. The Nazis wanted the prestige of a de Courmont publicly cooperating in running the de Courmont factories, but Monsieur Gerard refused. Like so many others, his refusal cost him his freedom."

Gaston had called her back as she walked dispiritedly towards the door. "There are many who need our help," he had said, in a low voice, "escaped prisoners, airmen who have been shot down, women of many nationalities fighting for *us*, Madame. They need to be smuggled out of the country. We are setting up a route through the South of France via Marseilles to Spain. They will need a place to hide along the section of coast and it seemed to my colleagues that the cellars beneath your hotel would be ideal."

"Beneath the hotel," whispered Leonie, "but the *Germans* are in the hotel!"

"Exactly! And therefore what better place? With the exception of von Steinholz and his staff the Germans and Italians staying at the hotel are only temporary. They are unfamiliar with its routine. They are officers on leave – resting from their labours. *They are there to have a good time.* To them the hotel cellars are only a place with an infinite supply of champagne. No one would suspect such audacity! The big problem is to link up the route from the north. And it is a problem."

Leonie hesitated. She longed to say yes, but there was Leonore to consider. If they were caught it was Leonore who was running the hotel. It would be *she* the Germans would take. And there was Peach, only seven years old. She couldn't risk putting the child in such danger.

"Please consider it, Madame Leonie," begged Gaston holding open the door for her. "We would be most grateful."

War could make heroes of the simplest men, thought Leonie, admiring his courage. "I'll discuss it with my granddaughter Leonore at the hotel," she promised.

Caro's letter, written weeks before, arrived the next day, hand-delivered by a farmer driving the sort of pony and cart that Leonie had ridden in as a young girl in her Normandy village and which had suddenly appeared again on the de-motorised roads of France. Only the rich black Mercedes, the big Citroëns and shiny dark de Courmonts used by the enemy were to be seen on French roads these days.

She'd kept the contents of the letter to herself for a day and for the first time she blessed the lack of communication that left Amelie in ignorance of her daughter's activities. But finally she had to tell Leonore why she was going to Paris.

Leonore had sat as if carved of stone and then she had begun to cry. "How could Lais do such a terrible thing?" she'd wailed, "*How could she!* But it's true, Grand-mère, I'm sure of it!"

Poor Leonore, the strain of keeping the hotel going while main-taining her position of aloof non-cooperation was beginning to tell. At first she had rebelled. Without telling Leonie, she'd stormed into the Commandant's office and told him she would do nothing to cooperate. The hotel could be closed.

"As you wish," von Steinholz had replied with his cynical knowing smile, "though of course the hotel will *not* close. It will merely be requisitioned. As will your grandmother's villa. And you and she – along with the little girl – will be interned." He'd consulted a chart on his desk. "There is a camp here, near the Italian border, that would be suitable I think." He'd smiled at her over the tops of his gleaming gold-rimmed spectacles and Leonore had known she was beaten. Even if she let go the hotel and even though she would consider internment for herself, she certainly couldn't be reckless enough to inflict such a thing on Grand-mère and Peach! And the villa was Grand-mère's treasured home, her refuge from the world. The idea of it being filled with enemy officers filled her with rage. Any rebellion on her part would have to be more subtle – and much more careful.

When Leonie told her of Gaston's conversation Leonore grasped at the chance. "We'll do it," she'd said eagerly. "The cellars are vast and with a little work they could connect with the villa. But we must think of how we can help to set up the rest of the chain."

"Meanwhile," Leonie had sighed, "something has to be done about your sister."

11

The Palacio d'Aureville was Florida's smartest hotel and even wartime restrictions hadn't managed to dampen its aura of glamour and excitement. Sunbronzed naval officers in tropical whites lingered for a few days R. & R. before heading back to base at Pensacola, enjoying the Palaçio's comforts – the luxury of a good bed, a decent bath and the splendid bar that never ran dry. Air Command pilots, glamorous in blue, with tense, tired eyes, waited for orders. And buff-clad army officers, Sam Brownes polished and battle-colours decorating their well-tailored jackets, tried to forget for a few brief days that the world was at war.

Amelie de Courmont pretended not to notice the tell-tale signs of nervous strain in her guests, the slight tremor of a hand, or the persistent small tic in the cheek or the strange, suddenly blank look in the eyes of men who had seen too much of the horrors of war. She simply did her best to give them everything they might need – rest, good food, a decent drink. The Florida girls who ran the always-open canteens for servicemen or worked long shifts in factories emerged beautiful and energetic as soon as they were freed from their toil to provide entertainment, companionship and affection. And, sometimes – love.

The design of the hotel was based on the Palace of the Alhambra at Granada with courtyards and fountains and beautiful gardens laid out in the manner of the Generalife, leading along delightful shady paths to the sea. True, the paths were a little more overgrown than they should be now that there were only two old men to help with the acres of gardens instead of the prewar crew of a dozen strong young ones. But even though the paintwork of the hotel was a little shabby, the linen sheets were still the finest; and no one seemed to mind the long waits for service because the staff were at a minimum.

Though Amelie de Courmont was physically a younger replica of her mother Leonie, somehow, with her air of alert efficiency and her ability to take care of a dozen tasks at once, she seemed all-American. In fact she was entirely French by birth – and completely Brazilian by upbringing and instinct. Amelie had inherited the good bone structure of her mother and she in turn had passed it on to her daughters – the straight positive nose, the slanting cheekbones, delicate jaw and wide-spaced eyes. And the same blonde mass of hair. But despite Amelie's feminine Brazilian charm, she had a steely determination that had made her a success in a man's world. When Amelie de Courmont wanted something, she usually found a way to get it.

Amelie put in long hours, rising at five every morning and falling exhausted into bed well after midnight. Showered and dressed smartly as befitted her role as manager and proprietor of the Palaçio, her blonde hair firmly held in place by one of the new velvet-mesh snoods, and with Gerard's enormous sapphire engagement ring that she would never remove, glinting on her left hand, she would walk across the gardens to the hotel. It would have been easier to move into a suite at the hotel now that she was alone, but she forced herself to return to her house every night, walking through its lonely rooms, blinking away the tears that she refused to let fall. She would cry when they all returned, she promised herself, and not before. Who would have dreamed that this would happen? How could she have known the day she fell and broke her hip and the decision was made for Lais to take Peach to France, that she would lose both of them? She'd gone over the "if-onlys" so many times that she didn't even bother any more.

After that terrifying telephone call when Peach was so ill and Gerard had left for France, she had tried to tell herself that it would be all right, that her little girl would survive and that her two grown daughters would return home with their sister before the axe of war cut off the escape route. Sometimes at night in bed, she would pray, offering to bargain with God. "I'll give away all this," she promised, "the hotels, the money, the luxury – everything. If you'll just give my children and my husband back to me, safe and undamaged." But her lovely, darling little girl Peach now walked only with the aid of a calliper. It hurt so much to think of those young, once-strong legs encased in steel and her recurrent nightmare was one in which Peach cried to her endlessly to "take them away, take them away, Maman", and she was helpless to do so. Of course Peach was now seven years old and Amelie had no concept of how she might really look. She had only her memories.

The gardens were particularly lovely this morning, trees and grass glittered with dew and the hibiscus and bougainvillaea were just beginning to open and show their gay pink and purple and orange colours. Of course the grass needed cutting and the paths should be edged, and the bushes were in dire need of pruning, but still, they were beautiful.

Amelie called in at the hotel's kitchens en route, picking up a cup of coffee and a fresh-baked roll which she munched as she walked along the corridor, safe in the knowledge that at this early hour she wouldn't be observed.

Her office was cool and pleasant though later it would become oppressively hot. Amelie used the air-conditioning only sparingly, conserving energy and reserving such luxury for her guests.

A typed list of matters to be dealt with waited on the desk, prepared last night by her secretary, and beside it, a list of *priorities*. Heavily underlined. Such as finding out about the liquor supplies, and where could they get replacements for the lawnmowers and what about lightbulbs? And they were desperate for a shipment of cigarettes!

Amelie put down her coffee cup carefully as the tears brimmed in her eyes. She'd held them back for so long, refusing to cry for Gerard, or even for Peach – and now she was crying over lawn-mowers and lightbulbs. It was all too much to cope with. *It was simply too much!* Sometimes it felt as though she were giving one long party at which she was an unwilling hostess. "Oh Gerard, Gerard, where are you? Are you even alive?" Shocked she heard herself cry out the question she'd never permitted to cross her mind. Gerard had to be alive. And Lais and Leonore? There had been a few scattered communications via diplomatic bags, but nothing positive, just that they were still in France, that at that moment they were all right. And Peach, her little love?

Picking up her pen Amelie dashed away the tears and began determinedly making notes as to whom to call that day. The only way to keep herself sane was to work, just the way she had when her first husband Roberto died. Work was the magic talisman of the lonely and desperate and it was only when she was working that she felt *real*.

The telegram from the Red Cross arrived at noon and its yellow envelope sent a chill through her heart. Her secretary, waiting by the door, watched apprehensively as Amelie turned it over and over in her hands before finally ripping it open.

"Oh," she gasped, and then, "Oh, oh, thank God. Gerard – is all right. He's been interned in some sort of camp in Belgium. A forced labour camp, they call it. But *he's all right*. Oh thank you, thank you," she cried casting a glance heavenwards. "Thank you, God."

Drinks were on the house in the Palácio bar that night and Amelie, sparkling with joy, flitted among her guests making sure that their happiness matched her own, however temporary either might be.

It was the old Senator down from Washington for a naval conference who gave her the plan – and it was his influence that finally set it in motion.

"Damned if I can see how you can be here and your little girl in France," he'd said thoughtfully. "At least if you were in Lisbon you might be able to get news of her."

"Lisbon?" Amelie stared at the Senator in surprise.

"An odd city," he replied, "I was there just a couple of weeks ago. Goddamn place is full of spies and counter-spies, Free-French, British, Germans, you name it, all eating in the same restaurants! And not too far away the same nations are killing each other! It seemed to me, Mrs de Courmont, that a person could get almost anything he wanted in Lisbon – whether it was a good meal – or a man killed. Or some information – for a price, of course. Yes. They would ask a high price.''

Amelie leaned forward grasping his arm excitedly. "I would be prepared to pay any money," she whispered, "to have news of my daughter. But, Senator, I'm here, in Florida. How can a woman like me get to Lisbon in wartime?''

The Senator's kind eyes met hers with a smile. He had girls of his own just a little older than Peach. "We'll just have to see what we can do about that, Mrs de Courmont, now won't we?''

12

Peach scrambled the last few feet to the top of the hill making for the patch of shade formed by the intertwined branches of the old olive trees. The sky was a hard bright blue and the mid-afternoon sun blazed with the intensity of high summer. Below her, the pink-arched hotel hugged the olive and cypress-studded headland like a coat of frosting on a wedge of rich dark cake. Its rectangular swimming pool glittered in the sun like an aquamarine and Peach watched swimmers splashing through the water then climbing out and shaking themselves in a shower of crystal drops. Like wet dogs, she thought contemptuously. White-jacketed German waiters carried trays of foaming ice-cold beer and a snatch of music drifted up the hill. If it weren't for the fact that there were no children around you might almost have thought it a normal holiday scene. But it wasn't. No children ever swam in that pool now.

Peach lay back and stared at the sky. Even the usually noisy birds and cicadas had been subdued by the heat, but a tiny breeze held the sweetness of mimosa and the tang of the sea and there was the scent of rosemary and thyme and a dozen different flowers. She hadn't been able to bear her room any longer. The long green shutters of the villa were closed against the heat, giving it a translucent dimness like being underwater. The white sheet was rumpled from her restless tossing, her book flung to the floor. Leonie had been gone for two days and Leonore was busy at the hotel. Madame Frenard was taking her siesta and the house had a strange empty silence that frightened her. She wished Leonie hadn't gone to Paris, it was so far away, and although they hadn't said anything, Grand-mère and Leonore had looked so worried. And, try as she might, she couldn't push away the thought that Papa had gone away just like Grand-mère, promising to come back soon. And so had Jim. *And they hadn't returned.*

Peach wondered what might she be doing if she were home in Florida with Maman? Leonore had told her that when it was daytime here in France it would be nighttime at home. Maman must be sleeping – maybe even dreaming of her. But it had been so long – what if she had forgotten her?

Peach sat up quickly. Of course Maman hadn't forgotten her – she was just being silly. Grand-mère had told her that when *she* had had to send Amelie away to live in Brazil when she was just a little baby, she had never forgotten about her, that she'd thought of her every single day. "Mothers never forget," she'd reassured her.

Her right leg in its steel brace felt hot and uncomfortable and Peach stared angrily at the ugly leather straps. "*Merde,*" she said, relishing the curse word. "*Merde* thing!" Leaning forward she pulled angrily at the buckles. There! She was free. She examined her legs anxiously. The right one didn't look too bad – only a little thinner. She still exercised every day and swam in the sea first thing in the morning before she went off to school in Monte Carlo, and again as soon as she got home in the evening. And that was the nicest part of the day!

She would sling her schoolbag on to the floor, discard her round straw hat and striped school smock, and pull on her pink cotton bathing suit. Then she'd hurry down to the beach below the villa as fast as her limp would allow, taking the steps in a sort of sideways rush that she had perfected over the past two years. And then the bliss of freeing herself from the calliper and of floating on her back in the clear water, letting her long hair drift coolly behind! After a few minutes she would turn over, cutting through the water with her strong arms, enjoying the feeling of *power* as she swam. The sea refreshed her, it made her feel strong again, and almost normal.

Picking up the calliper Peach examined it carefully. She'd bet the man who designed it had no children – if he had surely he would have used scarlet leather, or pink, or maybe even just pretty ribbons. She had told Grand-mère that she wanted to throw it in the sea, but Leonie wouldn't allow it.

Peach stared at the sea, so blue, so smooth. There was a place, just along the chalky path that led around the Pointe St Hospice, where the rocks shelved steeply and the colour of the water deepened to ultramarine. It would be the perfect spot.

Getting to her feet without the calliper wasn't as easy as she had thought, but by pushing herself on to her hands and knees and then grabbing a handy branch, she made it. The path up which she had scrambled an hour ago looked suddenly steeper. Cautiously, she tested her weight on the right leg. Her knee wobbled a bit but she had both feet flat on the ground. So far so good. She glanced doubtfully at the calliper lying on the scorched grass. She could always put it on again just to get down the hill. But no. She was never – ever – going to wear that *merde* thing again. Hauling it by its ugly leather straps she took a tentative step on the little stony path. Her left foot skittered on the loose stones, and she wobbled again, dangerously. Peach bit her lip, feeling the sweat trickle down the back of her shirt. A snatch of music and laughter came towards her on the wind and she glared angrily at the hotel pool. That odious von Steinholz would be there. And the even more odious Volker Kruger who was trying to give Leonore orders and boss her around. She'd heard Grand-mère and Leonore talking. The de Courmont girls were strong, they had said. They would never be beaten.

Half-scrambling, half-sliding with her legs scratched and bleeding, she made it to the bottom of the hill. Forcing herself to put her weight evenly on both legs Peach limped very slowly along the path that led around the headland. She was there. With a final contemptuous glance she lifted the calliper by its straps and flung it over the small cliff. The setting sun flashed from the steel brace as it dropped with only the smallest splash into the sea. Raising her arms over her head Peach gave a cry of triumph. The *merde* thing was gone. And never, *never* again would she wear a calliper.

13

Enrique García lit his fourth Gauloise in a half hour, checking his watch nervously. One of Lais's virtues was that she was always prompt. He'd give her five more minutes and then he'd make a phone call. Sipping a cup of ersatz coffee he wrinkled his nose at its acrid taste, wondering if the coffee in Barcelona still tasted as good as he remembered.

Lais slid on to the stool beside him in the small bar in Les Halles where they had first met. "I need a drink," she said shakily.

Enrique stirred his fourth cup of coffee. "Too bad," he replied, "it's a dry day."

"Damn! Oh damn!" Lais had forgotten that on three days a week the sale of alcohol was forbidden and for some reason the petty disappointment made her want to cry.

She looked pale and shaky, he thought. Combined with the lateness it wasn't a good sign. "You're getting spoiled, living in the lap of luxury with the Nazi boss," he commented, signalling the bartender.

"Enrique, it's just that this time I'm really frightened." The bartender placed a small coffee cup filled with brandy in front of her.

"An emergency," he murmured with a wink.

"We are all afraid, Lais. You get used to it." Enrique noticed her trembling hand as she lifted the cup.

"You don't understand. You can't possibly understand." Lais stared into her empty cup. "I'm afraid every time Karl looks at me, assessing me like a prize racehorse whose performance isn't quite what he was led to believe it would be for its thoroughbred background and the price he had to pay. I'm afraid every time he touches me – *physically afraid*. Karl's a sadist, he enjoys inflicting pain. Oh, so far there's been nothing that I couldn't bear – and maybe even enjoy," she added bitterly. "God, you don't know how I despise myself afterwards."

Enrique lit another cigarette, exhaling pungent blue smoke towards the stained ceiling.

"I can cope with the rest," said Lais as tears coursed down her face, "I can flaunt myself in my fancy couture clothes and make believe I don't see the contempt in people's eyes. I can drive around Paris in my chauffeur-driven car and dine on good food at the Ritz while others go without, wearing jewels that were probably looted from some charming French family to whom they had belonged for generations. I can smile when Karl puts his arm around me in public, I laugh at his witty conversation, act as his hostess and procure girls for his visiting comrades ... I've tried not to mind when he caresses my breast in a restaurant or a theatre, making sure that everyone understands what I am – and that he owns me. I just tell myself that next time – yes the *next* time, I'll take a knife and kill him!"

Her blonde hair was tied back in a blue silk scarf and she wore no make-up. She looked like a schoolgirl of sixteen. It shocked Enrique to see her so vulnerable. Lais had always played the role of the tough, arrogant little rich girl who didn't give a damn what anyone thought, living for the mood of the moment. Life had always come on her terms.

He gripped her arm, steadying its shaking and signalled the bartender. "You mustn't think like this, Lais," he said urgently. "You *must not* do anything foolish."

"My, my," Lais sipped the fresh cup of brandy and stared at him with tear-swollen eyes. "Anyone might think you cared."

"This is not a personal matter," Enrique replied coldly. "You have a job to do. You knew what you were taking on when you started. Now you are important to the organisation. We *need* you, Lais."

"Well, at least that's something," she said, finishing the brandy at a gulp, "at least I'm needed."

"How dare you feel sorry for yourself," said Enrique angrily, keeping his voice low, "there are hundreds of women in far worse situations than you. *You* are living in luxury. Others are hiding in the slums of Ménilmontant or Belleville, keeping just one step ahead of the Gestapo. They've lost husbands and sons. They *know* why they are working for the Resistance and *they can never forget*."

Lais stared at Enrique's dark, impassive face. He was right. She

71

had known what she was getting into; at first she'd been excited by the game and the thrill had been exhilarating. Flirting with danger had offered an excitement that was better even than a dangerous sexual flirtation with a man because with *that*, she always knew how it would end.

But Karl was clever, his sharp eyes missed none of her changes in mood. When he made love to her he searched her face looking for clues to her true emotions. Every time he made her beg him he would lift her face to his, watching her with that icy smile. And one night she knew he would go too far, past the point of enjoyment into cruelty. Lais felt the rush of fear up her spine. *It was herself she was afraid of.* She didn't know what she might do – or what she was capable of. "If I could just leave him," her eyes begged Enrique, "I could work somewhere else. I'd do *anything*, Enrique, anything!"

"It's too late," Enrique pulled the pack of Gauloises from his pocket. "You'll just have to put up with him until he tires of you, Lais. Meanwhile, you've got work to do." Lighting up the cigarette from the stub of the previous one he tossed the butt into the brimming blue ashtray. "So, who are these important visitors, Lais?"

She stared at the meagre display of bottles behind the bar. "General Guderian – the man who occupied and practically destroyed Reims, and Otto Klebbich, the man he appointed to control the champagne industry."

"Not such big fish," shrugged Enrique.

"There's to be a party tonight at the house. Goebbels is coming with his wife Magda, and Reichsführer SS Heinrich Himmler and someone called Speer, who is Hitler's Minister of Armaments and War Production. Along with their entourages and hangers on, of course." She took the cigarette from Enrique's fingers and dragged on it deeply.

Enrique's lips formed a silent whistle. "Do you have any idea why they are here?"

Lais shrugged. "There's a meeting tomorrow to discuss the movement of French workers into the armaments factories in Germany. I think Himmler and Speer are at loggerheads. Goebbels is here to show the pretty Magda the sights of Paris. I have been delegated to take her to the couturiers, the furriers, the hat shops, the perfumers, the jewellers . . . apparently she's a nice woman . . ." Her voice trailed off and tears coursed down her face. "I can't do it, Enrique, don't make me go on . . ."

72

"Just this once, Lais," he gripped her hand fiercely, "you *must*. You've done so well before, the information you have given us has been invaluable. You've saved many French lives through your work. Just do what you've done before, Lais. Listen to all the conversations – particularly those *after* dinner when they've been drinking and are likely to open up and discuss matters among themselves that should be kept for meetings behind closed doors. Observe everything, read any documents or papers left lying around before or after that meeting. We need *any* information we can get, Lais. And then I'll see what I can do about getting you out of this situation."

"You mean that?" she asked shakily. "Really Enrique?"

"I mean it," he promised. Damn that bastard von Bruhel! He'd broken her. And Lais had been one of their best sources of information, ensconced snugly among the ranks of Nazi power.

"Lais, you must promise me that tonight you'll be your old self. Karl von Bruhel's beautiful Frenchwoman, his charming hostess. Make the others envious of him, Lais, so that Karl will preen himself in his glory. And later, after you've 'made love' to him, drop this in his champagne." He held up a familiar little packet. "He'll sleep soundly and you can take the opportunity of inspecting his papers for tomorrow's meeting."

She managed a grin. "Lais de Courmont, super-spy."

"Lais de Courmont, a brave woman." He leaned forward and kissed her on the lips. "Take care, Lais. I'll be thinking of you."

He watched as she walked to the door, pausing to tighten the scarf over her hair, checking the street before she stepped out. He hoped she would be all right.

The great crystal chandeliers of the de Courmont mansion glittered a welcome as long gleaming limousines swung into the courtyard, disgorging elegant passengers. Karl von Bruhel, waiting impatiently at the foot of the curving marble staircase to greet his guests, glanced angrily upwards. *Where* was Lais? His guests were arriving, and he would have to receive them alone. Ah! *At last!* Lais floated down the stairs towards him, a vision in sea-green silk crêpe de Chine. The long gown left one gleaming shoulder bare, clinging to the curves of her slender, high breasted body, and affording a tantalising glimpse of her long silk-stockinged legs where the straight skirt wrapped around at the front. Enormous emerald drops hung from her small ears and the matching necklace, threaded with diamonds, circled her neck. The hairdresser had swept her blonde hair into two glossy wings that framed her lovely face – the face, dammit, that she had just spent an hour making-up when she should have been here by his side!

"It's good of you to come down, Lais, in time to meet our guests," Karl said acidly.

"And here they are." Ignoring the barb in his words Lais swept forward with outstretched arms and a wide smile to welcome Magda and Joseph Goebbels. Magda was older, sophisticated, blonde and attractive. Her husband was thin with a large, elongated head and a small man's strutting arrogance. His protuberant grey eyes swept over Lais in a way that made her blush. Joseph Goebbels was a notorious womaniser and he and Magda had separated several times, though the rumour was that Hitler had forbidden their divorce because it would set a bad example to the Reich. Reichsführer Heinrich Himmler, his chest a blaze of ribbons, high boots glittering, bowed over her hand.

"A pleasure to meet you, Fräulein de Courmont," he said, "especially since I also had the recent pleasure of meeting your stepfather."

Lais felt the colour drain from her face. Himmler's position as head of the SS gave him control of concentration camps. If he'd met Gerard could it mean that he had been moved from the "political" camp near the Belgian border into one of the concentration camps in Germany?

Taking her arm Himmler walked with her into the beautiful salon. She had filled the room with sweet-scented jasmine and tall aromatic lilies. Garlands of fresh bay were looped around a table containing a silver platter with a two-foot-high mound of Beluga caviare. White-gloved waiters offered champagne as Himmler helped himself to the shiny black granules, licking his fingers greedily. "A good man, your stepfather," he said to Lais, "a straightforward man. *Honourable.*"

"Yes, Gerard is an honourable man."

The caviare glistened between Himmler's teeth. "You should have a talk with him, my dear. Perhaps *you* could convince him that working for the de Courmont armaments production could only help to bring a quicker end to this war. The foolish man is quite adamant."

"My stepfather never had any interest in the business," said Lais. "He's an architect. What use would he be to you?"

74

"A de Courmont at the head of the de Courmont industries would be quite a coup for the Fatherland. Many other industrialists are already working with us – why not the Duc de Courmont's son? His name is known around the world – its prestige would be great propaganda against our enemies. Of course you are aware of the importance of propaganda?"

"My stepfather and I feel differently about this matter," Lais answered stiffly. "I'm sure I would not be able to change his mind."

Himmler sighed, wiping his mouth with a white damask napkin. "A pity. Life would be so much more comfortable for him if he would only see things our way."

"Please," Lais's hand rested softly on his arm. "Where is my stepfather?"

"Gerard de Courmont is in a labour camp, Fräulein, where I am afraid he must stay until he sees reason."

His thin lips smiled but his eyes had the same fanatic iciness she saw so often in Karl's. Lais looked around the salon of Gerard's family home, at the beautiful yellow silk curtains outlining the long windows, at the sparkling chandeliers, and the Nazis treading the lovely Aubusson rugs, at the silver and crystal and the obscene mound of caviare, symbol of luxury and power. She felt sick. Enrique had told her only that morning that there were other women who could never forget the reason they worked for the Resistance, they had lost husbands and sons – and fathers. Now Lais knew that she too would never forget. She must do what she could to help.

Lifting her chin she smiled sweetly at Magda Goebbels. "I hope you are ready to take Paris by storm, Frau Goebbels," she said, taking her arm, "I have made an appointment with the couturiers for Wednesday morning, and then I thought we might go to the fur salons. It'll be such fun. Now I have someone *very* charming sitting next to you at dinner." Her eyes were full of female conspiracy as she escorted Magda across the room to meet Ferdi von Schönberg.

Señor Goncalvez-Herrera drove his Hispano Suiza with its diplomatic licence plates that allowed him to ignore the curfew, slowly across the Pont Marie. Even from across the river he had noticed the lights and the activity on the Quai de Bourbon and as he turned into the Quai d'Orléans he pulled the car to the kerb and parked.

"Madame Jamieson, won't you please re-think this situation?" He gestured to the row of Mercedes and the waiting chauffeurs gossiping, the red tips of their cigarettes glowing in the dark, and at the armed guards patrolling in front of the house.

A snatch of music carried down the street and light spilled suddenly on to the courtyard as the door was flung open to admit more guests. Leonie boiled over with anger. How dare Lais give parties for the Nazis when Frenchmen were risking their lives for their country's freedom! "There is no need to wait for me," she said, stepping from the car and closing the door firmly behind her.

"I'll wait," he said with a sigh. He watched as she strode purposefully towards the de Courmont house, her back straight, head up. She looked indomitable. He hoped, for her sake and her granddaughter's, that she was.

"Halt!" A pair of bayonets barred Leonie's way as she turned into the courtyard. "Who are you? What do you want?" The sergeant pushed her roughly against the stone gatepost. "Where are your papers?" he demanded. "At once!"

Leonie had them ready. "I think you will find them in order," she answered calmly. "I am Mademoiselle de Courmont's grandmother."

The sergeant peered at her with small suspicious eyes. "Her *grandmother*?"

"That is what I said. Now kindly let me through. I wish to talk to my granddaughter."

"What is it? What's going on?" A young blond officer shouldered his way through the knot of guards that surrounded her, staring at Leonie in surprise.

"I am Leonie Jamieson," she said evenly. "I am here to see my granddaughter."

"Of course," Ferdi von Schönberg said quietly. "I know who you are."

Leonie stared at him puzzled. There was something familiar about him, but the soldiers all seemed to her to look alike, young, blond, strong.

"It's all right," said Ferdi, "this lady is who she says she is. Let her pass." He took Leonie's arm but she shook him away angrily.

Embarrassed, he led the way up the steps into the house. "If you will wait here, Madame, I will find Lais for you."

Leonie glared at his departing back. So, he called her Lais, did he? Was this the one then? No, he wasn't of high enough rank. Lais had gone for the top.

Inside the double front doors armed sentries stood at attention

76

and in the lofty hall guards were positioned at the entry to every room. This was surely no ordinary party they were guarding.

"Grand-mère!"

Lais, beautifully dressed and laden with emeralds, stood at the top of the staircase staring at her with an expression of horror. Or was it fear? Leonie felt a momentary pang of compassion for her wayward granddaughter. But this was no girlish madness. This time Lais had gone too far.

"Grand-mère, *what are you doing here?*" Lais ran down the stairs and flung her arms around Leonie, kissing her.

"Get your coat, Lais," Leonie said quietly, "I'm taking you home with me."

"Grand-mère! Don't be ridiculous. You know I can't do that. I can't leave now, we – I – have guests. Important guests," her blue eyes searched Leonie's face desperately. "Can't we meet tomorrow? We can talk about coming home then."

"Pardon me, Fräulein," Magda Goebbels interrupted, smiling at Leonie. "I am a great admirer of yours for years, Madame Leonie. I first saw you on stage in Munich years ago and I have remained your devoted admirer ever since. I never missed your concerts when you came to Germany."

"Grand-mère, this is Frau Magda Goebbels." Lais introduced them nervously.

Leonie ignored the woman's outstretched hand. "Thank you for your compliments, Frau Goebbels," she said coldly, "but that was a long time ago. Before the war."

Magda's blue eyes regarded her sadly. "I understand," she replied quietly, "these are difficult times. But I'm very happy to have met you, Madame."

As she walked towards the double doors that led to the salon an attendant sprang to open them for her. Leonie took in the white-gloved German servants, the elegant women, both German and French, the gaudy parade of Nazi hierarchy. And the great mound of caviare – ignored on its melting bed of ice. A pianist tinkled away at the grand piano and vermeil candelabra painted the scene with a soft unreal amber light. "My God, Lais," she whispered, "what are you playing at?"

"Grand-mère, it's all right," whispered Lais urgently, "Please believe me. It's not what it seems."

"What is not what it seems, *Liebchen?*" Karl's arm snaked around her waist, gripping her tightly just beneath her breast. "You have a visitor," he said jovially. "Magda told me. We are honoured, Madame Leonie, although this is a strange hour to pay an unexpected visit. Still, we shall be happy to have you join our little party, won't we *Liebchen*?" Leonie pretended not to notice his hand squeezing Lais's waist. "Some of us are lucky enough to be familiar with your stage performances," his cold eyes inspected her carefully. "And of course you are still as beautiful as ever."

"Grand-mère, this is General Karl von Bruhel," faltered Lais.

Karl offered Leonie his arm. "Come, Madame, my guests will be thrilled to meet 'Leonie'."

"Grand-mère?" pleaded Lais.

"I am here to take my granddaughter home," said Leonie, casting a contemptuous glance towards the salon. "This is no place for a de Courmont, nor for any Frenchwoman."

"I don't hear your granddaughter complaining," replied Karl angrily. "Well, Lais? Do you have any complaints?"

"No. Of course not," Lais shrugged, avoiding Leonie's eyes.

"Quite the opposite in fact," said Karl. "Lais is very content here. She is a clever woman, Madame Leonie. She has chosen her side well." With a bow, he walked back towards the salon. "Lais, you are being neglectful of our guests." His voice held a warning and Lais shot an apprehensive glance at his retreating back.

"Grand-mère," she whispered, "it's not the way it seems. *Please believe me.*"

"I came here once before to rescue you," Leonie took Lais's hand in hers, "when you were involved with that terrible Russian and didn't know how to get out of it. You said you felt trapped. Is that the way it is now, Lais?"

"In a way," Lais nodded. "A little like that, Grand-mère. It's more complicated," she added despairingly. "I can't come with you tonight, Grand-mère. I just can't."

Leonie's eyes searched her face. "I won't ask why," she said, "because there's no time for explanations. But I'm here to help you, Lais. I feel you are in terrible danger here." She felt Lais's hands trembling. "I'm at Caro's," she said quickly. "I'll wait there for you tomorrow. And then I'm taking you home, Lais."

"Yes. Oh yes, Grand-mère, please." Lais blinked back the tears as Leonie walked across the hall to the doors. An attendant flung them open and Leonie looked back with an anxious half-smile before she walked slowly down the broad steps into the night.

14

Karl von Bruhel awoke feeling calm and refreshed. He sat up in the big Louis XIV bed whose headboard was decorated with a charming painting of lords and ladies disporting themselves by a lake, and pushed the bell to signal that he was ready for his coffee. Running his hands through his crisp steel-grey hair, he glanced first at the clock and then at the empty place beside him. So, Lais was up already. A memory of last night came to mind and he smiled. Throwing back the sheets he padded naked across to the bathroom. Legs arrogantly apart he urinated into the bowl, remembering last night. Lais trembling and beautiful, begging him to stop, goading him on. He remembered that the party had gone well, too, apart from the visit by Lais's grandmother. No ordinary grandmother! Leonie was as firm-fleshed and beautiful and as coolly arrogant as she had always been on stage. She was his kind of woman.

Laughing, he stepped under the shower, turning the dial to cold, gasping as the freezing water hit his warm flesh. His thoughts switched to the meeting he was to have today at the Château Villelme, a very high-level conference in which he was to play a principal role. He had marshalled his plans for the deployment of French labour, and his notes and the agenda for the meeting, together with the comments of Goebbels and Himmler, were waiting in his briefcase in the library. It would be an easy day in which he would consolidate a pleasant victory, one that would place him more prominently before the Führer's eye, and maybe even put him in line for promotion to Reichsmarschall. That would upset Himmler! Karl towelled himself briskly. He despised Himmler, and as for Goebbels – just look at the man's behaviour towards his wife last night, flaunting that actress in front of her. They said he'd even brought the woman to live with them at one point. A man should not treat his wife that way.

There was a tap on the door and he looked up. Lais was dressed beautifully in simple blue-green linen that breathed Paris couture. Her shoulder-length blonde hair was brushed into a smooth curve framing her face and she wore dark glasses. "Up so early?" he commented, narrowing his eyes as he scraped the long-bladed razor across the stubble on his cheek.

"I thought I'd visit my grandmother this morning," murmured Lais.

Her voice sounded very small and he shot a glance at her in the mirror. "Take off the glasses," he commanded. Obediently she removed them. Her eyes were red and swollen. Karl sighed as he continued his shaving. "Crying? Again!"

Lais put back the dark glasses. "I thought as you were going to be away today and as Grand-mère is here . . ."

"Going to cry to your grandmother, eh? You're wasting your time. She's only here to tell you what a bad girl you are. And you are a bad girl, aren't you, Lais?" Gripping her wrist he pulled her roughly towards him. "You were *so bad* last night, *so very bad*." He forced back her head as his tongue explored her mouth. When he let go of her, Lais backed away towards the door. Her lipstick was smudged, and her hair in disarray. "Be home by six," commanded Karl, returning to the mirror. "We are going to the theatre and I want you to look your best. Wear the white dress with the rubies. I like you in that combination." He didn't say goodbye as she walked away.

Enrique García, dressed in blue mechanic's overalls, tinkered with the innards of an ancient Citroën in the forecourt of the wayside petrol station on the route between Rambouillet and Chartres. The old *patron*, in overalls and blue beret, sat in his office, sipping the brandy that Enrique had brought him, and dreaming of the days when his little garage had serviced a constant stream of vehicles, the tractors and farm machinery and the smart automobiles of the *maisons bourgeoises* and the *châteaux* that dotted the surrounding countryside. With petrol rationed and in short supply, and a scarcity of spare parts, most cars were off the road for the duration, and all he had left were his dreams. This was the old man's second war and Enrique had thought the brandy would help ease the pain of his losing everything he had worked for, *twice* in a lifetime. There were many men like this now, who had nothing left to lose, who would gladly do what they could to help the Resistance.

Enrique glanced up at the threatening sky. Even as he looked the first drops of rain began to fall, whipped into a flurry by a chill little wind. He pulled on a beret and stared down the empty road, then he checked his watch, frowning. He knew the car had left Paris exactly on time. It should be passing here within the next five minutes.

The Mercedes coughed suddenly and the chauffeur glanced at the dashboard in surprise. The car had been sluggish all morning. He listened, but all seemed well. No. There it was again. A sudden hiss came from the radiator and simultaneously the overheating signal on the dash flashed a warning red. Alarmed, he glanced through the glass partition that separated him from his distinguished passenger, but General Karl von Bruhel was immersed in his papers. The chauffeur wondered what to do. The boss was supposed to be at an important conference in thirty-five minutes' time and they still had twenty kilometres to cover through winding country roads. The Mercedes slowed to a crawl, steam hissing from its radiator just as the little garage came into view, twenty-five metres ahead.

"What is it?" demanded von Bruhel through the glass partition. "Why have we stopped?"

"Sorry General, but the car is overheating. I'm stopping at this garage to see if I can get some help."

Karl groaned, glancing at his watch. He'd left the time a bit tight deliberately, not wanting to arrive too early and therefore look too eager. It was a tactic he used often – but he hadn't planned on this sort of delay.

The chauffeur pulled the car into the forecourt in a cloud of steam and got out. Thank God there was a mechanic!

Enrique sauntered over, hands in pockets, a low whistle on his lips. "Monsieur," he said in a slow, country accent, "you are in trouble!"

"I know that," snapped the chauffeur. "What can you do to help?"

Enrique peered through the window at the passenger in the back and Karl glared at him. These damned French peasants were so slow! Enrique grinned cheerily at von Bruhel and Karl turned away impatiently, concentrating on his papers.

Enrique released the bonnet, standing back as the scalding cloud of steam escaped. Peering inside, he poked around expertly with a spanner.

"It's the water pump," he said finally. "Broken. *Kaput*." He laughed happily at his own little German joke. "You need a new one, Monsieur."

The chauffeur paled. Now he really was in trouble. Without the pump there was no way the car could run. "Then you must get me another," he commanded harshly. "General von Bruhel has important business at the Château Villelme. We must get there immediately."

Enrique shrugged indifferently. "Well, Monsieur," he said in slow country French, "I don't know if I can help you. We're not used to such cars as this nowadays and, as you are aware," he added with a shrug, "there are no spare parts for us French. But if you wait a minute, Monsieur, I'll see what I can find in the back."

He shuffled towards the jumble of rusting tools and parts at the rear of the workshop while the chauffeur paced the forecourt anxiously. He was dying for a cigarette.

Enrique emerged clutching a rubber pump. "Wait one moment, Monsieur, just one moment. I think we might be able to help you after all." He delved into the engine with his spanner, cursing loudly as he burned his hand. But in moments he had the defective water pump removed and was inserting the new one. "It's not *new*, Monsieur," he explained, "it must have been here for years. We used to service good cars in the old days. But it'll get you to your final destination."

Relieved, the chauffeur paid him a few francs and climbed back into the car. "Well?" asked Karl.

"We were lucky, Herr General," he replied. "The mechanic was able to fix it, but I'll have to drive fast, sir, to get there on time."

Karl sighed. "Very well then. Get on with it."

Enrique shook a Gauloise from the packet, placed it between his lips and lit it, watching the Mercedes retreating into the distance. Smiling, he returned to the cabin and removed his beret and his blue overalls, emerging in the pants and shirt of an agricultural worker. "*Au revoir*, Clémence," he grinned, clapping the old man on the shoulder. "Enjoy the brandy."

"I am already, M'sieur, I am already." The old man toasted him with his brimming glass.

Enrique headed through the field at the back of the garage making for the woods to the north. A delivery truck waited at a farm five miles away loaded with fresh vegetables that he would drive to the market at Les Halles. His papers were in perfect order. There would be no problems.

He jogged rapidly keeping close to the hedgerows and avoiding the open fields. Lais had kept her promise though at what cost to herself he would never know. They had the information and that was all that mattered. As he came to the woods, he paused to check his watch. Leaning against a tree, his listened. The explosion came exactly on time. It would have happened exactly where he had calculated. On the bridge. The car, with its passenger, or what was left of him, would be twenty feet beneath the river by now. Enrique cut through the woods towards the farm. He had kept his promise to Lais.

15

Lais sat next to her grandmother in the back of the Hispano as it ate up the kilometres between Paris and Reims. Goebbels himself had signed her travel papers under pressure from his sympathetic wife Magda, who had mistaken Lais's hysterical sobs for sorrow at Karl's death. But if Enrique hadn't killed Karl then Lais knew she would have done so. Her body still bore the bruises and welts of their final night together and she felt tainted with the mark of Karl's depravity.

And if it weren't for Grand-mère and Caro she didn't know how she would have got through the past few days, especially the questioning by the Gestapo. They had pounded on Caro's door where she'd fled for safety and a frightening young man in a black uniform with cold angry eyes that bored into her, had forced her to go over her movements on the day Karl died – over and over again. She could tell he didn't believe her when she said she had been here all day, with her grandmother, but thank God her story was true and there was no way he could associate her with Karl's murder.

Then she'd confessed to Grand-mère and Caro how Enrique had recruited her into the Resistance. Because of her unique position she had been able to meet socially most of the members of Hitler's

High Command. At first there were just snippets of information gleaned over the brandy, but later she'd gained access to Karl's papers and been able to find out important information about Nazi policy and troop movements and armaments. And as her work became more dangerous so did her relationship with Karl.

When Leonie had told her of Gaston's request for help in setting up an escape route, Lais had had the idea about the champagne trucks.

It had all clicked suddenly. The German love of champagne, the appointment of their own man to make sure supplies were maintained . . . therefore champagne was delivered regularly to all the hotels – including the Hostellerie. What better way to transport escapees south than in the delivery trucks? Leonie and Lais were on their way now to ask secretly for the champagne houses, cooperation with their plan.

German military police patrolled the streets of Reims and armed guards surrounded the champagne "caves". The town had suffered badly in the German shelling, the great grey cathedral had lost its windows and some of the famous carved angels around its vast doors were headless or had lost their wings. Certain streets were reduced to rubble with here and there a section still standing but split open, exposing intimate scenes – a bedroom with its pretty wallpaper intact, a broken bed stained from the dust and rain; a kitchen, its floor pebbled with broken dishes and a pan on the rusting stove.

The Boulevard Lundy seemed so normal. Ordinary-looking young soldiers bought postcards and took in the sights of the famous champagne houses, and the Brasserie Boulingrin by the fish market was open for business as usual. A bottle of good champagne cloaked in a white napkin to conceal its excellent label appeared unasked at their lunch table. "For old times' sake," they were told with a smile, "when Paris was still Paris and Leonie was its queen." And it was there they discovered who to contact in Épernay.

At the Café Billy by the post office in Épernay a game of ping-pong was in full swing and their contact leaned casually against the bar watching the players. Lais ordered a black coffee. "Capitaine Laurier?" she asked, lighting a cigarette.

Captaine Laurier sent them to number 20 Avenue de Champagne and Comte Robert de Vogüé, managing director of Moët et Chandon.

Moët et Chandon was the biggest of all the champagne houses

and its eighteen miles of caves, some of which dated from Roman times, had sheltered the refugees of many wars. The Comte de Vogüé, a debonair ex-army officer of World War I, led a risky life as spokesman for the industry to the occupying Germans and head of the local Resistance.

The plan was discussed in secret with his brave Resistance colleagues and fellow workers, and it was arranged that, with the cooperation of the drivers, the escapees would be transported either to the Hostellerie or to other hotels along the southern coast, via the delivery trucks.

And, in a charming little salon overlooking a pretty courtyard where Napoléon had once visited, they solemnly toasted the success of their "champagne funnel" with Moët's fabulous Dom Perignon '34.

16

Jim was stranded in Lisbon. He'd flown from London Northolt yesterday expecting to catch a connecting flight to New York en route for Washington DC, but there'd been a hitch in the plans. His plane had never arrived and no one wanted to talk about it. Grimly he assumed the worst – that it had been shot down over the Atlantic – and, leaving a message with the Embassy as to where he could be contacted, he took a room in a small hotel near the Rossio.

Lisbon's brightly lit streets and well stocked shops came as a shock after England's rationing and blackout. The smart cafés were crowded, there was traffic on the streets and the sound of a plane overhead wasn't accompanied by a screaming siren and a scramble for the shelter – it just meant that some lucky bastards had got their onward-flight. Lisbon was a city in transit – everyone was waiting to go somewhere else. Foreign embassies and consulates brimmed with people demanding visas and officers in the uniforms of half a dozen different countries, including Nazi Germany, passed through on their way to secret destinations. Red Cross workers impatiently whiled away the time in pavement cafés waiting for transportation to the war zones, and armaments dealers from South America talked contracts with anonymous men in sober business suits. Lisbon thrived on intrigue and double-cross, and spies and foreign agents conducted their business in the narrow streets of the old quarter, where secrets were bought and sold on street corners and in dingy bars, as well as in high-level offices and luxury hotel rooms.

Smart in his uniform of a major in the Eighth Bomber Squadron of the United States Air Force, Jim took the Victorian Gothic iron elevator of Santa Justa a hundred feet up to the Praça Luís do Camões. The narrow streets of the Chiado were lined with smart shops selling everything from the latest furs and fashions to caviare and cream-filled pastries. And, among the pretty smocked and flowered children's dresses in the window of "Modas do Crianças" was a charming little rag doll that would be just right for Peach. He could just imagine it tucked up in bed with her next to the teddy and the other half-dozen stuffed animals that made up Peach's menagerie.

Pushing open the shop door Jim collided with the woman coming out and they both stepped back politely, "Excuse me . . ." they apologised simultaneously in English, and then stared at each other.

"My God!" cried Jim, astonished. "*Amelie.*"

"Jim? *Oh Jim!*" Her parcels fell to the floor and she was in his arms, tears raining down her face and staining his immaculate uniform.

The shop assistant watched them curiously from behind the old-fashioned mahogany counter; you never knew what to make of these foreigners. The city was full of them, either laughing too loudly or crying too much. She ran to pick up the forgotten parcels.

"I came in to buy a pretty dress for Peach," sniffed Amelie, "my poor little girl."

"And I came in to get her a doll! But what on earth are you doing in Lisbon?"

"Trying to get to Peach, of course. And Lais and Leonore. Perhaps I may even be able to see Gerard . . . He's a political prisoner, you know, somewhere on the Belgian border." Amelie borrowed his handkerchief and wiped her tears. "Anyway, what are *you* doing here?"

"I'm waiting for a flight to the States – hopefully tomorrow. I was going to come to see you – after Washington. But, Amelie, you're not seriously thinking of trying to get into France, are you?"

They walked along the Rua do Carmo while Amelie explained

86

how the Senator had wangled her a seat on the plane and given her the names of contacts who might be able to help her.

Tension showed in the tight line of Amelie's mouth, the worried frown between her eyes and her new thinness. Jim had heard a disquieting rumour that Gerard had been moved to another camp in Germany, but decided not to burden Amelie with this news in case it were not true. She'd learn the truth soon enough, in France.

"Tell me," he continued, "how are you planning to get to France?"

"I was going to buy a car and drive across Spain. My Senator promised his contacts can get me the right documents – for a price. *Everything* has its price in Lisbon. *Except a car!* I've scoured this city from end to end – but no luck."

"Aren't you forgetting something?" asked Jim with a smile. "You're a de Courmont – and I'll bet there's still a de Courmont agency here in Lisbon. We'll get you a car, Amelie – though I'm not sure that we should."

"I'm going," she said fiercely, "even if I have to walk there. Nothing will stop me now."

17

Leonie's orphans were her second family. She had founded the home many years before when she was at the peak of her career, fuelling the old Château d'Aureville – which had been Amelie's father's old home – with money from her world-wide tours to keep the forty children in happy modest comfort, looked after by a staff of young and loving nuns. Leonie knew what it was like to have to give up your baby, never to see your child grow up. It had happened to her when she had given Amelie to the d'Aurevilles and they had had to flee to Brazil to protect her baby from Monsieur's wrath. The orphanage had begun as a way of atoning for her guilt, but had grown into a part of her life that she loved.

She had asked von Steinholz if he would give her permission to travel once a month to the château near Tours, as she had always done, to visit her children.

"We will do more," he had said. "A car and a driver will be at your disposal any day you wish to go."

Leonie could just imagine the consternation she would cause rolling up in a German car, a German chauffeur at the wheel. "It would be better if you gave me the proper papers and I drove there myself," she said. "After all, I wouldn't want to take a man from his more important duties."

"As you wish," von Steinholz had replied, but she had seen that he was upset by her refusal. Photographs of his wife and two pretty blond children were displayed in silver frames on his desk. Von Steinholz would have liked to be counted in on a charitable act for children and she had denied him that satisfaction.

"Your papers will permit you to travel three days out of the month, Madame Leonie," he said coldly. "That should give you sufficient time, I think."

"I would appreciate it if you could make an addition to those papers, Commandant," said Leonie calmly. "My little grand-daughter likes to go with me to the château."

Von Steinholz stamped the papers irritably, handing them over with a sigh. "Do you always get what you want, Madame Leonie?" he asked, sure that no man had ever refused her anything.

"Almost always," admitted Leonie modestly.

It was always fun at the château, thought Peach, staring eagerly out of the car window as they spun up the drive. *There! There they were*, lined up on the steps, waving excitedly. She leaned from the car window, waving back.

"Hello, Yves," she called, "hello, Monique. Hey, Véronique, you've cut your hair!" She had been coming to the château with Leonie for as long as she could remember. Leonie even said she had brought her here as a tiny baby to show the children. They were her friends, and when she came to the orphanage she became one of them.

Peach hurtled from the car and limped up the steps to embrace the Sisters. "Calmly, calmly, Peach," they protested laughing as she flung her arms first around each of them and then around each child in turn.

Peach felt so proud as the children politely curtsied and bowed to Grand-mère and then, throwing politeness to the winds, hurled themselves into her arms, eager to be swept up and kissed.

Leonie always brought presents, kites and balls and puzzles and books; then, in the huge wondrous garden, Peach helped the children pick tiny beans and carrots that tasted so good at lunch; and afterwards there were always the "goodie bags" of sweets – Madame Frénard's homemade toffees and fudge – given secretly under the discreetly turned backs of the Sisters.

Then upstairs in the children's pretty flowery-papered rooms with the windows open wide to fresh country air and the crisp cotton curtains blowing in the breeze, they exchanged stories and secrets.

Later Leonie inspected their schoolwork and listened to an account of their progress, smiling her approval.

In the car on the way home, Peach noticed the little smile still lingered on Leonie's lips. She knew that Leonie had worked hard for orphan children all her life, that her grandmother was famed around the world for the amounts of money she had raised for children's charities. "They adore you, Grand-mère," she murmured, resting her head against Leonie's arm. "It's not such a bad thing to be an orphan, is it?"

"It means," Leonie answered severely, "that there is no maman and no papa to spoil you and without people like the Sisters, and you and me, some children will grow up without love."

Peach closed her eyes, imagining what it must be like not to be loved. It was hard, she just couldn't capture the feeling. "It must be terrible," she murmured drowsily, "never to be loved."

It was a warm, clear evening at the Hostellerie la Rose du Cap. The last few fluffy pink clouds drifted towards the darkening horizon and the rustle and squeak of tiny night-flying bats blended with the crackle of the cicadas and the slow smooth rush of the sea. Peach walked from the villa to the hotel, through the cooling green gardens, sniffing the night-blooming stocks and the syringa blossoms and the tiny white starry flowers whose name she could never remember but which were her favourite. She had pinned up her heavy tawny hair on top of her head but she still felt hot. It was in weather like this that she had an urge to take the scissors and cut the whole lot off. She remembered her mother telling her the story of how, as a girl, she had done just that – and how upset her grandmother d'Aureville had been. Peach thought that maybe Leonie wouldn't be so very upset, but what if the war ended suddenly and Amelie were there and she looked so different with short hair that her mother didn't recognise her? It was Peach's recurring worry that she might have grown and changed so much that her parents wouldn't recognise her, that they might not even *like* her now she was growing up. On good days she laughed and told herself she was being stupid, but on the bad days she cried. It was then that Leonie would hold her close and tell her how proud Amelie and Gerard would be of her, proud that she had beaten the polio, proud that she had thrown away her calliper and exercised with weights until she walked with only the slightest limp, and one day that too would disappear. She was just like everyone else now, thought Peach, with the child's ever-present fear of being different. And now she was helping France.

Peach could remember how surprised she had been when she had followed the new kitten down the steps to the hotel's cellar and heard the radio. And it wasn't Radio Paris playing Wagner and spouting German propaganda, it was speaking English! Then she heard other English voices – right there, in their cellar! The two men looked just like truck drivers and she thought maybe they were delivering champagne, but then they smiled at her and said, "Well, hello love, who are you then?" It was their turn to be surprised when she'd answered them in English.

"I'm Peach, of course."

"Of course you are," they'd laughed. Then she explained that she lived at the villa and that Leonie was her grandmother, and Lais and Leonore her half-sisters.

Lais had been furious – not with Peach, but with whoever it was who'd been careless enough to leave the door open. But then Lais had to let Peach in on the big secret, and she had her *swear* never to tell it to *anyone* – whatever happened. Peach had felt a bit frightened when Lais had told her that their own lives, as well as many others, would depend on keeping the secret. She wished she had never gone down the cellar after the kitten, but she couldn't just have let Ziggie get lost, could she? She was *her* kitten.

Later it had become exciting. Lais, wearing a worried frown, asked her solemnly whether she thought she could carry a message for her. "A very secret message," she said. "I wouldn't ask you, but I'm sure that creepy Captain Kruger is having me watched and it would be too obvious if Grand-mère went suddenly into Monte

Carlo. Leonore can't go because she has to be at the hotel as the Italian generals are arriving today for the conference, and Kruger won't let her out of his sight; he's driving her crazy, demanding this and ordering that. It's desperately urgent."

Peach only half understood what she was doing but she had sensed Lais's anxiety as she watched her fold the tiny piece of paper into her pencil-box, tucking it safely into her brown schoolbag, and waving her goodbye on the bus. Peach joined the little crocodile of blue-smocked schoolgirls walking sedately through the streets of Monte Carlo to school. The box with its secret sat on her desk all day and her eyes were drawn to it time and time again, but Lais had warned her to tell no one and especially to speak to no one in the street. When the bell signalled that school was over, she quickly slid the piece of paper from the box into her smock. It felt as though it were burning a hole in her pocket – like the weekly allowance Leonie gave her which she liked to squander on ice cream.

He was waiting on the corner. A short man, rather fat and with a moustache, wearing the jacket of a croupier at the casino. The screw of paper slipped from her hand to the pavement as she strolled by, pausing a few seconds later to pull up her sock and peek back at him. He was already walking away, hands in his pockets, whistling. The piece of paper was gone! Thrilled by the success of her secret mission Peach skipped the rest of the way down the hill to the bus, proud that she had done well for Lais, proud of her work for France, proud of her strong legs that could skip. At the age of seven she was a member of the Resistance.

Leonore was waiting for her in the big pantry behind the hotel kitchens, busily checking supplies. Leonore always looked so calm, despite Captain Kruger's constant badgering and Kommandant von Steinholz's demands. There was just that constant tiny worried frown between her brows to show the strain. The sisters were so unalike that sometimes Peach wondered how they could possibly be twins. They were almost identical, yet they looked *different*. Leonore's calm expression, her cool deliberateness when confronted with a problem, were in complete contrast to Lais's vivid face and impetuous personality – Lais had always "leaped before she looked". And, of course, Leonore pulled back her blonde hair severely and wore only rose colour lipstick and sometimes she'd forget she had her spectacles pushed up on top of her head and think she'd lost them. Even her skin was different, paler than Lais's, who was always out in the sun, and Leonore always wore simple tailored dresses. Leonore was very pretty in a *gentle* sort of way, decided Peach. But Lais was flamboyant, and beautiful.

"Peach! I didn't hear you come in." Leonore glanced round to make sure that the doors were shut. Fishing a small box from behind a stack of jars of jams and honey, she pushed it to the bottom of Peach's schoolbag, covering it with her books.

"There's only one man in the cellars," she whispered, "and he's leaving tonight. These are his rations for the journey and his instructions. Make sure he burns them after he's read them, Peach. It's very important."

Peach nodded.

"It's impossible for me to go because Kruger is on the alert. He's making life *very* difficult at the moment," she added with a sigh. Her worried frown deepened. "Are you sure you'll be all right, Peach?"

"Of course," said Peach confidently. "No one cares about *me*, Leonore. Old Kruger barely knows I exist." Planting a quick kiss on Leonore's cheek, she slid through the door and into the garden.

As Peach turned the corner of the hotel, Captain Kruger emerged from the shadows by the parking lot, his boots crunching on the gravel. She felt the hot sweat of panic on her spine. Her eyes wide with alarm, she clutched the schoolbag closer. Did he know? Was he coming to arrest her? *To arrest all of them?* Suddenly she boiled with anger. She felt about Volker Kruger the way she had about her hated calliper. He was a *merde* thing. Tossing back her head, she began to skip down the path towards him, swinging her bag, humming to herself.

"*Guten Tag,* Fräulein Peach." Volker Kruger straddled the path in front of her, forcing her to halt.

"*Bonsoir,* M'sieur." Peach lifted her eyes reluctantly from his gleaming, oversize boots to his face. Volker Kruger had the short stocky legs of a peasant, tapering upwards to a narrow chest. His head was shaped like a lightbulb and his eyes were bulging green marbles. His stubbly hair was dark and dead looking with a sprinkling of white flaky dandruff, and he had a habit of standing legs apart, elbows akimbo, fists clenched at his hips in the small man's arrogant pose.

"And where have *you* been?" he asked, staring at her schoolbag. "Shouldn't you be home preparing your schoolwork for tomorrow?"

Peach shifted anxiously from foot to foot. "I'm on my way, M'sieur," she said dodging past him, almost tripping over his enormous feet. Resisting the terrible urge to run, she skipped down the path, away from him. "*Bonsoir*, M'sieur," she called sweetly.

Kruger caught a snatch of the song she was singing as she disappeared along the path, something in English – "She'll be coming round the mountain when she comes," carolled Peach gaily. Baffled, Kruger walked back to the big pink hotel.

Lais sat at her usual stool at the bar of the Hostellerie la Rose du Cap, sipping champagne, surrounded by a group of admiring officers. She looked wonderful, thought Leonore, wending her way through the usual pre-dinner cocktail bar crush to her sister's side. Lais had a golden tan and her hair was bleached even blonder by the sun. She wore a diaphanous amethyst dress that Leonore recognised as coming from Leonie's storage closets, and which must be at least thirty years old, but Lais managed to make it look chic and fashionable. Tossing back her long hair, Lais waved a hand to the barman for more champagne cocktails, calling to the pianist at his white piano to play louder so that she could hear him over the buzz of conversation and laughter.

From the corner of her eye, Leonore noticed Kruger, standing stiffly by the piano, a drink clutched in his hand, his eyes fastened on Lais. Kruger's jaw hung slackly and his tongue flickered across his wet open mouth. Leonore had never seen such naked desire in a man's face and she felt sick with apprehension as she pushed her way through to her sister. Forcing herself to be calm, she sat down next to Lais. Bending closer she whispered in Lais's ear, "Peach is doing her homework."

Lais lifted her glass in a mock toast and smiled at her sister. "Time for one more before dinner," she called to the officers. "And then who's going to the casino in Monte Carlo afterwards?"

Leonore watched Kruger watching Lais. His stillness was that of an animal sizing up its prey, waiting for the perfect moment to make its move. The crowd in the bar began to thin out as they drifted towards the dining room and she heard Lais fending off demands for her company, making easy excuses, promising maybe later, as the young officers turned away reluctantly. Slamming his glass down on the white grand piano so that the beer slopped over its sides, Kruger marched stiffly from the room.

"Lais, please take care," said Leonore urgently, "Kruger is crazy. And he's jealous."

"Jealous? Of what?" Lais gazed at Kruger's retreating back

contemptuously. "That disgusting little man knows I would never even look at him."

"Haven't you noticed the way he looks at you? *He wants you,* Lais!"

"He's nothing," said Lais, "just a small cog in a big wheel."

"He's unpredictable and he's dangerous," replied Leonore, but Lais just laughed.

"Well, don't say I didn't warn you," sighed Leonore. "I'm off to check my kitchens now."

"A woman's work is never done," Lais called after her mockingly. Fatigue swept over her as it did every night about this time when she'd played out her role as the darling of the High Command, ex-mistress of Karl von Bruhel, the de Courmont who knew which side her bread was buttered and who played along with the winners. But a steady stream of escapees and refugees, hidden in the delivery trucks, had already flowed along the champagne funnel from Épernay. And by keeping her ears and eyes open for gossip in the bar, Lais was able to come up with occasional scraps of valuable information. The memory of Karl still lurked in the back of her mind, coiled like a cobra, waiting to spring at her when she was alone, and leaving her vulnerable and shaken, but that was a face she never showed the world. She stared wearily into her drink. The champagne cocktail was part of her performance as Lais the gay charmer, von Bruhel's ex-mistress – and no one's lover.

"Lais? Do you remember me? We met in Paris."

Lais looked up, straight into the gold-flecked hazel eyes of Major Ferdi von Schönberg.

18

Volker Kruger inspected himself in the long mirror of the suite he inhabited at the Hostellerie, puffing out his chest and tightening his polished brown leather belt an extra notch. Clicking his heels together smartly he bowed to his image. The fact that he came only half-way up the mirror's height went unnoticed. What he saw was an officer of the Third Reich in a smart, freshly pressed uniform and gleaming high leather boots, the peaked cap denoting his rank planted squarely on his narrow head. *Power* was reflected back at him from that mirror, cancelling the pinched face that spoke of decades of deprivation and a slovenly family who spent what money they earned picking potatoes or helping bring in a harvest on cigarettes and beer.

Volker's mother had been a big, fat woman partial to a plate of coarse regional sausages doused in hot mustard and a brimming tankard of rich dark beer. She had a harsh guttural voice and an even harsher hand that she used frequently on her only son, whose puniness was a constant source of annoyance to her. Volker took after his father, a wiry little man, half the size of his wife and completely under her thumb. Until he'd had enough beer. Helmut Kruger's randiness "under the influence" was a source of much amusement to his wife, who tolerated his crude amorous advances the way she did a fly crawling over her body, flicking him off when he was done with a dismissive, "Little men, little pricks."

Volker had spied on them on Sunday afternoons after they'd washed down a crate of beer together, rolling half-naked on the sagging bed, her fleshy breasts hanging slackly over her sides. His father lay on top of her, desperately trying to contain them in his small hands while he heaved up and down, grunting. It always excited Volker seeing her breasts like that and he would shut himself in his room, standing on the chair anxiously inspecting his erection in the slab of unframed mirror on the wall, pulling on it desperately, hoping it would grow larger, and exciting himself until his sperm splashed stickily across the glass.

Volker's member stirred expectantly as he surveyed himself now, remembering Lais in the thin amethyst dress she'd worn last night, how it clung to her taut high breasts and the curve of her hips. He imagined her long slender legs that would end in a delicious warm triangle.

Volker put his hand on his groin tentatively, fingering the buttons on his fly. But no, there was no time for that. Tonight he would ask Lais de Courmont to have dinner with him. And if she knew what was good for her, she'd better accept. She was up to something, he was sure of that. It was *exactly what*, that he wasn't sure of.

He had kept his eye on her – and the other de Courmont women

95

– for the past month; he had them followed when they went to Monte Carlo or Nice, and made it a point to call on Leonore unexpectedly in the kitchens or her office. He kept watch on Lais out by the swimming pool and in the cocktail bar at night, and he even had young Peach followed on her way to school.

Kommandant von Steinholz's intelligence man suspected the baker, Gaston, of being involved with the Resistance and Volker couldn't understand why the man was still at large. *He* would have thrown the fear of the power of Nazi Germany into the whole community by sending a Gestapo truck in the middle of the night to arrest Gaston, with a judicious bit of violence to show them they meant business. A few bleeding skulls would mean a few less Resistance workers. But von Steinholz wanted to play a waiting game and see where the trail led him. Kruger sniffed contemptuously, patting the revolver at his waist. The Luger was as much his badge of power as the captain's insignia on his hat. With the Luger close at hand, he was in command. Snapping a smart "Heil Hitler" to himself in the mirror he marched to the door.

In the bar the pianist thumped out hearty German drinking tunes while a group of half-drunk young officers, fresh from the war-zone in Africa, sang along laughing nervously and slopping beer over the ivory keys, which the pianist wiped away every so often with an immaculate linen handkerchief. Volker's glance dismissed their antics as normal as he searched the bar for Lais. Her usual stool waited, empty. Strutting to the bar Volker demanded to know where she was.

"Sorry, Captain," replied the barman, "she hasn't been in to-night."

Fuming, Volker consulted his watch. He liked to dine promptly at eight. Ordering a beer, he took up his position by the empty stool. Of course Lais wouldn't want beer, she always drank champagne – a woman's drink, he thought contemptuously, ordering the barman to put a bottle of his best champagne on ice. The clock ticked towards eight and still Lais hadn't arrived. Kruger looked around the emptying bar nervously. Ordering another beer, he decided to give her until eight thirty.

Ferdi von Schönberg sat opposite Lais in the Café de Paris in Monte Carlo watching her devour a mound of tiny pink shrimp with sighs of enjoyment. Beneath Lais's brittle façade there was a childlike quality that brought out the protective instinct in him. He'd felt it

96

when he'd first met her as von Bruhel's mistress. Everyone was aware of von Bruhel's reputation as a sadist and it was even rumoured that somewhere in the past among the trail of broken women, there had been at least one with whom he had toppled over the brink into murder. Only von Bruhel's brilliance as an army intelligence officer had saved him from prosecution – that and his wife, a mature and charming lady from a socially prominent Bavarian family reputed to be close to those in power.

Lais finished the last shrimp with regret and drained her glass. Ferdi signalled the waiter to refill it and she looked at him suspiciously, aware that she was just the tiniest bit drunk. "Are you trying to get me drunk?" she demanded, placing the glass firmly away from her.

"I'm not sure that I have anything to do with that."

"What do you mean?" Lais leaned forward staring into his eyes. Marvellous golden eyes, no, they were green in this light.

"Getting drunk is your own choice, no one else's."

She sat back, considering his statement. "True," she said finally, "but sometimes there's no other way."

"No other way?"

"To get through the day, of course. Or rather, the night."

Ferdi waited for her to amplify the statement but she chose not to.

"Tell me," Lais said, hoping to provoke him, "what's it like to be an officer in the German Army? A conquering hero?"

Ferdi shrugged. "I'm simply a man doing a job. I have no choice in the matter. Like the French, I was called upon to do my duty for my country, whether I agree with its policies or not."

Lais looked at him in surprise. No Nazi ever breathed a word of criticism of the regime. Perhaps he was trying to trick her into talking by pretending to be sympathetic? Somehow she didn't think so. Not with those calm clear eyes, and that firm mouth. Ferdi von Schönberg looked the image of the ideal Aryan. Tall, with a well-muscled body that spoke of potential power and silky smooth Nordic blond hair, he seemed a thinking man, quiet, calm, authoritative. And gentle. "You shouldn't be saying things like that," she told him.

"I know. But it's the way I feel. I thought you would understand."

He did suspect. Now she knew it!

"The night of the party," said Ferdi, "the night before von Bruhel died. You went to the library very late, remember? The room was

97

dark, only one lamp left on over the desk where von Bruhel had been working. I couldn't sleep. I'd gone into the library and poured myself a brandy and I was sitting there, in the big wing chair in the corner, thinking. I suppose I must have fallen asleep. I woke up when you came in. I watched you go through von Bruhel's papers, making notes."

Lais stared into his eyes like a rabbit paralysed by oncoming car lights.

"It's all right," he said gently, "if you hadn't killed him, I think I would have."

"But I didn't kill him!" Her voice was rough with shock.

Ferdi shrugged. "Then I'm grateful to whoever did. Von Bruhel was a monster."

"What are you going to do now?" asked Lais, snapping open the gold cigarette case with her initials in tiny diamonds and taking out a cigarette with shaking hands. Ferdi leaned forward to light it.

"Why should I do anything? Von Bruhel deserved all he got. And I'm not in the business of spy-catching. Besides, I'm in love with you."

"Love?" queried Lais, bemused.

"I've loved you since the minute I first saw you at the house in Paris, leaning against the piano listening to Cole Porter. I wanted to peel away the lines of bitterness from your mouth, and make your eyes smile again without that watchful mask. I wanted to hear you laugh, Lais."

The cigarette burned forgotten in the ashtray, as she listened. She had accepted Ferdi von Schönberg's invitation because for the first time in months she had felt the thrill of a sexual attraction. Ferdi was a very attractive man. But what he was saying had taken her completely by surprise. "Go on," she commanded.

His hand gripped hers across the table and his voice mesmerised her. "I want to unpin your hair and let it flow in the wind, I want to swim naked with you in the warm sea, I want to stroke you and soothe you until all the painful memories are gone and you are a girl again, with all your life in front of you and no ugly stains in the past. I want to make love to you, Lais, and I want to love you."

Tears trembled on her lashes. "I don't know about all that," she whispered. "I don't understand love."

Ferdi smiled at her, his firm hand steady over her trembling one. "Then isn't it time you learned?"

*   *   *

Volker Kruger paced the gravel car-park in back of the Hostellerie angrily. It was almost midnight and she wasn't back yet. Yet her car was there, the blue de Courmont for which, to his intense irritation, von Steinholz provided petrol coupons. As the lights of a car approached he stepped back into the shadows, but it wasn't her, just a group of young men who'd been out on the town and were boasting to each other of their conquests in some back-alley bordello. Trembling with anger, Kruger recommenced his pacing, determined to wait until she returned.

At one thirty-five by his watch, a small Citroën drove slowly down the slope from the road, crunching across the gravel and stopping within feet of his hiding place. As the lights were extinguished he could see the silhouettes of two figures inside the car. Then the two heads merged in a kiss. Kruger held his breath, peering into the night to see who was with her, for he felt sure it was Lais. The driver's door opened and a tall man got out, walking round to the passenger side to hold the door open for his companion. As Lais stood up the man's arms slid around her. He held her so close that Volker thought they were one. Still he couldn't see who the man was. The couple began to walk across the gravel towards the Hostellerie, arms around each other and her head resting against him. Keeping to the grass so as not to be heard, Volker followed them curiously. *Who the hell was he?*

As they mounted the broad steps to the big revolving glass doors, Kruger hurried after them. Ferdi took Lais's arm and they strolled together towards the elevators. The metal grill closed behind them, caging them together and shutting him out and Kruger watched in stunned silence as the lift ascended from his sight.

Punching the elevator button furiously he waited for it to descend, then, stiff with anger, he stood at attention until it deposited him, alone, at his floor. In the quiet of his room, he cast off the peaked cap, the polished belt, and the smartly tailored jacket. He tugged off the high boots and, fumbling with the buttons, he removed his officer's grey-green trousers. Kruger stood before the mirror in his socks and baggy army issue undershorts and the vest with the two semi-circles of sweat at the armpits.

Lais was with Ferdi von Schönberg. Volker's puny body shook with anger. Of all people von Schönberg represented everything he hated. Ferdi's father belonged to one of Germany's oldest and most illustrious families. His mother's family owned the vast Merker iron and steel works; it was *their* rolling stock that sent Germany's armies across continents by rail, *their* tanks that waged war in foreign deserts, and armaments from Merker factories that brought German victories. Von Schönberg had had no need to fight his way up the ranks. Why he was still only a major was a mystery to Kruger, though there had been rumours that he was unwilling to accept promotion, preferring to stay with his men in battle than to take the higher rank and stay in an administrative job behind the lines. But Irene von Schönberg, Ferdi's mother, was a tough old woman who was known to have run her family with a rod of iron after her husband died. Using her influence, she had had her son removed from the front and von Schönberg became an aide to Klebbich in Reims.

It was easy for the von Schönbergs of this world to get the girls. Easy. All Ferdi had to do with Lais was ask. Lais was with him now, in his room. They'd be naked together on the bed. Ferdi would be kissing her, his hands would find the places Volker had only dreamed about. Shaking, Volker ripped off the shorts and vest and surveyed his erection in the mirror. *This* should have been hers tonight. He would have been so excited that it would have been bigger, big enough to fill her. His hands moved faster and Lais became entangled in images of his mother's obscene white breasts and flailing legs until he sagged against the glass, sticky and spent.

19

Lais rolled over in bed, still half-asleep, clutching the pillow close to her, afraid to open her eyes. She felt Ferdi's fingers trace the line of her lashes along her cheek and smiled. It was all right after all. He was no dream, he was still here, and she could feel his warm breath on her face as he bent and kissed her.

"Good morning, my darling," Ferdi said, smoothing her tangled hair gently from her face. Her eyes sprang open so suddenly that he laughed. Lais laughed too. "It's ridiculous to feel this happy," she murmured against his chest.

"Does the ridiculous feeling mean that you love me?" he asked kissing her again.

Lais knelt over him dropping tiny quick kisses across his belly. "I'd *love* you to make love to me," she replied between kisses.

"That's not what I asked," said Ferdi, groaning as her kisses moved lower. "I love you, Lais. I want you to love me."

Lifting her head she regarded him seriously, thinking of last night. He had helped her undress, removing each garment and stroking her body as tenderly as though she were some precious and exquisite art treasure. And when Ferdi was naked and held her in his arms he'd trembled with passion for her, but he'd held back, caressing her gently, kissing her mouth, her eyes, the fluttering pulse at the base of her throat, running the tip of his tongue over her eager nipples, and down her belly. He groaned with passion as his hands opened her yet he waited until her passion matched his. Then he guided her towards his body so that she could feel his desire for her throbbing in her hands and, unable to wait any longer, she'd pulled him towards her. Ferdi was a wonderful lover – like none she'd ever known. Curled against his chest, Lais sighed happily. It had been a perfect endless night of love-making. It wasn't just sex, as it had always been before, there was no desperate seeking for an ultimate thrill that didn't exist, and no meaningless unemotional gropings for mutual satisfaction as had happened so often. And there was no reluctant awakening to face herself in the mirror. But was it love? How could she know? "I've never been in love," she told him. "All I know, Ferdi, is that I've never felt like this before."

He held her so tightly she felt she would break. "That's love," he murmured in her ear. "I promise you, darling, that's love."

Amelie had been on the road for what seemed like a year, though in fact it was only ten days. She had taken the northerly route across Spain through Salamanca and Valladolid to Bilbao and San Sebastian, heading for the French border at Hendaye, where Jim's contacts had informed them it would be easier to cross. They had decided it would be better if she pretended she were *returning* to France after spending a few days in Spain. Her French papers, obtained with a large sum of money in a mere two days, bore the authentic stamp of the French wartime government official at Bordeaux and gave her permission to leave France for a period of ten days to visit her sick mother in Spain. And they were stamped with the date she had supposedly left France at another border town. They bore her name as a citizen of France, and the address of their Paris house on the Ile St Louis. There was no fuss at the Spanish side of the border. The Spanish officials had swung open their barriers, wishing her good luck and shaking their heads at her foolishness in returning to France. She had driven slowly forward to the yellow demarcation line and the frightening folds of barbed wire. German soldiers, rifles at the ready, commanded her to halt and obediently Amelie switched off the engine and waited. Ordering her roughly out of the car, they marched her to the command post where a fat sergeant, jowls wobbling over his tight collar, looked her up and down before inspecting her papers. Bidding her wait, he left her standing while he walked slowly to the car and inspected it. Amelie watched nervously through the window as the sergeant ran a plump banana-fingered hand across the bonnet, opening up the doors to peer inside and inspecting the trunk. There was only her one small suitcase and the bag with the dress in it for Peach. Picking it up he peered inside, glancing back at the concrete command post and then, still clutching the bag, he walked towards them.

"These things," he said laying the bag on the scrubbed pine table between them. "They are new. Where did you buy them?" Thank God the label on the bag said only "Modas de Crianças" without any address or the name of the city; her papers didn't give permission to visit Portugal. Taking a chance he didn't speak Portuguese, Amelie lied firmly, "In Bilbao, where I went to see my ailing mother."

His small piggy eyes, half hidden in folds of smooth pink flesh, examined her for a moment, then he said, "You are a Spaniard then?"

"French. My mother has lived in Spain for many years. She prefers the climate." Amelie felt the sweat trickling between her breasts as he peered at her in silence and for the first time she realised the enormity of what she had done. She was in occupied France and this was the enemy!

"And these things," opening the bag he poked at the dress and Jim's doll. "Who are these for?"

"My daughter," she replied quietly. "She'll be waiting for me, at home."

Thrusting the things back in the bag, the sergeant pushed it across the table. With a flourish he stamped her papers and handed them to her. "I have children of my own," his piggy eyes almost disappeared as he smiled. "I haven't seen them in almost a year."

"That's too long," said Amelie politely, "they will miss you."

He walked with her to the car and nervously she wondered why. He had stamped her papers, couldn't she just drive on?

"The car," he said, resting a hand on the dusty blue leather seat, "it's a de Courmont. The same name as you." Amelie's heart skipped a beat. De Courmont was an important name in France. With Gerard in a prison camp they might want his wife too.

"A coincidence," she laughed, settling herself in the seat, "worse luck! Take care of those children of yours." She waved as the car rolled smoothly forward. The sergeant stepped back, snapping to attention in the Nazi salute. She had seen it before of course in Lisbon, but somehow, here on French soil, it made Amelie's blood run cold.

It was late afternoon and the light was already fading but she pushed on to Biarritz, where knots of young German soldiers paraded along the promenade buying picture postcards to send to their families. A group of them, young and blond, in shorts and vests, performed supervised exercises on the beach, then waded laughing into the cold ocean.

Amelie decided to drive further up the coast, stopping finally at a delightful little fishing village where brightly coloured houses curved around a small bay and the tiny café on the harbour let rooms. She spent her first night in France curled up alone and sleepless in a big brass bed while the moonlight played across the pounding Atlantic outside her window. I'm almost there, she reassured herself as dawn broke and she finally fell asleep, I'm almost there.

It was noon when she awoke and, dressing hurriedly, she drank the cup of bitter imitation coffee whose only merit was that it was hot and milky. She dunked a piece of fresh crusty bread into it for her breakfast, and then she was on the road again.

Amelie didn't know why it should have surprised her to find Germans in every village and hamlet that she passed. Their presence was total and she noticed that the French were scrupulously polite to them without offering any extra warmth. In no village shop did she see the time of day passed with a German soldier, and in no bar or café were they treated with anything more than cold politeness.

Amelie pushed on through Dax, stopping overnight in remote villages and negotiating the various command posts nervously. At Carcassonne she found she was running out of her precious petrol coupons. The petrol station attendant told her to apply for more at the Kommandatur which turned out to be the old town hall. The queue of people inside was endless and, too tired to wait, Amelie sought a café and sipped a *citron pressé* in the shade of plane trees. Half a dozen old men argued over a game of *boules* in the square and a young girl cycled home from work, a lunchtime baguette in her basket. It could have been any peacetime scene in a small French town but for the swastika flying over the town hall and the uniformed Germans, some little more than boys, strolling through the quiet square.

Amelie suddenly remembered Jim's trick with the car. Hurrying to the post office, she checked the telephone listings for a de Courmont agency. She was in luck, there was one at Narbonne and if her luck held she would just have enough petrol to make it there.

At Narbonne the manager promised her the petrol coupons, though it would take him a few days. His house and hospitality were at her disposal. Pleasant though he was, Amelie couldn't face the prospect of making small talk with him and Madame. She preferred her solitude and her thoughts.

At last, stocked with petrol, she was on the road again. It was at Nîmes that the car refused to start. "Damn, oh damn," cried Amelie, furiously kicking at the tyre.

The mechanic at the garage just pursed his lips and said with a shrug, "Madame, there are no parts. It could take months to replace the cylinder head."

The railway station at Nîmes was crowded with German troops. Long trains full of them snaked endlessly through while civilian passengers waited patiently, hoping that their train would be next. Amelie sat on her suitcase all day, not daring to leave in case the train came. A fractious baby screamed in the heat as its tired young mother tried desperately to soothe him and an old woman dressed in peasant black sat stoically beside her wicker basket, knitting. The station closed at dusk but Amelie was there again the next morning at dawn, this time with a slab of bread and cheese and a bottle of water to sustain her. At three o'clock on the third day the train came and Amelie elbowed her way into a carriage, only to give up her hard-won seat to a desperate young woman clutching a pale, listless child. Amelie sat on her case in the corridor, staring out of the window at the flat landscape inching by, wondering when she would ever reach Cap Ferrat and Peach.

20

Walking up from the beach after their evening swim, Leonie and Peach noticed Lais strolling hand in hand with a young man along the chalky path that ran around the headland. Shading her eyes Leonie stared at their distant figures with a feeling of *déjà vu*. The tall blond young man reminded her of her first love, Rupert von Hollensmark. So many years ago they had walked just like that, young and in love around the Pointe St Hospice. They had dabbled their feet in the cool water of the rock pools, they'd kissed with the wind in their hair and he'd made love to her in the shadow of the sea grasses with the flickering sun warm on their naked bodies.

It had been Rupert who had first brought her here to the old inn on the Cap. The room that was now her bedroom had been theirs, filled with a big white bed where, with the shutters closed against the afternoon heat and with the windows open wide at night to the sound of the sea and the moonlight spilling across their warm naked bodies, they had loved each other and planned their future. But, yielding to family pressure, Rupert had returned to Germany, taking his love and his promises for their future with him. Leonie had never seen him again. The pain of her abandonment cut through her once more, the waiting and hoping, and the gradual realisation that Rupert was never coming back.

With an effort Leonie gathered her fractured dreams together.

"Who is that young man?" she asked Peach, who was skipping along at her side.

"That's Ferdi. I think Lais is in love with him, Grand-mère."

Leonie smiled at her. Peach was growing up. "And what do you know about being in love?" she teased.

"I know you sigh a lot and go around with a funny look in your eyes," Peach said, "and you look like you have a little light glowing inside you. At least Lais does."

So Lais was in love! With a pang Leonie realized that Ferdi must be German too. Oh Lais! She had done it again! Was she destined always to find the wrong man?

"Grand-mère," said Peach, holding out her hand to help Leonie up the steps from the beach, "I love you and Jim, and I love Maman and Papa and my sisters. So why don't I look the way Lais does?"

"It's different," explained Leonie, "when a man and a woman choose each other to love, it's a very *special* sort of love. It's something that can't ever be explained to you, but you'll know when it happens. You can't mistake it."

Peach scooped up the little brown kitten, Ziggie, kissing her. "I love you, Ziggie," she murmured into its soft fur. The kitten struggled, wanting to be free to run, leaping suddenly and leaving a thin red scratch along her arm. "Ow," winced Peach, rubbing the scratch. "If Ziggie really loved me, she wouldn't do that!"

"Peach," laughed Leonie, "you have a lot to learn about love."

Ferdi couldn't take his eyes from Lais, he wanted to drink in the fleeting expressions that crossed her vivid face and to be absorbed into the blueness of her eyes. When he was away from her, her face floated like a talisman in the back of his mind. He drove the long distance between Reims and the Riviera every weekend so that they had two days and two nights together, but it wasn't enough. He needed her all the time. He needed to touch her. He needed to kiss her, even just gentle kisses dropped on her wind-blown hair that smelled of sunshine and flowers. It was more than just a physical attraction, he'd known that immediately, the first time he saw her. Lais's fragile vulnerability had shown through the courageous façade, the brittle blonde woman with the smiling red mouth had seemed to him just a sad girl searching desperately for answers to questions she couldn't formulate.

Lais stopped and slid her arms around him, resting her head against his chest. The fear was gone from her eyes. She knew who she was now.

"I love you," she said, gripping him fiercely, "oh I love you, Ferdi von Schönberg."

"I thought you weren't sure – you didn't know if you could feel love," he teased.

"That was then," she murmured, kissing his chest where the shirt was unbuttoned, "a long time ago."

It had been just three months since that night in the bar when she'd looked into his eyes. "Do you remember me?" he'd asked. Now she would never forget.

Ferdi's hands gripped her shoulders as he said, "I want you to marry me, Lais. I want you to be my wife."

They both knew that it was forbidden for a German officer to marry a foreign woman and she sighed, saying nothing.

"I want you to know how I feel about you. You are in my life for ever, we belong together. One day all this will be over. The world will be at peace again. Will you marry me then, Lais?"

His face was so serious, his eyes anxious, afraid that because he was unable to marry her now, that because he was a German – *the enemy* – she would refuse.

"I'll marry you, Ferdi," she said simply, "whenever you say." An impish smile flitted across her face; she could never be serious for long. "All you have to do is ask!"

"Grand-mère, Grand-mère! Where are you?" Lais ran through the villa peeking into rooms as she passed. "Oh, hello Peach, where's Grand-mère? There's someone here I want you to meet."

"I'll bet it's Ferdi," said Peach, nibbling on the fig she had just picked in the garden.

"How did you guess! But where is Grand-mère?"

"In the garden I think."

Dressed in a simple cotton skirt with a battered straw hat to keep off the sun, Leonie was working on her plot near her beloved Bébé's flowering tree, tidying the borders and planting bright new flowers. "Grand-mère, Grand-mère," waved Lais. "He's here, I've brought him to meet you."

"Your German?" asked Leonie quietly. The sparkle died from her granddaughter's face so quickly that she wished she hadn't had to say it.

"Ferdi is German. He's serving his country because he has to. Exactly the way Frenchmen had to. It's not *his* fault! And Grand-mère, after the war is over and everyone is free, he wants to marry me."

Lais brimmed with the optimism of youth and love and Leonie wished she had Lais's belief in the future. Would she ever see Jim again in a free France? Would Amelie and Gerard ever be reunited? Or would Nazi Germany, of which this young man was a part, continue to tyrannise the world?

"Please receive him, Grand-mère, please," begged Lais, reaching out a tentative hand to Leonie. "I do love him so much, Grand-mère."

Leonie knew it was true. Lais was transformed. She was soft, sweet, proud with love for this man. And if he could transform her wayward granddaughter, then that was to his credit. "Very well," she said, setting down her trowel and taking off her gardening gloves. "I'll meet him."

"Oh Grand-mère, Grand-mère, thank you." Ecstatic with happiness, Lais threw her arms around Leonie.

"Give me five minutes," begged Leonie as Lais dragged her towards the villa, "just to wash my hands and tidy my hair."

Peach inspected the tall young man, waiting alone by the long windows of the salon. He was certainly handsome, tall and blond like the fairy-tale prince from her old story books. Perhaps he'd kissed Lais and woken her from a hundred years' slumber and wanted to marry her.

"You must be Peach," Ferdi said with a smile. "I know all about you."

"Oh? What do you know?" asked Peach suspiciously. She hoped Lais hadn't told him about her leg. She never wanted anyone to know about that.

"She said you were astonishingly pretty and very grown up for your age and, of course, I can see that she was right."

Peach blushed. Of course Papa and Jim thought she was pretty, but this was different. "Where do you live?" she asked, sitting on the window ledge beside him.

"In a castle on the Rhine."

"A castle!" gasped Peach.

"And sometimes in a house in a big city called Cologne. And temporarily, I live in Reims, here in France."

"I used to live in America," ventured Peach. "I think I still remember it."

"Well, I *think* I still remember the castle too – but only just. It's been a long time."

Peach looked at him sympathetically.

"Ferdi," Lais rushed into the room. "Oh Ferdi, she'll be here in a minute. She wants to meet you. Isn't it wonderful?"

Ferdi knew Lais had been worried that her grandmother wouldn't receive him and he'd been afraid of her disapproval. Lais had a very close relationship with her grandmother. She had said to him one day, "Grand-mère is my conscience. She knows my soul. She lifts me up when I'm sinking and helps me to float again. Without her I think I might have destroyed myself by now." Lais's wounds went deep.

He looked up expectantly at the sound of Leonie's light footsteps on the tiled floor. Leonie's hair was brushed back smoothly and she smelled of some soft distinctive perfume.

"Grand-mère," cried Lais, "this is Ferdi von Schönberg."

Leonie looked at the blond good-looking man before her; he looked so like her Rupert it seemed to her like an omen of ill-luck. Yet this was not Rupert, this was Lais's suitor, Lais's lover. And he so obviously adored her granddaughter. Leonie told herself it wouldn't be fair to inflict the shadow of her own past, or the bitterness of war, on two such happy people. She wanted to give them her blessing, though God alone knew how long they would have to wait before they could marry. She prayed for Lais's sake that the wait would not end as hers had done for Rupert, and that peace would come soon.

Leonore walked unhurriedly to the kitchen, aware of Kruger's eyes boring into her back. She paused, pretending to check the lunch menu. He was still there lurking behind her in the corridor, waiting to pounce, hoping to catch her out. Negotiating her way past the hot ovens she paused to give the pastry chef special instructions for the birthday cake to be presented to Commandant von Steinholz at dinner that evening. Out of the corner of her eye she saw Kruger push through the swinging double doors, and stand legs astride, hands on hips, glaring around the kitchen. No one took any notice and after a few moments he pushed his way back through the doors again.

Leonore slipped through the kitchen past the storerooms to the side door. The young boy was waiting, a box of freshly baked bread beside him. "Your order, M'mselle," he announced loudly, then leaned forward to whisper, "Gaston says there's danger, M'mselle. The Gestapo have put the Comte de Vogüé in prison in Chalons-sur-Marne, and the rumour is that he is to be executed. There have been many other arrests in Épernay but three Resistance workers managed to escape and will be arriving this evening on the champagne truck. They must be helped along the funnel to Marseilles, M'mselle. It is urgent."

Leonore stared at him horrified. Without the help of the people in Épernay their "champagne funnel" was finished. She only prayed that de Vogüé and the others would be spared.

She carried the bread into the kitchen, wondering what to do next. As she put the box on the table she suddenly sensed someone behind her and spinning around found herself face to face with Captain Kruger. "Er, we needed extra rolls for the party tonight," she explained flustered, "you know how your boys like to throw them around, after a few drinks."

"And of course they drink champagne," said Kruger silkily, "of which we seem to have a constant supply."

"The pastry chef would like to show you how he is decorating the Commandant's birthday cake," said Leonore, regaining her nerve, "he would like your approval. The colours are pretty, don't you think?"

Kruger grunted, licking his wet lips and eyeing her suspiciously. "It will do," he said grudgingly.

Amelie looked despairingly around the crowded bus station at Arles. Her suitcase had been there just a moment ago and now it was gone! "Pardon, Madame, M'sieur," she pleaded, "did anyone see my case? I just turned around to pay for my ticket, and it's gone."

Shrugs and averted eyes were the only response. No one wanted to know about a missing suitcase, they had their own problems. "Dammit!" thought Amelie, now all she had was what she stood up in, a dusty print dress and a pair of sandals. But she still clutched the bag from Modas de Crianças with Peach's presents and, thank God, she had her purse with her money and papers. All was not lost.

In the station café she consoled herself with a cup of bad coffee and a stale bun and with forethought bought a couple of apples and some fresh figs for the journey.

Surprisingly, the ancient bus was almost on time and Amelie fought for a place with the others, using her elbows to push her way through. She had learned fast that those who pushed got on the bus and good manners were not going to keep her from Peach! Squashed into a seat next to a spotty-faced youth, Amelie could scarcely breathe. Strong wafts of garlic mingled with the odour of onions and stale sweat in the stifling heat and she battled unsuccessfully to open the crusted window, finally settling back with a sigh of frustration as the rattling country bus meandered slowly towards Aix-en-Provence and the next step of her journey – the route along the southern coast of France.

21

The big truck covered with a green tarpaulin marked "Champagne, Épernay" rolled to a stop in the rear courtyard of the Hostellerie. Volker Kruger strutted forward importantly. He'd heard the news about the round-up of the Resistance workers at Épernay. This was the third champagne delivery in as many weeks and, if his suspicions were correct, they were being used to carry more than champagne. "Your delivery list!" he barked, holding out a hand.

The stocky Frenchman gazed at him impassively, fishing a pack of cigarettes from the top pocket of his blue overalls. Offering one to his mate, he lit them both from a single match.

"Your list!" demanded Kruger.

"You got the list, Jacques?" asked the stocky one, indifferently.

"Me? No. I thought you had it," replied the other, coughing.

Kruger eyed them furiously. They were tall, broad-chested men used to lifting heavy crates of champagne, and they had succeeded in making him feel small and insignificant. "If you drive a delivery truck, you have a list," he shouted. "Get it at once or I'll have you both arrested."

"Arrested? For not having the delivery list?" laughed Jacques. "That's a new one!"

"Come on, Jules," he said, ignoring Kruger, "we'll get ourselves a bite of supper in the kitchens before we unload, it's been a long drive."

Kruger stared after them angrily. They *knew* he could have them arrested and they didn't care! Or were they trying to put him off the scent? Something was going on tonight, he was sure of it.

Apparently many of de Vogüés associates were on the run. It would have been a clever notion to smuggle them down here on the champagne truck. Or even cleverer if they pretended to be drivers. He'd never seen those two before. For all he knew *they* could be the escaping Resistance workers – they had seemed a bit too casually confident, a touch too smart for truck-drivers. Well, he'd show them where the power lay.

Fifteen minutes later six powerful motorcycles screamed to a halt in front of the Hostellerie, followed by the ominous black Gestapo wagon, its dark windows covered with wire mesh. Waiting on the steps, Kruger shouted his commands, "To the kitchens," he barked, marching the helmeted and jack-booted Gestapo men through the elegant pink marble foyer under the noses of surprised German officers.

The two truck-drivers lifted their eyes from giant bowls of bouillabaisse. Jacques tore a chunk from the baguette in the middle of the table. "Well, well," he said, chewing, "brought the big boys to fight your battles, have you?"

The busy kitchens had ground to a halt and the chefs watched nervously, wondering what was going on. With the Gestapo one could always expect the worst.

"These are the two men," cried Kruger, "inspect their papers please."

The Gestapo captain glared at Kruger witheringly. "You mean you haven't looked at their papers yet?"

"They'll be false, I'm sure of it," Kruger cried triumphantly. "Search them."

"Captain Kruger. Please!" The Gestapo captain didn't like Kruger giving him orders. The man was only an office worker after all. Didn't he know that the Gestapo were the cream of Hitler's troops? "Stand up," he commanded. The two drivers rose slowly to their feet, wiping their mouths on the backs of their hands. "Your papers?" the Gestapo captain held out his hand.

Leonore ran down the corridor to the kitchens, slamming through the double doors in a panic. She took in the scene at a glance and then, through the window, she saw the champagne truck, parked in the courtyard. It was unguarded.

"*Bonsoir*," she said politely to the Gestapo captain, "I am Leonore de Courmont and this is my hotel. May I suggest that whatever the trouble is we sort it out in my office? My chefs are preparing dinner and we are interrupting their work. As you probably know," she added with a smile, "there's a special birthday celebration for Herr Kommandant von Steinholz this evening. We wouldn't want a delay, would we?" Glaring at each other, Kruger and the Gestapo captain followed her from the kitchen with the two drivers and the jackbooted soldiers marching behind them.

Lais hitched up her long green crêpe de Chine evening dress above her knees and tied it with a piece of string, leaving her free to run. Slipping on a coat she made her way down the back stairs into the storeroom and closed the door behind her, waiting in the dark. Her heart was pounding and she realised she was afraid. Since she'd met Ferdi she was no longer able to regard this as a game. It was life and death – and life was too sweet to risk now. She thought of de Vogüé, imprisoned in the notorious Gestapo headquarters at Chalons-sur-Marne and condemned to death. She knew she would go on risking everything, just as he and many others had. Because they must. Life lived on these terms was no life. If she was ever to marry Ferdi, France must have its freedom.

The door to the store cupboard opened a crack. "Lais?" It was Peach's voice. Relieved, Lais slid through the door and they ran together along the corridor to the rear courtyard.

"They're in Leonore's office," gasped Peach. "She said we've got five minutes."

Lais fiddled with the locks on the back of the truck and the flap swung down with a loud crash. They stared at each other apprehensively. Through the kitchen windows they could see the chefs, busily preparing dinner. "Quick," whispered Lais, "I'll give you a leg up."

Clinging to the edge of the truck, Peach boosted herself up. Balancing precariously for a moment, she edged cautiously forward over the tops of the crates. At the fourth crate from the back, on the left, she knocked twice. An answering knock came from inside, and taking the screwdriver from her pocket she unscrewed the crate expertly. There were three crates, three men, and it took her two and a half minutes. "Quick," she called as the men stood up, stretching cramped limbs and groaning softly. "Follow my sister." She watched as they scrambled from the truck, running after Lais, wishing their footsteps didn't crunch so loudly on the gravel. Quickly she rescrewed the cases and jumped from the truck. Lifting the flap she wound the chains around it and slipped on the padlocks. Loud voices came from the hotel. Through the windows she could see Kruger in the kitchens with the Gestapo men. Oh God, he was coming this way. The key fell from her suddenly nerveless fingers, dropping with a small tinkle into the darkness of the gravel by her feet. Peach glanced desperately towards the kitchen window. *Merde!* What had she done! She hesitated only a second. Kruger was already at the door. She was around the side of the truck in a flash and heading for the trees before Kruger had the door open.

Lais led the three men down the steps from the courtyard and into the cellars, weaving through endless corridors past racks of fine wines and champagne. The cellars ran the full length of the hotel and to those unfamiliar with them, they were as intricate as a rabbit warren, made even more so by the new series of false walls and dead ends. Shining her torch Lais led them along a small dark tunnel, lugging aside a pile of crates to reveal a manhole. Silently, she tugged at the metal ring, lifting the flagstone to reveal another flight of steps. "In there gentlemen, quickly," she whispered. A dim light came from the single electric bulb in the ceiling of the room. It was small, only about nine feet by eleven, but an attempt had been made to make it comfortable. Bunk beds stood along two walls with clean blankets and pillows. A square wooden table with four chairs held bottles of wine and water, bread, cheese and fruit. And on a bench by the wall stood a radio-transmitter.

"Thank God," cried one of the men. "We must get a message through to Marseilles at once. It's vital, Mademoiselle. Vital!"

Lais picked up the earphones and switched on the set. It crackled for a moment and then fell silent. She could feel their tension and their eyes on her as she flicked the tuner across the dial desperately. It was no use, the radio was dead.

"An escort will be coming to take you along the coast tonight," she said. "With luck you'll be in Marseilles tomorrow night. Can it wait till then?"

"The Germans are planning to blow up the *Vieux Port* in Marseilles *tomorrow*. They want to flush out the Resistance workers and the guerrillas – as well as the deserters from their own army. They've tried to search that rabbit warren but it's impossible. This is their answer. If we don't get a warning through many men will perish and much valuable equipment will be lost."

Their tired, unshaven faces were haggard with worry, their eyes red and bloodshot. They had left behind wives and families not knowing when they would see them again, and their very future hung in doubtful balance, yet still they were concerned for the welfare of their comrades.

"I'll see that the message gets through," Lais promised. "Give me your contact there and it will be done."

22

Peach zig-zagged down the hill from the village, the schoolbag jolting against her back as her long suntanned legs covered the ground in urgent leaps. At the gravelled courtyard in the rear of the Hostellerie, she paused to catch her breath, deciding against sneaking in by the kitchen door and risking bumping into Kruger who was bound to be lurking near the champagne truck. Instead she made her way through the gardens towards the front of the hotel so that anyone might think she had just come from her grandmother's rather than all the way from the village.

The graceful pink hotel stood outlined against a clear electric-blue sky, framed with the black silhouettes of palms and umbrella pines. The familiar notes of Beethoven's "Für Elise" filtered from the bar. It was still early and the bar seemed strange without voices and laughter and the clink of ice in tall glasses. Taking a deep breath to steady herself, Peach slid through the french windows from the terrace. Kruger's bulging marble green eyes followed her from his position at the piano as she wound her way through the tables to where Lais sat at her usual stool at the bar.

"Hello little one," Lais said patting her sister's tousled head. "You look thirsty," she added as Peach wriggled onto the stool next to her. "We'll have champagne," she called loudly with an eye on Kruger, "after all, we just received a truckload of it."

Her derisive laughter rang across the quiet room and Kruger glared at her. Draining his beer, he stalked from the bar. The Gestapo captain had checked the papers of the two truck-drivers and found them in order. Under Leonore's eagle eye he had examined the suddenly produced delivery note and made only a cursory inspection of the truck. He had departed half an hour later after releasing the men and with a case of good Brut champagne in his car. The Gestapo captain had made his feelings about Kruger quite plain, accusing him of wasting the Gestapo's time. Kruger was still seething and Lais was enjoying the success of their red herring and Kruger's embarrassment.

The tense-looking Italian major who had thought he was making decent progress with Lais before the child arrived, insinuated himself pointedly between Peach and Lais, resting an elbow on the bar, picking up his flirtation where he had left off. Peach glared at his back furiously, wishing Ferdi were here; it would have been so much easier to talk to Lais. Her anxious eyes signalled her desperation but Lais didn't seem to catch her gaze. "Lais," she said at last, "I think I have something in my eye." She rubbed her left eye ostentatiously.

"Allow me, please." Flourishing an immaculate white linen handkerchief the Italian major tilted back Peach's head, instructing her to roll her eye first up, then down. "Nothing," he said, mopping her now streaming eye, "it's all right now, *bambina*." His smile was directed at Lais.

Peach glared at him with her good eye. She was no *bambina*! She was almost eight years old going on eighteen. She was fighting for France along with the grown-ups. *And she had an urgent message for Lais.*

"Lais," she tried again. "I'm not feeling very well. Will you take me to the powder room, please?"

Lais's eyebrows rose. "Poor darling," she murmured, putting an arm around Peach's shoulders, "it must be the champagne that's upset you."

From his position near the reception Kruger watched the comings and goings both in and out of the hotel and the cocktail bar. Spotting Peach and Lais he followed them down the corridor that led towards the back of the hotel, catching up just as they swung through the doors into the ladies' powder room. Rigid with frustration, he leaned against the wall, waiting.

With a finger against her lips, Lais checked the pretty, mirrored pink powder room and then the stalls of the lavatories to make sure they were alone. "Gaston says the escort for the escapees can't come tonight," blurted Peach, "they will have to wait."

"*Wait!* How long?"

Peach shrugged. "Gaston said maybe a week."

"Impossible! They must get to Marseilles in twenty-four hours otherwise they'll be stranded. When the Germans blow up the old quarter everyone will be scattered, there will be no 'safe' houses . . . we don't even know if our contacts will still be alive!"

"That's the other thing," said Peach. "Gaston can't get the message through, there's too much static on the radio. He thinks it's being blocked and that the Germans might know its location. He's closing down for at least a week and hiding the set."

Gaston was the mainstay of the Resistance movement in the region and Lais knew that if he thought that things were becoming too dangerous for him to operate, it must really be bad.

"He says it's up to you to get the message *and* the men to Marseilles," went on Peach, "but that he cannot help you."

Lais flung herself despairingly into the little pink wicker chair banging her first angrily on the dressing table. "How?" she stormed. "But how? Dammit!"

"There must be a way," said Peach, upset.

The answer came to Lais suddenly. "Of course," she cried, "the croupier."

Peach recalled the fat moustached man in the croupier's jacket who had picked up the note she had delivered on her way home from school.

"The croupier is *from Marseilles*! He knows the route and the contacts. *He* could do it!" Lais jumped up and made for the door. She stopped suddenly, her hand on the door handle. Of course it was impossible for her to go to Monte Carlo to alert the croupier, Kruger wasn't letting her out of his sight. She remembered the anger in his glassy green eyes. And Leonore couldn't go either. If she weren't there to supervise Steinholz's birthday dinner, Kruger would *know* something was up. Lais sank despondently into the wicker chair. "Then who?" she asked Peach, "who can contact the croupier in Monte Carlo and bring him here?"

Leonie drove the long, dark blue de Courmont easily along the Corniche, resisting the urge to push down her foot and get there faster. With a scarf over her hair she could be taken for Lais, on her way to meet some friends at the casino, as she so often did. The Nazis knew Lais, and knew that von Steinholz personally supplied the petrol coupons for her car. They knew her reputation and of her German lover. Lais was accepted.

Monte Carlo glittered with lights, but the wedding cake façade of the casino looked shabbier than she remembered. Leaving the car in the drive Leonie strode up the steps to the imposing entrance, swept suddenly back into the past by the memory of the first time she had ascended these stairs, with five francs tucked into the top of her stocking as insurance, and the kitten Bébé on a length of pink velvet ribbon trailing behind her, seventeen years old and prepared to gamble all she had in order to survive.

Touching the statue by the door for luck, as thousands had done before her, Leonie strolled into the salon. A few men wore evening dress, but many more were in the hated grey-green uniform. Though Monaco was neutral, the Nazi presence, as well as that of the Italians, was strongly felt. At the outbreak of the war most of the international set had flown off to more settled climes and without them the casino lacked its old glamour, when the jewels blazed more brightly than the chandeliers and all the men looked debonair and handsome in white tie and tails.

Leonie had dressed discreetly tonight in a simple dark silk dress, so as not to be too noticeable, and she took a seat at the third table as Lais had instructed. The croupier was short and overweight. A film of moisture glistened across his forehead as he sweated under the lights and he dabbed at it with a handkerchief. With her eye fixed on him Leonie pushed across her money, receiving the plaques in exchange. The croupier glanced back at her with the bland indifference of his trade. There were just three other people at the table, a German officer with a young Italian woman, and a man in evening dress who looked Armenian. It was eight o'clock – too early yet for the post-dinner crowds. Leonie had exactly one hour to accomplish her mission. Quietly, she placed her bet.

At eight fifteen she was fifteen hundred francs up. At eight thirty the German and his companion left to have dinner. Shooting a quick glance at the Armenian, Leonie knew she had to take a chance. Crooking her finger she beckoned the croupier. "I'd like to cash in my plaques," she said.

"Bien sûr, Madame. Un moment." He raked the plaques towards him."

"For you," said Leonie. She thrust the customary tip towards the croupier with a slip of paper wrapped around a plaque. His eyes met hers for an instant and then he covered the plaque and the note swiftly with his hand.

Tucking her "ill-gotten gains" into her purse, and without a backward glance, Leonie swept from the casino. It was only when she reached the car that she realised that she was trembling and she prayed that the Armenian had not seen her pass the note. She slammed the car into gear and drove through the hilly back streets of Monte Carlo watching through the rear-view mirror to see if she were being followed. The street was empty and, swinging the car around, she drove back down to the seafront and parked in a dark corner by the Hotel de Paris, waiting.

Amelie hadn't thought her homecoming would be quite like this. Of course she hadn't really ever thought of *how* she would do it, just of being there with her family. The last three nights had been spent in tiny hot rooms without even a functioning bath and her blonde hair was matted with the sweat and dust that had wafted through the bus windows, and she felt sure she smelled of the garlic and onions, cigarette smoke and body odours of her travelling companions. The skirt of her cotton print dress was crumpled and stained and one sleeve was ripped where she had caught it on a wicker chicken cage in a village market place. Amelie grinned as the farm cart rolled slowly onwards, pulled by a meek-looking bay horse whose two speeds were slow and slower. She had given up trying to make conversation with the old man driving it, his answers to her questions having consisted merely of grunts and the occasional nod. But at least he was going to St Jean and had been willing to give her a lift. She knew her way from the village to the villa like she knew her own face. Her sore feet and broken sandals would be forgotten, as she ran along the dusty white lane, back home to Leonie as she had done before in her life when she was desperate. And soon she'd be with her girls, with Lais and Leonore. And her baby. Peach.

Commandant von Steinholz surveyed the blue and white birthday cake Leonore carried in, candles burning brightly, in the darkened room. Smiling, he acknowledged the applause and the strains of Happy Birthday sung loudly and out of tune in German, and then in one breath he blew out the candles. Volker Kruger's eyes were on Lais as she clicked on the lights. Von Steinholz plunged the knife into the birthday cake and cut the first piece. Lais was up to something, thought Kruger; she was as tense as a coiled spring, despite her casual smile. A waiter leaned across him to pour champagne and he shifted his gaze. "None of that," he commanded brusquely, "I'll have beer." When he looked up Lais was gone.

"Your cake, Captain Kruger," said Leonore with a smile, thrusting a plate in front of him. "Now, now, Captain," she said, leaning her weight on the back of his chair as he attempted to push it back from the table, "you can't run away before the Kommandant's speech. I'm sure he would never forgive you."

Kruger sank back into his seat, unsmiling, as von Steinholz, champagne glass in hand, stood up and addressed the table.

"To our leader, the Führer," he toasted amid a scraping of chairs. "Heil Hitler!"

"Heil Hitler!" Collars unbuttoned, slopping champagne down their jackets, they toasted their leader drunkenly. Even von Steinholz was far from sober. Kruger stared at them with contempt. How dare they toast the Führer in such a state.

Standing to attention he raised his glass. "To Commandant von Steinholz," he said with a fixed smile. "A very happy birthday to you, sir."

Von Steinholz stared at him superciliously. "You are toasting in *beer*?" he asked disbelievingly.

Kruger felt the hot blood rush to his face as laughter broke up the table. "Kruger toasts in *beer*," they repeated, "thinks he's at home I suppose."

Kruger's hand slid to his belt, resting on the gun. The Luger felt warm from contact with his body, reaffirming his strength. Trembling, he pushed back his chair and strode from the room, ignoring Leonore de Courmont who hurried after him through the door.

"Captain Kruger," she called urgently, "what about the Commandant's speech?"

As he turned to look at her, her anxious expression slid into one of innocence. What had she been thinking only moments before, he wondered? And *why* was she so anxious for him to stay in that room? *And where was her sister?* "I have heard the Commandant speak before, M'mselle de Courmont," he snapped. Turning on his heel he collided with Lais. She flung out her arms to steady herself, clinging to him. He could smell her hair, her mossy perfume, the skin of her arm was satin under his rough fingers . . .

"Captain!" she said, smiling at him. This close her eyes were bluer than he could have imagined and her mouth had the tempting lasciviousness he'd dreamed about so often, the red lips slightly parted and moist, just as she would be in that other place . . .

"You saved me," she said lightly, "I almost fell."

Kruger's belly contracted and he felt himself stiffen, throbbing with sexual desire. Sweat filmed his forehead and beaded his upper lip. His eyes dropped to her breasts, smooth curves that disappeared into the sea-green silk as soft as her skin; he could just imagine burying his head in them, tasting her nipples . . . His face flushed suddenly and his hand shook as all his nights of erotic dreams of her climaxed in a moment and with a groan the juices spurted into his pants as his eyes met hers . . . She knew what had happened – she could tell . . .

"Well, well," murmured Lais, stepping away from him, "really Herr Kruger, you should be more . . . careful."

Kruger stood frozen to the spot, feeling the cold stickiness on his belly. He heard her mocking laugh as, arm in arm with her sister, she strode off down the corridor.

Peach waited by the gate to the villa, searching the dark road anxiously for the lights of the car. Her grandmother was fifteen minutes late and every minute had seemed to Peach like an hour. At last! The low beams of a car flickered as it curved the bend in the road.

The man sitting next to her grandmother wore the distinctive sharp-peaked cap of the Gestapo and Peach froze with horror. As they got out of the car she heard Leonie speaking French to him and then she heard his answer – also in French. In the light of the dashboard she recognised the croupier.

"Grand-mère," she whispered relieved, "I'm here."

"Peach," said Leonie concerned, "you shouldn't be out here, I thought you were in bed."

"I have a message from Lais. It's impossible for her or Leonore to get the men out of the cellars. Kruger is watching them like a hawk! I am to bring the escapees here to the villa and the croupier must take them on from there."

"I can't let you do that!" The cry came from Leonie's heart. "I shall bring the men back here myself."

"You can't, Grand-mère. Lais said that Kruger has been told that you were not feeling well and couldn't go to von Steinholz's reception. Kruger is suspicious of everyone. Except me." Her eyes pleaded with her grandmother. "Don't you see, I'm the only one!"

"I can't allow it, Peach," she protested, but Peach had already slipped away into the night.

*   *   *

Peach ran lightly across the gravelled courtyard, skirting the oblongs of light from the steamy kitchen windows, making for the steps in the yard used by delivery men. The wooden board that covered the flight of steps into the cellars was held in place by a bolt that felt stiff under her small fingers. She gripped it more firmly, tugging with all her weight and still it didn't move. "*Merde*, oh *merde* thing!" Standing up she kicked at it angrily. Her foot in its canvas tennis shoe stung like mad but to her surprise the bolt had moved a little. She kicked at it again. And again more forcefully. Her foot throbbed but the bolt had loosened and she tugged at it with both hands. It gave suddenly and Peach sat down surprised on the hard gravel. She waited a moment listening, and then holding up the wooden grate over her head with one hand she climbed down into the hole. With a miaow the little brown kitten jumped down the steps in front of her and disappeared into the dark. Damn! Ziggie had followed her! Peach settled the board in position over her head. Switching on her torch she began to wind her way through the cellars under the hotel. "Ziggie," she whispered, flashing her torch right and left. There she was! But the cat scampered out of the beam of light.

Peach knew the way like the back of her hand. She'd carried many messages, brought food, listened to the BBC in London on the radio. It would be easy to get the escapees along this maze of tunnels and out into the yard. And if Lais and Leonore created the promised diversion the plan would go like clockwork. There would be no trouble. If only Ziggie hadn't dashed in after her. Ziggie didn't know her way through the cellars, a kitten like that could be lost for ever in here. Anxiously Peach flashed her torch along the corridors on either side. "Ziggie," she called softly, "Ziggie."

The men clambered up the cellar steps after Peach and pushed back the wooden board, slamming home the bolt securely. Bent double they followed their small guide across the open courtyard to the circle of trees. Peach paused, letting her eyes adjust to the night. "We're going down there," she whispered, pointing out the villa, "but we must take a roundabout route up through the trees on the headland and come down on the other side. The path is too conspicuous."

"Right, little one," murmured one of the men. "Let's go."

Peach threaded her way expertly through the trees, pausing every now and again for them to catch up. She half-ran, half-walked, taking a wide curve around the villa and dropping back down towards it on the western side. Fifteen minutes later they made their way cautiously through the garden towards the house. Peach laughed as she remembered an American expression of her mother's. "It was a breeze!"

The croupier was waiting in the kitchen. He had changed into workman's overalls like theirs. "*Eh bien*," he said to the men, "we have no time to lose. We must go through the woods and fields on foot as far as St Maxime where we will pick up working papers. From there we will travel by farm truck, delivering milk, vegetables," he winked at Peach. "In war one must also be an actor." The three Resistance workers shook Peach's hand and told her she was a brave girl and they would never forget her. Turning out the lights Peach held open the door as they filed into the night.

"Good luck," she whispered after them.

She sat with Leonie in the silent kitchen, sipping milk and eating a piece of cake. The bleached pine longcase clock in the corner ticked minutes into the silence and the lamplight gleamed on Madame Frénard's polished copper pots and pans. Bunches of herbs hung to dry from the ceiling beam, scenting the air. It was so calm, so secure. And yet out there in the night – was danger. Peach shuddered, and took a gulp of her milk. Leonie caught her eye and smiled at her. "I wasn't scared, Grand-mère," she said.

"Nor was I," said Leonie. "Not until afterwards."

Peach said in a small voice, "I hope they'll make it, Grand-mère."

She sagged back in her chair, yawning. She felt so tired suddenly. Ziggie must already be curled up on her bed waiting for her . . . "Grand-mère!" she cried, leaping to her feet. "I must go back to the hotel. It's Ziggie. She's lost in the cellars." Grabbing her torch she was out of the door before Leonie could stop her.

Kruger took a place next to her and Lais leaned away from his stale beery breath as he stared silently into the mirror behind the bar. The Italian major who had been pestering Lais for a week elbowed his way through the crowd pushing himself in front of Kruger, slopping beer over him and Kruger glared angrily at the man's back as he wiped off his jacket. Of course he wouldn't bother to turn round and apologise. And Lais was deliberately ignoring him. Well, she wasn't going to make a fool of him again! Kruger's face burned at the memory – how could he have lost control like that? *And she had known* – he'd seen the expression in her eyes. He stared at his own face in the mirror, purple with humiliation. Lais leaned forward whispering something in the Italian major's ear, laughing. Laughing at *him*! Turning on his heel, Kruger pushed his way savagely through the crowd.

In the hall Kruger took out his handkerchief and mopped his perspiring face. He'd always hated crowds, always been a loner. From the corner of his eye he saw the small de Courmont sister hurrying along the corridor towards the back of the hotel and the kitchens. Going to find Leonore, he supposed. She probably wanted a piece of cake. All children were greedy. He walked across the marble hall to the revolving doors in search of some air and then stopped, replaying what he had just seen in his head. The little girl, in shorts and a shirt, hurrying down the corridor. *And in her hand was a torch.*

A triumphant smile lit his perspiring face as he strode along the corridor to the kitchen. If Peach de Courmont had a torch it meant she was going somewhere dark. *Like the cellars.*

Coming out of the kitchen Leonore saw Kruger heading purposefully towards her. "What is it now, Captain Kruger?" she snapped.

"Where is she going," panted Kruger, "the young sister?"

"She's going home, of course," lied Leonore easily, "where else would she go?"

"To the cellars?" suggested Kruger.

Leonore froze. Peach had promised her she wouldn't go after the cat tonight, she knew that it was wrong, that it was risky even though the men had gone. But the poor child had been distraught . . . tonight had been too much for her.

"Nonsense," she said, "why on earth should Peach want to go to the cellars?"

"She had a torch," cried Kruger triumphantly. He knew that only the main cellar areas were lit. The winding tunnels at the back had never been wired for electricity.

"Of course she has," Leonore managed a laugh, "she's walking home to the villa, it's a dark night, Captain."

"I shall go to the villa myself and check," said Kruger.

"You certainly shall not," stormed Leonore, "I *forbid* you to do that. My grandmother will be sleeping."

"*You forbid me?*" Kruger's eyebrows bristled.

"*I* forbid you – and if necessary I shall have the Commandant forbid you. My grandmother was not well enough tonight to attend the Commandant's birthday party and I don't think she would appreciate a mere Captain disturbing her rest." Leonore knew she was on safe ground, von Steinholz's youthful admiration for Leonie still held fast.

"Then I shall inspect the cellars." Kruger marched back up the corridor.

"Captain Kruger," Leonore called after him. "There is only one key to the cellars and I have it. I refuse to allow you to inspect my cellars simply because you have seen my young sister carrying a torch. Your suspicions are ludicrous. I shall report you to the Commandant immediately." Leonore pushed past him and headed for the cocktail bar. Von Steinholz had been drunk at his birthday party two hours earlier. With any luck he would be past all understanding by now.

"Ziggie, Ziggie," called Peach, "here kitten, come here to me!" The racks of bottles glimmered in the thin beam of her torch and she stopped to listen, hoping for the patter of paws, or an answering miaow. She pushed further into the winding corridors. "Ziggie," she whispered, "here darling, here Ziggie." A faint squeak came from in front of her and swinging her torch around Peach stepped eagerly into the darkness. The tiny miaow came from somewhere over her head. The cat's yellow eyes gleamed in the beam of light and she miaowed again piteously. "Come here you rascal," Peach said, reaching up to pick the kitten from the top of the wine rack, "poor little thing." The kitten pushed its tiny head affectionately against her face and she kissed its soft fur. "You mustn't ever run away again," she scolded as she wound her way back through the cellars, "promise me."

Leonore had never seen the bar so crowded. It was like the worst sort of cocktail party, one where people refused to leave and that had gone on far too long. The press of bodies and the smell of polished leather and the heavy cologne used by the Germans was overpowering. Wrinkling her nose, Leonore slid through the crowd towards Lais. "I've got to talk to you," she murmured, a hand on her arm.

Lais followed Leonore through the crowd.

"It's Peach," whispered Leonore, standing by the door. "Ziggie got shut in the cellar and she insisted on going in to get her. Kruger spotted her with a torch and he's demanding to inspect the cellars. I think I've put him off, but I'm not sure."

"Damn the man," cried Lais furiously, "oh damn that disgusting

125

man. Look Leonore, *there he is!*" Kruger stood at his usual observation place by the reception desk. "At least the escapees have gone! Peach is looking for her lost kitten, that's all. It'll be all right, Leonore."

Ferdi von Schönberg was very tired. The drive from Reims was a long one, but it was still better than taking the slow train down from Paris. Lais hadn't expected to see him for at least another two weeks and he couldn't wait to see the look of surprise on her face. A glance at his watch showed that it was exactly ten thirty as his black Mercedes swept round the curving drive in front of the hotel. She would be in the bar, playing her game of diverting the enemy. She was brave, his love, as well as beautiful. Her eyes would widen when she saw him, the way they had that first time, and then she'd smile at him, a private smile whose message only he understood. Ferdi slammed the car door and buttoned his jacket, sniffing the clean soft Mediterranean night air appreciatively. It was good to be back.

Kruger seethed with frustration. He *knew* the girl was in the cellars and if he waited here long enough she would have to come out again. His instinct had been sound, they were hiding escapees in the cellars, the child was the go-between. He knew there'd be a radio down there. He'd show Lais and her sisters now – *and* he'd show von Steinholz and those lousy aristocratic "officers" what a beer-drinking Captain could do. He'd catch the Resistance group under their very noses while they lounged drunk and idle in the bar. Hitler's Germany was meant for men like himself, men like Hitler! The Führer came from a simple background, he would be a man who drank beer, not wine . . .

Kruger paced the marble floor, his boots clicking harshly on its smooth surface. His eyes rested on Lais and Leonore, standing by the arched entrance to the bar. *He had them now! All three of them.* It was all so obvious he didn't know why he hadn't worked it out before. Lais's blonde head was bent close to her sister's. Their profiles looked like matching cameos as Lais whispered in her sister's ear. She would be whispering about him! Lais threw back her head and laughed. The sound ricocheted around the hall, bouncing from the marble walls, piercing his throbbing head. She was laughing at him, telling her sister how he'd shamed himself in front of her . . . her long smooth throat rippled with laughter like the pulse in his head . . . Kruger's hand trembled on the Luger, he wanted to kill Lais, rip her beautiful laughing throat to pieces.

Peach hurried along the corridor towards the hall, the kitten tucked under her arm. "Don't ever run away again, Ziggie," she scolded, "I was so worried about you."

"Halt!" screamed Kruger. His bulging eyes fixing her maniacally as he advanced, his hand on the gun at his belt. Peach's eyes met his, glazed with terror. This was what they understood, he thought triumphantly. *Power! His power.* The Luger slid easily from the holster into his hand. The very symbol of his superiority! Not even the de Courmonts would dare to argue with him now! Peach's shrill scream of terror cut through his thoughts as she fled past him into the hall. She had ignored him, ignored his gun . . . even the little one had no respect for him. "Halt!" he cried, lumbering after her, "Halt!" *She had known!* he thought bewildered, she had known he couldn't shoot, known he was a coward just as his mother had always told him . . . he should have shot them all, all three of them . . .

"A gun," shrieked Lais, "*Kruger has a gun!*"

He should shoot her now, kill that blonde tease who plagued his sleeping as well as his waking moments. Sweat dripped from Kruger's purple face. His shaking hand pointed the gun at Lais as she flung herself in front of Peach. Pull the trigger, he told himself, PULL IT! With a groan of defeat he slumped back against the reception desk, jamming his elbow against the counter. The Luger jumped in his hand and his nerveless finger danced on the hairspring trigger. The shot echoed around the room, repeating itself, echoing over and over and over in his throbbing head . . . and the sound of a woman's scream, dredged from some horror deep inside her.

Ferdi von Schönberg leapt the last three steps, his gun already in his hand. Peach was huddled on the ground holding a girl whose familiar sea-green silk dress was already soaked scarlet. Lais's long blonde hair tumbled across her face and Peach, splattered with her sister's blood, brushed it back softly.

Here was Lais's prince, she thought, come to awake her again with a kiss, but now he couldn't . . . Peach's eyes, dark with shock, met Ferdi's. Somewhere she could hear men running, shouting . . .

"She's dead, Ferdi," she whispered. "Kruger shot her."

Kruger sagged trembling against the reception counter, staring at them, the gun on the floor at his feet and Peach watched in horrified fascination as Ferdi raised his right arm, steadying his gun with the left as he took aim. She didn't want to look, she mustn't look . . . but her eyes followed Kruger as with a terrified scream he turned to run. The shot deafened her and a neat hole appeared in the centre of Kruger's back, small and very black. Ferdi's second shot spun Kruger around, a jet of blood spurted from his mouth as he fell to the ground. Peach caught the glitter of tears in Ferdi's eyes as he looked once more at Lais. Then he turned and strode for the door.

As if released from a spell, men surged from the bar, shocked from their drunkenness. Crouched on the floor Leonore searched desperately for Lais's pulse, tears streaming down her face, blinding her. In a strange petrified calm, Peach cradled Lais's head in her lap, wiping the splattered blood from her face with her sleeve, stroking her sister's hair. She felt miles away, locked out of this awful reality . . . it was a dream too terrible ever to speak of . . .

Coming up the steps with Amelie, Leonie called out to Ferdi but he didn't answer. He didn't even seem to see her. He just kept on walking. And wasn't there a glimmer of tears in his eyes?

"Who is he?" Amelie asked, nervous now that she was finally to be reunited with the children.

"He's your future son-in-law," answered Leonie, puzzled. And then she heard the shouting and the commotion.

The crowd parted before them and they stared, unbelieving, at the three girls on the bloodstained pink marble floor. The bag that Amelie had clutched protectively all the way from Lisbon fell to the ground and the innocent child's rag doll lay there, unnoticed.

"Maman," whispered Peach, her shocked eyes meeting Amelie's. "Oh Maman. Kruger has shot Lais."

Part II

Part II

23

"I can do nothing with him," Mr Hill stormed, thrusting Noel through the door of Mrs Grenfell's office. Still gripping Noel by the neck he shook him violently, incensed by his apathy. Noel had just *walked* the five mile cross-country run, taking his time about it and arriving back at base more than two hours after everyone else.

"It's not just that," Hill thundered, "he stands around on the basketball court like a bump on a log, he refuses to run on the football field and as for baseball! Ahh!" He thrust Noel towards her desk.

Noel's vacant gaze settled on a point somewhere above Mrs Grenfell's head. Sitting back with a sigh, she patted her tight, grey-speckled, permanent wave and stared at Noel from over the top of her gold-rimmed glasses. Elvira Grenfell was plump bordering on obese with deep cushions of fat across her shoulders that gave her a hunchbacked appearance and enormous thighs that, when she was seated, offered a lap wide enough for any child to cuddle in. But Elvira was not a cuddly woman, there was a steely edge to her glance, a sharpness to her voice and a cut of sarcasm to her words that wilted the children into self-doubt and insecurity. Still, Elvira considered herself a good woman, she had given her life to these children, she saw that they were brought up to be good Christians, ready to take their place in the workforce of society. It was boys like Noel who let her down. The non-conformers, the non-doers of the world. And the child was ugly too. Hastily she thrust the thought away as unworthy – but really, the boy looked so white and pinched, his eyes were so deepset she couldn't read them and his nose jutted in a most unchildlike way. And he was so thin, visitors would think she starved him!

"Well?" she asked sharply, "what have you to say for yourself? Why are you causing Mr Hill all this trouble?"

Noel's gaze remained in the air. "I'm not good at sports, ma'am," he muttered.

"He doesn't even try," stormed Hill, "he makes a laughing-stock of himself – and of *me*. The other boys snigger when they see him ignore my instructions – and they pick on him because he's such a runt. He needs to toughen up, make a man of himself."

Noel blocked out their voices. He had almost perfected the art of not being there. The person in the world he would have most liked to be was the Invisible Man – then he could have wandered the world, aloof and alone, looking at things, watching people like insects under a microscope . . .

"Well?"

Mrs Grenfell's voice had risen an octave.

"Answer me!" she demanded. "What things are you good at? What do you do, Noel Maddox, to contribute to our society here?"

Noel shrugged and dropped his gaze to the floor.

Mrs Grenfell and Mr Hill looked exasperatedly at each other over the top of his head. Really the boy was hardly worth bothering about.

"Very well then, when the others are enjoying their sport you, Noel, will help with the work around here. You can clean out the garage. I want the shelves cleared and washed and everything replaced neatly. All the tools will be cleaned and stacked in their proper places. My car will be washed and polished. Then you can do the staff cars . . . that should keep you busy. Maybe then you'll discover that sports are a better way of improving both your social communication and your physique – and I must say you could use it." Her glance expressed her distaste for his appearance. "You can start this afternoon. Mr Hill will inspect your work and report to me later. Now be off with you." Pushing up her spectacles she turned her attention to the coffee tray carried in by her secretary. It smelled good and rich and there was cook's special cake today – it really was childish of her to like angel cake so much but she just couldn't resist it. Her hand hovered greedily over the plate.

Noel walked quickly from the office, his face set and grim. They could think up any punishment for him, give him as much work as they liked, he didn't care. Maybe they'd send him away, get rid of him – he was uncooperative, a nuisance, he embarrassed them. The older boys ignored him, the younger ones laughed at him. And the girls never even acknowledged his existence. He wished he was dead.

Alone in the garage Noel cleared shelves reluctantly, dawdling over the job, but the car drew his attention like a magnet. It was a prim, solid, high-bodied automobile – not new, but in good shape. Noel's trips in motor vehicles had been limited to the hired bus on the few occasions the children had been taken to the county fair – the treat of a local civic group – or on the annual picnic. *He had never ridden in a private automobile.* The bucket of water and the brushes were forgotten. In a flash he was behind the wheel. The car smelled of leather and a faint whiff of mothballs and cologne – Mrs Grenfell. He gripped the wheel, joggling the gearshift, peering at dials that told you how powerful the car was and how fast it could go. He was filled with a sudden surging excitement. *God, he loved it.* He wished more than anything that the car were his. He had cut emotion from his life when Luke departed, but he wanted this car so badly he could cry.

Tears dripped suddenly on to the leather seat between his bony knees as though somebody had turned the tap on Niagara. He couldn't stop. He sat there with the tears streaming down his face for at least half an hour. Then he wiped the leather seat with the cleaning cloth and blew his nose on it and felt better. Better than he had in years.

Noel fiddled around until he found the lever that opened the bonnet. The engine was beautiful, a perfect, simple and yet complex piece of machinery. He sniffed the hot smell of oil and gasoline, consumed with a desire to understand how it worked.

Later, he borrowed books from the library, taking them with him to the garage, checking the diagrams against the engine, tapping nuts and bolts experimentally the way a mechanic would, filled with a sense of satisfaction.

Mrs Grenfell's attitude diminished from anger to indifference as Noel ceased to be a problem to be dealt with by her. He had finally become useful cleaning the cars.

Six months of Saturdays spent at Old Joe's Garage and Body Shop in town when the other kids were on the football or baseball field taught Noel the beauty of precision engineering. And those Saturdays replaced any need in his heart for human companionship. It was enough to watch the mechanics turn the engines from grimy, malfunctioning, ill-used objects into gleaming, powerful efficiency. In between pumping gas, of course, because that's what Noel did, Saturdays.

24

Stripping bare the flower boxes on Carolina Montalva's balcony, Peach tossed the blossoms on the heads of the liberating American troops rolling through Paris in their jeeps and armoured vehicles, laughing as they grinned up at her. "I'm American too," she yelled, returning their thumbs-up signal delightedly.

The people of Paris cheered and sang and the city sparkled shabbily in the spring sunshine. Every now and then the jeeps stopped to allow pretty young girls to kiss the liberators.

"Paris is alive again," cried Leonie, "they're embracing in the streets, Caro, just the way they used to."

"The terrible thing is," said Caro, "that I'm getting too old to take part in it. Now," she went on briskly, "what time do you think we might expect Amelie and Gerard?"

Leonie glanced at the Meissen porcelain clock whose pretty gilt hands had ticked away Caro's life for as long as she had known her, and now it was ticking away the minutes to Gerard's return.

"Soon," she said smiling, wishing it could have been a true homecoming at the house on the Ile St Louis. But that was now the headquarters of an American general and his staff.

Peach looked at the table set for her father's homecoming lunch. The old damask cloth gleamed with Caro's silver, reclaimed from its wartime hiding place beneath the flagstones of her country house. A posy of zinnias decorated the centre like a brightly coloured mosaic and celebration champagne cooled in ice buckets on the sideboard. Peach knew that she was one of the fortunate ones – her father was returning. They knew so many other families for whom there would be no celebration and whose posies of flowers would be placed on cold graves and watered with tears.

"They'll be at the hospital now," she said, unable to contain her own happiness, "and soon – *Papa will be here!*" She danced across the sapphire blue rug, suddenly mad with joy. *"Papa's coming home!"* If only Lais were able to share her joy. But Lais lay in the white hospital bed with all the complicated weights and pulleys and the dangling bottles and tubes that fed life into her through her arms and her throat. Lais was surrounded by ugly steel tables that held little kidney shaped dishes and there was always a smell of antiseptics and fading flowers. And in poor Lais's twilight world the curtains were always half-drawn to keep out the sun. At home Lais's room had always been a wonderful clutter of paintings and books and small pretty objects, it had been filled with colour and scattered with her clothes, smelling of powder and perfume and nail polish. But now Lais lay pale and weightless, her eyes closed to the hospital ugliness, her long slender legs covered with the neatest white sheet that never, *never* got crumpled.

Every day when she went to see her, Peach would remember to wear her smile in case Lais woke up and saw her there. She was *sure* Lais knew she was there. It was just that she had never opened her eyes since that night.

Peach had protested over and over again that it would have been her in that hospital bed if brave Lais hadn't run in front of her, and even though Leonie explained that Kruger had aimed his gun at Lais and it had gone off by accident, still Peach felt sure that it was all her fault. If she hadn't gone back after Ziggie, if she hadn't panicked . . . Most often the guilt would sneak up on her at night when she was alone in bed and despite herself she would re-live the horror of those moments. The scent of blood would be in her nostrils and Lais's thin eerie scream would split her ears. There was the cold, terrible look in Ferdi's face as he turned the gun on Kruger and the fountain of blood that spilled from Kruger's throat – so much blood for such a little man! It was Leonore who had found Lais's fluttering pulse, and Leonore who had screamed for someone to get an ambulance as the German doctor tried to staunch the flow of blood from Lais's side . . .

The bell rang at last. "He's here, he's here," cried Leonie, hurrying to the door.

Peach hovered on the balcony, suddenly shy. It had been five years since Papa had seen her, she had been just a little girl. Now she was eleven and tall for her age. He might be expecting his baby and all he would get would be this gangling half-child.

Papa was shockingly thin, so thin that she'd bet she could count his ribs. His hair was mostly grey where it used to be so glossy and dark, and his blue eyes were weary, even though he was smiling. He leaned heavily on a silver-topped cane and Amelie held his arm protectively.

Peach's eyes met his across the room and the years fell away. The cane dropped to his side, forgotten as Gerard held open his arms and she ran into them. "I thought you'd be all grown-up," he murmured into her hair in between kisses, "but I see you're still my little girl."

"Always Papa," whispered Peach hugging him madly, "I'll always be your little girl."

The doorbell rang suddenly and for a moment there was silence. It was still too soon to have forgotten when the unexpected ring at the door meant terror. "Hope I'm not too late for lunch," said a familiar voice in the hall. Wearing the uniform of an American Air Force colonel, Jim breezed through the door. "Well, well," he said taking in the lunch table, the champagne, the assembled family. "I see you were expecting me."

"Jim! Oh Jim!" cried Leonie. Sweeping her off her feet, he crushed her to him as though he'd never let her go again.

"Why didn't you tell me?" she protested. "Why?"

Jim's laugh boomed around the elegant salon, "I was under orders, ma'am. I'm one of your liberating soldiers. Of course they didn't believe me when I said I was just off to see my old friend Caro. They figured I must have a smart mistress tucked away somewhere in Paris." He grinned at Caro. "I must admit I didn't expect to find all of you here. I'm as surprised as you are."

"And Papa's home too," cried Peach, "and Maman. Oh Jim. It's a miracle, a true miracle."

"It's our second miracle today," said Amelie. "I took Gerard to visit Lais at the hospital. Gerard was holding her hand talking to her quietly, saying he was home, that he would look after her now and that everything would be all right. 'Back to square one, Lais,' he said. And then he kissed her and we turned to go. At the door we looked back at her – *and Lais's eyes were open!*"

25

Wearing a faded blue shirt and his best grey flannel trousers that were two inches too short and had belonged to Tom Robinson last year, Noel poked in the car's engine with a wrench, frowning as he noticed the oil stain on his newly starched sleeve. He would rather be in his overalls down at Joe's Garage but Mrs Grenfell had said the visitors were special and that the lady raised enormous sums for charity. *Charity!* Noel despised that word. Charity only made you feel good when you were bestowing it. When you were on the receiving end it meant being grateful for things others took for granted and always having to say "thank you" for your daily bread, it meant wearing trousers that were too short and flapped around your skinny ankles.

The bell rang summoning them to the assembly hall. Mrs Grenfell had given instructions for them all to be dressed in their best and neatly brushed and combed. Noel rubbed at the oil stain on his sleeve despondently. He doubted it would ever come out and he knew he'd be in trouble with Matron again. The bell summoned him a second time and wiping his hands on the cloth he walked reluctantly back towards the house.

Peach shifted her eyes from the flat vista of wheat under a leaden sky, to her grandmother. Leonie's hands gripped the wheel tightly, arms extended, sitting well back in her seat in the proper position for driving. The big Chrysler covered the empty road at twenty-five miles an hour and Peach sighed. At this rate they wouldn't be there before four o'clock.

"No need to sigh," said Leonie, "we'll get there." She'd brought Peach on the tour of the American orphanages instead of Amelie, because Amelie had wanted to stay at the hospital in New York where Lais was undergoing treatment. But Peach was an impatient traveller. No sooner were they in the car than she expected to be there!

Peach grinned. "Can't we at least go thirty-five?"

Leonie glanced at her eleven-year-old granddaughter. "It's just that I'm not used to driving these big American cars," she said apologetically, "there was always a chauffeur, or Jim . . ."

"Come on, Grand-mère," teased Peach, "yours was the horse and carriage era."

"You're right," admitted Leonie. "I watched the world change with the automobile – and your grandfather made some of the finest cars in France. Why, I remember the night Monsieur took me out in the very first de Courmont car. I can see it now, it had soft cream leather seats and little Lalique flower vases. It was a bright red, a dozen coats of special polished lacquer, he said, with big brass lamps and leather straps around the bonnet . . . I wore a red silk dress to match and Monsieur had bought jasmine for the vases . . ."

Peach waited, scarcely daring to breathe, for what Leonie would say next. Was she going to tell her at last, about her and Monsieur?

"We caused quite a sensation outside the theatre that night," said Leonie.

"Not only *that* night," said Peach quickly, "you were always sensational, Grand-mère."

Leonie smiled. "Not always. And anyway it was Monsieur who was the sensation – *he* was the one in the public eye. He was a very clever man, very powerful." Leonie's fingers gripped the wheel tighter.

Encouraged by Leonie's sudden intimacy Peach asked the question that had burned in her mind for a long time. "Why didn't you marry him?"

She looked so sad Peach wished she hadn't asked. "Maybe I'll tell you one day, Peach, if I must. Oh, I wish I could spare you all the traps that women fall into. Wait. You'll know too soon that *love* is the most complex emotion of all – and it makes *fools* of us all."

"Still," said Peach, "if I loved someone, I'd marry him . . ."

"Good," replied Leonie briskly, shutting out the past, "just bring him to meet your grandmother first so that I can give my approval. Now look, Peach – there on the horizon. That's the first building we've seen in half an hour – that must be it. The Maddox."

The harsh clanging of a bell greeted them as the car swept through the iron gates, held back by a two well-scrubbed young boys. Peach surveyed the squat grey buildings with a sinking feeling in the pit of her stomach. No flowering creepers attempted to soften their outline, and no carefully cultivated roses or azaleas bordered the paths the way they did at the Château d'Aureville. And the group of children drawn up behind the staff to welcome them looked grey too, pinched from the everlasting wind from the plains. They didn't smile as the car came to a halt.

"Grand-mère, I can't," whispered Peach.

Leonie looked at her in surprise, "Can't what, darling?"

"I can't go in there." A flash of fear at the thought of what it would be like made Peach feel sick. "I don't like it . . ."

Mrs Grenfell's face loomed nearer, false teeth gleaming in a sudden shaft of sunlight.

Leonie glanced at Peach, alarmed. "Do you feel ill?"

"No, no. But please don't make me go in, Grand-mère. Please?"

Leonie looked at the Maddox Charity Orphanage, at Mrs Grenfell's expectant face and the grey children lined up in front of that grey building. She understood why Peach didn't want to go inside. "Wait here then, darling," she said opening the car door. It was her duty to go in, to see what her organization could do to help. She wished now she hadn't brought Peach with her.

Leonie shook Mrs Grenfell's hand, a warm smile lighting her still beautiful face. A small girl in an unbecoming print dress offered a stiff bouquet of gladioli wrapped in cellophane. Leonie bent to kiss her and the child stared at her, mouth open in amazement, a hand on her cheek where she had been kissed. Leonie progressed down the rows of children, smiling, shaking hands, pausing to pat the head of a little one, questioning the older ones. Her interest was real and her concern genuine and Peach thought she almost shone with love for those poor children.

Peach slumped back against the seat with a sigh of relief as they filed inside. She couldn't have borne to sit with them and have lunch, the way she did at the Château d'Aureville. This place terrified her. Somehow she knew how it would smell without even going in there – of strong disinfectant and stale food – and unhappiness. Sitting up she stared out of the window at the closed front door. The steel letters glittered in the wavering sunlight. Maddox Charity Orphanage.

A skeletal face appeared suddenly at the car window, its eyes as light and steely as the letters over the door. Peach pulled back with a gasp of alarm.

"Sorry," the boy muttered, "sorry. I just wanted to look at the car." He walked away, head down, hands jammed in his pockets.

Peach rolled down the window and stared after him. He didn't seem very old. The boy's grey trousers were too short and flapped around his skinny ankles and his cropped head looked vulnerable and pathetic. Sliding quickly across the seat, she called after him. "Wait a minute."

Noel walked on, blinking to clear his eyes of the vision of her. He must be dreaming that she had called him.

"Please," called Peach, "wait a minute, wait for me."

Noel heard her light footsteps on the gravel and felt the slight pressure of her hand on his arm.

"Hello," she said. "I'm Peach de Courmont. Who are you?"

She was even more beautiful than at first glance, a glowing girl with a cloud of russet hair. Her skin looked soft – not red and chapped from the wind like the girls he knew; and her eyes – oh her eyes were this marvellous deep, dark blue – the blue of summer lakes he had never seen but knew must exist. For other people, not for him.

Peach smiled at him tentatively. "Well?"

Noel hung his head. "Well, what?"

"What's *your* name?"

"Noel."

"Noel – *who*?"

"Maddox – Noel Maddox."

Peach's glance rested on the steel letters over the door. She wished she hadn't asked. "Why aren't you inside having lunch with the others?"

Noel thrust his hands deeper into his pockets. "I wanted to look at the car, that's all," he muttered, hanging his head.

"Well, come on then." Peach took his arm, "Come on, I'll show you."

The shock of her touch made Noel shiver, so that the hairs on the back of his neck bristled. Shyly he allowed her to lead him towards the car.

"Look all you want," she said. "I couldn't tell you how fast it goes because Grand-mère never drives over thirty miles an hour."

Her high sweet laugh sent shivers down Noel's spine. "Can I . . . I mean would it be okay if I looked inside?"

"Of course." Peach flung open the door and stepped back.

"No. No I mean *inside*. Under the hood."

"You want to see the *engine*?" She had thought he would want to admire the luxurious interior. "I'm not sure how to open it," she confessed.

"Here, let me." Noel located the lever and walked around the front of the car. Lifting the hood he gazed at the immaculate, still hot engine.

Peach leaned companionably over the side. "What's so fascinating about engines?" she asked.

Noel's hungry gaze took in the details of the machine's construction and capacity. His hand itched for a wrench, he could have poked around in that engine for hours. "Don't you see?" he murmured. "It's all so perfect. The plugs, the hoses, each little piece plays its part in creating power. It's all so logical and so easy."

"It certainly looks complicated to me!"

Noel lifted his gaze from the engine. Peach's arm rested on the rim of the car next to his hand. It was faintly golden from the kind of sun that never shone here, with a scatter of blonde hairs. Noel gripped the edge of the car tighter and his voice deepened as he answered. "That's because you're a girl."

Peach tossed the hair out of her eyes, laughing. "Ah, but I'm a *de Courmont* girl."

The name rang in his head with the impact of the fairground bell struck with the full blow of the hammer. "*De Courmont!* You mean the *automobile* de Courmonts?"

"That's us," smiled Peach, meeting his stunned gaze. Really he had nice eyes when he lifted the veil of defence and allowed you to see into them, a light grey and with long, dark lashes. "My grandfather practically built the first one himself."

"They're *wonderful* cars," said Noel, awestruck. "If course, I've never seen one for real . . . just in books."

Peach sighed. "We're not sure that there'll be any more now. The factories were destroyed in the war – there's not much left."

Noel tried to imagine what the de Courmont factories must have looked like. They were important enough to be destroyed in the war . . .

"*Noel!*"

He spun round as Mr Hill's familiar tread crunched across the gravel.

"Noel! What are you doing out here? You're supposed to be inside with the others. You've missed Madame Leonie's talk and your place is conspicuous by your absence in the dining hall!"

"Sorry," mumbled Noel, hanging his head.

Peach looked at him in alarm, it was as though somebody had turned a switch, cutting off the burning eagerness in his eyes. He was dispirited, disinterested . . . "It's my fault," she smiled, holding out her hand. "I'm Peach de Courmont, Leonie's granddaughter. I didn't feel too well," she gestured towards the car. "Noel noticed and stayed behind to see if he could help me."

She could see the man didn't believe her, but she was Leonie's granddaughter. He would have to accept her explanation. He shook her hand politely.

"Is there anything I can do for you, Miss de Courmont?"

Peach shook her head. "Thank you, I'm feeling better now. I'll just wait here in the car, for my grandmother."

"Then you'd better come with me, Noel, lunch has already begun."

"Goodbye, Noel," called Peach. Their glances met as he turned to follow Mr Hill to the house and Peach closed one eye in a conspiratorial wink, grinning as she climbed back into the car.

When Leonie re-emerged on the steps of the Maddox Orphanage an hour later her face still wore a smile but Peach thought she looked tired. It wasn't surprising, her grandmother was almost seventy and the Maddox looked enough to exhaust anyone.

With a final goodbye, Leonie climbed into the car and switched on the engine. "Wave farewell, darling," she murmured, still smiling, as they drove smoothly down the drive towards the tall iron gates, held open for them again by two small boys.

"Thank God," she breathed, tears stinging her eyes as the gates clanged shut behind them. "Oh thank God, Peach, that you never had to belong in a place like that."

Noel lingered by the gate watching until the car was no more than a speck on the straight road that led to the horizon. One more instant and then it was gone. Peach de Courmont was a golden girl, as unattainable to him as a dream. Her world was one of love and laughter, freedom and success. The fields of wheat rippled under the wind and a sigh as deep as eternity swept through his thin body. A sigh of longing. He now had two things he knew he wanted from life. He wanted to work with automobiles. And he wanted a girl like Peach de Courmont.

26

The Pan-Am Clipper from New York landed late after a bumpy eighteen-hour flight and Leonore trudged thankfully through the Paris rain to the Le Bourget terminal. New York was not her city, it was too fast, too glossy, too *new*. A few days of New York's pace left her drained and reluctant to leave her hotel room. It was the same with planes. Flying was fast and efficient but why did it leave her body feeling as though she were still in New York when her eyes and her mind told her she was home?

In the taxi to the Ile St Louis she decided she would take the train south to the Riviera the following morning. The door was opened by Oliver, the new English butler. "A gentleman called to see you this afternoon, Mademoiselle de Courmont," he told her.

She hadn't been expecting anyone. "Did he leave his name, Oliver?"

"No, Mademoiselle, he merely said he would call again."

Leonore trailed tiredly up the curving staircase. All she wanted was a hot bath, a cup of tea and bed. But the house was so *quiet*. She hadn't realised just how used she had become in a few weeks to New York's constant backdrop of traffic and sirens and parades. Hands thrust in the pockets of a fluffy white towelling robe, she pressed against the window pane, searching the familiar view. The river Seine wore its decoration of lights and car headlamps formed patterns across the bridges and avenues, yellow one way, red the other. Everyone in Paris seemed to be out tonight. Leonore knew that the cafés of St Germain would be crowded. Street entertainers would be out in force making little befrilled dogs jump through hoops or walking on stilts or juggling plates and playing jazz on out-of-tune saxophones; and someone would be singing softly to a guitar as lovers tossed coins into their waiting caps.

And on the smart Right Bank beautifully gowned women would be arriving at grand restaurants on the arms of handsome men, and lovers would walk hand in hand along the banks of Paris's magical river. How could she possibly go to bed at eight o'clock when Paris waited? Pulling on a pair of black trousers and a fine jade green cashmere sweater, Leonore fastened its tiny pearl buttons hurriedly, as though she were late for a date. She unpinned her long blonde hair from its familiar chignon and shook it free. She would taste Paris on her own, go for a walk, maybe drop into a café for a drink . . .

Her loafered feet took the stairs two at a time and slinging her purse over her shoulder Leonore ran across the hall, through the big double doors into the warm Paris night.

A man was turning into the courtyard as she came out and they side-stepped each other quickly to avoid a collision. "Excuse me," he said in German.

"Pardon," she said simultaneously in French. The street lamp outlined his tall figure, the straight light hair . . .

"Ferdi," she gasped.

"Lais. Oh Lais."

Ferdi's arms were around her, his mouth on hers. She was pressed against his body, lost in his kiss . . .

Leonore struggled free, pulling her mouth away from him. "Ferdi, no . . . no. Please, Ferdi."

He held her face in his two hands, "Lais," he said wonderingly, "it's really you. I thought Kruger had killed you. They put me in prison, you know, after I shot him. But someone told me there were rumours that you were in hospital, that they had taken you away to America. Others said you were dead . . . I wanted to believe you were alive, I hoped you'd be waiting for me. I came back to find you as soon as I could. Oh Lais, Lais . . ."

"Ferdi. *Please*," begged Leonore. "*Please listen to me*. I'm not Lais. I'm Leonore."

Ferdi picked up a strand of her long blonde hair, running it through his fingers. "No," he said. "No." Leonore's hair wasn't like this.

Leonore realised suddenly that tonight she did look like Lais, wearing casual clothes and with her hair loose. Leonore was the one with the tight-pulled hair, buttoned into the business suit. But her eyes were different, Ferdi would know she wasn't Lais when he saw the colour of her eyes.

"Here Ferdi," taking his hand she lead him to the street lamps. "Now look at me!"

He looked so deep into her eyes she felt he must be willing them to change to blue, waiting for some magic that would make her Lais. "I'm sorry Ferdi," she whispered as his hands fell from her shoulders.

"Then it's true," he said quietly. "Lais is dead. It was too much to hope for."

Leonore hesitated only a moment. Lais lay in the hospital in New York suffering tortuous treatments in the hope that she would recover from the shock that had left her silent since the shooting. Hopes had faded that one day the pieces of her puzzled mind would suddenly fit together and she would be their old Lais. And she never really could be, for there were no treatments that would ever help Lais to walk again. It would be better for Lais if Ferdi never saw her the way she was now, better he thought her dead.

"I'm so sorry Ferdi," she whispered.

He patted her head absentmindedly. "You were always a good sister," he replied gently.

"I'd like to know what happened to you, Ferdi, how your life has been since it happened."

They walked together across the little Pont Marie, finding a quiet café on a corner where over a bottle of red wine he told her of his arrest and court martial. He had been sentenced to ten years' imprisonment and stripped of his rank, but his family had used their influence to have his sentence commuted to house detention for the duration of the war, pleading that he was needed in the family's important steel works. By then the power of the Third Reich was already crumbling. Every night Ferdi had watched the Allied planes dropping shoals of bombs on to his city, destroying his factories, the armaments plants and steel mills. *And all he had felt was joy.* He had thought Lais dead, but then someone said no, she had been taken to hospital, first in Nice, then Paris. He had followed the trail here. "I couldn't go back to the Hostellerie," he explained, "I couldn't bear to see where it happened. I would always have an image of her lying there, her eyes closed, covered in blood. I came here looking for a ghost . . ."

Leonore recalled Peach's childish fantasy of Ferdi, but he was no longer the handsome young prince. Ferdi's face was lined and his blue eyes stared blankly as though he were searching his memories and finding them cold.

When he took her back to the house on the Ile St Louis, Ferdi shook her hand. "I must apologise for the kiss," he said.

145

Leonore felt the blush sting her cheeks. "It was understandable."

"Leonore, tonight was the first time I've talked to anyone about things. Thank you for listening. I feel now I can face the future without her. I had to know for certain, you see."

Leonore nodded, avoiding his eyes.

"Can I see you again? I promise I won't talk about me all the time."

His smile was boyish, a little wistful, and Leonore remembered his mouth on hers. "I'd like that," she said quietly.

Ferdi bowed over her hand, always the German gentleman. "I'll telephone you tomorrow," he called, striding across the courtyard.

Leonore leaned against the closed door, a smile playing around her mouth. There had been eagerness in Ferdi's eyes, a ray of hope when he'd asked her if he could see her again. Truly it was better that he thought Lais dead. Poor crippled Lais, her mind locked away in some other world. There would be no more schoolgirl silver trophies for diving and running, no more singing and dancing, no driving along the Corniche foot pressed hard on the pedal of the big dark blue de Courmont. Lais had her own world.

The last thing she thought of that night before she fell asleep was Ferdi's mouth on hers, the firmness of his lips, the warmth of his body pressed against her.

Three weeks later Leonore sat beside Ferdi in a cinema on the Champs Elsyées. In the flickering light from the screen she could just make out Ferdi's hand gripping hers. She wondered if he knew how tightly he held on to her, as though he were teetering on the brink of a cliff and her hand was his lifeline – only she could stop him from falling. Of course she had meant to return to the hotel but instead she had lingered in Paris, waiting around the house all day, afraid to go out in case she missed his call. Ferdi had called every day. Leonore never asked him to the house but always arranged to meet him at seven at the Café Deux Magots where the waiters now gave them the grudging nod and half-smile they permitted their regulars, bringing the wine they preferred without asking.

It was all perfectly innocent, Leonore told herself. She and Ferdi were simply friends. The *only* reason he had kissed her was because in his disturbed state of mind seeing her suddenly like that in the half-light, her blonde hair flowing free the way Lais used to wear it, he had *wanted* to believe she was Lais. Even though, as he told her later, he had known that she must be dead.

Leonore had felt no guilty pang listening to him talk of Lais as dead. And every night she saw Ferdi and he talked of Lais, it seemed more and more real. She could almost *believe* that Lais was dead now.

"Ferdi," she said as they strolled through the Tuileries Gardens later that week, "it's time I returned to the Hostellerie. I'm a working woman, you know."

"But I don't want you to go!" Ferdi's lean, strong-boned face looked suddenly desperate. "You can't imagine what it has meant to be being able to talk to you, Leonore. You've made me see that life must go on. It's all thanks to you," he clasped her hands tightly. "Don't leave me, Leonore," he pleaded, "not just yet."

A fitful wind tossed a strand of hair in her eyes and Ferdi brushed it aside tenderly, running his hand along her soft cheek, tracing the delicate curve of her eyebrow with his finger, and then her mouth. Their eyes met and for an instant they gazed at each other, reading each other's needs.

"Leonore," he said softly, and then his lips were on hers. Wrapped in his arms, away from the buffeting wind, Leonore knew this was what she wanted.

She had expected a bachelor's *pied-à-terre*, or a hideaway in some picturesque Left Bank street, but the Merker family had always maintained an apartment at the Ritz and with the end of the war, it had become Ferdi's second home. Leonore wandered the apartment's impersonal opulence nervously, touching the stiff flower arrangements, wondering if they were wax. She was horrified by the apartment's impeccable neatness. There was no coat thrown casually over a chair, no shoe peeking from beneath a sofa, no newspaper tossed impatiently aside. There were no personal photographs on the desk, and even the blotter was unmarked. Ferdi's bed had been turned down neatly by the chambermaid and a carafe of water with a glass stood on the bedside table.

Ferdi helped her undress and when he was naked he took her in his arms and they stood, warm body next to warm body, and Leonore thought that this was the way it must be for the "*filles de nuit*". An anonymous hotel room and a man who replaced your face with another's while he took your body. Ferdi's mouth was on her breast, his hands pressing her closer. Lifting her he carried her to the wide bed. The linen sheets were cool on her back and then his heat filled her and she was dying with pleasure, moaning her lust the way any whore might.

When it was over he lay quietly beside her for a moment, without speaking. Taking his cigarettes from the bedside table he lit one, offering it to her.

"But I don't smoke," said Leonore in a small voice. It was Lais who had smoked.

She took the train south the next morning, leaving a message for him with Oliver, the butler, that she had been called to the Hostellerie urgently and expected to be away for some time and would be too busy to see him.

27

Noel's dedication to the art of boxing took Mr Hill by surprise. He showed up with the other kids one Saturday afternoon, put on the gloves when his turn came to spar a round and he took a beating without complaint. Not only that – *Noel fought back*. Of course the lad was puny and slow and he didn't stand a chance, but he was plucky in the ring, taking his punishment silently. And he came back again the following week – and the week after. This time Hill refused to let him in the ring – the kid would just get whipped again. Instead he took him on one side at the end of the session and asked him what the big idea was? Did he want to get himself punished? Was he some kinda masochist, or what? The kid just looked at him with those unfathomable light eyes and said, "I want to learn." And that was it. Hill set the kid on a course of weight training, road-running, skipping and shadow-boxing that would've soon told him whether Noel meant business or not. And by golly he meant it! He stuck with it, practising with weights every night and getting up early to run four miles before breakfast – even in the winter's bitterest cold, until the snow put a stop to it for a few months, and then he worked out in the hall, running on the spot, push-ups. The kid had proven a marvel – and now, at just fourteen, he could whip the best.

Mr Hill's eyes held genuine warmth as he presented the cheap silver-plated cup to Noel. "For the winner of the Maddox Boxing Tournament – a true champion," he said, smiling.

A spatter of admiring applause came from the audience of Maddox boys as Noel shook hands with Mr Hill. "Thank you, sir," said Noel holding the trophy firmly.

"Give it back to me next week boy, and I'll see your name engraved right there along with your title, Junior Boxing Champion, Maddox Charity Orphanage, 1946," promised Mr Hill. "It was a good, clean fight, Noel, you did real well. Congratulations."

"Thank you, sir."

Noel slid his way under the ropes, walking through the ranks of boys seated on wooden benches towards the showers. Placing his trophy carefully on a chair, he stripped off the sweat-soaked shorts and turned on the water.

The hot spray stung the fiery red welts on his back and shoulders and Noel winced, forcing himself to stand there silently and bear the pain. After a few minutes he turned the shower to cold, gritting his teeth as the icy water flowed over him. Throwing back his head he let it stream over his face and through his short dark hair while he soaped his wiry, muscular body, willing himself to take the punishment of the frigid water. He counted off the slow minutes. Three exactly. Then he stepped from the shower, rubbed himself briskly with the thin towel and dressed rapidly. Standing in front of the mirror he combed his hair. Hill had said it was too long for a boxer, ordering him to crewcut it like everyone else, but Noel had ignored the command. His critical gaze in the mirror showed a thin but well-muscled lad of just fourteen – or he could have been fifteen, thought Noel. Maybe even sixteen. It was important to look older because you had to be older to work. At a proper job, that is, not just a Saturday one. And Noel was going to need a proper job.

He glanced around the shower room, taking in the scabby green wooden chairs and the old brass pegs that held the sweaty paraphernalia of sport. Picking up his trophy he made quickly for the door just as the other contenders in tonight's boxing tournament arrived.

"Hey Noel," they called, "great stuff, you sure had him beat."

"Thanks," said Noel, walking down the brown linoleum corridor.

They watched him with puzzled eyes. "Gee, you'd think now he's champ he'd loosen up a little," grumbled one.

"Ah, he's always been a loner," someone replied. "Not even boxing'll change *him*."

Noel had decided to take nothing with him but the parcel of food he'd managed to save over the past week. That way he would avoid arousing suspicion. He wore dungarees, a denim shirt, a pair of new high-top sneakers – requisitioned by Mr Hill as part of his necessary equipment as a sports jock and which were the only thing in his entire life that had brought Noel pleasure of possession. A grey windcheater jacket and a woollen scarf completed his leaving outfit. Knotting the scarf, he pocketed the trophy and picked up the brown paper sack with the food.

Taking the five dollars – two notes and some small change – from its hiding place in a shoe, he slid the money carefully into the pocket of his jeans.

It was nine o'clock on a Friday night. Lights still burned in the Maddox Orphanage and boys chatted in the dining hall over the special treat of cold milk and cookies to celebrate the boxing tournament. Even the younger boys had been allowed to stay up for the event. Of course the girls were in a separate building and Mrs Grenfell and Matron had no wish to watch such a masculine sport. It was quite easy for Noel to walk down the rarely used front staircase into the darkened hall. His sneakered feet made no sound on the black and white polished tiles and he turned the big lock carefully. It was very dark outside. The full moon was hidden behind dense scudding clouds, pushed by a wind that moaned across the bleak landscape.

Without a backward glance Noel closed the door behind him and walked down the worn stone steps. Keeping to the thin border of grass that ran alongside the gravel drive, he walked rapidly to the gates and rattled the latch impatiently. It must be stuck. Noel gasped as the full moon surged from behind the clouds lighting the driveway like a stage set. He could see that the gates were locked! Hesitating for a minute, he stuffed the parcel of food in the front of his windcheater then walked back a dozen paces. Turning he sprinted for the gates, hurling himself up half their height, clinging like a monkey and scrabbling his way up – and over. He dropped lightly down on the other side, and dusted the rust and paint from his hands. Straightening up he set off at a brisk jog down the road that led straight as a die, between the wheatfields to freedom.

28

Peach pushed Lais's wheelchair through the arched cloisters of the Palaçio d'Aureville in Miami, swivelling her sister around to face the splashing, blue-tiled fountain guarded by sturdy stone lions – copies of those in the Court of the Lions at the Alhambra. "Look Lais," she called, "do you remember when I was three and fell in and you had to rescue me?" The pond was shallow at the outer edge but the tiles were slippery and Peach had slid all the way to the centre where it was quite deep. Lais's eyes had been frightened when she fished her out. Peach laughed. "You were more scared than I was," she said, "I only had time to be surprised, it all happened so suddenly."

Kneeling beside her sister's chair Peach searched her empty eyes for a response. Now that all the curves had melted away, Lais's pretty face was gaunt, the cheekbones appeared too prominent and her wide mouth soft and vulnerable. Lais's eyes seemed to look at the fountain but Peach couldn't be sure. There was no glimmer of recognition, no smile. With a sigh Peach took her place behind the wheelchair once more, pushing Lais along the shaded paths. The green ocean sparkled in the strong Florida sunshine and a dozen little sailboats tacked across the horizon in the breeze. Closer inshore sunbronzed holidaymakers dived into the cool Atlantic surf. At the swimming pool Peach stopped to watch a boy climb the diving platform, balancing for a moment, arms outstretched, toes curled around the edge of the board, flexing his leg muscles before he dived. He cut through the still pool with barely a splash. There was a flash of his seal-sleek body under water a second before he broke the surface in a scatter of crystal drops.

"Perfect!" she called admiringly. "That was just perfect!" She pushed the wheelchair away from the pool, wishing that her sister could have seen him dive, that she could have sensed the physical pleasure of such a moment. With a sudden shock she realised that instead of as always facing front, Lais's head was turned slightly to the left. *Lais must be looking at the pool!*

Peach hunted eagerly through the closets in Lais's room, tossing garments from the drawers as she searched for a bathing suit. Throwing the clothes back into the drawers she ran across the room to Lais. Her sister lay on the special chaise-longue by the window leading on to the terrace, gazing at the view. Except, thought Peach angrily, you couldn't *tell* if she even *saw* the view. "Lais," she said, putting on her cheerful smile, "I have to go out. I'll send Miz in to be with you." Miz was Miss Z. (for Zena) Foley, Lais's Scottish nurse/companion, though Miz always said when Peach was home from school there was no companioning needed. Peach had christened her Miz right away and it suited her small, wiry stature and the sharp personality that she used to protect Lais from the curiosity of the public – and also served to cover her infinite kindness.

"Do you think she even knows what I say, Miz?" asked Peach following her back into the bedroom and staring despairingly at Lais's indifferent cameo profile.

"Maybe she does and maybe she doesn't," said Miz, briskly fluffing up the pillows behind Lais's head, "but it's my belief that you haven't yet found out what she wants to hear. One day you'll say the right thing and she'll wake up again."

"Like the sleeping princess in the story book," said Peach, "when she was kissed by the handsome young prince." But Ferdi hadn't looked like the handsome young prince when he'd shot Kruger; his eyes had been cold and dead, and Lais had lain bleeding in her arms . . . And Ferdi had *never* come back to claim his princess again. He'd disappeared for ever.

The screen door slammed behind her as she ran down the steps and across the grounds to the hotel. The smart little shop had a selection of fashionable bathing suits and remembering how painfully thin Lais was, Peach picked out one that seemed pathetically small. But it was in Lais's favourite sea green and it was sleek and pretty and meant for swimming, not decorating the poolside.

Out of breath from running, she hurtled back to the villa, doors slamming behind her, grinning as she heard Gerard protest from his study.

"Look Lais," she said, holding up the bathing suit. "We're going swimming!"

Miz glared at her, scandalised. "What are you saying, Peach, you know the poor lady can't swim?"

"Lais was the best swimmer in our family – apart from Grand-mère," retorted Peach. "Miz, oh Miz, at the pool today we stopped to watch a boy diving and *Lais turned her head to watch!* I'm sure of it."

Miz took the bathing suit from her quietly. "I dare say it was just the sun in her eyes. You know she doesn't like that."

Peach gazed at her, crestfallen. She had been so *sure*. She watched sadly as Miz tucked the sea-green bathing suit into the drawer. Then she walked silently to the door, turning to smile at Lais – just in case. Lais's wheelchair waited beside the chaise-longue, its ugly steel bars, its huge wheels and stiff black leather screaming its function. Peach remembered her hated calliper. She had longed for it at least to be pretty. Well, even if they wouldn't let her take Lais into the pool, there was something she could do for her. Lais would have a surprise waiting in the morning!

Gerard insisted that the family breakfasted together because it was the only time he could be sure of having them all in one place at the same time. It was remarkable, thought Amelie, pouring herself some coffee, how quickly Gerard had recovered physically from the ordeal of the forced labour camp, though she knew its memories would be with him for ever. Gerard hadn't yet become strong enough to return to his architectural practice but lately she'd found him at the drawing board in his study, poring over plans and occasionally sketching new ideas. Gerard was healing. If only Lais were getting better too. It was hard to accept that Lais, her quicksilver extrovert daughter, could be this silent stranger for the rest of her life, dwelling in the solitary caverns of her mind, hiding from the world's pain.

"Good morning, Maman." Tiptoeing up behind her, Peach slid her arms around Amelie's neck and kissed her. Amelie could smell the sea on her skin.

"Have you been swimming already?" Amelie laughed.

"Mmm," Peach helped herself to papaya and melon from the sideboard. "I had a date at seven o'clock."

"*A date?* You mean with *a boy?*" Amelie asked laughing.

"Of course, Maman. You don't have *dates* with girls," retorted Peach scornfully. "I met him yesterday at the hotel. He's a terrific diver and he's promised to help me."

Amelie realised with a pang that Peach was growing up. She seemed so much older than just twelve. They had missed so many years together, and yet now Peach longed to go back to Europe. Gerard had put her off firmly. "When you're fourteen we'll talk about it," he'd said, "meanwhile we would like to have you around." But Amelie knew that Peach had her heart set on the school in Switzerland.

Peach lifted her face for a kiss as Gerard came in, newspaper under his arm.

"Where's Lais?" he asked, surprised. Lais and the punctual Miz were always the first down, beating them all to the breakfast table.

"She's late," said Peach. "That's probably because of my surprise." It suddenly occurred to her that maybe Lais hadn't liked it, but even *not* liking something was better than just nothing.

"Here we are then," Miz pushed Lais to the table in her wheelchair.

"Why Peach," gasped Amelie, "it's wonderful!"

Peach had covered the metal bars of the wheelchair with brightly coloured ribbons, winding them round and round and leaving streamers to dangle in the breeze. She had glued pale green satin from one of Amelie's most luxurious Paris nightdresses over the backrest and she had tacked together a cushion of golden yellow lace. She'd dug into her mother's jewellery box and pinned diamonds and emeralds on the corners of the chair and she'd padded the footrest with bright green velvet.

"It's a throne, Lais," said Peach excitedly. "A throne for you. You are the princess, you see."

Amelie saw the love in Peach's eyes as she spoke to her sister. And Lais's eyes were bright too. *There were tears on her cheeks . . .*

"Peach," said Lais, her voice thin, and rough from long disuse. "Peach," she said again, a little stronger this time. "Peach."

29

"Motor City" was what they called it. And it was booming. Detroit's plants were operating night and day to feed a postwar nation's thirst for newer, bigger, glossier vehicles. The giant corporations, Ford, Chrysler, General Motors, US Auto, and the Great Lakes Motor Corporation, buzzed like queen bees at the centre of the sprawling city's hive of activity, fuelled by a network of smaller factories and workshops producing machine tools, nuts, bolts, batteries, paint – anything and everything needed to feed the massive ever-rolling assembly lines that churned out thousands of automobiles every year.

It had taken Noel two weeks to get there. Two weeks of walking, hitching, riding the rails along with bums and vagrants, two weeks of freezing November weather sleeping rough and trying not to feel hungry. He'd hit Detroit the previous night, riding the cab of an automobile delivery truck that was returning to the city empty of its load. The driver was young, twenty-five or so. He'd done a stint with the fifth Armoured Division and had been one of the first into Paris. He kept Noel awake – telling how great it had been, what the girls were like, how much brandy and champagne he'd drunk. It was great to be back though, just great. Noel's eyelids were drooping with fatigue and the warmth was creeping back into his numb feet, but still he wondered who needed a place like Paris when there was Detroit? The truck-driver was great, though, he'd assessed Noel's shabby shivering state quickly and after an hour he pulled in at a diner, bought them both eggs, bacon, hashbrowns, rolls and about three gallons of steaming hot coffee. Noel hadn't been able to keep his eyes open after that. He hadn't eaten in two days and he had just twenty-five cents in his pocket that he had been keeping for emergencies. He dozed for a couple of hours, waking as the rhythm of the truck changed from the smooth onward roll of the highway to the stop and start of the city.

"You looking for a job?" the driver asked, waiting at a red light.

"You know of one?"

"The plants are real busy, but there's a lot of guys after the jobs – all the veterans back on civvy street y'know. They get priority. You'd be better off trying one of the small places that make automotive parts for the big plants. I can tell you where to go."

"No," said Noel firmly. "*I want to go where they make the cars.*"

The driver glanced at him, surprised. "Listen kid, a job's a job – a few bucks in your pocket at the end of the week'll make you feel like a man whether you earned 'em making bolts or sticking the bolts in the car."

"I want to work on the cars," Noel repeated stubbornly.

The driver shrugged, "Okay, kid, it's your life."

Because he was driving for General Motors he dropped Noel there, and gave him directions to the gate nearest to the hiring office, wishing him luck. But Noel's luck had run out. "Try again tomorrow," the guy on the gate said. "Come earlier next time, kid."

Noel spent the cold night huddled in a doorway near the plant. He was afraid to leave the area in case he'd be late at the hiring office next morning. City life came as a shock. The grinding squalor of the streets Noel wandered that dawn only replaced the flat, infinite wheatfields as a new symbol of loneliness in his mind.

There was no job the next day either. "Try Chrysler," they told him, "maybe they're hiring." Noel felt weak, he wasn't sure he'd be able to make it to Chrysler's plant. With his last twenty-five cents he bought himself a doughnut from a street stand and a cardboard container of coffee that he piled with three spoons of sugar, devouring them standing in a doorway out of the icy wind. Then he began to walk. The hot sugared coffee and sweet doughnut gave him the spurt of energy he needed. Detroit awaited him.

He had been walking for what seemed hours. Dusk was closing in around the city and the sidewalks were hard under his worn sneakers. Noel stared down at his feet. The new high-tops that he'd prized were grey and stained. Lifting a foot he looked at the sole. Its ridged pattern was worn smooth and thin. Pushing both hands in the pockets of his windcheater to keep them warm, he looked around him. There was no doubt about it, he was lost. Tall featureless buildings lined the quiet streets and lights burned in the empty windows of offices whose workers had long since departed for their comfortable surburban homes and a waiting wife and kids with a steak on the dinner plate and a bourbon or a beer to take away the winter's chill. The freezing wind cut ferociously at Noel's face, bringing tears to his eyes. Turning his back to its force, he stared down the empty street in despair. A car rolled along the road towards him, stopping at the light, and Noel looked up startled as the horn honked and a man leaned from the window.

"Hey kid, you lost?"

Noel shuffled his feet. "Yeah," he mumbled, hanging his head, "sort of."

"Where are you heading? Perhaps I can give you a lift?"

The car was a white Chrysler with chrome trim that gleamed under the streetlights. Noel saw that the upholstery was black leather. It was beautiful. "I'm trying to get to the Chrysler plant," he said moving towards the car.

The man whistled, "Well, you're sure out of your way."

Noel stood on the sidewalk beside the car, leaning forward a little as he spoke. The harsh orange-yellow streetlight lit his bony face, carving shadows beneath his cheeks, outlining his wide frost-bitten mouth and strong nose. His shadowy grey eyes burned with a gamut of emotions – fear, uncertainty, admiration – as he ran a rough-skinned hand along the car's gleaming paintwork.

"Get in!"

Noel ran around the car as the light changed and jumped in, slamming the door shut as the man pulled away from the light. Noel examined his saviour. He was a tall man, grey-haired, confident. He looked sort of *distinguished* – like those ads about executives in magazines. Running a bit to fat though, thought Noel, tightening his stomach muscles instinctively, though there was not an ounce of excess flesh on him.

"What's your name?" The man's light blue eyes took in the stained dungarees, the thin windcheater, the cheap woollen scarf knotted at his throat.

"Noel."

"Noel what?"

Noel hesitated and the man smiled. "Okay," he said, "It doesn't matter. I'm Scott Harrison. Nice to meet you, Noel."

Noel was silent because he didn't know what to say.

"Been on the road long?"

The question came out of the blue. "A couple of weeks," Noel mumbled. The luxurious car stopped at another red light, engine purring softly, and Scott flicked on the radio. "Seven o'clock news," he explained.

Noel leaned back against the cushions, running a surreptitious hand across the smooth texture of the seat, breathing the luxurious smell of good leather and the light, citrusy fragrance of Scott's cologne. Noel blushed, suddenly aware of how dirty he was. He must look terrible.

The car surged away from the light and Scott turned down the volume of the radio. "Nothing dramatic," he said, "cars are still being produced in Detroit – that's all that matters around here." The news finished and was replaced by the soft sounds of a Mozart quartet. With a sigh of pleasure Scott relaxed. "That's better," he said, turning the big car on to a freeway. They passed a vast illuminated sign announcing the number of cars produced that year, changing every minute as more and more cars rolled off the production lines.

Noel gasped. "Is that for real?"

Scott laughed. "It sure is. This is Motor City, Noel. This is the 'Big Time'!" He glanced sideways at his young companion. "Are you hoping for a job at Chrysler?"

"Yeah. I've tried General Motors two days running and it's no good. I can't hang around there any longer – I've got to get a job."

Scott looked thoughtful. "You hungry?" he asked finally.

"Kinda," said Noel uncomfortably.

Scott pulled the big car off the freeway, heading for the drive-in hamburger stand whose bright yellow neon sign lit the night sky. "Double cheeseburger, fries and a chocolate shake," he said rolling down the window for the waitress.

Noel could feel saliva filling his mouth just smelling the hamburger. The ice cold shake hit his stomach with a jolt and he took a bite of the burger hastily.

He finished it in a couple of minutes and Scott told the waitress to bring another. The boy had a strange face, haunted-looking, but powerful. He was thin and undernourished but he stood and walked like an athlete. Scott wondered where he'd run away from – but he wasn't going to get into *that*! "How old are you, Noel?" He lit a cigarette, waiting while Noel finished chewing.

"Sixteen," lied Noel without hesitation. He'd practised it often enough.

Scott blew cigarette smoke through his nose, leaning back against the leather seat. "I know someone in Personnel at Chrysler," he said.

"If you like I could give him a ring, put in a good word for you."

Noel stopped in mid-bite. "*You* can do that?" he asked awed.

"Sure," Scott glanced at him speculatively, "but you'd better clean up your appearance before you go there."

Noel felt his heart sink. Putting the rest of his hamburger back in the container he stared out of the car window across the street. Gaily coloured pennants decorating the used car lot blew in the wind and the cars gleamed under the overhead lights, their prices displayed in bold letters on the windshields – sums that Noel could never imagine earning.

"It's all right," said Scott gently, "I can see the situation. Look kid, I have a flat here in town – I use it when I have to stay late. My wife and family are out in the country but sometimes it's difficult for me to get home. How about if you come on back with me? You can take a shower, get yourself cleaned up a little – get some rest. I'll get you to Chrysler in the morning."

Noel looked doubtful.

"Finish the hamburger," Scott said, starting the car. "Let's get home. We'll have a drink and talk about your job."

The apartment was in a tall discreet grey building and there were offices on the lower levels. The lobby was empty and stark with grey carpets and dark grey metal elevators. They stopped at the fifteenth floor and Noel followed Scott down a grey-carpeted corridor, waiting while he fitted the key into the lock of the heavy wood-panelled door. "Come on in," Scott called over his shoulder, flinging his coat on to a chair in the hall and dropping his leather briefcase next to it. "What'll it be, Noel, drink first or a shower?"

Noel had never had a drink in his life, so he decided it had better be the shower.

The bathroom was compact but luxurious and locking the door carefully behind him, Noel cast off his clothes and stepped under the comforting spray of pure heat. He let it drip onto his spine, thawing his raw nerves, and then his belly, glorious, relaxing heat, penetrating his being. Noel *never* wanted to be cold again. Lathering his body, he scrubbed the grime of two weeks on the road from his skin, his nails, his hair. Satisfied that he was clean, he stepped from the shower and dried himself with a huge white towel, marvelling at its size and softness.

"Hey Noel," Scott's voice came from outside the door, "there's a robe behind the door there. Why don't you put it on for now and we'll see what we can do about your clothes?"

Noel wrapped the grey and black striped robe around him. The material felt light and yet warm and very soft. A label on the inside read "100% pure cashmere". What, he wondered, was "cashmere"? Whatever it was, he liked it. Smiling, he emerged from the bathroom, leaving his grimy clothes in a heap on the floor.

Scott's blue eyes assessed him quickly. "What'll you have, Noel?" He gestured to the table and an array of bottles. "Scotch, bourbon? Or are you a Martini man, like me?"

The drink in Scott's hand was colourless and not too big and Noel decided a drink that size would be easiest.

He sat on a white sofa with a glass in his hand looking out at the lights of Detroit, a different Detroit from the one he'd seen the night before, huddled in a stinking doorway and pacing its streets trying to keep his blood circulating. He sipped the drink, coughing. It was aromatic, sharper than he'd expected. Noel coughed again to disguise the first one.

Scott prowled the room, drink in hand, smoking. "You look like an athlete, Noel, you've got a good pair of shoulders there. Too light though for football. What was it? Track? Baseball?"

"Boxing." Noel's eyes lit with a spark of enthusiasm. "I won a trophy – once."

"Really? Where was that. At school?" Scott's eyes were hooded, but his question was sharp.

"Yeah, just before I left. A year ago," lied Noel. He took a mouthful of Martini. It tasted better now.

Scott sat beside him on the sofa, sizing him up. The kid was wiry, his thinness had concealed a strength that was apparent now under the light robe. And he had such an *interesting* face – despite the fine bones there was a brutal quality to it that was intriguing in one so young. Was he sixteen? Scott shrugged away the question – maybe he was, maybe he wasn't.

Noel's head had begun to ache and his eyes burned. Despite the shower and the warm apartment he felt chilled.

"Are you all right?" asked Scott sharply. The colour drained from Noel's face and the glass dropped from his hand spilling its contents across the thick grey rug.

"I don't know," Noel said, "I don't know what's the matter. I guess I'm just tired, I haven't slept in three nights."

"Then you'd better get some sleep," said Scott levelly. "The bedroom's over there, can you make it?" He caught the hesitation in Noel's eyes. "I'll sleep out here," he added quickly, "I often do when friends stay over. Go on, get yourself a good night's sleep, we'll talk about your job some more in the morning."

He helped Noel across the room, supporting him easily, waiting until he rolled on to the bed and closed his eyes. Clicking off the light, Scott walked back to the drinks table and fixed himself another Martini. Noel's glass lay on the carpet and he picked it up and put it on the tray.

Noel woke to a room filled with light. He could smell coffee and hear a radio faintly. Still wrapped in the cashmere robe he walked through the living room to a minuscule kitchen. Scott was drinking juice and watching the coffee perk. "Hi," said Noel.

"Feeling better?" Scott smiled at him.

"I feel great," said Noel, accepting a glass of juice.

"Tell you what, Noel," Scott glanced at his watch, "I have to leave in a minute. Why don't you take it easy here today, you still look really whacked? I'll see what I can do about getting you some new clothes so you can go for your job tomorrow. Have some coffee, help yourself to whatever's in the refrigerator, have another shower." He grinned. "I'll be back around six and we can talk about your job over some steaks."

The phone rang, shattering the small silence as Noel weighed Scott's suggestion. Scott hurried to answer it, speaking in low tones into the bright red receiver. He glanced at his watch again and Noel heard him say, "Oh all right. I'll be there in fifteen. Right. 'Bye."

He put down the phone and walked back to the kitchen. "I've got to go, Noel, I'm late." He let his hand rest lightly on Noel's shoulder for a moment, smiling as Noel's shadowy eyes met his. "You know what," said Scott, "you should keep that robe – it looks better on you than it did on me. See you this evening, Noel." A slight pressure of his hand on Noel's shoulder and he was gone.

Noel took in his surroundings. Wrap-around windows framed views of a Detroit that bore no resemblance to the inner-city decay he knew, and a high sun shone in a clear, winter-blue sky. He prowled the luxurious apartment, opening doors, peering into cupboards and inspecting the rows of immaculate suits and polished shoes in the closet. There was an envelope on the dresser addressed to "Mr Scott Harrison, Vice-President, ARA Advertising Co." at an address in Detroit. Next to it lay some loose change. Noel counted it without touching. There was almost six dollars. Then he walked to the bathroom, found his clothes lying where he had left them

161

and got dressed. He went back into the kitchen and poured himself some coffee, peeking into the refrigerator. There was some cheese – a sort he'd never seen before, runny with a white crust, a jar with some olives, and a carton of milk. In a cupboard he found cereal and some crackers. He ate four bowls of cereal and drank two cups of coffee. Then he spread the cheese on the crackers and placed them in the empty cereal box. Walking back into the bedroom he placed the change in his pocket. After a search he found a pen next to the phone and wrote on the back of the envelope on the dresser, "Scott. Thank you. I will repay this money. It is $5.43. Noel."

The apartment looked warm and sunfilled as he glanced back from the doorway. Noel had observed what went on between some of the boys at the Maddox and he knew what Scott expected from him if he stayed. Scott was nice. He was generous and kind. And the apartment was warm and luxurious. It would be dangerously easy to stay. Closing the door quickly Noel hurried down the corridor to the elevator. It stopped at his floor and he got in avoiding looking at the woman already in there. He clutched the cereal packet with his cheese "sandwiches" close to him, realising suddenly that the cheese smelled very strongly. Wrinkling her nose the woman moved a step away from him. Noel stared down at his feet. He was glad when the elevator bounced to a gentle stop and without waiting for her, he was out of the elevator, out of the building and on the streets of Detroit once more.

At the US Auto plant four weeks later, Noel put down his power wrench with relief as the buzzer went, signalling the lunch break. Wiping his hands on a piece of rag, he watched the men climbing down from the bright skeletons of cars on the assembly line, downing tools, and heading as fast as they could for the canteen areas. Noel followed them slowly. Working on the line was beginning to drive him crazy. In the cheap hostel where he had a bed, he would dream of the nine-mile-long assembly line. Brightly coloured embryo automobiles moved steadily forward and, armed with his power wrench, Noel would try desperately to fit a bolt or tighten a screw – always too late. It was always the same job, always the same dilemma – the line moved too quickly. In his dreams it would get faster and faster and he'd be left, helplessly watching the cars flash by. The sense of urgency as he raced alongside the line, desperate to keep up, made him break out in a sweat and he would awake, shivering and afraid. Afraid he'd lose the job he hated. The job he'd been so lucky to get. Because every Friday he got a paycheck. And today was Friday.

Noel stood in line, piling his tray with food when his turn came around. He carried it to the far corner of the room and ate, eyes on his plate, looking at no one. The food was all right, better than at Maddox, and he ate enough to last him the day so that he wouldn't have to spend money at night.

When his shift was over he would walk back to the hostel. The sharp cold air cleared his head of the sounds and smells of the plant. At the hostel he would take a shower, change into his other clean dungarees and shirt and head for the library where he would stay until closing time, reading books on cars and about the founders of the automobile industry. Then he would walk back through the cold streets, strip to his underwear and climb into the narrow bed, ignoring the other residents who sat smoking or talking to each other in the still brightly lit room. Noel would pull the thin blanket over his head and sleep, dreaming his terrifying dream until it was time to get up for the day shift and repeat the whole process again.

Morosely chewing a mouthful of franks and beans, he stared at his plate. A paper rustled – the sound of a page turning. Noel glanced up. The guy on the next table was young, probably eighteen, and he was absorbed in his book, chewing steadily as he read. The men had only a half hour break and most of them grabbed the chance to relax, reprieved temporarily from the devastating monotony of the past hours, gossiping about the football game, shouting comments, laughing. But this guy never lifted his eyes. Noel stole a glance at the book. *Physics!* The guy was reading about *physics*. Feeling his gaze the young man looked up.

"Why are you reading that?" The question was out before Noel realised it.

"I'm learning about stress on metal," he replied, "got a test tonight."

Noel looked puzzled.

"Night school," he answered Noel's unspoken question. "I go right after work, every night of the week. Gonna get myself a better job than this one some day." He jagged a derisive thumb towards the assembly line. "Don't wanna end up my days on the crazy-farm, hammering imaginary rivets." He stood up to leave.

"What do you want to do then?" asked Noel.

The guy tucked the book under his arm, swigged a final mouthful of coffee and headed back to the line as the whistle went. "Gonna be

163

an automotive engineer," he called out over the racket of hundreds of departing men.

Noel progressed from fitting bolts, to installing steering wheels, crankshafts and windscreens. He had a spell in the paintshop, he learned to weld and, deafened and scarred from burns and cuts caused by his own clumsiness, he worked his way through every job on the assembly line. After the first six months the foreman realised that he could rely on Noel to fit in wherever the pressure was heaviest, but particularly on the welding. After a few months, however, Noel realised that he was getting nowhere, that there was no future for him on the assembly line. He wasn't going to get promoted, though he had got a rise in pay. He sought out the young guy in the canteen and asked him about night school. After work he went down there and enrolled. He had a long way to go to become an engineer – his education, such as it was, had stopped at thirteen.

Noel put the same energy he had put into boxing into his studies; he never missed a night. He moved from the hostel where he had remained for its cheapness to a rooming house where he had his own room and could study. He ate sparingly, using the money he had saved from his salary to buy books, and he studied far into the night, rising again at six to make the shift. He was shabby, underfed and overworked. He had no friends – he had neither the time nor need for them. He was a young man with an aim in life.

It took over a year, but he emerged at the end with a High School Diploma. When they congratulated him at the school and wanted to know what he was going to do now that he had his education, he asked them how to get into college. He was not quite sixteen.

30

It was as though a mist had cleared from Lais's mind and she looked at them for the first time. Doctors had been summoned, examinations made, tests and X-rays taken. Voice therapists began to work with Lais, re-teaching her everyday words that seemed strangely to have been forgotten. Peach read her stories from old baby books, stringing together words as she would for a child, and Lais eagerly learned to recognise once-familiar sounds and symbols until after months of work she was able to read and write again.

As she progressed Lais began to pick up her old zest for life, demanding to be taken to the best shops so that she might order pretty clothes, having her hair cut in a fashionable curving shoulder-length bob, applying make-up with the old skill while Peach watched breathlessly from her usual position on the rug at her feet.

Lais simply seemed to accept the wheelchair as a part of her life, never once asking the reason for her paralysed state, and when Amelie worriedly sent her to a psychiatrist, he told her that he was up against a stone wall. Either Lais had forgotten her past, or she simply refused to remember.

On a clear blue Florida morning over breakfast, Lais announced in her new soft, husky voice that she wanted to return to France. "I'm perfectly well now, Maman," she said as Amelie's eyes met Gerard's. "I can't stay here forever like a child."

Gerard knew what she meant. At home with them, she was protected, cosseted, made much of. She was the sun at the centre of their world and they revolved around her like attendant planets. Lais wanted her old independence back. "Lais is right, darling," he said to Amelie, "it's time she went out into the world again."

"Then I must go with her," said Amelie, already planning which liner to take.

"No," cried Lais sharply. "I want Peach to come with me."

Peach's eyes widened with excitement. "France," she squealed, "terrific!"

"But Lais, you'll *need* me," objected Amelie, "I can't just let the two of you go alone."

"Let them go," said Gerard calmly. "Lais is perfectly capable of managing with Peach and Miz to help her." He reached across the table and gripped Amelie's hand reassuringly, "And, besides, I need you here with me."

The liner *Queen Mary* sailed from New York on a brisk spring morning and Lais grinned up at Peach standing by her chair. "Remember when you were five and I was in charge of you? Now it's you who'll be dancing and flirting all night and who will have to send me to bed with my glass of milk and a teddy."

* * *

165

"You should never arrive at dinner or a party too early," Lais counselled as Peach hastily flung on her new coral pink taffeta dress with the bows on the shoulders and full, frothy skirt. "You must learn to make an entrance." Peach brushed her hair firmly, restraining its bronze waves with a pink headband and then, deciding it made her look too young, letting her long glossy hair flow free to her waist. Tall and slim, in flat ballet pumps, she looked like a Giselle escaped from the forest. And also, she thought with a sigh, not a day over her fourteen years.

She shifted impatiently from foot to foot as minutes ticked by and still Lais sat at the dressing table, adding an extra blush to her cheeks, brushing her hair until it fell into a shining blonde bell that swung smoothly as she turned her head. Clipping graceful emerald leaves into her small ears, Lais lifted her arms for Miz to slide the brilliant green silk dress over her head, waiting while Miz hooked the fasteners up the back. The spreading bouffant skirt made her waist look even tinier and emphasised the new curves of her bosom. Fastening the big emerald and diamond pin given to her by Gerard and Amelie as a going away present just where the low bodice curved into her breast, she added a final dab of Guerlaine's "L'heure bleue".

"There," she said, as Peach sighed with relief. "Now we're ready."

Peach blushed as pink as her dress, sliding quickly into her seat, as every head in the dining room turned their way. Lais took her place on the captain's right, flashing her most dazzling smile, and the famous red-haired movie star who sat on his left stared at her coldly. In her low husky voice Lais apologised for their lateness and was instantly forgiven by every man at the table.

It was as thought someone had pressed the right button and all Lais's half-remembered reflexes began to function agin. With Peach pushing her wonderfully decorated chair, Lais went to all the cocktail parties, charming everyone with her unselfconscious ease. She didn't try to pretend that the wheelchair wasn't there, she simply never made it an issue that she was any different from anyone else. She took part in all the shipboard activities and gleefully won $500 on the wager of how many days, hours and minutes the ship took to reach Cherbourg. She tapped her fingers in time with the swing band playing popular Glenn Miller tunes, smiling as she watched the dancing. And she sat at the bar afterwards, drinking champagne cocktails and flirting outrageously with all the men, her eyes sparkling with a touch of her old wickedness. Peach felt sorry for young Tom Launceton, sitting next to her at dinner, who was so badly smitten with Lais he could barely eat.

"You should try this," said Peach scooping up chocolate soufflé.

Tom merely sighed, pushing his plate towards her. "Have mine," he said, "you look as though you need filling out a bit."

Peach glanced down at her slender figure indignantly. True, her bosoms were small but they were growing and she had hopes for them. She wasn't such a *stick*, was she? She finished his soufflé, frowning.

"Aren't you enjoying it?" he asked, removing his eyes from Lais for a second to smile at her.

"Very much," admitted Peach. "I see you admire my sister," she added.

"Who doesn't?"

"I bet you don't have any sisters," guessed Peach intuitively.

"Brothers," Tom said with a grin, "one older – that's Harry, who's up at Oxford. And one younger, Archie, who'll leave Eton next year and go on to Sandhurst."

"And you?"

"I'm just travelling around before I go up to Cambridge. I've been working on a ranch in Colorado and before that I worked in a bank in Hong Kong and on a sheepfarm in Australia. It's supposed to give you a feeling of real life between school and university."

Peach was enchanted to hear he lived in an old rosy-brick Queen Anne house called Launceton Hall in a village called Launceton Magna. "I suppose I'm a bit homesick for it," Tom admitted, "I've been away almost a year."

"It doesn't sound like the sort of place that will have changed much," observed Peach comfortingly.

Tom asked her to dance and Peach forgot her self-consciousness as they swung around the parquet floor to the latest show-tunes. Tom told her he was nineteen and was going to read History at Cambridge, but that what he truly wanted was to farm. Launceton Hall had many hundreds of acres and three different farms within its feudal realm, and Tom wanted one day to be in charge of the estates. "No use relying on Harry for that," he grinned, "Harry's the talented one. He published his first novel at seventeen and everyone says he's a genius." Peach thought the genius didn't sound like too much fun.

167

"Shipboard romance?" teased Lais as Peach flung herself exhausted on to the bed.

"Of course not," she scoffed, "it's you he's in love with, Lais, like all of them."

Two days later, watching the shores of France emerging from the morning mist, Lais said suddenly, "Did the Nazis really blow up the *vieux port* in Marseilles?"

Taken aback, Peach stared at her in surprise. "Yes," she admitted, "they blew up the whole quarter, street by street. Ten thousand people were evacuated. They said you could see the fleeing rats swimming across the harbour with the German deserters." Hesitating a moment she added, "Most of the Resistance workers escaped."

Lais stared at the grey outline of the horizon and Peach waited anxiously for her to say something, afraid to ask any questions. *How much* did Lais remember, she wondered? *And did she remember Ferdi?* But Lais said nothing more.

Lais greeted Oliver, the butler at the Paris house, as though she had known him for years and Peach wondered if she mistook him for Bennet. She approved of her new room in what used to be Monsieur's downstairs study, admiring the new green and white flowered curtains and the silk bedspread and exclaiming at the special bathroom with the bathtub and the sink at the proper height for her chair. Gerard had seen to it that nothing was forgotten. Lying in the centre of her old bed with its scalloped seashell headboard, watching the firelight flickering in the hearth, turning carved marble nymphs and trailing vine leaves to amber, Lais sighed contentedly. "It's good to be home," she said.

Leonie and Jim arrived the next morning and to Peach's surprise Lais clung to them tearfully. *"But she never cries,"* she whispered, bewildered and upset.

They took Lais for long walks through the Bois, stopping for lunch beneath the chestnut trees, and they strolled in the Tuileries Gardens. From the terrace you could see the true heart of Paris, the Place de la Concorde and the obelisk, a gift to the city of Paris from Egypt at the Great Exhibition of 1884. The statue of horses, "Les Chevaux de Marly", stood at the foot of the Champs Elysées and on the western side of the square was the magnificent façade of the Hotel Crillon where the Nazis had once had their headquarters. Lais stared at it for a long time, her face emotionless.

*   *   *

They took the overnight train south, waking to find blue skies and the Alpes Maritimes, still snow-capped, framed in their windows. Peach waited eagerly for the thin blue line of the Mediterranean to appear on the horizon, longing to smell the sea and the jasmine and oleanders. The train wound along the coast and suddenly the Côte d'Azur sparkled before her like a jewel beneath a cloudless sky. "Almost there," she called excitedly to Lais, but Lais's eyes were closed, and her face pale as she leaned back against the cushions. If she heard she didn't answer.

Leonore paced the garden in front of the villa waiting for them to arrive. She wore a tailored grey suit and a crisp blue blouse buttoned to the throat. Her hair was tied back with a dark blue velvet bow and she wore large horn-rimmed glasses. She looked every inch the efficient businesswoman. Taking a blue linen handkerchief from her breast-pocket she wiped her damp palms, telling herself there was no need to feel nervous. She had checked her appearance in the mirror before she left; no one would ever suspect that this efficient woman in her thirties would be capable of a secret passion. No one would suspect how she responded lustfully in a man's arms. *No one could possibly know about Ferdi.*

Leonore had meant never to see him again, but Ferdi had begged her, saying she was the only person who could help him. They arranged to meet at an old hotel in Provence. Arriving before him, Leonore sat nervously on the edge of a chair in the hall, reluctant to go up to their room in case he had changed his mind. But he hadn't.

In their pretty bedroom they drew the flowered curtains across the sunny afternoon, holding each other naked in the vast four-poster bed that seemed to Leonore to seal them in their own private world. She left her hair loose, even brushing it the way Lais had, so that it fell over one eye, and she'd brought a nightdress in a soft sea-green chiffon. She didn't know whether she was deliberately playing the role of Lais so that she could keep Ferdi with her, or whether he wanted her only because she looked like Lais. All she cared about was that she wanted him. She wanted Ferdi's firm hands on her breasts, she wanted to stretch her nakedness against his, she wanted to run her tongue along the groove of his stomach, and take him in her mouth. "Anything," she murmured, as he thrust himself into her, "do anything you want with me." Her body curved to his rhythm exploding into crescendos of trembling excitement that she never wanted to end.

Ferdi never said he loved her. And he never called her Lais. But he was always tender and gentle, considerate of her needs. Over dinner he talked and talked – about himself and about Lais, the past and the future. He was thinking of taking his place as head of the war-shattered Merker steel mills. Soon he would do it, soon.

They met every week at the little hotel and the flowery room overlooking the park became their room, the curtained four-poster, their bed. And Leonore, the cool businesswoman, lived for those hidden sensual weekends.

Ferdi had said he would never return to the Hostellerie. He had been gone a month now. His letter crackled in her pocket. "My dear Leonore," it said, and "Yours Ferdi", at the end. In between was a report of his progress at work, and a brief, "I'm missing our talks." No one could mistake it for a love letter, no matter how hard they tried, thought Leonore bitterly. But she had known that from the beginning. Now she must write and tell him it was over.

Peach bounded along the terrace towards her, waving madly. Her long russet hair swung in a thick glossy pigtail and she looked very tall. "You're growing up," accused Leonore smiling.

"Hello, Leonore," Lais's voice was different, deeper. Sexy.

"W . . . w . . . wel . . . welcome home," stammered Leonore, a guilty blush staining her cheeks, as Lais eyed her quizzically. "W . . . welcome home, Lais."

31

Peach wound her way slowly up the hill at the back of the villa, Ziggie at her heels, both of them wilting in the summer heat. Flinging herself into a patch of shade, she turned over on her stomach, resting her head on her arms and watching a little trail of ants march determinedly up the gnarled olive tree and disappear into the hole in the bark – just like the escapees into the cellars beneath the hotel. It was odd how life then had continued so normally on the surface when beneath were such dangerous secrets. She had to admit that helping the Resistance had leant an undercurrent of excitement to her schoolgirl life and she had quite enjoyed the game – until that awful day when it was a game no longer.

Peach buried her head in her arms, shutting out the memory. She didn't want to go through the pain of it again, *and the everlasting guilt!* She never talked about her feelings to anyone, but she thought that perhaps Grand-mère understood. It was Grand-mère who stopped her from devoting all her time to Lais, forcing her to find company her own age. "There are lots of young people at the Hostellerie," she said, "put on your bathing suit and go to the pool, you'll soon find some young companions."

School would be starting soon back home in Florida but Peach didn't want to return. If only Maman and Papa would let her go to the school in Switzerland. In the prospectus she'd sent for, it sounded exciting. There were students from many different countries and they skied in the winter term and swam and sailed on the lake in the summer. If only, if only . . . Peach jumped to her feet, her mind made up. If anyone could persuade her parents, Grand-mère could.

The past forgotten in her plans for the future, Peach began to jog back down the hill, slithering down the steeper bits and jumping the rocky areas until she came to the chalky path that snaked its way back to the villa. And then she and Ziggie ran, leaping every few steps. It was fun to be alive on a day like today.

Jim arrived back from a tour of the de Courmont automobile plant looking worried. Production was way down on prewar levels and the new designs lacked the flair and imagination of their Italian and American competitors. Tools and machinery in current use in the plant were old-fashioned and there was no money available to invest in up-to-date tooling, which in turn meant that the cars coming off the line were using virtually the same technology as before the war. Yet in the States, Ford's famous V8 engine was revolutionary and the body designs from US Auto, Chrysler and Great Lakes Motors were new and exciting.

Fiat and Citröen had cornered the European market on the small car scene leaving de Courmont's long-bodied, heavy cars with only the upper end of the market. Competition from Rolls-Royce, Aston

Martin, Bristol and Jaguar was strengthening in Britain, and Mercedes were already pushing to regain their top-of-the-line market from Germany. The future for de Courmont did not look good.

Worried telephone calls to Gerard had produced an indifferent, "Do whatever you think necessary, put in new management if you wish. Take the company public." Gerard didn't care. With memories of his father's devotion to the pursuit of power and gain at the expense of family life, Gerard had opted out of the de Courmont industrial empire. "I held out against all my father's bribes and bullying years ago," he told Jim on the phone from Florida, "so nothing you can say now will get me into the business. Do whatever you want with it all – the rolling mills, the foundries, the automobile plant . . . I don't give a damn."

"But it's Peach's inheritance," protested Jim, "you should protect it for her sake."

Gerard's laugh boomed down the phone. "Somehow I don't see Peach at the head of an automobile empire. She'll have enough money to make her happy, Jim. I've never seen any reason for having more."

Jim discussed the problem with Leonie as they prepared for bed that night.

"I understand," said Leonie, remembering Monsieur's fanatical devotion to building his automobile empire. And she knew, too, that Gerard had always held his father to blame for the faulty design that had led to his brother's death in a car crash on Armand's twenty-first birthday.

"I'll have to sell factories off at a loss to raise money but it's better than letting the automobile plant slip out of the family's hands," decided Jim. "We must do what we can to save it for Peach."

"It's about time that someone thought of Peach," said Leonie, dabbing scent behind her ears and on her throat.

Jim looked at her surprised.

"Do you realise that that child has taken a back seat most of her life? You know that Peach longs to go to this school in Switzerland, L'Aiglon? I think we should persuade Amelie and Gerard to let her go."

"It won't be easy," said Jim. "First they've had to let Lais go, and now Peach. But if you think that's what's best for her they'll listen." He was watching Leonie brushing her hair, fascinated by the way it sprang out in a golden halo of energy around her face.

"Such beautiful golden hair," he said touching a strand gently.

"As much silver as gold now," said Leonie truthfully.

"Still beautiful," Jim murmured, burying his face in the scent of it. "Do you know how much I love you, Leonie Bahri Jamieson?"

Leonie turned into his arms. "*I think so*," she murmured teasingly, "I think I do."

The sprawling chalets that made up L'Aiglon bordered a lake of smooth polished steel under a leaden autumn sky. Blue-grey mountains soared behind, tipped with mist, and terraced gardens, planted with precise Swiss neatness in symmetrical blocks of bushes and flowers led to a jetty with a dozen kayaks drawn up on its wooden planks. On a clear day, of which there were many, you could see the urban sprawl of Geneva at the far end of the lake.

Peach fitted into the life of the school as though she'd been there for years instead of just one term, making friends quickly with the other girls. There were two other Americans, Nancy and Julie-Anne, but mostly they were French or English. And it was Melinda Seymour, an English girl, who soon became her best friend. They were room-mates and doubles partners in tennis, they sat next to each other in the dining hall and Peach helped Melinda with her French prep and Melinda helped Peach with science. They exchanged life stories and secrets and Peach was thrilled to have someone her own age at last who "understood" her. They often walked to the village together to buy delicious Swiss chocolate bars which they devoured in their rooms at night along with the latest flimsy paperback romance, an endless supply of which circulated around the school, filling their heads with dreams of tall, ruggedly handsome men with smouldering dark eyes and firm passionate mouths. "Do you really think men like that exist?" asked Peach, hugging her old teddy to her chest as Melinda turned out the lamp.

"Of course they do," replied Melinda sleepily. "I know one."

Peach shot up in bed. "Melinda! You *know* a man like that?"

"Well," yawned Melinda, "maybe he's a bit younger than the ones in the books, but he's divine."

"Who?" demanded Peach. "Melinda, don't go to sleep. Tell me, who is he?"

"His name's Harry," murmured Melinda burrowing down beneath her eiderdown.

Peach fell back against the pillows clutching her teddy closer, a smile on her lips. "Harry," she whispered, "Harry." He'd have dark wavy hair and smouldering eyes like the man in *Passion's Playground*, and an intense serious face with a firm jaw. He'd be as tall and broad-shouldered and passionate as the hero of *Dangerous Kisses*. And his name was Harry. She dreamed about him that night.

Romance filled the heads of all the teenage girls at L'Aiglon. On Saturdays they would take the little lake steamer into Geneva or sometimes Montreux to do their shopping, and would loll around in cafés, eating enormous ice cream sundaes and examining each man intently, discussing his potential as a lover in whispers and giggles, and blushing furiously when they received an amused stare back.

Julie-Anne was petite and cute with soft dark hair that fell over one eye in what she assured them was a very sexy manner. Julie-Anne was a true flirt, and knew *everything*. Melinda and Peach would trail after her on their trips into Geneva as she ogled the boys on the steamer, the waiters in the cafés, and the sales assistant in the jeweller's where she took her watch to be repaired. "But how do you do it?" they said, baffled by the mystery of why, when Julie-Anne opened her eyes wider and brushed her soft hair from her eyes with graceful fingers, smiling a tremulous little half-smile, she should get such electric response.

"It's sex," said Julie-Anne loftily.

Peach found herself wondering about sex in the middle of classes, while staring at bewildering algebra equations on the blackboard, or absentmindedly boiling bubbling liquids over a bunsen burner in the science lab, or while reading Shakespeare's sonnets. "I think I like romance more than sex," she admitted finally to Melinda. "I mean it all sounds so complicated and silly, doesn't it?"

There seemed to be no answer to that one.

When the first snows came they packed excitedly into the school bus for a week on the ski slopes. Julie-Anne in figure-hugging blue ski-pants and a scarlet fair-isle sweater soon had a host of willing young men eager to help her up if she fell and to carry her skis back to the chalet at the end of the day.

It was the ski-pants, decided Peach and Melinda, heading into the village to purchase some. But somehow they didn't look quite the same, Peach simply looked all long skinny legs and Melinda looked dumpy. "Let's face it, Peach," commented Melinda, "I'm too fat and you're too thin. No boys in their right minds will ever look at us twice."

Every afternoon after skiing they went to the café where Peach drank giant mugs of hot chocolate floating with cream, consuming enormous fattening pastries in an attempt to gain weight while Melinda, tightening her belt, dawdled over a cup of black coffee, trying not to look. But at the end of the week they weighed just the same. "So much for that," said Melinda, tucking thankfully into an enormous wedge of chocolate cake, "I've had enough of romance and sex, give me food!"

"Peach?"

The masculine voice had a familiar ring as Peach looked up.

"Tom," she said, surprised.

"Tom Launceton," echoed Melinda.

Tom pulled up a chair, laughing. "It seems we all know each other," he said cheerily. "Peach and I met on the *Queen Mary* last spring. I must say you've grown up a bit since then," he said, eyeing her appreciatively. "And Melinda and I are country neighbours."

"Country neighbours means we live within twenty miles of each other in Wiltshire," explained Melinda. "We went to all the same children's parties although it's Archie who's more my age. And then, of course, there's Harry. Tom's older brother."

The same Harry? signalled Peach's surprised eyes as Melinda nodded.

"Why are you sitting here stuffing yourselves with cream buns?" demanded Tom. "You should be up on the slopes. Come on Peach." Taking her hand he marched her to the door, and grabbing both their skis, crunched off down the icy village street towards the ski lift.

It was fun skiing down the black runs with Tom, although really she was only used to the more moderate red runs. But with Tom beside her, Peach felt safe. Swinging over the valleys in a chair lift was somehow more fun with a boy than with Melinda, and she felt a funny little crackle of excitement when he held her bulky leather-gloved hand in his. "Have supper with me this evening," he said as dusk fell and they trudged tiredly back through the village.

"But I can't," she protested, "I'm in the school chalet. It's like a fortress, they never let us out at night."

"We'll see about that," Tom said.

He was such a man of the world, thought Peach back at the chalet as the lodge-keeper palmed Tom's Swiss francs with a wink, promising to leave the gate open. Even so she felt a bit guilty, though she knew Julie-Anne and some of the older girls managed to sneak out every night. Julie-Anne's latest romance was the young bronzed ski instructor with the broad shoulders and compelling eyes of his equivalent in *Sun Valley Secrets.*

Tom was nice, though, and he was fun. *He* told her about life at Cambridge and *she* told him about life at L'Aiglon and they ate tons of *rosti* and drank a lot of fruity white wine so that her head whirled.

He walked her back to the chalet at midnight. "So your skis won't turn into a pumpkin," he grinned and then he kissed her.

It was nice, thought Peach with her eyes closed, counting the seconds so she would remember to tell Melinda how long the kiss lasted.

"Night, young Peach," said Tom cheerfully. "I'll drop you a line from Cambridge."

Peach waited and waited for that letter, dashing to the table in the hall and sifting the pile of letters eagerly every morning, hoping for one with a Cambridge postmark, but it never came. "Why?" she asked Melinda.

"I suppose he's found someone else," answered Melinda gloomily, watching Julie-Anne devouring her latest letter from the ski instructor, who seemed to write every day.

Peach sighed. "I've been spurned," she cried dramatically, "after a kiss that lasted thirty-two seconds. I swear I shall *never* fall in love again."

Peach prowled through Geneva's old quarter one Saturday searching for birthday gifts for her sisters, admiring the pieces of handblown glass etched with small, exquisite mystical landscapes, in a smart gallery and wondering if she could afford one for Leonore. Of course Lais would need something different, something amusing to make her laugh.

Making her way to the desk she glanced at the tall silver-haired man browsing through a catalogue. His back was towards her but Peach knew it was Ferdi. Her heart pounded as she shakily placed the tiny bottle with its waving trees and curling river on the table.

"Ferdi?" she said, her voice quavering.

He looked at her. "Peach?" he said at last. "Is that really you?"

She nodded, not knowing what to say. He looked different. His thin face was lined and his blonde hair silvery white, but he was still handsome in an older sort of way.

He took her to a café by the lake and Peach stirred cream into her hot chocolate, watching him doubtfully. Why had he never returned to see Lais? Was he afraid because she couldn't walk?

Didn't he know that something like that couldn't change a person like Lais, that she would still be as beautiful and wonderful and exciting as she had always been? Oh, how could Ferdi be so *cruel!*

Ferdi asked her questions about herself and school and she answered sullenly, wishing that she had just made an excuse and disappeared out of the gallery.

"And do you still live in the castle?" she blurted after an uncomfortable pause.

"Part of the time," he said with a smile, "but mostly I live in Cologne to be near my work. And what were you doing in the gallery, Peach?" he asked, lighting a cigarette, watching her sip the steaming hot drink.

"I was buying a birthday present for Leonore," she replied, "it's her birthday – *their* birthday next week."

Ferdi glanced away from her across the lake.

"You should go and see her, Ferdi!" The words burst from her suddenly and she slumped back against her chair in relief. Lais had never once mentioned Ferdi's name but Peach just knew that all these years Lais had been waiting for him, hoping he would return . . . she was sure of it. "You should go to the Hostellerie, speak to her, explain . . ."

"Explain what?" asked Ferdi bewildered, wondering what this child could know about his relationship with Leonore.

"Why you never came back," said Peach. "She needs to know, Ferdi. She *needs* that."

"It's been a long time, Peach," said Ferdi, "and you don't understand, you can't possibly understand what happened."

Pushing back her chair Peach glared at him tearfully. "I thought you were the fairy prince who would wake her with a kiss," she cried, "but you're . . . you're just a *traitor!*"

"Peach," he called, hurrying after her, "Peach." But she was racing down the street, bumping into passers-by and dodging the traffic as she hurtled round the corner out of his sight. Ferdi returned to his table staring silently at her still-full glass of chocolate and the long handled silver spoon in the saucer beside it. *But he was seeing Peach crouched over Lais, covered in her sister's blood, her eyes wild with terror.* What had she meant by "she *needs* to know"? Tossing some coins on to the saucer in payment he strolled down to the lake. Ferdi stood for a long time just watching the birds wheeling over its glassy grey depths and the tiny steamer in the distance, puffing its way along the shores filled with happy Saturday shoppers.

177

32

Noel scraped into the University of Michigan by the skin of his teeth. Of course he had to lie abut his background, he didn't want anyone to know about the Maddox Charity Orphanage. He wanted the stain removed from his record as though it had never existed, so that maybe one day, it would cease to be a reality.

He would have to work as many hours as God sent and even so he was the shabbiest guy at the school, but he made sure that one of his jobs was in the cafeteria so he had enough to eat.

No one wanted to share a room with Noel Maddox. The guy from New York who was supposed to be his room-mate rarely showed up, spending most of his time with his friends and avoiding Noel's eye on the chance occasions they were in the same room together. Noel didn't blame him. He knew he looked strange. He was still very thin, his face was gaunt and fleshless and in reaction to the years at Maddox when his hair was cropped, he wore it longer than the crew cut that was the norm. He had three shirts and two pairs of jeans and wore sneakers winter and summer with an ex-army parka to keep out the cold. And his slate-grey eyes glittered with an intensity that was unnerving.

One thing he needed was some form of physical exercise. He wanted release from the pent-up tension of his studies and the strain of the extra workload he took on to cover his costs – and also from his physical cravings. Noel had discovered a sexuality in himself that sometimes shocked him by its urgency. He tried to bury it in his old standby, training. He lifted weights, he ran track, he skipped and punched away his passion. And his body responded, muscling out, becoming sleeker, adding inches to his height with his upright, athletic posture.

*　　*　　*

"Noel Maddox has a great body." Four pairs of female eyes watched from a table in the cafeteria as Noel effortlessly hefted a tall stack of trays and carried them back to the counter.

"Trust you to notice."

Jeannie Burton smoothed her blonde hair and smiled at her friends. "It's true though, just take a look at the shoulders under that shirt . . ."

"That *disgusting* shirt," mumbled one through a mouthful of bacon, lettuce and tomato sandwich, dripping with mayonnaise.

"Not 'disgusting'," said Jeannie, eyeing Noel thoughtfully, "just . . . cheap."

"Yeah, well, I guess that's what the guy is – *cheap*."

"How do *you* know what he is?" demanded Jeannie. "Have you ever spoken to him?"

"No," she said, munching her sandwich, "and I don't know anyone who has. He's the mystery man. The Enigma Engineer of the University of Michigan."

"I've seen him around," said Jeannie as they watched Noel shrug on a jacket and make for the door, a half-dozen books under his arm. "He's in the undergrad library till all hours, studying."

"He works out all the time too," said her friend, "he's on the track a lot. No teams though – and *no football*." At the University of Michigan football was a passion and the players were gods. On game days the town of Ann Arbor, through which the university spread, was deserted, and the parties on those nights were *the best*. "Hey," she teased, "I think Jeannie Burton's got a thing for our poor engineer. You're wasting your time, sweetheart – he never even *looks* at a girl, and he certainly doesn't *date*."

"Doesn't he?" queried Jeannie, recalling Noel's shadowed gaze as he'd passed.

"Listen," said her friend, "that guy wouldn't even notice Rita Hayworth. Nobody could get a date with him."

Jeannie sat back and lit a cigarette, blowing the smoke lazily. "Is that so?" she said.

Jeannie Burton had long, straight blonde hair and round blue eyes. She wore soft pink or pale blue cashmere sweaters and a string of tiny pearls whose lustre emphasised her smooth pale neck. Her short, pleated skirts swung with the rhythm of her walk and she wore saddle shoes with little tassels on her small narrow feet. And she had the greatest legs ever.

Noel had been aware of Jeannie's legs for months. Whenever she appeared in the cafeteria he managed to find an excuse to hang around where he could observe her and he stored the image in his head for later that night when, alone in bed, he would re-run the interlude like a roll of film until it dissolved into his fantasies of her. The shock when Jeannie spoke to him caused him to tremble.

"Hi," said Jeannie, "I've noticed you around for ages. I'm Jeannie Burton."

"Hi." Noel stared at her dumbfounded.

"I know you're Noel Maddox," she continued with a smile. "Look, we're walking the same way, could you give me a hand with some of these books?"

"Sure. Sure." He took the books she handed him, and fell into step beside her.

"So," she said, "what do you do with yourself, Noel? You're quite a mystery man."

She was wearing some kind of perfume that smelled fresh and flowery. "I work. At my studies. And then the jobs. Sometimes I wonder which comes first."

"Chicken or the egg!" she laughed. "But I hear you're a great athlete too." Her eyes flicked over him boldly. "You must work hard at that too, to be in such good shape."

Noel Maddox blushed. "I like to box," he said, "so I train, but I don't get enough time to enter tournaments – I spar with the other guys, now and then."

Jeannie stopped in front of the Undergraduate Library. "This is where I'm going. Thanks for helping with these books."

Noel handed them over and their hands touched.

"Say Noel, why don't you and I get together for a pizza and a beer," smiled Jeannie, fixing him with her round blue gaze. "When are you free."

"I . . . er, well," stammered Noel.

"Tomorrow? Seven o'clock then. Let's meet right here." With a wave, she ran lightly up the steps.

Noel was unable to study the rest of that day. His concentration was shot. He didn't sleep for thinking about her, remembering the way the pearls rested against her warm neck, the long legs swinging up the steps away from him, her blue eyes smiling at him. He worried about what he would say to her when they met, how to behave on a date, what they would talk about, and how much it would cost for pizza and beer. And he worried about touching her.

He took two showers within an hour, put on a clean pair of jeans and a new chequered shirt. He folded ten dollars into his pocket and walked over to the Undergraduate Library. It was only six forty-five.

"You're punctual," Jeannie greeted him twenty minutes later. She wore a white wide-necked sweater and a light blue skirt and her blonde hair shone. "Come on then, I'm starving."

Jeannie drank red wine and only picked at her pizza. "I thought you were starving," said Noel, staring regretfully at the neglected pizza.

"I was," said Jeannie, lighting her fourth cigarette, "but I talk too much to eat." She took another sip of her wine. "Do you know, Noel Maddox, that you have a very interesting face?" Her finger traced the length of his cheek gently. "And," she leaned closer, "the most wonderful eyes. Sometimes they look intense and smoky – that's when you don't want people to know what you're thinking – and other times they're light clear grey, almost like glass. That's when you're relaxed and enjoying life. Like now."

Noel listened, fascinated. His eyes had never been the subject of such a close scrutiny before.

"And your mouth," she said dropping her finger to his lips, "strong and firm – that's a passionate mouth, Noel Maddox." She lifted the cigarette to her lips and drew on it, then she offered it to him. Noel didn't smoke but he took it because it had touched her lips. It tasted of her pink lipstick.

Jeannie sipped her wine and he finished his beer in one enormous swallow.

Jeannie laughed. "Well," she said, "I've told you all about me. Let's talk about you now. All I know is your name and you're twenty years old."

Noel stared at her, a feeling of panic creeping over him. What would she say if she knew he were only eighteen? What would he tell her? What did she want to know? She'd prattled on about her home in Grosse Pointe, told him about her father who was a president of an internationally known stockbroker's, about her mother's horses and her sister who'd left Mt Holyoke and got married last year to this great guy who was going to be a fantastic neurosurgeon one day. They had a summer cottage at Martha's Vineyard and in the vacation she sailed and swam and got a great tan.

"There's nothing to tell," he murmured, looking down into his empty glass. "My parents are dead. I've always been alone."

Jeannie stared at him, her smiling chatter stilled. "Oh Noel, I'm so sorry."

Noel shrugged. "That's okay."

She took his hand across the table. "Then that's why you keep to yourself, you're still hurt because of . . . was it an accident, Noel?"

He nodded.

"And that's why you have to work so hard – because you're all alone." She squeezed his hand sympathetically. "Now I know what that look is in your eyes, when they are shadowy and remote. You must be thinking of *them*."

Noel avoided her eyes, glancing around the crowded café.

"Let's go," she said suddenly, "I feel like walking."

Outside the pizza place Jeannie kissed him very lightly on the mouth. She took his hand as they walked back through the streets of Ann Arbor and in a shadowy corner she put her arms around him and pressed herself close. "Kiss me properly," she commanded.

It wasn't as difficult as he had expected, kissing a girl. Somehow his face fitted against hers; and his mouth searched for her lips. They felt soft against his and warm. When she opened her mouth for him his tongue found her instinctively and he pulled her closer, wrapping her against him, lost in his passion.

She could feel his erection, of course, and normally she wouldn't have let a guy get this far on a first date, but there was something about Noel Maddox, a hungriness. It was a dangerous kind of appeal.

She pulled away finally, smoothing her bruised lips with fingers that trembled. Noel stepped back from her. "I'm sorry," he said, "I didn't mean to do that."

Jeannie smiled, fumbling for her cigarettes. "That's okay," she said lightly, "I liked it."

Noel stood rigidly, watching her. If he moved he might not be able to control himself, he could still feel the pressure of her small breasts against him, the curve of her stomach and the way she'd opened her legs slightly so that his erection rubbed against her. God, he couldn't stand it! Jamming his hands in his pockets he stared at the ground.

"I'd better get back," said Jeannie. "Call me tomorrow, Noel." She leaned forward and kissed him on the cheek and was gone. A

trace of her flowery perfume mingled with the cigarette smoke in
the cool night air. He waited until she had disappeared into the
house and then he began to walk, then his step quickened into a
jog. Noel jogged through the darkened campus until he came to the
track and then he began to run, round and round on the cinder
track, running until he was exhausted and there was no energy left
for passion.

Noel couldn't figure out what Jeannie saw in him. He hadn't called
her because he couldn't afford to take her out again. So she'd called
him. He'd never had a telephone call before and when the guy down
the hall yelled his name he'd been astonished. "Hi," Jeannie said,
"don't you like me any more?"

He met her and they sat for a couple of hours over a beer just
talking – or rather she talked. She talked abut herself and about
him, embroidering his meagre story with a romance of her own
imagination, the lost loving parents, no family to help him. And
she really liked his eyes.

They met several times after that but she insisted they go dutch
because it wasn't fair he should pay for her. Noel couldn't even
afford to pay for himself, he was using money allocated for important
things, like books – but he told himself he'd get two jobs in the
summer break to make up for it. And he wasn't spending as much
time studying as he should, even when he wasn't with her he was
dreaming about her.

They kissed a lot, in a booth in the café, or behind the cafeteria,
or in a hallway. In the darkened movie theatre she took his hand
and placed it on her breast. He could feel her breathing, feel the
tautness of her nipple under his fingers through the blouse. As if
driven by some compelling force he bent his head and kissed it.
Jeannie moaned softly and pushed him away.

They began to see each other every night; even when he was
studying in the library she would come with her books and take a
seat next to him and their eyes would meet, longingly. Her friends
were astonished by her behaviour. "Remember it was a *joke*,
Jeannie," they exclaimed, "*Noel Maddox was just a joke.*"

"You don't know him," she replied, her eyes fevered with the
remembered contact of his mouth on hers. "You don't know what
he's *really* like."

They eyed her doubtfully. Noel Maddox was alien, rough. Jeannie
shouldn't be going out with him, she didn't know what she was

getting into. You couldn't tell with a guy like that, nobody knew anything about him. And her father would go crazy if he knew!

It was six weeks after they met that Jeannie told him that some friends who had an apartment off campus were going away for the weekend – to the big football game at Harvard. "Come on over," she said casually, "I'll get some wine and we'll have supper."

She was wearing a flowery skirt and white silk shirt with nothing on underneath it and Noel couldn't take his eyes from the hard points of her breasts beneath the smooth fabric. They drank red wine and talked nervously. She offered him cheese on a wooden board and he recognised the kind he'd made sandwiches with when he'd run away from Scott's apartment. But he didn't run this time, though in her own way Jeannie was as dangerous as Scott, because he wanted her, desperately.

The light faded outside the windows to a dusky blue-grey and Jeannie lit a candle in the wax-encrusted Chianti bottle and drew the curtains. It seemed as if he were seeing her in slow motion when she knelt before him and unbuttoned her blouse, sliding it over her shoulders, waiting. The pearl necklet gleamed against the warmer tones of her skin and candlelight gilded her breasts. His hands found them and she leaned back, gasping as his lips closed over her hard little nipples. He never wanted to leave them, he wanted to lick them, nuzzle them, bite them.

Jeannie pushed him away and their eyes met. Without removing her gaze from his she got to her feet and slowly removed her skirt. She stood for a minute, tall and slender in her white panties and then she unbuttoned his shirt. Running her hands over his chest she bent and bit his nipple. Noel felt a shudder run through him. Her hands fluttered at his belt, and then on the buttons. Her eyes fastened on the bulge in his underpants. Then she was in his arms and they were lying on the rug together in the candlelight. His face was buried in her fragrant hair while his hands explored her body. She was soft, smooth, damp. He was consumed with the need to taste her, and she trembled and leapt under his urgent tongue. It was too much, too much . . . he had to have her. He pressed himself against her, seeking entry . . .

"No," she gasped, "no . . ."

His fingers found her, opened her . . . "No," she cried, "Noel, don't . . . I can't . . ."

Noel lifted his eyes and stared at her, bewildered.

184

"Here," she said taking him in her hand, "here, like this." His eyes burned into hers as he came.

Jeannie couldn't keep away from him. Her friends had taken to getting her alone and giving her earnest little lectures on Noel's unsuitability and how her parents wouldn't like it, but she didn't care. She couldn't help it. She *had* to see him. She spent hours locating people whose apartments would be free for a night or even a whole weekend and she would buy some wine and cheese and light the candles and wait for him, until whatever hour he'd finish work. The transformation when Noel shed his cheap old clothes and stood naked in front of her was startling.

"All men are equal," she said to him once, "in God's eyes. But Noel Maddox, without your clothes, you are a king."

His lithe strong body tempted her, and the touch of his hands and mouth became more dangerous. He wanted her so badly, so very badly. Jeannie gave in, moaning her pleasure as he entered her.

Afterwards, they lay side by side, not touching, aware of each other's still-rapid breathing. There was a silken glaze of sweat on his chest and she put out a hand to touch it. Noel leaned over her, gazing intently into her eyes, not speaking.

"You did that *then*," she said, touching his lids, "you looked at me like that!"

He kissed her gently. "I love you, Noel," she murmured as he kissed her again.

Very few people knew about their affair. Her friends, worrying about her reputation, covered for her. But Jeannie was a very pretty, very popular girl and she was missed at the parties and football games.

"You're missing all the fun," the friends protested.

"Am I?" she would answer dreamily.

At the end of the fall semester Noel's grades dropped drastically. He had never before had anything but an A. He stared angrily at the paper with the scatter of B's and C's. He'd been neglecting his studies because of Jeannie. He'd kept up with all his campus jobs because he had to have the money – but the *real work* had suffered. For the first time in four years he was behind his goal. Jeannie had wanted him to meet her in the vacation but he had told her truthfully that he had to work. He was going back on the assembly line during the day and working a shift at a bar at night. It was as good a time as any for making the break.

When they returned to college she called him on the phone and said, "Hi, let's meet." He walked along beside her, kicking at the ice along the path, avoiding her gaze. "You didn't call," she said taking his hand. "I missed you."

"Yeah," he said, avoiding her eyes. "Me too."

"Noel," she pleaded, "what's wrong?"

He shrugged. "Nothing. Nothing. I guess I'm just too busy that's all."

Jeannie just stood there, fighting the tears and said, "You don't want me any more."

Her blonde hair swung in the wind and her face was pale. "I need to work Jeannie," he replied stonily.

"I thought I knew you," she said, tears clouding her bewildered blue eyes.

"You *don't* know me, Jeannie, not the *real* me. *The real me doesn't exist. Yet!*"

"Damn," she cried. "Oh damn," and she took off down the path, blonde hair flying, skidding a little on the ice.

Noel watched, eyes hooded and remote, until she disappeared and then he went back to his room and his studies. Work would always have priority. But Jeannie never knew how desperately he missed her. He was lonelier now than he'd ever been before in his life.

33

Pale sunlight filtered through the chestnut trees fringing Launceton Hall's south lawn, dappling Peach's upturned face and long outstretched legs with a shifting mosaic of colour. The lawn stretched smooth as striped velvet to distant rose gardens and terraces and beyond them the house.

Launceton Hall had been built in the reign of Queen Anne by Sir Edward Launceton, the third baronet. Tucked into a fold of the verdant Wiltshire hills its rosy brickwork glowed against the green of the park that had been laid out by Capability Brown. There was a fine avenue of elms and a series of silvery cascades tumbling down the hillside into a lake, spanned at its narrowest point by a bridge copied from a Chinese porcelain plate; a Grecian "folly" surmounted the slope overlooking the eastern bank affording spectacular views of the house at the sunset.

Launceton Hall's many windows were flung wide to the afternoon sunshine and its lawns were dotted with summery figures drifting towards the tea-tent. White-flannelled cricketers made their way thankfully from the pitch amid a spatter of applause and small children shrieked and laughed, spilling lemonade on the grass, while overheated dogs slobbered anxiously for forgotten morsels of cake. In the shade of the ancient chestnuts the Launceton Magna Silver Band, red-faced beneath their smart peaked caps, perched on tiny metal chairs, puffing jovial Gilbert and Sullivan melodies into the warm blue English afternoon.

Peach lounged in a deck-chair, her eyes half-closed, her bare toes curling into the cool, infinitely green grass. It was the perfect English scene – and perfectly boring. She'd come here today with Melinda and Mrs Seymour, hoping that she might see Tom, but he was away at Cambridge. When Melinda had invited Peach to stay she had made English country life sound so enticing. Peach had envisaged morning strolls through fronded woods with perfectly trained dogs running at heel, and afternoon tea and crumpets in front of blazing log fires, and maybe long summer evenings in the romantic green English half-light where she would meet some handsome and romantic Englishman. It hadn't turned out quite like that. Unless you were dedicated to horse-riding, besotted by badly behaved dogs and adored life in damp, sprawling, vaguely shabby country houses that hadn't felt the winds of change for at least a century, then country life was not for you.

Peach sat up straighter in her striped canvas deck-chair, lifting her heavy hair languidly from her warm neck. Sometimes the English bewildered her. Take Melinda, for instance – sixteen years old, the same age as herself, munching away at those awful sticky cakes that were already ruining her shape and wearing a cotton dress that must be last year's because she seemed about to burst out of it. And yet Melinda was sweet and uninhibited, full of charm and totally nice. She'd probably be married at eighteen, thought Peach gloomily, and have a brood of babies to drool over.

Of course that wasn't Peach's future, she'd already decided that. Thank God, she was over her "romantic period". When she'd turned sixteen she had suddenly bloomed, the breasts she'd despaired of for so long emerged from mere buds to roundness, her hips gained curves, her legs became long and slender instead of sticklike. It was pleasing when the boys at the dances organised at L'Aiglon rushed to ask *her* to dance, and surprising to find that she knew how to flirt. Watching Julie-Anne practising all that time must have rubbed off on her. And it had been oddly pleasing to notice that Julie-Anne was a touch jealous of her. Suddenly boys were always around, and sometimes it was pleasant – and sometimes it bored her – especially at the parties where everyone drank too much because they thought it meant they were having fun and then drifted off into darkened rooms together to do who knew what?

There would be no time for men in Peach's life for years and years. She was going to go to Radcliffe because it was a good college and because Uncle Sebastião do Santos lived in Boston and Maman said he could keep an eye on her! And after that she'd take business affairs and management courses and then she hoped to be able to help Jim with the ailing de Courmont industries and restore them to their former glory. Maybe she should buy a pair of those horn-rimmed spectacles like Leonore's to make her look more business-like?

At the house on the Ile St Louis Peach had studied the portrait of her grandfather, Monsieur, seeing herself in his face. She had his eyes, though without that intimidating stare.

"Grand-père," she had told him, "I've heard all about how you built your first car, and how beautiful it was. I heard how you brought the rubber for tyres from Brazil. I know about the dozen coats of special lacquer applied carefully and sanded smooth and then another and another until the cars shone with a depth of colour no others had. Trust me, Grand-père," she'd promised, "de Courmont automobiles will run on the roads of Europe again, and maybe even in America. And they'll be beautiful. I won't let you down."

Applause rippled through the crowds as the cricketers returned to the pitch, refreshed by their tea. Closing her eyes Peach slumped back in her deck-chair, lulled by heat and boredom into drowsiness.

The labrador licked her bare toes lavishly but she felt too lazy to push him away.

"Wake up Peach," whispered Melinda, "wake up. *Open your eyes!*"

"Why?" murmured Peach comfortably, "things must look exactly the way they did half an hour ago."

"No they don't! Quick Peach, *you must take a look at him.*"

Melinda must have fallen for someone – again. It was a habit she had. Smiling at the urgency in Melinda's voice, Peach opened her eyes a mere slit.

The cricket match was in full swing again and the bowler was just striding down the wicket. He was tall and slender with thick fair hair which he pushed back with an impatient hand only for it to fall silkily back over his tanned forehead. Eyebrows knitted in concentration, measuring his distance, the bowler paced backwards. Then swinging back his right arm he ran forward and pitched the ball powerfully towards the batsman.

"Isn't he *wonderful!*" whispered Melinda.

Peach's heart was pounding, her cheeks were flushed with a heat that wasn't from the sun, and her eyes were dark with excitement. He was the most graceful, most beautiful man she had ever seen in her life.

The bowler strode back again, catching the throw easily from the fielder at mid-on. Peach admired his easy masculine stride, the long slope of his back as he flung the ball, the muscles tense along his forearm.

"But *who is he?*" she demanded of Melinda.

"That's Tom's brother. You remember I told you about him ages ago – the one from the romantic novels."

"Harry?" Peach whispered the name reverently.

"Harry," confirmed Melinda. "The squire of Launceton Magna's eldest son – and no doubt he's wreaking havoc with the village maidens. I just wish he'd wreak some havoc with me," she added with a sigh. "Not only is he beautiful," continued Melinda, "he's brilliant too. He's only twenty-five and he's already published three novels – they're not the sort you and I read in bed at L'Aiglon, though. He gets marvellous reviews and he's published all over the world. They say Harry Launceton's destined to be one of Britain's great men of letters. But his father, Sir Piers Launceton, told Daddy that he's damned if *he* understands them. They're all about gnostic visions and beliefs and medieval myths in the form of a novel. I don't even know what 'gnostic' *means.* I'm afraid the way to Harry's heart may be through one's intellect and in that case I'm sunk."

Melinda's chatter bubbled across the surface of Peach's consciousness as Harry Launceton relinquished the bowling to his successor. Pushing back his fair hair with a boyish gesture he strolled across the brilliant green turf towards them.

"God," squealed Melinda, "he's coming this way! And I look such a mess." She smoothed her too-tight cotton frock desperately.

Peach sat very still, her relaxed pose and half-closed eyes disguising her inner tension. Any observer would see a young girl, a little sleepy from the sun, idly watching the cricket.

Harry Launceton waved a casual hand in Melinda's direction as he walked by, turning his head to smile at Peach. His eyes glinted in the sun like green moss under the waters of a running stream. Nerve endings that Peach didn't know she possessed trembled as she looked into his eyes and a dark feeling of excitement swam in the pit of her stomach. *This must be what love was!* It made her want desperately to touch him, to run her hand along his tanned neck and curl her fingers into his hair. She wanted to be alone with him on a desert island, locked in his embrace . . . *She was in love with Harry Launceton.* Instantly and overwhelmingly in love with him!

Quick calculations flashed through her head, she was sixteen and he was twenty-five. He might meet someone else before she was old enough to marry! No matter. She would wait until it was time. Her previous plans and ambitions were forgotten. And when she said her prayers over the next couple of years it would be that Harry Launceton would wait to fall in love with *her*.

34

Lais powdered her nose, added lipstick and a final spray of "L'Heure bleue", and inspected the result in the triple mirror of her crystal dressing table. The table had been a present from Leonie when Lais had moved into her own penthouse at the Hostellerie and had once belonged in the fabulous collection of some Indian prince. Its graceful faceted-glass legs and serpentine front glittered in the setting sun like a thousand big carat diamonds reflecting little shimmers of rainbow colours into her blue eyes.

In her pale silk dress with its narrow straps and voluminous silk skirt designed for her by Dior you might almost think she was human again, thought Lais bitterly. She glanced at Peach sitting on the rug, arms wrapped around her knees, watching her just as she had always done. She remembered when Peach was just a child, trying to get rid of her, telling her she was a little pest. But Peach had stuck to her like a limpet and she was still here, holding out the earrings and then the bracelets. Lais's helper.

It was Peach's self-imposed task to escort Lais downstairs every evening to the cocktail bar, wheeling the beautiful white leather chair into the private elevator that took them without stopping to the ground floor. And it had been Peach who had suggested the penthouse. Gerard had designed it specially and Lais's view across the bay with its green headlands encircling the ever-changing sea and the blue expanse of sky was better than a gallery full of paintings. Lais's penthouse and her pretty little roof garden were her territory, the place where she was really herself. And Peach was the only one to see that true Lais.

Yet if it weren't for Peach she might not be in the wheelchair. Lais tried to stop the thought coming into her mind, as she always did . . . but wasn't it true? If it weren't for Peach . . . *Stop!* What happened had nothing to do with Peach – Kruger would have made his move at some point. And it had been *she* who got Peach involved in the first place. She had always gambled with danger. What happened was simply a stroke of fate, that's all.

And what about Ferdi? Lais bit her newly scarlet lips to stop herself from crying out his name. Not even Peach knew that she dreamed of Ferdi every night, and that these dreams were now her reality. In them she was her old self, running hand in hand with Ferdi along the beach, dancing in his arms, curving her body into his as he made love to her, wrapping her long slender legs around him pressing him even closer. She was still a woman, she could still respond, and those warm scented sexual memories springing unbidden from her sleeping brain aroused her needs – and her longing for Ferdi.

But Ferdi had never been to see her when she was in that awful waking-trance from which she had been unable to free herself.

191

Afterwards she had asked Leonie what had happened and Leonie had been forced to confess that Ferdi had killed Kruger and disappeared. He had never tried to see her, never even written. No one knew where Ferdi was. "I can have Jim find him, if you wish," Leonie had said, "it can't be too difficult. If he is alive, he must be back with his family in Cologne." But Lais had gone suddenly cold with fear. If Ferdi hadn't come back for her, it meant he hadn't wanted her. Or maybe that he *knew*. Of course she couldn't blame him for not wanting her now. *She was a cripple!* Underneath that pretty flowing silk skirt were two slender useless legs. Shrugging off her memories Lais turned from the mirror. Ferdi was probably married by now to some tall strong girl with a brood of beautiful children. And *she* had her life such as it was. Lais was queen of the Riviera's smartest American cocktail bar.

With a tilt of her chin and a jaunty smile she turned to Peach. "Hurry up then with the earrings. We're late."

Scrambling to her feet Peach handed them over, running a frantic hand through her mop of bronze hair. "Am I tidy?" she asked anxiously.

Lais looked at her little sister, remembering how passionately she had hated her when she was born. Peach was growing up but she was still sometimes, like now, a child. And at other moments so unconsciously elegant. And quite beautiful.

"What would I do without you?" she said simply.

Peach grinned, tossing back her thick hair and skewering it into place with enormous grips without once looking in the mirror. "Come on then," she said, "we're late!"

Lais de Courmont played her game well. Perched on her high stool at the Terrace Bar she seemed in her element. No one would have guessed that her wonderful clothes, her great style, her wide smile and witty remarks disguised her inner loneliness the way her full silken skirts hid her useless legs.

Lais had made the Terrace Bar of the Hostellerie famous along the Côte d'Azur, importing Max, the New York barman, to make his White Ladies and Green Goddesses and the driest Martinis this side of Madison Avenue. Max had created a special champagne cocktail for her – a sugar cube drenched in Marc, a dash of bitters, a splash of rosewater topped with Moët's special Cuvée. And she'd hired Murray, the American pianist, to entertain nightly with his repertoire of Jerome Kern, Noël Coward and Cole Porter in his slightly off-key, half-singing, half-talking intimate style. To be included in Lais de Courmont's inner circle at cocktail hour was *the* smartest thing, and those who weren't cast envious glances at the laughing, witty, elegant crowd that surrounded her, remembering the stories they'd heard about her, and wondering . . .

Lais bent her head to light her cigarette, smiling into the eyes of the man who held the flame for her. She was smoking too much. And she was restless. Her eyes searched the bar – *looking for Ferdi?* Did she one day expect him to walk in and reclaim her as though the years between had never happened? Fool, fool, Lais!

Sliding a soft arm around the neck of the man who had lit her cigarette she whispered something in his ear. His eyes met hers and he smiled, smoothing a hand along her upper arm, letting his fingers move softly across the warm curve where blue silk met naked flesh.

The buzz of conversation, the tinkle of ice in glasses and Murray's off-key voice crooning, "I get no kick from champagne . . . mere alcohol doesn't thrill me at all, so tell me why should it be true, that I get a kick . . . out of you . . ." greeted Peach as she pushed her way through to the magic circle that surrounded Lais. Worldly sunbronzed men in white dinner jackets interrupted their conversations of business and power, of yachts and motor cars and other men's women, to smile at Peach. And soft malicious women whose gossip was of who was having an affair with whose husband, and the cost of other women's dresses and jewels, stared after her, envying her youth.

Peach's cheeks flamed as she averted her eyes from the man with Lais, aware that his fingers were resting on the white curve of Lais's breast. They were expected at Grand-mère's for dinner, otherwise she would have waited quietly outside until Lais was ready. "It's time for dinner," she said.

Lais consulted her exquisite diamond-studded Cartier watch, frowning. Peach knew the rules. "Come back in half an hour," she ordered, "there's plenty of time."

Peach hesitated. Grand-mère hated it when they were late – but the bar was still crowded and no one was making the move towards the next phase of the evening – dinner, then dancing or a party at some villa along the coast. And Lais never left until the others had gone. Or at least, all those who mattered.

"Sweet, that little one." The man's fingers slid beneath the strap across Lais's naked back as he spoke. "She looks so worried about you."

Lais shrugged away his hand impatiently, ordering another champagne cocktail. "Silly child," she murmured irritably, "she's always been a nuisance."

Waiting on the terrace Peach checked her watch nervously. At last the crowds were beginning to drift off. She watched them climbing into long, elegant cars, hating the women in their high golden shoes and slender strapless dresses, hating them for having what Lais no longer had. "Come with us, Lais," she heard someone call. "No, no," waved Lais laughing, "I have another appointment." She made it sound like an assignation.

The bar was almost empty, just a few quiet drinkers – unknowns – left in the corners. Peach wheeled the chair from its hiding place in the corner behind the bar, and Max put his strong arms around Lais, lifting her from her stool into her chair. As Peach pushed her across the hall a group of revellers, waiting for their cars by the big double doors, called to her, "Come with us Lais . . ."

"Sorry," she called, "but dancing is the one thing I'm no good for any more."

The man came over to her. "You're as light as a feather," he murmured in her ear, "I'll hold you so close no one will ever know . . ."

"You are standing," Lais remarked coldly, "on the exact spot where I stopped the German bullet. Isn't that right, Peach?"

Peach nodded her head miserably.

"And you know what?" added Lais. "It didn't even hurt! Isn't that odd?" She swung her chair round abruptly. "Come on Peach, we're late for dinner."

35

Leonie had closed the green shutters against the afternoon sun and lay propped against the pillows of her wide white bed. Jim was away visiting the de Courmont factories at Valenciennes as he did several times a month, supervising the board and management meetings of the complex group of companies. His work had not been easy since the war. Steel foundries and armaments works had suffered direct hits in the bombing and much of what was left had been destroyed by the retreating German armies. Only the automobile plant had survived more or less intact and it was there that Jim was concentrating his energies, aware of the need in a postwar world for transportation. The de Courmont auto plants now produced lorries and buses in addition to cars, and the foundries were gradually being built up again. It had been hard work for Jim, but he loved it. Leonie had never known Jim without a project – and always one on an enormous scale on which he could expend his vast energies. He had already run through three successful careers by the time she met him – and he was then only twenty-seven! Son of a genteel but out-of-funds family from Savannah, Georgia, prospecting for gold had brought Jim his first wealth and when he got bored with that he'd tried his hand at wildcatting for Texas oil. Lucky again, he'd parlayed his wealth into property holdings and for years he had commuted between the continents, crossing the Atlantic Ocean to work as easily as other people crossed cities. Finally, he'd left it all to settle here with Leonie. Jim always boasted that he knew every liner on the transatlantic route as well as he knew his own home.

Leonie hated it when Jim was away, missing him as much as she had in the throes of first love. Pushing her hair back from her damp forehead she sat up, staring across the shadowy room at Sekhmet. The smooth granite statue from the Eighteenth Dynasty of Egypt's history stared back at her from its marble plinth. Its proud lion head with the backflung mane of hair had a cool impersonal beauty and the solar disc glowed like a halo in the silvery light. This statue and the one of Bastet, the sacred cat, had been Leonie's legacy from an Egyptian father who had disappeared when she was born, escaping back to the flamboyant circus-world he came from. They had been her "dolls", all she had had in the way of toys in her poor childhood and, when she had run away to Paris at the age of sixteen, they were the only things she valued to take with her. And she had always believed that it was when she ran away to Paris that the Goddess Sekhmet took over her destiny. Her life from then had seemed to echo the goddess's legend. It was Jim who had finally convinced her that it all was her imagination. Or – more truthfully – she had allowed Jim to think he had convinced her. Secretly, she still believed.

With a sigh Leonie swung her feet from the bed and padded over to the window. The little brown cat followed her, blinking as Leonie flung back the shutters and sunlight flooded the room. Leonie absorbed the warmth of the sun's caress, feeling better. But it wasn't just Jim being away that was upsetting her. It was her granddaughters. Behind Lais's extrovert façade was a bitter loneliness that she refused to acknowledge, even to her grandmother. And now Leonie hardly ever saw her other granddaughter, Leonore, except in passing. Leonore was always "just on her way to do this or that", or simply, "had to sort out a problem here or there" Work seemed to claim her every waking moment and Leonie knew Leonore well enough to understand that she was piling on work and pressure so she wouldn't have time to think about her true problems. But what were her true problems? For years, thought Leonie wistfully, her granddaughters had confided all their troubles to her. She knew them as well as she knew herself. Now only Peach, still the chatterbox, told all.

"Grand-mère," Peach had said just this morning. "Oh Grand-mère, I *must* tell you. *I'm in love.*"

With her long hair swinging in a fat braid, and her long suntanned legs, scratched from her walks in the hills, Peach looked about thirteen. Biting her lips to stop from laughing, Leonie listened attentively while Peach poured out the story of Harry Launceton.

"He's so *beautiful*, Grand-mère, just *so* beautiful. He has this thick silky hair that slides over his eyes all the time and he pushes it back – like this. And his eyes are the greenest – I mean *true* green, Grand-mère. He's a *famous* writer – and he's only twenty-five. Grand-mère, I *knew* as soon as I saw him that I would marry him. *I just knew.*"

"Peach, Peach," protested Leonie laughing, "you don't even know Harry Launceton! I'm sure he's as attractive as you say and I suppose he's very talented, but maybe you're just a little impressed by it all. Fame *and* beauty combined can be very heady stuff even for people older than you. After all, you are only sixteen." Even as she said it Leonie remembered that at sixteen she too had been madly in love – with Rupert von Hollensmark.

"Grand-mère," protested Peach, jumping to her feet, "I told you about Harry because I felt sure you were the only one who *wouldn't* say, '*you're only sixteen!*' I didn't even tell Maman because she would never understand, even though she married for the first time when she was *seventeen!* Oh of course I'm not old enough for Harry yet –

but I will be. Each year that goes by brings Harry and me closer together. And when I'm old enough – eighteen or nineteen – then Harry Launceton will marry me."

Despite herself Leonie laughed. "And does Harry know this?"

"Of course not, but he will, when I'm ready."

Leonie stared at Peach, seeing in her shining dark blue eyes a glimpse of Monsieur's passion. And his obsession. "And what if Harry should fall in love with someone else in the meantime?" she asked. "After all, he doesn't know he's supposed to be waiting for you."

Peach shrugged her shoulders. "No matter," she said airily, "he'll fall in love with me when he meets me. I'll make him love me."

Leonie hadn't known whether to laugh or cry. If this were anyone but Monsieur's granddaughter she would have dismissed it as schoolgirl nonsense. But Peach's words had the ring of truth. She believed what she was saying. Remembering how Monsieur's obsession had cast a shadow over her own life, Leonie was worried.

"Eighteen is old enough isn't it, Grand-mère?" Peach did a little pirouette of sheer exuberance, stopping in front of Leonie, a smile lighting up her lovely face.

"Oh Peach," said Leonie sadly, "you have lots of growing up to do. Forget about Harry Launceton and enjoy your life."

Caro Montalva always preferred to travel south by train. She enjoyed boarding the long, important monster at Paris's Gare de Lyon and being pampered by attentive stewards who knew her well. She enjoyed dining in the elegant restaurant car with its intimate rose-shaded lights and fresh flowers, its gleaming silver and its excellent food. And like a child, she enjoyed curling up in the spotless linen sheets, with the dark industrial north speeding by the windows, only to wake to southern sunshine and the train running alongside the sea with the blue mountains in the distance and puffballs of yellow mimosa promising warm Mediterranean weather.

This time she was travelling with a companion. Maroc, Leonie's oldest friend – who had emerged from his sprawling retirement palace on a hillside in Tangier to pay his annual visit to Paris, and then to Leonie. Maroc's eyes were closed. His face was unlined and his dark hair was as thick and crispy curling as when she first saw him working with Leonie as the little parcels boy at Madame Serrat's lingerie shop on the rue Montalivet. Could it really be fifty years ago? Caro sighed. They were all getting old, no denying it. And she was the oldest of all. Her bones creaked protestingly when she got up in the mornings and her glossy black hair was silver-white – a colour she had never cared for. Why couldn't hair turn to say sapphire blue when one got older? It would have suited her much better. But her back was still straight, her legs still good and she was always dressed by Dior – although she did admit to having a little flutter at Balmain every now and again. She was seventy-four now, after all, and it simply meant she had to plan things well ahead so that she had the time and energy to prepare for them. Going to Leonie's had taken a month's preparation – two weeks for her to get used to the idea of leaving her apartment and venturing forth – she who had travelled the world as though she owned it! And two weeks planning her clothes, having her secretary organise tickets, and just simply looking forward to it. Even better, Edouard d'Aureville's sons, Jean-Paul and Vincente, were to be there – the first time she had seen them since Lais and Leonore were children. And probably the first time Lais and Leonore had seen them in years, too, for though they were cousins the d'Aurevilles lived thousands of miles away in Rio de Janeiro.

The train began to slow down as they approached the outskirts of Nice. "Wake up, Maroc," said Caro, digging him with the tip of her lizard-skin shoe. "We're here."

Jean-Paul d'Aureville was the image of his father and Leonie's eyes returned to him time and time again across the dinner table. He had the same strong bones. It was Edouard d'Aureville to whom she had entrusted her baby Amelie, convinced that Monsieur was out to destroy them both, and it was Edouard who had brought up and loved Amelie as his own, and not just his brother's, daughter. Later Edouard had married the beautiful Cuban girl, Xara, and with their twin sons had moved from Brazil to Florida, where Edouard had built the hotel Palaçio d'Aureville, one of the first and grandest hotels in the then village of Miami. Amelie had married their distant cousin, Roberto do Santos, and, when she was widowed at a young age and left with two small daughters – Lais and Leonore – she had taken over his job of running the hotel.

Vincente d'Aureville was dark, like his mother Xara, with her large brown eyes and olive skin. He was a paediatrician, and Jean-Paul, like Leonore, was a hotelier, running the d'Aurevilles' other famous old hotel in Copacabana, Rio de Janeiro.

"My father is working with yours, you know," Jean-Paul was saying to Leonore. "He's had this idea brewing for years and now they've drawn up plans for a new hotel in Switzerland. He's always been intrigued by what you achieved with your Hostellerie, I think it's been a big influence on their new designs."

"In Switzerland?" Leonore was interested. "In Geneva or Zurich?"

"Neither. In a little town on top of a mountain. It's to be a winter resort hotel but father's planning summer activities too – a golf course, maybe even a race-track."

"That sounds like Edouard," said Leonore, smiling.

"And Gerard," added Lais.

"They build dreams," said Peach suddenly. "What they really want is to make people happy."

Jean-Paul looked at her, surprised. "You're right, of course," he said, "just think then, Peach, I'll be managing a dream."

Leonore laughed and Leonie realised suddenly that it was a sound she hadn't heard much of lately. Leonore was looking especially pretty tonight in a simple blue and white printed cotton dress with a tight bodice that showed off her slenderness and a full skirt that swished gracefully around her pretty legs. And if she weren't mistaken, Jean-Paul had definitely noticed that fact. Leonie watched them, pleased, and then her eye met Caro's.

"Plotting again?" asked Caro with a raised eyebrow.

"Leonie is always full of plots," responded Maroc, "she re-writes the scenarios for all our lives."

"She certainly re-wrote mine," said Jim cheerfully. "I drove all the way back from Valenciennes at her request specially to be here with you all."

"It was worth it," Leonie smiled as he bent to kiss her. Jim was home again and she was happy.

36

Rain was falling steadily from a leaden sky and, from his fifth-floor apartment at the Ritz, Ferdi had a bird's eye view of striped and spotted umbrellas hurrying along slick grey streets and the traffic surging round the Place Vendôme. Klaxons blared as impatient Parisian drivers battled against the elements and each other, but Ferdi barely noticed. His mind was on Peach.

Leonore couldn't possibly have told Peach about their affair, yet Peach knew something. What happened between him and Leonore hadn't been a *love* affair. There had been no romance – just a generous comforting gesture by Leonore, the only woman who could possibly understand his pain. That and a mutual sexual need. When he had received her message that she would prefer him not to try to see her again, he had understood it was over. Their physical and mental longings had been assuaged. Then *why* had Peach said – so fiercely – that he should go back and *explain*?

Ferdi paced the floor worriedly. He lay awake at night brooding about Leonore and trying to analyse his feelings for her. It was so different from what he felt for Lais. Lais had blazed into his life like a ray of pure sunlight, thawing him with her warmth. Until then his life had been a serious business, burdened with family obligations and duty. Born just as his father was killed, Ferdi was the only son in a family of sisters, but their frivolous activities had never been allowed by his mother's family, the powerful Merkers, to intrude on his solitary life. As heir presumptive to the Merker iron and steel works with its factories spread throughout the Ruhr, Ferdi was groomed for his future role like a prince destined for the throne. His young life was bound by tutors force-feeding his brain with work until the work-ethic became the vital element. Physical instructors coached him in swimming, fencing, riding and gymnastics so that he would be strong and fit for his role as master of Merker.

Ferdi had never known his father but he'd heard stories from his grandparents and from his mother, of Klaus von Schönberg's capacity for hard work – and his gift for enjoying life. Klaus had been sensitive, Ferdi's grandmother said, perhaps *too* emotional, but in the end he'd buckled down to a "proper life". Ferdi had always wondered what she had meant by a "proper life", but assumed it was the sort of life he too was destined for. The first crack in the superficial façade of the correct, well-educated young German born and bred to succeed in his duty had come with the outbreak of war. Ferdi's refusal to take his proper place as head of the Merker factories had ripped through his family with a tidal wave of shock. For them *nothing* – not even so transparent an evil as Hitler's – mattered more than maintaining Merker's wealth and position. When he had been drafted into the army and accepted only the status of a lower grade officer, his mother refused to speak to him. He had disgraced his family.

When he first saw Lais at the party in Paris her brittle façade of gaiety had seemed about to splinter and sensing her vulnerability Ferdi had been drawn to her. And when they had met again at the Hostellerie the powerful sexual attraction between them had merged into love.

Looking back Ferdi couldn't remember much laughter in his life except when he was with Lais and he would trade the whole of the Merker empire to laugh again with her.

Then what should he do about Leonore? If he'd hurt her he hadn't meant to. He cared about Leonore more now than any other woman in his life. He probably loved her. It was just that it was so different from the way he felt about Lais that he didn't recognise it.

Striding to the desk Ferdi picked up his pen and paper. "My dearest Leonore," he wrote, "Forgive me for not writing to you before and if I've hurt you then I'm sorry. I needed time to think about things – about *us*. I have never been able to bring myself to return to the Hostellerie since that night, but now, knowing you are there, I shall plan to visit you as soon as I am able in order to discuss our future. Please believe me, dearest Leonore – I didn't mean to hurt you. Ferdi."

37

Peach swung the telescope on Lais's terrace towards the beach, focusing on the couple strolling at the edge of the waves. "It's Leonore and Jean-Paul," she called excitedly, "he's just taken her hand, Lais. They've stopped to talk . . . oh, I believe he's going to kiss her."

"*Peach!* It's unfair to watch them."

Reluctantly Peach swung the telescope around. "Do you think he wants to marry her?" she asked wistfully.

"They barely know each other."

"But you don't need to *know* each other to fall in love."

Lais looked at her sister thoughtfully. "Perhaps that's true," she admitted, "but when you're older Peach you don't fall in love easily. And certainly not like you – with a man you've hardly met."

Peach blushed angrily. "I *do* love Harry Launceton, why don't you believe me?"

"Because I don't think you know what love is," replied Lais.

"And you do, I suppose!"

"It took me a long time, but yes, I do."

Peach stared at her remorsefully. "Oh Lais, I'm sorry, I didn't mean to say that."

Lais smoked her cigarette saying nothing.

"I know I'm young, and I know that I've never even spoken to Harry," whispered Peach, crouching at Lais's knee, "but it must be love, Lais. What else can it be? I just want to touch him, to be by his side, to listen to his voice, smooth his silken hair. I know what it will feel like when he kisses me. I'll melt away inside and I'll want him never to stop . . . Isn't this love, Lais?"

Their eyes met as Lais said, "Only you can tell, Peach. And if you think it's love, then take it. Take all you can from it – it may not last."

*　　　*　　　*

202

Jean-Paul d'Aureville was a man who knew what he wanted. He was thirty-nine years old and with his busy gregarious life running a luxury hotel he had so far avoided marriage to one of any number of willing and beautiful Brazilian girls. In Rio Jean-Paul was known as a bit of a playboy, always throwing parties on his boat or dinners for two in Rio's most intimate restaurants. The dark-haired beauties and their eager mamas considered Jean-Paul quite a catch and he had become famous over two decades for eluding their nets. And now here he was, falling for the tall blonde cousin he'd known since he was a child – and he couldn't even tell if she cared.

He sat alone at the corner of the Terrace Bar, sipping a dry Martini and waiting for Leonore. She had promised to have dinner with him, warning him that she would probably be late. "I'll wait," he'd promised – he who never waited for anyone. Yet the anticipation of seeing her was pleasurable. He was actually *enjoying* waiting for Leonore. "You're too mysterious," he'd told her that first night when they were alone on the terrace at the villa, "so cool and calm and efficient. But there's another side to you that you're not letting anyone see."

"You're imagining things, Jean-Paul," she replied avoiding his eyes, "or maybe you're confusing me with my sister. Lais is the multi-faceted character."

"Lais is as easy to read as an open book," he contradicted, "there's no confusion in my mind. Is there in yours, Leonore?"

He must have triggered a signal on some painful nerve end because Leonore glared at him, stricken, and then hurried back in to the lighted salon and Leonie's other guests.

He'd apologised the next day, prising her away from what seemed a million and one urgent commitments, by simply brushing them aside. "You can't fool me with your excuses," he'd grinned, "you forget I run a hotel too. Leave it all and have lunch with me." To his surprise Leonore accepted. They ate at a tiny village restaurant high in the hills above the coast, sitting for hours beneath a shady grape arbour, protected from the hot sun by its dense glossy leaves, eating fresh figs and goat's cheese and sipping a clean, stinging white wine, while Leonore talked.

She told him about Lais and how Lais had always been the one who claimed all the attention, how she'd always protected Lais, how much she loved her and how it tore her apart to see Lais play-acting nightly at the bar, pretending it was all the way it used to be. "I would do anything," Leonore said passionately, "*anything* to turn back the clock."

"Clocks can't be turned back," he said gently, taking her hand and feeling her flinch from the contact. "You have to go forward adapting as best you can to the new circumstances. Life is made up of changes, strokes of fate, circumstance, destiny – call it what you will."

"You don't understand," Leonore had said pulling her hand away. "*Lais was in love!* Truly in love this time. But when she was shot Ferdi never came back for her, he thought she was dead . . ."

Jean-Paul waited for her to say more but Leonore's voice trailed off and she sat there, eyes cast down at the purple fig on her neglected plate, her smooth blonde hair pulled back into a white ribbon, looking a troubled young girl.

"Leonore?" he asked. "Why did you never marry?"

Her shocked amber eyes met his. "But Ferdi wanted to marry Lais," she blurted out and then, realising what she'd said, she blushed, turning her head away but not before he'd seen the glimmer of a tear on her lashes.

So that was it! Jean-Paul didn't need her pathetic admission fleshing out with details – he understood. He waited a few moments and then said, "It was all a long time ago, Leonore. Life goes on and love changes, sometimes at a faster pace than you might think. Why not try living in the present – not the past or the future – but right now? Here we are in a sunny arbour up in these lovely hills with a view of the whole beautiful Mediterranean coast below, drinking cold wine and eating delicious fruit – and just being with each other. Being with you at this moment brings me as much pleasure as I've ever known. Can't you try just to enjoy the day? And enjoy being with me?"

Leonore smiled gratefully as she answered, "Of course I'm happy with you, Jean-Paul."

Since then he'd spent as much time with her as she would give him. Leonore told him it was the first time in all her years running the Hostellerie that she'd ever delegated her work to others and she was a little put out to notice that the hotel seemed to run just as smoothly without her there. But then she began to enjoy "playing truant", as she called it. Together they toured the length of the coast, driving over the border into Italy for dinner, looping back via fishing villages and hillside hamlets, pausing to admire local monuments and the works of struggling artists, making a purchase here and there, bickering happily over their choices. And he'd kissed her once or twice – lightly. But it wasn't like brother and sister.

Jean-Paul sipped his Martini and glanced at his watch. Leonore was already a half-hour late. No matter, he would wait.

Leonie stared aghast at Leonore. Of all the things she could have told her, this was the most unexpected. She had been filled with happiness and relief, seeing Leonore blossom in the company of Jean-Paul these past few weeks. When Leonore said she had something important to tell her Leonie had hoped that maybe she had come to confess her love for Jean-Paul. It would all have been so perfect . . . but now this desperate tale of her passion for Ferdi and their sad *affaire*.

"I would never have told you – or anyone – *ever*," confessed Leonore, "except that this letter came from Ferdi this morning." She handed over the crisp white sheet of paper stamped with the heading, Hotel Ritz, Paris.

Leonie read it quickly. Poor Lais, oh poor Lais. And poor Leonore! How could this ever have happened! "And what do you intend to reply?" she asked Leonore.

"A few weeks ago, I would have *wanted* to see him, though of course I wouldn't," she admitted. "You can't imagine what sort of state of mind we both were in, Grand-mère. It was like living a dream."

"The dream where you finally had that which belonged to your sister," Leonie replied cuttingly.

"Grand-mère, please, oh please don't be angry. I know it was wrong. I'd give everything for it never to have happened – especially now."

"Because of Jean-Paul?"

"Yes. And because of Lais. She's so brave, and so – damaged. I couldn't bear to hurt her. That's why Ferdi must never come here, Grand-mère. He thinks Lais is dead. And Lais would never have wanted him to see her like this, she would hate him to know that she is a cripple."

"*Don't ever call your sister that!*" Leonie had never raised her voice in her life to Leonore before and her granddaughter flinched. "The only thing that excuses you, Leonore, is that you took something your sister had finished with. Lais has never mentioned Ferdi's name in all these years. It's better to let things stay the way they are. Try to forget what you did. *Live your own life, not Lais's!* There's a wider world out there for you, if only you'll take the chance and be your own woman."

205

Leonore's arms were around her, her tears wet against Leonie's cheek. "I will, Grand-mère, oh I will. I promise." She sounded just the way she had when she was a little girl, so young, so sweet.

Leonore simply had to write the letter before she saw Jean-Paul. Then she could go to him free from her guilty past. Her pen flew across the thick blue paper in a fast scrawl. . . ."It's not in your interests or mine, Ferdi, for us to meet. Please don't try to see me . . . it was all my fault, I am the one who must apologise for making a fool of myself. Please don't feel guilty about me. It is for the best. Leonore."

She posted the letter to Ferdi in the box in the foyer on her way to the bar to meet Jean-Paul, watching it slide down the glass chute and out of her life. A glance at the hall clock told her she was an hour late, but Jean-Paul had promised to wait. A great feeling of relief lifted the burden from her heart as she hurried to meet him.

38

Ferdi drove slowly along the lower Corniche Road to Monte Carlo glancing occasionally at the red disc of the sun dipping into the already darkening sea. In a few minutes the vermilion and gold glow would change into the gauzy blue of a warm Riviera dusk.

It had taken a month of worry over Leonore's letter before he had made his decision. Then, without giving himself time to reconsider, he'd packed a bag and jumped in the car and driven down from Paris. He had behaved selfishly in the past and once he had decided that Leonore had a right to his love and support, he couldn't wait.

Now that he was almost there, his foot had eased off the accelerator and the big Mercedes idled along the winding road. It was returning to the Hostellerie he was afraid of. He'd walk into the pink marble hall and Lais would be there, lying in a pool of blood, Peach beside her, wailing those words into his soul, "She's dead, Ferdi, Kruger shot her . . ."

Grimly Ferdi pushed his foot down, sending the car surging forward in a growl of power. He could put off the moment no longer.

A young parking valet in the pink shirt of the Hostellerie la Rose du Cap took the Mercedes from him and Ferdi walked slowly up the broad steps. Everything was different. The big plate glass revolving doors were gone and in their place heavy carved wooden ones stood open to the warm night. The reception counter had been removed and in its place stood a graceful antique table and chairs. A young girl with polished bronze hair was sitting with her back to him, talking to the reception clerk. There was no one else around. Ferdi stared at the large handmade Portuguese rug that covered the centre of the big hall where Lais had fallen, its soft colours hiding the terrible memories. The hall was calm and serene, filled with the scent of flowers, and there was the sound of a piano from the bar.

It was as though nothing had ever happened. Life went on for those who were left, he thought grimly.

Waiting for Lais as usual, Peach turned from her conversation with the desk clerk, noting the man crossing the hall. It couldn't be . . . it wasn't possible . . . She could swear that it was Ferdi. And he was going to the bar – *to see Lais!* Oh my God! *After all these years.* Leaping to her feet she sprang for the door. She must get Grand-mère.

Walking into the buzz of conversation and laughter in the bar, Ferdi felt as though time had stood still. She sat on a high stool at the bar wearing a flowing dress of sea-green silk, her wild blonde hair flung back, laughing at a remark from someone in the crowd next to her. Someone was playing softly on the piano, singing Lais's favourite song . . . "I get no kick from champagne . . ."

Standing at the door of the crowded room, Ferdi felt as though he were in a waking dream. The voices around him came from the end of a long empty tunnel. "Leonore," he said puzzled. "Leonore?"

The crowd fell back as Ferdi pushed his way urgently towards her. With a jolt like an electric shock Lais's eyes locked with his and she was suspended between dream and reality, drowning in memories. He had come for her. Ferdi had come back for her at last. Trembling she accepted his kiss. "*Leonore,*" he murmured, "I'm so very sorry." Lais's wide blue eyes, dark with shock, stared into his.

Ferdi paced the terrace of Leonie's villa, listening grim-faced to the story of Leonore's deception. "But the fault was not all Leonore's, Ferdi," said Leonie quietly, "you never came back to find Lais, never even wrote. You offered no explanation to us, her family."

"I thought at first she was dead," he groaned, "then I heard rumours, I went to Paris to find the truth. And when Leonore told me she was dead, she was only confirming what I already believed. I knew you were not altogether happy about the marriage because I was German . . . I thought you blamed me. And you would have been right."

Leonie sighed. The whole sad saga had been one of misunderstanding. "The accident wasn't your fault," she said more gently. "When Lais told me that she loved you I gave you my blessing."

Ferdi stared broodingly out to sea, hands thrust in his pockets.

"Do you really love Leonore, Ferdi, is that it?"

"Leonore has been very good to me. I owe her the dignity of marriage."

"You and Leonore both took what you wanted – or what you needed – from each other," answered Leonie. Her slim hand slowly caressed the little brown cat on her knee. "And as you can see, Lais's life is different now. She'll not thank you for your pity."

Ferdi stared at her, agonised. Leonie seemed to read his mind, unmasking him, leaving him defenceless.

"I shall take care of Lais," said Leonie softly, "as I always have done. You are free, Ferdi, if that is the way you want it."

Ferdi turned away from her. "Forgive me," he said. He glanced back once when he reached the path. Silhouetted against the light on the terrace, Leonie stared out to sea. There was something indomitable about her slender figure, a strength that Ferdi envied. Turning on his heel he strode on.

39

No one would tell her anything! Peach marched angrily along the path around the Pointe St Hospice, with Leonie's cat, Chocolat, and her own cat, Ziggie, following at her heels like devoted hounds.

Leonore had gone off to Switzerland with Jean-Paul the very next day before Peach had even had time to ask any questions. Jean-Paul wanted to show Leonore the village where the new hotel would be built. And Lais had locked herself in her penthouse with only Miz as her link with the world. When Peach had asked her grandmother where Ferdi was, and what he had said and what had happened, and all the dozens of questions that were popping in her brain like bubbles in champagne, she got no real answer. Just that, "it was a mistake on Ferdi's part".

"But what about *Lais*?" cried Peach. "Ferdi came back for her, after all these years."

"I don't know why he came back," Leonie answered evasively.

"But *I* know," said Peach, "I saw him in Geneva. I told him that he should at least come back to see her, to explain . . . to say he's sorry."

Leonie stared at her aghast. "*You* told Ferdi to come here? Oh Peach, what have you done!"

Tears stung Peach's eyes as she clambered over the rocks, kicking angrily at pebbles in her path. What had gone wrong? Naturally it was a shock for Lais, but *Ferdi had come back*. Why couldn't the years have been just swept away and everything be as it was before – the way it would be in the romantic novels she read at school? The truth struck her like a blow. *Ferdi didn't want Lais because she couldn't walk.*

She couldn't bear it any longer. She *had* to find out the answers. And if Leonie wouldn't tell her, then she must ask Lais.

Miz refused to let her in. "Lais doesn't want to see anyone," she told her. "I'm keeping her in bed today. The doctor says she needs a good rest."

"But I need to see her," begged Peach. "Please Miz. It's only me – she'll want to see me, I know it."

"Not today Peach," said Miz firmly, closing the door.

She tried the next day and the next. Then Lais sent a message asking to see her grandmother. Peach hovered anxiously outside the door waiting for her. "Well?" she demanded as Leonie emerged.

"She'll see you now," said Leonie, "I told her that you'd seen Ferdi in Geneva. She understands now why he came." But Peach sensed that Leonie wasn't telling her everything.

Lais was sitting up in bed wearing a plain white nightdress with her long hair braided into pigtails. She wore no make-up and her lips looked pale without her usual bright lipstick.

"It's all right, Peach," she said with a little smile, "it wasn't your fault."

"Oh Lais, I just don't understand why he didn't come before."

"He thought I was dead," said Lais softly, "all these years he thought I was dead."

Peach stared blankly at her sister, a memory of her own words ringing in her ears . . . Lais was dying, there was blood everywhere, a wisp of smoke from Kruger's gun still pointed at them . . . every detail sprang to her mind like a painting on a gallery wall . . . "She's dead Ferdi," her voice was saying. "Kruger shot her. Lais is dead . . ."

Ferdi hadn't come back to find Lais because of her.

"You mustn't blame yourself." Lais's voice was calm. "Now his life can go on, and so can mine. All the ghosts are laid."

Looking guiltily at her sister, Peach wondered.

Lais's face was as pale as her hair as she lay on her special chaise-longue in her shady roof garden, an open book on her lap, pretending to read. But whenever Peach glanced at her Lais was gazing towards the blue horizon, with a remote expression, as though she were far away from here. She avoided the busy hotel and no longer went to the Terrace Bar at night. She ate in her suite with just Miz or Peach for company.

Peach knew that Leonie and Jim were worried about her. "I think we should send for Amelie," suggested Leonie.

"The girl doesn't need her mother," replied Jim, "she's pining for Ferdi."

Peach thought if that were true then it was up to her to do something about it. It was she who had got them into this position, only she could get them out. If only Leonore were here to talk to! Peach just couldn't understand why she'd gone away at such a crucial time.

It took her two days to compose the letter to Ferdi and when she finally posted it she immediately wished she could get it back. She had told Ferdi the truth. That Lais was no longer herself, that she was pining for him. That now their ghosts were laid, couldn't they at least write to each other . . . and that Ferdi must never tell anyone that she had written.

She was at the Hostellerie every morning by seven thirty when the post arrived, sifting anxiously through Lais's letters to see if there was one from him. A week later it was there, postmarked

Paris, with his name inscribed on the flap in blue ink above the words, Hotel Ritz. Peach carried it upstairs carefully, arriving with Lais's breakfast tray.

"A letter for you," she said, propping it on the tray in front of Lais. And unable to contain herself, "It's from Ferdi."

"Ferdi?" Lais's hand shook as she took it and tore it open.

It wasn't a very long letter, Peach noted, just one page, but it was taking Lais an awful long time to read it. At last Lais folded it and placed it on the table by the bed. "Well?" demanded Peach impatiently.

Lais smiled at her – just a half-smile, but it was encouraging.

"He was sorry he upset me but he was shocked to find me still alive. He would like me to write to him. Perhaps we can get to know each other again and then maybe one day, when we are used to the idea of each other again, we could meet . . ."

"Oh," sighed Peach, "oh Lais. Will you write back?"

"I'll see," she replied. "I'll think about it."

But glancing back as she dashed off to tell Leonie and Jim, Peach saw that Lais was reading the letter again. From then on letters came regularly from Ferdi, delivered with Lais's breakfast by Peach. She noticed that they were often postmarked Cologne or Essen and assumed that Ferdi was back working at the Merker offices. Of course Lais didn't tell her what the letters said, though Peach was consumed with curiosity. And Lais still avoided the Terrace Bar and the company of her old friends. Still she looked more like her old self in pretty silk trousers and soft shirts with a touch of coral lipstick brightening her pale face. And there was a different light in her eyes.

It was the week before Peach was due to leave for Florida to spend the last weeks of her summer vacation at home with her parents that the letter came from Paris. "Ferdi wants me to see him," Lais said, holding the thick letter tightly, "he's in Paris. Oh Peach. What should I do?"

Paris had the hot summer emptiness of a city deserted by its population for the beaches. Lais had refused the see Ferdi alone and, pushing her chair into the cool lofty halls of the Ritz where they were to meet Ferdi for tea, Peach was so nervous she felt sick. Lais looked beautiful, but different. Her hair was smoothed back and tied with a navy velvet bow and she wore a tailored white linen jacket from Chanel with navy trousers and navy suede shoes. But she smelled divinely of the same *L'Heure bleue* – the romantic very French perfume by Guerlaine whose name described that hour between sunset and dark – the blue hour – when star-crossed lovers met, made love and parted again . . .

Ferdi was at the table, waiting. He stood up as they arrived, taking Lais's hand in his and kissing it. "Lais," he said softly, "thank you for coming."

"It's good to see you, Ferdi." Her voice shook a little.

They looked at each other, assessing the effects of time and change, and Peach shifted nervously from foot to foot, not wanting to break their spell. "I'll be going," she said finally. "I'll come back in half an hour, Lais," and she sped off before they could stop her.

When she looked back they were sitting opposite each other at the round table. She couldn't see Lais's face, because her back was towards her, but Ferdi was smiling.

She was back in exactly half an hour, hurrying anxiously across the room to them.

"Peach," said Ferdi, "you didn't even give me a chance to say hello!" He really was a handsome man, thought Peach, even though he looked so much older now.

"Goodbye then, Ferdi," said Lais offering him her hand.

Taking her hand in both his he kissed it, and then he leaned forward and kissed her on the lips. "We'll see each other again?" he asked. Peach thought he looked so eager, as if he couldn't wait.

Lais's face as she said goodbye was calm, with none of the radiant joy Peach had expected.

"But why, Lais, why?" asked Peach in the car on the way back to the Ile St Louis. "Why not see Ferdi now?"

"You don't understand," said Lais, "Ferdi and I can never go back to where we were. We are different people. We both need time to see if what we're looking for in each other really exists."

But at least, thought Peach, it was a beginning and if Lais and Ferdi came together again, then she would at last be free of her guilt.

Part III

Part III

40

Peach knew she was going to enjoy Radcliffe college – and it wasn't just because there were all those good-looking Harvard "men" practically next door, though that helped.

Of course at first she'd felt like a "foreigner", because her life had been so different from the other girls', but she never spoke about the war or the Resistance in case they thought she was showing off. She bought pleated skirts and pale cashmere sweaters and loafers so that she would look exactly like they did, but somehow she still looked French.

After the first two semesters she grew bored with their "uniform" and began to find her own style. She wore skinny black sweaters and tight black ski pants with little ballet slippers, or full sweeping skirts and bright silk shirts with a fabulous belt from a smart Paris shop. Sometimes she swept her bronze hair up in a sophisticated style, thinking she looked very woman-of-the-world, and other times she let it hang loose around her shoulders in a glossy bronze cape, so that she looked fifteen instead of eighteen and very vulnerable. And when she was pressed for time, which happened a lot what with Radcliffe's hectic schedule and *her* hectic social life, she simply dragged on a battered broad-brimmed black felt hat managing to look delightfully dishevelled and hopefully slightly mysterious. Peach carried her books in a vast shabby leather bag from Vuitton and she wore Miss Dior perfume.

Life in her house at Radcliffe was a lot like life at L'Aiglon in Switzerland but without the restrictions. The girls were like sisters, sharing secrets and having endless, involved discussions about boyfriends, though whereas at L'Aiglon they'd discussed romance, here the talk was of sex. But of course they only *talked* about it. Nobody ever *did* it.

215

The little town of Cambridge was on the opposite side of the Charles River from Boston and its squares and greens and winding cobblestone or brick-paved streets were dotted with colonial church spires and bookstores and coffee houses where the girls from Radcliffe met the boys from Harvard. Peach found herself invited to football games and parties but she always went in a group with the other girls. She danced and flirted and got herself kissed in the front seat of battered sports cars but never in the back because that was dangerous territory. She'd heard stories of what happened in the back seats of cars and she wasn't ready for that. Besides, she was saving herself for Harry.

To her chagrin she hadn't yet contrived to meet Harry. She often went to stay with Melinda but whenever Peach was at Launceton Magna, Harry was away. He was off in Latin America researching a book, or tramping round Australia to gain authentic experience, or lecturing, dazzlingly, coast-to-coast across the USA and being lauded at literary lunches in New York and San Francisco and Washington DC.

Harry Launceton had made the news by winning three major literary prizes in two years and his name featured prominently in the gossip columns linked with a succession of beautiful and eligible girls. Peach scoured the newspapers, clipping out every mention of Harry and culling his photographs from magazines. He always looked handsome and aloof in a dinner jacket, with the lock of silky hair falling across his brow, and always with a different pretty girl on his arm. Peach severed the girls with a sharp snip of her scissors and stuck Harry's pictures into her fat scrapbooks, jammed with clippings. She knew Harry Launceton's every move.

The day she read about Harry's marriage to Augusta Herriot, Peach hurled her scrapbooks into the boiler-room fire in a storm of tears, condemning Harry's handsome face into the flames, hating him for his treachery.

"You're crazy," laughed her friends who knew the story. "You're obsessed with a man who doesn't even know you exist! The best thing you can do is to go out with Jack Mallory – he's been calling every night – lucky girl."

Jack Mallory's father was a self-made man who had ascended rapidly from local Philadelphia politics into Federal Government, treading his scruples underfoot and making a fortune in imported liquor on the way. His career had reached a pinnacle with his appointment as Washington's Ambassador to France – though he would have preferred London and the Court of St James – and the young Jack had lived for several years in Paris. When Jack was thirteen his father suffered a stroke and the family had returned to the US.

Jack was handsome in a square-jawed, blue-eyed Irish style and like his father, he knew what he wanted. Peach stood high on his list. He'd been laying siege to her for weeks, contriving to be there when she came out of class, walking with her across the Yard, dropping casual references to his time in France, and bombarding her with telephone calls – none of which she had answered.

"Why?" he asked, amazed, when Peach picked up the phone this time.

"What do you mean – why?"

"I must have called every night for a month and you always sent someone with an excuse. You were studying, or washing your hair."

"Well tonight my hair is clean," said Peach, "and I'm free. Are you the lucky man, or shall I accept someone else?"

"No, no, it's me. I mean yes. Oh gosh. What I mean, Peach, is can I take you out to dinner?"

Peach suddenly realised she was starving! She had been so upset about Harry that she'd barely eaten in a week and a vision of hot comforting food overwhelmed her. She could almost smell a tangy Boston chowder and taste the freshness of Maine lobster . . . "Lock-Obers," she said, knowing he could afford it, "at seven thirty."

Jack couldn't figure her out. At dinner she silently ate enormous quantities of food while he watched in amazement. "Would you like some more?" he asked politely as she spooned up the last of her baked Indian pudding with vanilla ice cream. Peach felt better. While Jack had struggled to make conversation she had been thinking about Harry and now she had it all straight in her mind. It didn't matter that he had married Augusta Herriot. After all, she and Harry hadn't really even met yet and she had her studies to finish. Radcliffe was important to her. She must learn all she could about literature so that she could discuss things with Harry on a proper intellectual level. When the time was right they were destined to meet and then she was sure everything would fall into its proper place, though she didn't bother to map out exactly what Augusta's place would be. Meanwhile she might as well go ahead and enjoy herself.

"That was wonderful," she said, smiling at Jack at last, "but no more, thank you." Encouraged by her smile Jack wondered if he dared take the hand that rested on the table. She wore a tiny gold ring on her little finger and a hoop of small brilliant diamonds on her index finger and her nails were painted a startling fuchsia.

"I think I must be getting back," Peach said as he took her hand. "I have an early class tomorrow."

It was snowing outside, blustering in thick little flurries that caught on their eyelashes and melted in their mouths as they skidded hand in hand along the slippery sidewalks to his white Jaguar sports car.

"Not quite up to a de Courmont," he apologised, holding open the door.

"Probably better than a de Courmont right now," she retorted, folding her long legs into the Jag and thinking of the de Courmont's recent lack of success.

Peach hummed along with Beethoven's Pastoral Symphony being broadcast from Boston's Symphony Hall while Jack concentrated on the icy roads.

He parked outside her house and slid an arm along the back of her seat. "When shall I see you?" he asked.

Peach could feel his warm breath on her face, and his Irish-blue eyes looked darker in the glow of the dashboard lights. Most of the girls at Radcliffe thought Jack Mallory was handsome. At six foot two with the wide shoulders and heavy build of an ex-football player he had a virile all-American appeal. With his white sports car and his rich family, Jack was a "catch" – and he knew it.

"Thursday perhaps," she said, "if I can manage to get free. Call me."

Thursday was five days away. "What about tomorrow," he pleaded, "or Monday, or Tuesday?" His tweed jacket was rough against her cheek as he pulled her closer. "Please Peach," he said, his mouth hovering over hers, "tomorrow?"

His lips were cool as the snowy night and then warm as his mouth forced hers open. Peach's heart lurched, thudding in her chest so that she thought he might hear it as their mouths clung together. What was he thinking? she wondered frantically as his lips moved over hers. What *did* men think when they kissed like this? Jack's fingers caressed her neck and she put a tentative hand to his face and he pulled her closer. Hastily she drew back.

"Don't go," he said, "beautiful Peach."

She was out of the car in a flash, slamming the door behind her, running up the steps to the house.

"I'll call you tomorrow," cried Jack standing by the car. He looked handsome in the snow, thought Peach, turning back for a last look. Tall, good-looking, all-American. What more could she need to practise on for Harry?

Lying in bed that night she went over the evening step by step . . . or at least the last part. She blushed at the thought of how she had ignored him and then she went hot all over remembering his kiss. It wasn't the first time she'd kissed a boy but the others had all been youthful teasing games. Jack Mallory was twenty-one and his kisses were serious. Jack Mallory had *wanted* her! And that strange tingling of the nerve-ends, the sudden sliding lurch in the pit of her stomach, the melting feeling meant that *she had wanted him*! All the girls in the dorm were virgins. No one – absolutely no one – played around, though they talked of it often enough for God's sake! Peach snuggled further under the blankets, staring out of the uncurtained window at the snow falling steadily. When he called tomorrow she'd answer the phone, and talk to him for a while. But she would make him wait until Thursday.

On their fifth date Jack took her to the Harvard/Yale game. It was Boston's turn to host and the crowds were out in force. Sipping whisky from Jack's silver flask, wrapped in a fur jacket and Jack's Harvard scarf, Peach crouched shivering in the stands trying to summon up enough warmth to cheer Harvard and laugh at Yale's bulldog mascot. She didn't envy the pretty cheerleaders prancing the frozen field one bit and she would have given anything, *anything* to be lying in a hot bath. Still, she felt pleased to be the girl with Jack Mallory, aware that other girls envied her. But when he touched her breast the way he had last night, Jack Mallory was *dangerous*.

She'd rationed their meetings because she knew she really should stop seeing him, but she dreamed about him even in class. Or rather, she dreamed of him kissing her . . . and more. Harry was still there waiting in the shadows of her dreams, but Jack was *immediate*. She hadn't understood about *desire*. When she thought of Harry she wanted to be with him holding his hand, talking to him, being allowed to just admire his beauty and catch the crumbs of his genius. Jack Mallory disturbed her.

When Harvard scored a winning touchdown in the last few seconds, the stands erupted in yells and cheers and Jack flung his arms around her exuberantly. "Great game," he yelled, "great, just great. Come on," he added noticing her frozen expression, "we'd better get you inside."

"Where are we going?" she asked, following him obediently.

"Where? To the parties of course!"

The Men's Bar at Lock-Obers opened its door to women only on the night of the Harvard/Yale game and its masculine mahogany sanctity had already been invaded by the revellers. Jack seemed to know everyone and Peach watched jealously as a pretty dark-haired girl flung herself into his arms and Jack kissed her firmly on the mouth. Quite a *long* kiss. "It's been a while," said the girl dreamily, her arms around his neck. "A long while," added Jack, his arms around her waist.

Turning away from them Peach stared angrily at the enormous painting of a naked woman over the bar. Jack had told her that when Harvard lost, the nude's ample charms were draped with a black scarf, but tonight the lady remained undraped, looking pleased and eager – just like the dark-haired girl. *Merde*, thought Peach. Now that she'd become aware of it, sex seemed to beckon from every angle. In a dark corner of the bar a couple embraced, and she watched them wonderingly.

"I'd like another Ward Eight," she said to Jack, interrupting the brunette's whispered conversation.

"Another?" he said. "That's pretty powerful stuff." Lock-Obers had concocted a Ward Eight cocktail to celebrate the election-eve success of one of Boston's most famous political wards years ago, mixing grenadine with a whisky sour to give it a pink glow.

"You forget that I'm French," said Peach haughtily, "I was drinking wine mixed with water when you were still on milk."

Jack disentangled himself from the girl, laughing. Pushing through the dark, smoky room, he elbowed his way through the crowd at the bar. "Two more Ward Eights," he called to the barman.

Noel Maddox hurried to fill the order. He must have made hundreds of them tonight. He'd been called in at the last minute to help with the big game crowds and welcomed the extra income. Every dollar helped towards his goal.

With a good degree from the University of Michigan under his belt he'd gained a place at the Massachusetts Institute of Technology. MIT was Boston's most prestigious science and engineering college and the closest place to heaven Noel could imagine. And each week studying in the hallowed halls of MIT brought him closer to his goal – just like each hard-earned dollar. In two years he would have a Master's Degree in Automotive Engineering. And in two years and one day he'd be back in Detroit calling on the personnel managers of US Autos and the Great Lakes Motor Corporation, as well as Ford and General Motors, selling himself. Only this time the price would be higher than that of the skinny kid in the stained blue overalls wielding his power drill and hopping in and out of those ever-moving assembly-line car bodies like some crazy ant!

Grimly Noel slammed the drinks on to the glossy mahogany counter and Jack Mallory glanced at him in surprise. "Thank *you!*" he commented, taking the glasses and pushing his way back to their crowded table.

Wiping the counter Noel caught the eye of the woman sitting at the bar. "Great game," she said, taking a cigarette from a pack of filter Camels and placing it between her lips.

Noel flicked his lighter, holding the flame to her. She was older but *very* attractive, blonde like Jeannie with that same long fall of straight hair and wide eyes. She wore no make-up and looked fresh and outdoorsy in the smoky bar room. A high-class woman up for the game.

"You don't work here full-time."

It was a statement not a question and Noel continued serving orders expertly. He'd worked as barman every night for six months at Boston's smart Copley Plaza Hotel – its grandeur had come as a shock after serving beer and whisky chasers at Nick's Saloon in downtown Detroit. In the Copley Plaza's luxurious surroundings he had begun to gain an insight into another world – a world of affluent ease, of self-assured men and elegant women. It was a world he wanted to be part of.

"You're too good for this," Hallie Harrison remarked.

Noel looked at her in surprise. Her comment had matched his thoughts exactly. "I'm an engineer," he said. "I'm at MIT."

"Another car freak," she said with a sigh.

Noel raised her eyebrows. "Another?"

"I'm from Detroit," she explained. "My husband is in advertising and he's associated with the motor industry. You might say it rules our lives," she added with a laugh. "As it will yours too one day, Mr Engineer."

"Noel," he said.

"Noel. I'm Hallie. Up for the big game with my husband. He's a Yale man and he seems to have disappeared again. It's not unusual," she added as Noel looked at her in surprise, "I often end up on my own."

Her widespaced eyes were greeny-blue with dark pupils and she had a smooth tanned skin – probably from some winter vacation in the Islands. Her breasts were full and round under her white cashmere sweater and she wore discreet pearls at her ears and throat. *Real* pearls, Noel knew. Her un-lipsticked mouth had a full passionate underlip and Noel suddenly longed to touch it. Hallie's small teeth gleamed prettily as she smiled at him. "Perhaps we could get together later, Noel," she said, "I'm at the Copley Plaza but it might be a bit too crowded there. Maybe you have an apartment?"

She was picking him up! Desire jolted through Noel and he poured himself a shot of Scotch, tossing it back and catching the warning frown of the head barman. He couldn't take her to his terrible room. "We could go to a motel," he said, "I'm free at midnight."

"Like Cinderella," laughed Hallie. "Tell me where, Noel, and I'll be waiting."

"I'll make a call," promised Noel, slipping out from behind the crowded bar to the staff phone. Noel prayed she had a car, he couldn't afford cabs *and* a motel.

Hallie was still sitting at the bar but there was a man with her. Noel stared at her companion with a shock of recognition.

Scott Harrison hadn't changed much, just a few extra pounds distributed here and there. The recognition was mutual. "So," Scott said, "the young runaway. We meet again. Noel, wasn't it?"

"Yes sir." Noel mixed a dry Martini and placed it in front of Scott, meeting his eyes. "This is on me," he said, "with thanks." He had remembered that dry Martini was Scott's drink because the one Scott had given him was the first liquor he had ever tasted in the first smart apartment he had ever seen – and he had slept in Scott's bed. Alone. He could tell Scott remembered too, by the wry smile that crossed his face.

"Did you ever make it to the assembly line?" asked Scott.

"Still do – in vacations. I'm at MIT – automotive engineering."

Scott whistled. "I had a feeling you had what it takes," he said, toasting him with his glass.

Hallie Harrison watched them quietly. "Any luck," she whispered as Scott turned away. "With the phone call?"

"Sorry," Noel said, avoiding her eyes, "no good."

Hallie gathered up her purse and her mink jacket. "I see," she said bitterly, "that's the way it is. I didn't understand."

"Wait," cried Scott, "hey, just a minute Hallie." Setting down his glass he elbowed his way through the crowds after his wife.

Removing their glasses Noel wiped the counter clean. Scott Harrison had helped him when he needed it most and he wasn't going to repay him by seducing his wife. Beautiful though she was.

41

Someone had turned out the lights and the room was dark and crowded and too smoky. Couples were wrapped around each other dancing smoochily to records and Peach had a hazy memory of being introduced to their host, but he had disappeared earlier in the evening with a big-breasted brunette he'd picked up at some other party. They had run out of whisky and people were drinking beer but no one actually seemed drunk.

She was wrapped in Jack's arms and they were dancing cheek to cheek barely moving and Peach wanted the night to go on for ever. Her breasts were pressed against Jack's chest and every now and then his mouth fastened on hers hungrily. Closing her eyes Peach clung to him. Radcliffe seemed light years away, and Harry was forgotten. Without speaking, Jack took her hand and led her out of the room.

Peach's legs suddenly didn't seem strong enough to support her and her head was whirling. He opened a bedroom door and they peered into the darkness. They could hear mysterious rustlings and giggles, and she drew back, pulling at Jack's hand. "We'll try another," he whispered, guiding her along the corridor, his arm around her waist, stopping every now and then to kiss her again. Peach leaned against the wall while Jack opened a door and looked in, closing it again quickly.

"No good," he whispered. "Tell you what, let's go to my place."

Peach's fuzzy head rang with shock at the idea. Then Jack's mouth closed on hers again. She sagged against him and Jack pressed his body closer. His hand was on her breast and he was kissing her. "Let's go," he whispered. Outside Peach gasped from the cold. She had forgotten her fur jacket. "I'll get it," said Jack diving back into the shadowy hall. Left alone Peach shivered in the icy night air, but it wasn't just the cold she was feeling, it was fear – fear of her own sexuality.

Peach could hear music and voices from other parties along the street and a couple ran past skipping over the rain puddles with whoops of joy. They looked young and carefree. The way she had been a few weeks ago – before Jack. But she didn't want to feel like this. She wanted to be young and silly and carefree too! If she went with Jack Mallory there would be no going back. Tears streamed down her cheeks as she began to run. She was eighteen years old, she was Peach, and she belonged to no one but herself.

"You all right, Miss?" the cab-driver said, screeching to a halt at her frantic signal.

"Yes, oh yes. I am now," Peach gasped, sinking shivering on to the shabby plastic seat.

"If anybody's been bothering you, Miss, I'll take care of him for you," said the burly Irish cab-driver, eyeing her sympathetically in his mirror.

"No. No thanks," sobbed Peach. "It's all right really. It was my own fault."

"Well . . . If you're sure. Where to then?"

Where to? She couldn't go back to Radcliffe at this hour. She remembered Uncle Sebastião. "Beacon Hill," she said firmly.

Sebastião do Santos's small narrow house on a sloping street on Boston's Beacon Hill was painted white with grey trim and had a view of the Charles River from its first-floor drawing room windows.

Huddled on his grey velvet sofa Peach sipped hot coffee, mopping away her tears every now and then with Uncle Sebastião's large white handkerchief.

Sebastião thought she looked like a twelve-year-old waif – but she was a waif in trouble and he hoped it wasn't as drastic as it seemed. He could remember playing this same role of helpful uncle with Peach's mother Amelie.

Sebastião do Santos had always been in love with Peach's mother but Amelie had married his wild younger brother. After Roberto's tragic death Sebastião had hoped Amelie would turn to him, but like a fool he had introduced her to Gerard de Courmont; he might have known they'd be right for each other. Once again Sebastião had had to watch a man he cared for marry the woman he loved.

The troubled young girl sitting opposite him now might easily have been *his* daughter if he hadn't played the game of love like a loser. Unlucky in love – lucky in money – wasn't that what they said? It was certainly true of him. He was one of America's foremost architects. Large international companies as well as wealthy private individuals vied for his services. He was an honorary professor at Harvard and his name was followed by so many letters they had spoiled the perfect symmetry of his letterhead, so that now the plain white pages were inscribed simply in the lightest grey – "Sebastião do Santos". And that was it. The address and telephone number were in minute lettering at the foot of the page. Sebastião thought that the design of the paper was exactly like the lifestyle he had created for himself. Simple perfection.

He sighed as Peach's hand shook and coffee spilled on the immaculate velvet of the pale grey sofa. Perhaps perfection needed a stain or two to humanise it. And at least the stain would always remind him that Peach came to him when she was in trouble.

"Do you feel like talking yet?" he asked, taking the cup from her.

"What about school?" whispered Peach, worried.

"I already called them, told them you were safe with me and that it was all my fault. I said you thought I had already asked permission for you to stay out."

Peach heaved a sigh of relief. "Thank you. Radcliffe means a lot to me. I'd hate to lose it for a silly mistake."

"Is that all it was then, a silly mistake?"

"Oh Uncle Sebastião," she cried, hurling herself at his feet and leaning her damp cheek against his knee, "I almost made such a fool of myself."

"Well thank God for the 'almost'," he replied drily.

"His name's Jack Mallory," said Peach, the story spilling from her, "I'd never met anyone like him before. I mean he's older, and he's not like the boys I'm used to . . . with them it was just fun. *You know*. But with Jack I felt different. It was like a battle between this new person who wanted him so badly and the old me who never wanted anything to change."

Sebastião's hand stroked her thick glossy hair absently as she told him the story. Poor little girl. Life's first lesson had been a hard one for her. "You're young, Peach, enjoy the fun of parties and dating," he said, "you'll know when you meet the right man. And then you won't need to run away."

Peach sank back on her heels, relieved. "I've already met him," she murmured yawning. She was so *tired* suddenly. But now everything was all right again and her life was back on course.

42

Noel's room was in the basement of a grey five-floor walk-up in a littered treeless dead-end street. Its two advantages were that in return for janitorial duties it was free – and it was located next to the boiler room and therefore was always warm. It was also within a mile of MIT and saved on subway fares.

It hardly mattered that the room was small and dark, it suited Noel's needs. It contained a single burner hot plate, a scarred saucepan and a mug stained brown from endless cups of coffee when he stayed awake all night to study. There was one clean plate, one knife, one spoon and one fork, a can-opener next to a couple of cans of soup and a jar of instant coffee. An old iron-frame bed stood in the far corner, its dingy mattress covered with a blue sleeping bag, and behind the door hung an old tweed overcoat bought second-hand for five dollars from a departing student and which also served Noel as a bathrobe on his treks to the bathroom two flights up.

A scarred table under the sunless window was where Noel worked, losing himself in the beautiful logic of engineering, and while one part of his agile brain tracked scientific theses and mapped rapid calculations, absorbing like a sponge all that could be poured into it, another part of him would conjure up his dream automobile. Not all at once, of course, just piece by piece. He'd analyse the radiator on the latest model Ford and then figure out what he would do to improve its design, he'd spend hours re-designing the seating of the new Chrysler or analysing the Jaguar's aerodynamics. He'd make improvements to hub caps and bumpers as well as engines.

He covered large thick expensive sheets of paper with sketches and calculations, filing them neatly in a big black portfolio. And he spent as many hours as possible at MIT, working in the libraries when he wasn't in class or at his job as a barman. Noel had a brief, businesslike acquaintance with his fellow students but he was still the loner. Except with women.

To his surprise expensive upper-class girls found him attractive. They liked his off-hand attitude, mistaking his silence for a smouldering sexuality. But Noel kept his mouth shut because he had no small talk and he didn't know how to act with girls. They took him as he was – raw and muscular, silent and virile.

They'd pick him up in the bar of the Copley Plaza or in the university libraries or in coffee houses and it was because of them that Noel became aware of his need to do something about his lack of culture. He knew nothing of the latest novels or biographies but now he began to borrow them from the libraries, trying to make time to read them. He had never been to an art gallery in his life and his first visit to Harvard's Fogg Art Museum so overwhelmed his senses that he went every day for a month, spending exactly one allotted hour of his time there, absorbing paintings so intently that he seemed to be imprinting each brushstroke on to his memory. He bought the cheapest student seats for the Boston Symphony and, drunk on the power of music, he went as often as he could afford, losing himself in an emotionally uncharted world.

He met Cassie Plumpton at Symphony Hall. Noel had noticed her there on a couple of occasions before she spoke to him. You couldn't miss Cassie. She was twenty-nine and told him she was considered by her smart Boston family to be "on the shelf". She wasn't exactly pretty but she was so beautifully groomed that she always looked attractive. She had short, dark, curly hair, fluffy as a poodle's, large brown eyes and a penchant for wearing shocking pink.

"Who are you?" she demanded, approaching him in the foyer of Symphony Hall. "I seem to see you *everywhere*. Don't you work at the Copley Plaza?"

Over a drink Noel told her the old story about his parents being killed in an accident years ago and having to make it on his own through college and MIT and she was sympathetic but not really interested. Cassie liked his rugged looks and unintentionally rough manner. "You're like someone who's been locked out of civilisation," she'd told him after their first time in bed together, "an urban peasant!"

Noel despised himself for not knowing how to behave, even in bed. Where did you go to learn the sort of manners these women expected?

"But you mustn't ever think of changing," Cassie warned him, "it's part of your charm."

They'd been seeing each other for several months on and off – whenever Noel permitted himself to break free from his work schedule. He took her to art galleries and coffee houses and Cassie took him to the theatre and for dinner in out-of-the-way little restaurants. Noel didn't mind the fact that Cassie paid for dinner, but he was self-conscious about his shabby clothes; yet when she suggested she take him to Brooks Brothers for some shirts and maybe a new jacket, he was furious. "I am what I am," he snarled, "I've paid for everything I've ever had by working for it and until the time I can afford better, I'll wear what I have."

"I don't mind, if you don't," she replied. "I just wanted to give you a present."

Then out of the blue she asked him to escort her to the party tonight. "It's Boston's welcome to Harry Launceton," she told him. "You know – HARRY LAUNCETON?"

Noel shrugged. He'd never heard of him.

"He's to be Harvard's youngest ever writer-in-residence. Because of his social background – he's *Sir* Harry now that his father has died – and the fact that he's probably a genius – to say nothing of his good looks – Boston society is taking him to their bosom. It's black-tie, darling, so you'll need a dinner jacket."

Noel had often played the role of hired barman at these sort of parties, handing around drinks on a silver tray, but this would be his first time ever as an invited guest. Cassie was part of smart Boston society and he knew he would be meeting her friends.

He shaved carefully, hoping his beard wouldn't grow in too fast and give him that blueish unshaven look, and inspected his appearance in the bathroom mirror. He had an athlete's body, medium height, wide-shouldered, well-muscled – and one thing he had learned from his expensive girl friends was how to use it to good effect. Dressed in the hired tux that didn't fit too well Noel thought he looked pretty good – but he still didn't look like a man born to a dinner-jacket lifestyle. Turning uneasily from the too-honest mirror, Noel headed for the door. One day he'd be a part of that smart society. For tonight he'd just have to pretend.

*　　　*　　　*

Sebastião do Santos was waiting for Peach in the bar of the Copley Plaza and as usual she was late, though after the way she'd bombarded him to get her invited to Harry Launceton's party the least she could do was to be on time.

The evening would be a mixture of academia, publishing and old Boston snobbery and Sebastião would have declined if it hadn't been for Peach. "How wonderful," she'd said, laughing at Sebastião's bewilderment, "oh how simply marvellous. I've been waiting for this for years."

Sebastião spotted her by the door of the bar. You couldn't miss her in that dress. Jesus Christ!

"Here I am," said Peach, kissing his cheek.

"So I see."

"Well, what do you think?" Peach looked at him doubtfully. She'd spent hours deciding on this dress, wondering if she had the nerve to wear it. She wanted Harry to notice her and the strapless scarlet dress was cut very low – by Boston standards anyway – and its slender skirt, scalloped like a tulip petal, hugged her as though silk knew it belonged next to her skin. Sebastião was uncomfortably aware that Peach was the centre of the bar's attention.

"I'm not sure about the dress," he said.

Peach lifted her chin haughtily. "Nobody would think twice about wearing a dress like this in Paris."

"But I bet you did," Sebastião said with a smile, "you look terrified of it. Let me tell you a little story, Peach. When your grandmother was a young girl she was about to go on stage for the very first time and she was wearing a very skimpy costume. She hung back in the wings, shivering and afraid, but she had to go on – she needed the work and the money. It meant survival to her. Something one of the other showgirls said changed her whole life. 'If you have to do this,' she told her, 'be proud of yourself. Stand tall, put your chin up, pretend you're a queen.' And it seems to me, Peach, that if you're going to wear that dress then that's how to carry it off."

Peach stared at him, amazed. "You're right," she said with a grin, "of course you're right! Come on, Uncle, we'll be late for Harry's party." Head up, back straight, and with a queenly smile to the curious drinkers in the bar, she strode towards the door, every eye upon her.

Harry Launceton really didn't like parties. He much preferred a quiet dinner with a few friends to this mob-scene. However his wife

Augusta, over there in the corner talking to that sharp old dame in the brown lace with the immense rubies decorating her withered chest, loved parties. It was for her sake that he'd agreed to come. "So that we can meet everyone all in one go, darling," Augusta had said. "After all, we're going to be living here for a year. It's all right for you," she'd gone on, "immersed in your work and meeting all those people at Harvard, but I shall be stuck in that big rented house on my own."

Harry had given in and here they were. He smiled politely at the persistent woman next to him, who wanted him to speak at the very next meeting of her little literary circle, and avoided the tall, distinguished-looking man who looked like a banker in a Hollywood movie, who asked him how much money there was in publishing these days, pushing his way through the crowd to the buffet where at least there were a couple of pretty girls.

Augusta Launceton watched her husband through narrowed eyes. She and Harry had known each other since childhood, their fathers had been at school together and her brother had been at Oxford with Harry. They had always moved in the same social circles but everyone had been surprised when he'd married her. Quiet little Augusta Herriot. So competent and charming. "That's exactly why I'm marrying you," Harry had laughed. "Women are dangerous creatures. At least with you I know what I'm getting." And of course Augusta understood the importance of Harry's work. But Harry also liked pretty women.

Noel stood quietly at Cassie's side, taking in the splendour of the high-ceilinged room and its pale silk-lined walls and solid antique furniture. He refused champagne and canapés, he was afraid to drink anything in case it loosened his tongue. Cassie kept trying to draw him into the conversation but, beyond admitting he was at MIT Noel managed to avoid their probing questions. He saw how the game worked, though, how all these people meshed into the same network. "I hear you're from Ohio, do you know the so and so's?" they said, or, "I went to prep school with a guy from there, name of so and so – father's in railroads. Know him?" If you did then you had your credentials and you were accepted into the magic circle.

Wait, thought Noel, *just wait! One day he'd show them all he didn't need a past to qualify for their world.*

He noticed the girl, at once. She wore a red dress and she was looking around the room with a breathless look of anticipation on her familiar face. Peach de Courmont hadn't changed that much. Of course she was very tall now, taller than Noel, but she still had that mass of shiny reddish-brown hair and the eager little girl expression. Even in that wild red dress she didn't look more than sixteen. She still looked like the golden girl of his childhood dreams. His symbol of freedom. The man with her was older, handsome, distinguished. A man at ease in his surroundings and Noel watched them jealously. But of course Peach de Courmont wouldn't even notice him, much less remember him from their one chance meeting at the Maddox Charity Orphanage seven years ago. He looked different now. *He was different!* The orphanage was buried in his past and no one in his life would ever know about it.

When she saw Harry Launceton Peach's heart pounded so fiercely she thought she might faint, but then a wave of pure happiness swept through her. Harry was here and her plan was finally coming to fruition. Edging through the crowd she moved closer to him.

Harry stared at the stunning girl in the red dress hovering on the fringe of the circle around him, trying to concentrate on the professor who was explaining Harvard's literary tradition to him.

"Mr Launceton," called Peach, her voice breathy with excitement. "Hello. We've met before at Launceton Magna . . ."

She was enchanting, a nymph in scarlet silk with a tumble of hair the colour of tawny port. Feline and feminine and dangerously young . . . "I know!" Harry said holding out his hands to her. "The cricket match."

Peach gazed at him in delight, both her hands captured in his. "I was with Melinda Seymour. I didn't think you'd remember."

Ignoring the professor, Harry tucked Peach's arm through his, drawing her from the crowd. "How could I forget? You looked like some exotic creature lost on England's docile green lawns. You belonged in a tropical rain forest running barefoot and wrapped in animal skins or on a soft white beach, naked but for a lei of scarlet hibiscus flowers."

"Do all writers talk like this?" she asked, mystified.

"This one does," Harry replied with a smile, "it's a hell of a lot better than answering questions on how much money I make from writing and dodging old ladies who want me to speak at their little literary lunches. Now. Exactly who are you?"

Standing by the long windows he turned her to face him and the touch of his hands on her bare shoulders made Peach shiver. "I'm

Peach de Courmont," she replied, her voice sounding very small in the buzz of conversation around them.

Harry's eyes locked with hers. "And where are you to be found, Peach, if not on a sub-tropical island?"

"I'm at Radcliffe," she murmured, feeling inadequate for not living up to his exotic image of her. "I'm reading English."

Harry laughed. "Another one," he cried. "They all love me for my words, never myself."

"I don't," said Peach truthfully, "I can't read your books. It's you I love."

Augusta Launceton downed her glass of champagne and headed purposefully towards her husband. When Harry laughed like that it meant he was enjoying himself and that girl was too pretty to ignore. "Harry," she called. "Harry, we really must leave now. We're going on to the Westmacotts' for dinner."

"We shall meet again," he whispered to Peach. "Radcliffe, wasn't it?"

"Yes," she breathed, "oh yes."

"I'll call," he said, his eyes sealing their secret.

Blushing, Peach avoided Augusta's piercing glance. She felt hot and excited and a little bit frightened as she made her way to the buffet to get a glass of wine. Her eye caught that of the dark-haired man standing with a crowd of people and she had a sudden feeling that she knew him. It wasn't the kind of face you forgot.

Peach circled the buffet. Maybe love made you hungry. Or excitement. Or it could be that she hadn't eaten that day? Oh Harry, Harry, she sang to herself, how beautiful you are, and how clever. She tried to remember what he'd said about her, about jungles and tropical flowers in England's docile greenness. But what about his *scary* wife? The sweet English rose with a backbone of iron! "I'll call," Harry had said. She would live by the phone tomorrow.

Who *was* that man? He kept staring at her and it really made her feel quite strange. He was part of the crowd – but not really. He looked so uneasy. Yet she was sure she knew him. She *had* to find out who he was.

"Hello," she said confidently to Noel, "I'm Peach de Courmont. I'm sure we've met, I just can't remember where . . .?"

"You must be mistaken," said Noel, uncomfortably. His voice sounded harsh in the sudden silence and Cassie and her friends stared at them interestedly.

232

Peach stared into the shadowy grey eyes and the bony jutting face of the boy at the car window all those years ago. "*Of course!*" she cried into the waiting silence. "The Maddox Charity Orphanage. *You're Noel Maddox!*"

Noel felt sure the whole room must have heard her. Now everyone knew his carefully covered secret. Everyone knew of his non-existent beginnings. They all knew that he was a non-person. His fists were clenched, and his face frozen with anger as Noel stared into Peach's innocent blue eyes. *He wanted to kill her!*

43

Peach was curled up in the chair pretending to read *Past Configurations* by Harry Launceton and waiting for the phone to ring. Just holding his book and looking at the words he had written made her feel close to him. Harry had taken his passion for the myths and legends of the past and transformed them under a microscope of present-day psychological beliefs into "a novel of depth and wit, dissecting human relationships with a visionary sword" – or so the reviewers had said. Peach felt proud to be the one who was waiting for his call.

For the tenth time she looked at Harry's photograph on the bookjacket. He was smiling, his eyes narrowed against the sunlight, and he looked boyish and very handsome. Closing her eyes, Peach relived their meeting at the party for the hundredth time. Harry had looked exactly as she remembered him. If only Augusta hadn't been around she felt sure he would have whisked her away there and then . . . Oh dear, she didn't want to think about his wife. The phone rang and she hurtled across the hall to be there first, but the call was for one of the other girls. Sagging with disappointment she padded back to her chair.

She hardly dared go to classes these days in case she missed his call and she left endless messages as to where she could be found, and that if a man phoned to say she would call him back if he would leave his number. But Harry didn't call.

It must be Augusta, decided Peach, making excuses for him, or he was busy in his new role at Harvard and probably in the throes of writing some wonderful book. Genius couldn't be harnessed to time. But thinking it over in bed she decided that it wasn't going to be quite as easy as she had imagined. If she wanted Harry, she would have to do something about it.

She called him the next morning and got Augusta on the phone. "Hello," said Peach nervously, "I'm calling for the Radcliffe Literary Society. I wonder if I could speak to Mr Launceton, please?"

"Hello?" said Harry.

His voice sounded even deeper on the phone. "This is Peach de Courmont," she told him.

"Really?" he sounded pleased. "Is it really you? I thought it was the Radcliffe Literary Society."

He didn't mention about not calling her and Peach bit her lip nervously. "The society was wondering if you would be able to fit in a talk for us? On your new book, *Past Configurations.'*

"Have you read it?" he sounded amused.

"Yes." Twisting the telephone cord around her fingers Peach added, "But I admit I didn't understand it. That's why I need you to explain."

Harry laughed. "Well then, if you *need* me, I'll have to see what I can do. Look, there's a gap in my diary on the eighth – that's next Tuesday night. How does that suit your society?"

"Wonderful," gasped Peach. She hadn't expected it to be so soon. "That would be perfect."

"Good. About seven thirty. Just drop me a note and let me know where. See you then."

The phone buzzed emptily in her hands and Peach stared at it in surprise. He hadn't even mentioned the party where they'd met, or not calling her or anything. But she'd be seeing him – next Tuesday night.

Harry sat on a sofa being plied with very small glasses of very bad sherry by very charming girls. He'd talked for an hour about his life, his career and his latest book and they'd listened raptly and afterwards some of them had even asked intelligent questions. It had all been most enjoyable – and young Peach de Courmont looked dazzling in tight black pants and a high-necked black sweater. She had braided her hair and wore no make-up and looked quite different from the confident beauty in the revealing red dress. Lovely. Quite lovely. Harry sipped the terrible sherry and pulled a face.

Peach had heard that Harry didn't drive a car because he found driving on the right-hand side of the road confusing and had once almost crashed. "I'd be pleased to drive you home, Mr Launceton," she said, "when you're ready."

"That's very kind of you," he replied looking at his watch.

Squashed into her small, sporty, dark blue de Courmont, Harry suddenly associated the names. "Not *that* de Courmont?"

"'Fraid so," she replied.

Harry whistled. "My father told me he once saw old Gilles de Courmont – 'Monsieur' – at the Hôtel de Paris in Monte Carlo. He'd survived a terrible car crash and a stroke and he still looked stronger than ten men. How did he build his empire – through a reign of terror?"

"Probably," said Peach, "but I heard he was always kind to his servants. They stayed with him for years."

Harry laughed. "You must admit he was a scandalous man," he said, "all those court cases and delicious women."

Peach switched on the ignition so she could see his face in the lights of the dashboard. His arm lay along the back of her seat, just touching her shoulder, and he was looking at her.

"The court case was about my mother," she said abruptly, "and the delicious woman in his life was my grandmother."

"Sorry," said Harry, squeezing her shoulder, "I didn't mean to unlock the family secrets. It's the writer in me, I pry into people's lives."

"I can't tell you the secrets," said Peach, "because I've never heard the true story. But all my life I seem to have heard rumours, whispers, snatches of conversation that suggest the tip of an iceberg of some monumental romance between the two of them. Monsieur died before I was born and Leonie never talks about him. I did ask her once, but all she said was that if she ever thought I needed to know, then she would tell me."

Harry leaned back in his seat with an exaggerated sigh. "Then I shall never know," he said.

"And I don't know where you live," said Peach. "I'm supposed to be driving you home. Unless you'd like to take me for a pizza.

I'm starving." Harry's eyes met hers. "I can tell you more stories of the scandalous de Courmonts," she promised.

"You're on," he agreed, laughing.

Peach drove to Pansy's Pizza in Back Bay, a place where she knew few of her fellow-students were likely to be. Or Harry's acquaintances. The restaurant was typically dark and Italian, with red-chequered cloths and dripping candles in Chianti bottles. In a high-backed red velvet booth she felt in a private world with Harry. He ordered a pizza for her and a bottle of Barolo which they sipped out of thick greenish glasses. She barely touched the pizza.

"I thought you were starving," he complained, leaning forward to touch her thick braid. "It's the colour of conkers on the autumn chestnut trees at Launceton," he commented.

Harry continued to stare at her, sipping the wine. "You're a beauty, Peach de Courmont, and I should warn you I'm susceptible to beauty."

"I know," she said. "You write about it in your books. Beautiful women. And making love."

They gazed at each other in the flickering candlelight. He thought her eyes were the most luminous blue he had ever seen. "You shouldn't believe everything you read," he said lightly, "writers never write about themselves." She just smiled at him. "Time to go," he said, signalling the waitress.

"Thank you," said Peach, "for the pizza and the wine."

She was lovely, he thought, as they drove back across the Charles Bridge, and she was very tempting. Her smile as he said goodbye was wistful, and he almost succumbed and kissed her. But he didn't. Peach de Courmont was a very dangerous young woman.

It seemed suddenly that she was everywhere. He saw her at a lecture, sitting on the aisle near the back of the hall wearing a scarlet sweater. And when he was walking through Harvard Yard with old Professor Gunniston he spotted her all bundled up in a tweed jacket and wound around with enormous scarves. She looked cold, as though she'd been waiting for ages for someone, and he waved to her. Then she was at the symphony looking very French in a blue suit with her wonderful hair piled in gleaming waves on top of her pretty head sitting next to a nice-looking young man and another couple. He spoke to her briefly at a reception for some other visiting literary luminaries but had no time for more than a mere "How are you?" And then she was at Sebastião do Santos's dinner.

"I'm your hostess," she told him smiling. "Sebastião is my uncle." She looked delicious in a black silk dress, long-sleeved and tight-skirted, that should rightly have been worn by a woman twice her age. On Peach it looked both demure and sexy at the same time. He could feel Augusta prickling with irritation at his side. Poor Augusta never looked like that in black – or any other colour. Augusta was at her best in tweeds and sweaters, rain upon her cheek, walking a brood of golden labradors at Launceton.

Harry sat next to Peach at dinner, with Augusta at the bottom of the table on Sebastião's right. "I keep seeing you," he said. "Every time I turn my head you're there."

"That's because I'm chasing you," said Peach demurely. She'd decided that honesty was the best policy with Harry, since subtlety was getting her nowhere. It had taken her weeks of persuasion for Uncle Sebastião to give this party and it was her only chance.

Harry wondered if she could be serious? God, she had the bluest eyes, and that wonderful skin, touched with gold. She was very, very tempting . . .

"Well," he said lightly, "you may just have captured me."

Flicking a careful glance at their dinner companions to make sure they were engrossed in their own conversations, Peach said to him, "Will you meet me later – after this? I need to talk to you."

Harry sipped his wine – a good Haut-Brion. Sebastião do Santos's taste in wine was as excellent as in everything else. Could she possibly know what she was saying? And how old was she anyway – no more than seventeen, eighteen maybe?

"Please," said Peach, resting her hand lightly on his knee.

"Where?" he asked.

"I'll write down the address and give it to you after dinner."

He couldn't concentrate after that. She wasn't the first girl to run after him, in fact, without being conceited he was used to it. It got a bit boring sometimes, when he'd really rather be concentrating on his work, but he'd always been susceptible to a pretty face. But Peach de Courmont was more than that. She had a luminous quality – a sort of shining innocence – even though she was playing dangerous grown-up games.

"I feel I've been a poor guest tonight," he told Sebastião as he was leaving.

"No doubt another great novel brewing in your mind," said Sebastião shaking his hand, "but you were more amusing than my usual company."

On the way home Harry told Augusta he was going to his office to finish up some work and she dropped him off there. Taking the piece of paper Peach had slipped into his jacket pocket he called a cab and was there within ten minutes.

"It's a friend's apartment," Peach said, taking his coat. A fire burned in the grate and she'd put a Vivaldi concerto on the record player. One lamp was lit by the armchair and she chose to sit under it. In its pinkish light her hair, which she wore loose tonight, looked the colour of tawny port decanted against a flame. Harry felt he could paint her in words. Golden flesh. But not sapphires for eyes – maybe those old-fashioned Victorian paste brooches that had so much more brilliance were more apt. Eyes like blue paste brooches didn't sound too good for a writer-in-residence and literary genius. He'd have to do better than that. What was he thinking of! He'd come here because she'd asked him and he assumed she wanted him. And he certainly wanted her.

She handed him a glass of the wine she'd taken from Uncle Sebastião. "The Haut-Brion," he said, recognising it.

Peach sank to the floor at his feet. Wrapping her arms around her knees she said, "I wanted you to come here because I have something to tell you." Taking a deep breath, she hugged her knees even tighter. "I'm in love with you, Harry Launceton. I've loved you since I first saw you at the cricket match at Launceton Magna. I know it sounds foolish and you'll think I'm just a silly schoolgirl, but there it is. I had to tell you. It's no accident that you see me everywhere you go. It's because I follow you."

Harry was stunned into silence and Peach stared nervously at the rug. "I want you to marry me," she said. The Vivaldi quivered in the background, its gentle seventeenth-century melodies gilding the silence.

"Come here," said Harry holding out his hand, "sit next to me on the sofa." The way she uncoiled herself in a single movement and rose to her feet was the most graceful action he had ever seen.

"I'm a married man, Peach," he said gently. "And I'm also a man married to his work."

"I know that," she said, her eyes fixed unwaveringly on his.

Her deep smooth lids with their long curve of lashes closed as his mouth fastened on hers and Harry felt her sigh. Her mouth was silken soft, pliable and tender. The kind of mouth that would bruise with passion.

She clung to him, her arms locked around his neck as his hand slid across the smooth upward curve of her breast.

Unlocking her hands, he stood up and took off his tie and unbuttoned his shirt. He took a drink of the wine and offered her a sip. "No," she said, "I want to remember all this. I want to know that it wasn't just the wine . . ." She sat curled up on the sofa watching him as he undressed, her eyes catching the glow of the flames. And when he was naked she made no move to touch him. "Let me help you," he said gently, unbuttoning the sophisticated black dress. Underneath she wore girlish white cotton pants and bra and she looked suddenly vulnerable. But as he slid the straps from her shoulders she reached up and kissed him. When she was naked they lay on the rug in front of the fire. Its flames had sunk into a red glow and in its reflection with her golden skin she looked like a child of the sun. She didn't touch him, just lay there, staring at him with those huge luminous eyes, searching beyond the moment. He stroked her gently, trembling with his own passion, caressing her soft mound with its drift of soft hair. "Are you sure Peach," he whispered, his mouth on her breast, "are you sure this is what you want?"

"Yes," she breathed. "Oh yes, Harry. This is *truly* what I want."

44

Peach woke up with her arms around Harry, his head resting on her shoulder. Cautiously, so as not to wake him, she wriggled her left arm free, wincing as the blood circulated through its numbness shooting prickles of pins and needles through her fingers. Remembrance rushed through her body in a wave of happiness as she gazed at Harry's hands, remembering how they had caressed her, and then, daringly, her eyelids travelled the length of his slim muscular body. How strange love was, she thought, that it could transform a man's body into an instrument of pleasure. She longed to touch him but was afraid of waking him. Somehow watching Harry's sleeping face was more intimate than looking at his nakedness. He slept with the slightly open-mouthed contentment of a child, breathing evenly, his smooth hair falling over his forehead. A faint stubble of darker beard had appeared on his chin and he looked more vulnerable than his confident daytime self. Peach wanted to kiss him.

Last night Harry's face had looked so different. She remembered how it had contorted in the final moments of his passion as though in agony. She had kept her eyes wide open, wanting to remember their very first time for ever. And if her passion had seemed less than his, she put it down to the fact that she was a virgin.

Harry had been shocked. "Why didn't you tell me?" he groaned afterwards.

"But I thought you'd know," Peach said, angry that he might have thought otherwise. "I don't do this with everybody, you know."

"Of course you don't," he said contritely, "I didn't mean that. I meant – well, I should have taken more care with you."

"You mean I'll have a baby?" asked Peach.

Harry laughed. "No," he told her, "you won't. And a bloody good thing too."

"I don't want a baby," said Peach, nuzzling his neck, "I only want you."

He kissed her. "Well, you've got me."

"Not just this. I want to marry you."

Harry laughed. "This is better than marriage – we'd only get bored with each other."

"Like you and Augusta?"

"Let's not talk about Augusta. Let's talk about us." And he kissed her again and again. Peach was more daring this time and she ran her hand down his body. "It's so different," she'd said wonderingly, curling her hand around him and feeling him stir again with new life.

"You're no good for me, you know that," Harry had said, pulling her across him so that her length covered his. Then he'd run his hands down the clean golden line of her back and across the curve

240

of her hips. "You're too beautiful, Peach de Courmont, and you're too young and far, far too distracting."

Now, watching him sleep, Peach thought she would remember him just like this, for ever.

"You're staring at me," said Harry accusingly.

Laughing, Peach kissed his closed lids. "I'm *so glad* you're awake," she murmured, her kisses travelling to his mouth and down his neck to the base of his throat. Her fingers tugged at the light brown hair on his chest as her mouth continued down across his belly, coming to rest in the crisp darker hair. Lazily her tongue travelled the length of his erection and instinctively she took him in her mouth.

"God," murmured Harry, "oh my God, who taught you to do that? Wonderful, wonderful . . . Peach."

"I have to run," he said, climbing out of the shower and towelling dry. Picking up his watch he glanced at it. "Seven thirty. I'll go straight to my office. I'll tell Augusta I worked all night – I often do."

Peach watched him jealously. "Shall I see you tonight?"

"Can't make it tonight, sweetness, there's a dinner or something." Thrusting his feet into polished brown moccasins he tied his tie expertly without looking in the mirror. "Look," he said gently, "I'll call you sometime this evening." Putting his finger beneath her chin he tilted her face to his. "All right, Peach?"

"Yes," she said quietly. Harry turned and waved as he closed the door. "Love you," called Peach. But she didn't think he heard.

45

Lais stared at the stack of Ferdi's letters in the drawer of her desk. They were all carefully re-folded in their white envelopes and tied with red ribbon. There were eight letters for every month – two each week. Even at first when she didn't reply, Ferdi had continued to write about his life. Not about *them*, just day-to-day things. Ferdi told her about how he'd ridden in the forest and seen a badgers' set, about re-planting the ancient myrtle whose great sprawl of roots was undermining the south wall. He described the castle with its turrets and towers and the commanding view of the river Rhine, and the house in Cologne that was still dark and stuffy the way it had been when he was a boy, filled with heavy old furniture and dark velvet hangings he'd always hated. He wrote about the long tedious business meetings at Essen and Bonn and the complex decisions to be made, and he described the Merker steel mills, like caves in hell, where slabs of white-hot metal licked with fiery orange flame hissed angrily as they were plunged into vats of cool water, boiling it instantly with their heat and sending up clouds of scalding steam. Ferdi told her everything about his life. But he didn't write about the past and he never mentioned the future.

Today, as she did once every month, Lais was to be driven to Paris to meet him. Ferdi stayed at his apartment at the Ritz and Lais went home to the Ile St Louis. After they'd met again at the Ritz she'd invited him to dinner at the house, just the two of them, with candlelight sparkling on the silver and the view of the ropes of lights along the Seine. Lais had thought she wouldn't feel nervous because their letters had strung a subtle connecting web between them. But when Ferdi came towards her across the blue Aubusson carpet in the salon her heart had jumped and she had wanted desperately to be able to run to meet him. Ferdi had taken her hands in his and then he'd kissed her and for a moment the familiar feel of his kiss and the scent of his cologne, the texture of his skin had eliminated time. But Ferdi hadn't spoken of love. He had simply treated her as a treasured friend.

Ferdi took her everywhere in Paris, untroubled by the curious stares of passers-by at the beautiful, elegantly dressed woman in her wheelchair. He pushed Lais's chair unselfconsciously to the smart shops on the rue de Rivoli and the Faubourg St Honoré. They went to galleries on the Left Bank and they lunched in simple street cafés. And they went to the theatre and dined in their favourite restaurant or in crowded noisy brasseries.

The journey to Paris was long but Lais didn't feel tired when she arrived this time. She was looking forward so much to seeing him. It didn't feel strange being with Ferdi any more, not now they had had time to become friends. In fact she felt she knew him better now than before. "I never knew what books you liked or your favourite artists," she told him over dinner. "I didn't know the name of your tutor when you were a boy and that you wrote in red exercise books and your fingers were always stained with black ink. Or that you took size ten shoes and hated wearing a wristwatch."

"Lais, what would you like most in the world?" interrupted Ferdi suddenly.

"You want to know how to buy me?"

"No, I'd just like to give you whatever it is you want most."

Lais looked at the man she loved. She didn't see the lines of pain and harsh experience on his fine, lean face, nor the prematurely silver hair. She remembered the young blond officer, smart in his uniform, leaning against the piano at her party in the Ile St Louis, the young man walking with her along the rocky headland near the Hostellerie, his strong hand holding hers, and the young virile lover who had held her in his arms and promised her their dreams would come true. It would be unfair to expect Ferdi to marry a cripple. She must be content to remain his friend.

"It's impossible, Ferdi," she said quietly. "You see, no one can turn back the clock."

Oblivious to their surroundings they stared into each other's eyes. He had thought for a moment it could be the way it used to be, that Lais would take down the barriers and let him back into her magical world. But she refused to put back the clock – she couldn't. For her it was impossible. And for him? He still loved her, he knew that now. He'd marry her tonight if he thought she'd have him. But she'd just told him it was impossible.

"I'm sorry, Lais," said Ferdi at last. "I'm so sorry."

They left the restaurant and Ferdi lifted her carefully into the car, waiting while the chauffeur folded her wheelchair, placing it in the trunk of the big old-fashioned de Courmont that had been Lais's since before the war. They sat silently holding hands as they drove along the Boulevard St Germain, veering left on the Quai de Tournelle. The Seine looked smooth and black beneath the lighted bridge and the grey façades of the ancient buildings on the Ile St Louis loomed like a prison fortress.

Lais couldn't bear his silence. What had he meant? Was he sorry for her? Or sorry because he didn't love her the way he used to? If only she could run she would have wrenched open the door and raced away from the car, away from the wheelchairs and specially adapted rooms and the fuss that surrounded the once simple events of living. She would have run away from the silent man she only thought she knew.

Her half-averted cheek burned as he kissed her goodnight. "I'll telephone tomorrow," he promised as the door closed.

"Miz!" called Lais. "*Oh Miz*, Miz, where are you? *I need you.*"

Her hair in metal curlers, wrapped in a salmon-pink wool robe, Miz hurtled across the hall towards her. "Dear me," she gasped. "I was just in a doze, waiting for you. Whatever is the matter?"

"We must pack," said Lais, tears streaming down her face. "We're leaving tomorrow."

"Leaving? But we only just got here. Do you want to go back to the Hostellerie already?" queried Miz, sensing disaster.

"Not the Hostellerie," replied Lais. "We're going home. Whatever ship sails tomorrow for New York, we'll be on it."

Ferdi couldn't get a straight answer from Oliver, the de Courmont butler. "Mademoiselle Lais had packed and left very early this morning, sir," and "No, I do not know where she was destined," was all the response Ferdi received to his surprised questions.

Ferdi paced his apartment overlooking the Place Vendôme, hands clasped behind his back, his face tight and expressionless, analysing the previous evening. Later he placed a call to the Hostellerie only to be told that they were not expecting Lais. *Then where was she?* Ferdi continued his pacing, watching the phone like a hawk, waiting to pounce on it when it rang.

Unable to stay indoors any longer, he took a taxi to the Bois and walked aimlessly, watching the children play and staring at the posters on the kiosks advertising concerts and the circus. Head down he paced the sandy paths, seeing nothing of the splendour of the autumn trees. He didn't feel the chill wind that had sprung up or notice that the sun had disappeared behind banks of grey clouds.

Life without Lais looked bleak. He lived for her letters and for their meetings in Paris. He had told himself that he could be happy with only her friendship because Lais would want nothing more. But her disability had become so much part of his way of life that it scarcely mattered. *Except when he wanted to hold her in his arms.* They who had been passionate lovers were now just friends. And when Lais had finally spoken of the past his façade of pretence had shattered.

At a little outdoor café Ferdi sank on to a green-slatted wooden chair, running a hand distractedly through his hair.

"Monsieur?" A waiter appeared at his side, a metal tray balanced on one hand as he cleared the small table of glasses.

"Whisky," demanded Ferdi, suddenly aware of the edge of ice on the wind. There were a few other people on the little green chairs. Solitary people. A man in a dark overcoat reading a paper, another, younger man, staring into space, lost in his own thoughts.

Ferdi pushed back his chair abruptly. What a fool he was. What a goddamn fool. He'd re-built their shattered relationship, not daring to look back at the past. They were two people who had been struck down by disaster *and who had survived*. He was a lucky man to love Lais. He wasn't going to lose her again!

Amelie and Gerard were surprised to have Lais so suddenly. She arrived with Miz by plane from New York and although she said she was happy to see them she looked so miserable they wondered what was wrong.

"It's that young man of hers – Ferdi," Miz told them. "They've been writing to each other for a long time and she sees him every now and again in Paris. But now something has upset her and she's not saying what."

A week went by and still Lais was silent and brooding. She smiled and was pleasant but they felt that it was an effort, and when they questioned her she said nothing was wrong.

When Ferdi von Schönberg arrived on their doorstep one morning and told them he had flown in to see Lais and that he must speak with her at once, it was urgent, they greeted him with relief.

"At least there'll be some action," said Amelie, lurking outside Lais's door, "good or bad."

"For her sake, let's hope good this time," added Gerard.

Lais sat in her chair by the window, a ribbon in her pale hair and no make-up, looking like a shocked child, waiting for the blow to fall.

"I'm sorry I startled you – but I didn't realise I'd *frighten* you!" exclaimed Ferdi, still standing by the door.

"I'm afraid of what you're going to say," whispered Lais.

"Then you know why I'm here?"

"Yes . . . no . . . Oh Ferdi, I don't know . . . ."

"I'm not taking no for an answer, Lais, you realise that?" He walked across the length of white carpet that seemed to her as long and infinite as a road she would never walk again. "Please marry me, Lais," begged Ferdi, dropping to his knees by her side. "Please say you will?"

Her hands were imprisoned in his and his firm warm touch still gave her that old thrill and, when he looked at her like that, the old magic still played its tune in her brain, leaving her breathless. "Ferdi, it's not possible . . . Look at me . . . realise what you would be getting . . ."

"It's you I want, Lais," he said, his eyes steadfast as they locked with hers, "you and only you. I want to help you, to take care of you . . ."

"You see," she cried, anguished, "you see – you pity me. And I can't bear it, Ferdi . . . not after the way I remember it, the way it used to be . . ."

"Let me finish!" her commanded her, harshly, "let me finish, Lais. I sympathise with your condition, but I don't *pity* you. You are here, I can take you in my arms, I can love you – you're still my Lais. And I love you. My life has been empty without you. Please don't run away from me again. Marry me, Lais!"

His kiss bruised her lips and Lais gasped, responding to his passion. Then, blushing like a young girl as he lifted his mouth from hers, she murmured, "Ferdi, if you're sure . . .?"

"Say it!" he demanded, smiling.

"Yes," she whispered happily, "I'll marry you."

The door opened an hour later and the two of them emerged smiling.

"Is everything all right?" asked Amelie cautiously.

"Everything's fine, Maman," said Lais. "Ferdi and I are engaged."

"Engaged? Oh, how wonderful! How very wonderful!" Amelie bit her lip to stop from crying.

"You mustn't start planning the wedding yet, Maman," warned Lais. "I want Ferdi to take his time and make sure he knows what he's getting into, marrying someone like me."

Amelie's heart ached for Lais.

"That's Lais's idea, not mine," said Ferdi. "I'm doing my best to change her mind."

"Oh dear," said Amelie as the tears spilled over, "I'm sorry I'm crying. I was just thinking how pleased your grandmother would be."

*   *   *

Lais and Ferdi were married six weeks later in a simple ceremony in the gardens of the Palaçio d'Aureville. Peach flew down from Boston to be her sister's bridesmaid and Leonie and Jim flew in from France. Leonore was in Switzerland and couldn't get away but she sent her good wishes for the couple's happiness.

Peach thought Lais looked wonderful. She wore a wheat-yellow dress and a gardenia in her hair and she was smiling as though all the happiness in the world belonged to her.

But Peach knew better. She'd cornered some of that happiness for herself.

46

Harry Launceton flung down his pen and stared at the blank sheet of paper in front of him. Damn it, he couldn't concentrate. Every time he tried to follow a train of thought he ended up thinking of Peach instead. She was constantly in his mind. He went to sleep at Augusta's side wondering about Peach, and he woke in the middle of the night panicked in case she refused to see him again. She had infiltrated the most important part of his life. His work.

Peach wasn't the first girl he'd had an affair with but inevitably they bored him and he always returned thankfully to his wife. Cool, sensible Augusta who protected him from the daily household problems and who, when he was writing, always fended off the visitors and the endless requests for interviews, the invitations to lecture or to dinner parties. *Augusta understood him.* She knew he had a weakness for a pretty, available face and without saying anything, she tolerated his little escapades. And behind that cool façade, she was surprisingly inventive in bed. He'd always enjoyed sex with Augusta. He still did.

His affair with Peach had been going on for six months but on the surface life continued as normal. He had breakfast with Augusta, hiding behind the airmail edition of *The Times*, he prepared his lectures or worked on his novel in the mornings, and they went to dinner as usual at friends' houses and to the theatre or the concert hall. *But underneath it all he was going quietly crazy.*

He lived for the long luxurious afternoons making love to Peach in a friend's borrowed apartment, or their quiet dark evenings together in some out of the way country inn. Peach's lithe girlish body with its small high breasts and long golden legs fascinated him and her innocence was charming. Sometimes, trembling on the brink of passion, he would open his eyes and meet her unnerving blue gaze as though she were searching for his soul and in the very act of love.

But it was *afterwards* that he felt inspired. Peach would lie, curled in the tumbled sheets, watching his pen fly across the pages writing page after page in a scrawl only he could decipher. He wrote about *her* – about her feline grace, about the way she walked naked across the room in her long pantherlike lope, about the sloping bones of her face and her small flat ears. He wrote of the colour of her russet hair contrasted against the leaden grey of a winter sky and about her watching him writing, lying there like a sleepy animal.

This would be different from any other Harry Launceton book. It was a novel of the senses, the story of a man and a girl and her entrapment of him in a love affair. It was Colette or Proust, fleshed out with sensual details. It would be his masterpiece and without Peach he couldn't finish it.

Harry stared desperately at his empty page, then he picked up the phone and dialled her number He could hear the girl who answered the phone calling her. "It's your Englishman," he heard her tell Peach . . . the whole of Radcliffe probably knew about them by now!

"Hello," Peach's voice was breathless. "Harry, is that you?"

"I love you, Peach de Courmont," he said gritting his teeth. "Damn it all, I love you!"

"Ohh. Oh, Harry, I love you too."

"Can you meet me right now?"

"Harry, I should work."

"Please," he said quietly. "I need you."

The month that Peach flunked her exams was the same month that Harry Launceton's extraordinary new novel was published to rave reviews. And Boston rocked to the fact that Harry had run off with Peach de Courmont.

Augusta Launceton took the news calmly enough. Harry's letter had been brief but apologetic – he would always love her, he said. She read the gossip columns in the papers the way she had before and accepted the calls from "friends" wishing to sympathise or find out the juicy details. "It's just Harry," she explained, "when he's writing he becomes so confused about reality. He'll come back." Then she packed her bags and returned to England to wait. It came as quite a surprise a few months later to find that Harry had obtained a Las Vegas divorce and had married Peach de Courmont.

47

Noel was probably the only person in Detroit who liked the city in winter when its grimy streets were covered in thick frozen snow that turned in a matter of days from virgin white to big-city pollution black. Detroit's angles and intersections and the sharp spears of its tall buildings splitting the sky lent thrust to his ambition. He needed the constant reminder that life was an upward struggle until you reach the very top of one of those towers. Noel knew that it was on the executive floors that Detroit's power games were played out against a backdrop of high tension and luxury and the players were men in custom-tailored suits from London, men who drove "special" model supercars customised to their requirements, men who returned each evening to their million-dollar homes in Grosse Pointe, homes crammed with expensive antiques and fine paintings where beautiful elegant wives waited for them.

At least that's how Noel visualised it. And that's exactly what he wanted. Meantime he had a job as assistant research engineer at Great Lakes Motor Corporation at a salary of $12,000 a year. Good money for a new guy, but he had an excellent degree from the University of Michigan and a masters from MIT. He had a small furnished studio apartment on a decent street in a suburban area with its own kitchen and bathroom and the day he'd paid the deposit plus the first month's rent and had opened his own front door with his own key, had been a milestone in his life. 22b Cranbrook Street was his first real home.

He prowled its square, compact, freshly carpeted area feeling the thrill of possession and then he took the bus into town and scoured the art galleries until he found a couple of inexpensive prints, a Kandinsky whose jagged geometry and flashing colour appealed to him and a huge black and white Mondrian with thin lines of scarlet and electric blue bisecting its squared design. Their angular compositions pleased him as he drank his solitary cup of coffee in the morning, or when he came home from work – late as always. It was a sort of welcome.

A sympathetic bank manager advanced him money on his first paycheck and he bought himself half a dozen blue Oxford-cloth button-down shirts and a plain dark Brooks Brothers-type suit. He chose two muted striped ties and a pair of black lace-up shoes. Like a kid starting a new school, he wanted the right uniform.

He bought a three-year-old Chevrolet with payments spread over a three-year period, though of course he didn't expect to keep it that long. He would be moving up in the car world.

Not bad going for the orphan kid, Noel thought as he drove out of downtown Detroit west towards Dearborn. *But not good enough.*

As assistant research engineer he sat in on meetings with designers and product-planners, thrashing around ideas based on market research as to what the public wanted from their cars. They discussed the social changes and fashion trends and the economics until a concept for a new car was born and a cost target projected. Noel's job was to help devise the engineering guts of the car, the "power-pack", suitable for the new design.

Working on his first car was a thrill that filled his waking and sleeping moments. He worked late every night refining his concepts, consulting with the toolmakers and the body designers and attending endless more meetings, while endless more changes were discussed and made. Designers' drawings were adapted and refined until finally a clay model of the proposed car took shape in the studio.

The new car was a small compact model aimed at the middle range of the market and Noel's personal view was that the design was unexciting. Despite all those stimulating meetings, its body lines were little different from previous models and an excessive amount of chrome trim had been added to the design in an attempt to jazz up its visual appeal, though Noel doubted the public would be fooled. Of course he kept his mouth shut and voiced no criticism. Permission was given to take the car to the next stage and a few months later a "mock-up" of the car awaited directors' approval. At this stage the car was merely a fibreglass shell moulded from the original clay model and sprayed a harsh bright blue – one of the latest colours. Spotlit dramatically on matching blue carpet the car still looked insignificant and Noel turned away disappointed. It wasn't only the way the new car looked. Limited by costing and design dimensions, the engineering concepts had been whittled down until the power-package was virtually the same as the previous model. He felt as though all his hours of work had been for nothing.

Pulling into a liquor store Noel bought himself a bottle of J&B scotch and drove to his apartment. Closing the front door behind him he headed for his tiny kitchen, took a glass from the cupboard and some ice from the refrigerator and poured himself a hefty drink. Glass in hand he prowled the small rented space he called home. The Kandinsky and the Mondrian on the bare white walls looked suddenly like the cheap framed prints they were. Disillusioned, Noel poured a second glass of whisky, staring out of the window at the neat, grass-verged suburban street, feeling trapped. For the first time since he was thirteen a year of his life had gone by without progress. He was twenty-two years old, claiming to be twenty-six, and in the mirror he looked dark and drawn and closer to thirty. He was assistant research engineer at Great Lakes Motor Corporation and maybe, if he could keep his mouth shut about the way he felt about the designers and the production chiefs, in another year's time he could expect a promotion to full research engineer at $20,000 a year. *But that wasn't what he'd worked for all these years!* Then how – *how* – did you get from assistant engineer to be the one who could give the nod of approval to an innovative design that would revolutionise the car industry?

Walking to the table he opened the big black portfolio that contained all his ideas and drawings from the past four years. He knew they were good. But he would need more than that. He needed to know more than just engineering and design to make it to the top in this town. He would need to know how the business worked.

Slumping on to the brown vinyl sofa that converted into his bed at night Noel sipped his scotch and contemplated his problem. His game-plan had reached a major set-back and he wasn't as prepared for the world he sought to command as he had thought. The grey dawn of Detroit appeared in his window and the bottle of scotch was finished by the time he finally fell asleep on the sofa.

Noel didn't show up for work the rest of that week. He called in to say he was sick and then he made a few more phone calls. Noel knew now what he would have to do, but it was no use planning on years of night school in Detroit. He would have to go for the top. Packing his curriculum vitae, his business suit and a blue shirt into a bag, Noel topped up his car with petrol and headed east.

He felt uneasy back in Boston again. He was used to industrial complexes, inner-city decay and automotive plants, and Harvard's leafy brick-paved squares felt alien. He found a small rooming house where he arranged to stay for one night, then he showered, changed into his dark suit and crossed the Anderson Bridge into North Harvard Street. Two hours later he emerged from Harvard's Graduate School of Business where he had been accepted for a course in business administration.

In Boston that evening Noel walked through Copley Square to the Copley Plaza Hotel. Ordering a Martini from the young barman he silently toasted his new life. He sat for a long while, watching that anonymous barman serving the smart customers, remembering how it felt.

The next day he set off on the three-day drive back to Detroit, stopping at roadside diners for cups of coffee and sleeping in the car. As soon as he arrived he gave up the lease on his apartment, sold his car and took a room in a cheap rooming house close by the plant. He saved every penny he could from his salary and in July he gave in his notice at Great Lakes Motor Corporation. Then he went to speak to the guy in the personnel for the assembly line at US Auto to make sure he would have a job in the breaks from school.

In September he started his new courses and picked up his old job as barman at the Copley Plaza. He had come full circle.

48

It rained all the time in England, decided Peach. There was green rain in the summer when all the leaves were on the trees and Launceton Hall's emerald lawns glimmered under pools of water. And there was grey rain in winter when the trees were bare and the cold flower beds displayed only sodden grey-brown earth.

It seemed to her she spent all her time just staring out at endless rain falling on the same unchanging vistas thinking longingly of the blue skies and warm sunshine of the Riviera. She longed for hot days and the harsh summer sound of cicadas and the smell of the sea and the pines and jasmine. And she dreamed of warm nights with the waves murmuring in the darkness outside her old room at the villa and the glorious golden dawns when you just knew it was going to be another perfect day.

If she weren't pregnant she would just pack up and go there but Harry wouldn't hear of her travelling.

"Of course you can't go," he told her, astonished that she had even suggested it. "The baby's due in two months. What if anything happened to you? You know that Launceton babies are always born here at the Hall."

Of course she knew that, he'd told her often enough. It had come as a shock to Peach to find that the avant-garde literary man who was famous for the progressive new concepts of his books, lived for family tradition. At Launceton Hall there were no decisions to be made and no choices. The elder Launceton son and heir, Harry in this case, always inherited the title and the estates and lived at Launceton Hall while his widowed mother moved out into a cosy flat in London that Peach secretly envied. Tom, who was the middle brother, lived at Launceton Magna Farm and managed the three large thriving farms that belonged to the estate and Peach was jealous of his way of life. The youngest son, Archie, whom Peach

253

barely knew, was at Sandhurst preparing for a career in the Army. That was the way it had always been in the Launceton family. And to Peach's surprise no one ever seemed to question it. Tom, whom she had thought would be her friend, led his own life with a much younger crowd of people than Harry and their paths crossed only at Sunday lunches or family get-togethers.

Her baby had already been registered at the schools he would attend, and his names were pre-planned, William Piers Launceton. Her shy suggestion over the Sunday lunch table that she liked her grandfather's name, Gilles, brought dismissive stares from the family and her mother-in-law's reply, "My dear, I don't think there have been any *Gilles* in the Launcetons' history."

And of course no one *ever* considered the possibility that the baby might be a girl. I mean, she might have a sweet little fair-haired feminine version of Harry who she would name something exotic like Jessamy or Eloise. But even with a girl she'd be voted down by the family in favour of Caroline or Elizabeth.

Merde! Peach glared at the rain moodily. Getting pregnant just wasn't something she had planned on. Making love was a private matter between her and Harry and their passionate nights had nothing to do with this baby. She resented the great bulge under the blue smock she was wearing and when she bathed she tried not to look at herself in the mirror because she looked so odd and ungainly. She couldn't blame Harry for not wanting to make love to her any more. *Merde*, oh *merde* thing! She hadn't wanted to admit it, but it was true. Harry *didn't* want to make love to her.

In fact, she scarcely saw Harry these days. He was locked away in his study writing his new novel, all about a city in the past that was like ancient Rome but with modern characters and present-day evils which all boiled down to the fact that life really hadn't changed much over the centuries. It was all so different when Harry had been writing *her* books.

It had been exciting being Harry's inspiration although after a while it became a bit disturbing. Sometimes she would wonder when he made love to her if it was going to turn up on his pages for all the world to read about and she would blush when Harry introduced her as his "muse" at publishers' parties.

And sometimes when she had been lying there on the bed still wrapped in the afterglow of his lovemaking, watching Harry's intense beautiful face as he wrote about her, she thought that this was what she liked best of all. She had felt a part of Harry's world

254

when she shared his thoughts as well as his body. In those moments she had everything she'd ever wanted.

With a sigh Peach turned away from the window. Giving the sullen log in the fireplace a kick to stir its greying embers into flame she slumped into a vast wingchair that was as old as the house and pulled a bundle of knitting from behind the cushion. It was blue knitting and was meant to be a baby's jacket, but its lacy pattern was full of holes that weren't meant to be there and it was already grubby from her hot hands as she struggled to master the pattern. "Oh *merde!*" Ripping the stitches from the needles she flung the knitting on to the fire, watching miserably as it crumbled into ashes. The marble clock on the mantel ticked loudly into the silence. It was only three thirty and it felt like eight or nine! The November greyness outside was already becoming dark and Harry wouldn't emerge until at least half past six and even then he'd probably just have a drink and ask her to have the housekeeper send something to eat into his study because he'd be working late. And when he hadn't joined her by ten Peach would put aside the book she'd been trying to read and turn off the record player and the music she'd been hoping to share with him and she'd just climb the stairs and go to bed alone. Again! She was twenty-two but inside she still felt like the eighteen-year-old she'd been when she met Harry. And here she was having a baby and living the life of an old married woman. It was a lonely, lonely life.

Picking up the phone she called Melinda.

"Come for tea," said Melinda, "and tell me about it."

Life at the Seymours' was informal and the house always seemed to be bursting at the seams with people and animals. Dogs rushed to greet Peach as she stepped into the hall and voices shouted a welcome over the sound of the latest record being played at top blast by Melinda's younger brother. Peach liked the way people just dropped in for tea at the Seymours', for drinks, or even supper without waiting to be asked, and there was always somebody there to recount the latest local gossip.

It was so different from life at Launceton Hall where people were invited formally and dinner parties were meticulously planned by Harry so that he had a balanced group of guests from the literary and academic worlds, who could provide the sort of stimulating dinner-table conversation that you really had to think hard about to catch on to what they meant. The house parties were the worst, though. Harry would invite a dozen people to spend the weekend and Peach would dread their arrival. Thank God the cook knew how to churn out the sort of meals they were used to and there was always a rice pudding with stewed fruit after lunch and a meringue for dessert after dinner! Harry said it was what they all got used to at school but Peach thought it revolting. The worst part was that she had absolutely nothing in common with any of them. She would wear what she thought was pretty and appropriate for dinner in the lovely panelled dining room where the long refectory table seated twenty – or thirty when all the leaves were pulled out – but all the other women would be wearing long patterned dresses in brown and sage green or that electric blue that they all seemed to like and which killed their pink complexions. They'd stare at her beautiful red Dior silk with a "what can you expect – she's French" look, and talk to her as though she knew nothing about life or literature. And the men would pay her intellectual compliments before dinner and then talk about events that had happened before she married Harry, dropping Augusta's name carelessly and then glancing at her apologetically.

"I can't stand it any longer!" she complained to Melinda as they sat before a roaring log fire toasting crumpets on a long brass fork.

"Here's yours. Catch." Melinda tossed the hot crumpet to her, burning her fingers. "Of course you can," she said, buttering hers lavishly and taking a large bite. "It's just that *you* are pregnant and *Harry's* busy. After he's finished the book and the baby's born you should get him to whisk you away to somewhere wonderful for a holiday. Barbados is lovely in winter – hot and sunny, just the way you like it."

"Barbados! I can't even get him to take me into *London* with him! Harry goes there every couple of weeks when he can't stand writing any more. He has lunch with his publisher or his agent and then he has dinner at his club and chats with his old friends. He says that he needs to get away. And he tells me I'm too pregnant to take up to town. Besides, if I went we'd have to stay at his mother's and Harry hates that. He has a hundred reasons for not taking me with him. Harry likes to think of me at home waiting for him, waiting for his child to be born. I feel like an actor in a play he's creating."

"Well, in a way you are. I mean you are his inspiration."

"Not any more," replied Peach gloomily. "He's gone back to ancient Rome. Melinda, do you know what I'm going to do after the baby is born? I'm going to buy a place in London. In Chelsea perhaps, or maybe one of those pretty little mews houses in Belgravia. Then Harry and I will have a home of our own in town."

"I doubt that Harry will want to spend money on a town house," said Melinda. "I hear he spends it all buying more acres for the Launceton estates. Harry's land-rich."

"I'll buy the house myself with my grandfather de Courmont's money," said Peach, suddenly enchanted with her idea. She knew exactly what she wanted, she'd noticed one just like it last time she was in London. A low, white house with a front door painted glossy black and a brass knocker. She would have two bedrooms just in case she wanted to bring the baby to town, and a sweet little kitchen where she could cook a surprise for supper. Or maybe Harry would take her out to dinner at one of those charming little restaurants in Belgravia. She could see it all now ... and she'd have such *fun* choosing wallpapers and curtains and, of course, a lovely big bed, and soft rugs for their bare feet. It would be their love nest and everything would be just the way it was before. And it would be her secret until it was finished. It would be her grand surprise present for Harry.

"Harry will love it," she said, beaming, "I just know he will."

Melinda sighed as she looked at her friend. There was a lot Peach didn't know about Harry.

49

It was one of the coldest Januarys on record but Peach didn't care. She lay snug and happy in her four-poster at Launceton Hall with a cheerful fire burning in the grate, the snow falling outside her window and her baby sleeping soundly in his crib beside her bed.

He wasn't a beautiful baby – he was too masculine for that, but he *was* very handsome and she didn't think he looked the least bit like Harry. He had her dark blue eyes but everyone told her that babies' eyes change colour so she was waiting to see what they would turn out to be, and he had masses of very straight dark hair and a nose that was a proper nose, not just some baby pudge. And she loved him like crazy. Peach couldn't think how she could have resented him when she was pregnant. She thought that if everyone knew what they were getting at the end of those nine months and the ordeal of the birth then they'd feel a lot happier about feeling sick and getting fat and clumsy.

Best of all, her mother and father were here. They came over to spend Christmas and stayed on for the birth. Her mother had been the star of all the Christmas parties, dazzling the locals with her glamorous good looks and fitting in with everyone much better than Peach ever had. She'd gone to the Christmas ball looking superb in yellow satin and she'd sparkled at sombre dinner parties in sapphires and blue silk and she'd eaten lunch at the Seymours' kitchen table, helping to clear off afterwards, and she hadn't minded when the dogs clambered up on to her elegant tweed lap slobbering and shedding hairs and probably a few fleas as well.

Amelie had been there to hold Peach's hand through the worst of the pains and she was there smiling at her, holding out the baby to her afterwards. Peach didn't know what she would have done without her.

And when Peach told her father what she wanted it was Gerard who sorted out the baby's name. "I know you won't mind if I insist," he said, smiling charmingly at Harry and his mother, "but the name Gilles has been in the de Courmont family for generations. It would be an honour for us to join it with the Launceton family names." Of course they had no choice but to accept.

Peach thought maybe Gerard hadn't been too keen on her giving the baby his father's name but it suited him. And at the christening a few weeks later, with the baby clasped in his godmother Lais's arms and yelling in what Peach felt sure was a very untraditional manner, he was named William Piers Gilles Launceton. And somehow he was always called Wil.

Nanny Launceton, who had brought up Harry and his brothers, was summoned back from her position with a nice family in Hampshire a month before the birth to prepare *her* nursery. Of course Peach had already done it the way she wanted it. It had been the only aspect of her pregnancy that she had enjoyed. She had gone to the White House in Bond Street and bought a lavish layette with dozens of little vests and nighties and heavenly little smocked jackets and tiny embroidered boots and bonnets in silk. She'd bought a wonderful crib and a lavish shawl and then she'd gone to Harrods and chosen new nursery furniture for when the baby was a bit older, a cot and a high chair and gaily painted wooden blocks, and all kinds of things that she would enjoy playing with herself. Harry complained she'd squandered a fortune when there was already plenty of stuff in the attics from the years before but Peach didn't care. She felt happy thinking of their new little baby in his all-new yellow-painted nursery with its crisp cotton curtains and soft blue carpet.

Nanny Launceton took one look at the new nursery, tut-tutting and shaking her head and said, "This will never do, Mrs Launceton. Oh dear me, no." She'd had the new blue carpet up the very next week and plain blue linoleum laid in its place. "You need to have surfaces that can be kept clean and free of dust, Madam, for a new baby," she'd said severely when Peach protested.

The new cot and the high chair were sent back to Harrods and Harry's old ones brought down from the attics. "No use wasting good money on this flimsy new stuff," Nanny Launceton said, kindly enough, as though Peach were another child. "This was good enough for Master Harry and his brothers and no doubt it'll see another generation of Launcetons through until they're old enough for a proper bed." Peach refused to part with her new crib from the White House though. She placed it firmly beside her bed in her room, daring Nanny to say anything, and when Nanny saw how determined she was she smiled and said, "Well I dare say it's all right to have a new crib, the old one in the attic would need mending anyway. And it is very pretty." Peach had smiled at her in relief. Perhaps she and Nanny could have a truce, although she knew they would never be friends.

Peach couldn't breast-feed the baby, there just wasn't enough bosom and enough milk. Nanny Launceton took him away from her and prepared bottles full of rich-looking formula and soon he was thriving and getting plumper and more like a person. Sitting in a chair by the nursery fire Peach held his bottle, watching him guzzling and gurgling. "Greedy little pig," she said happily.

"Time for Master Wil's nap now," said Nanny, sweeping him from her arms and burping him expertly.

Peach soon gave up the battle of the bath, which anyway always coincided with the time Harry emerged from his study for a drink, and Nanny triumphantly brought the baby to show his father, dressed in the plain serviceable cream Viyella nighties that she preferred. "Much more suitable, Mrs Launceton, than all those fancy French things," she said, dismissing the adorable blue and yellow and white ones with the silk ribbons that Leonie had sent her great-grandchild.

Peach thought that Harry seemed quite pleased with his son. Not thrilled and jumping-up-and-down with excitement but, still, he was pleased. He stroked the baby's hair gently and said very un-literary things about him, such as, "Good bones. Strong too. Look at those shoulders – he'll make the rowing eight at Eton, maybe even the rugger squad too." Or, "The lad's a Launceton, no mistaking that face." Peach had expected poetic descriptions of his emotions as a new father but Harry just seemed to assess his son the way he might have a new horse . . . sound chest, good fetlocks, strong hindquarters. She felt a little sorry for her baby.

Harry was wrong too. The baby didn't look like the Launcetons. He looked like his namesake and grandfather, Gilles de Courmont.

With Nanny in charge of the baby Peach had time on her hands. She prowled her big bedroom that still looked exactly the way it had when it was Harry's mother's room (before his father died and she moved into the London flat) and that Harry had refused to let her change. "Until Mother goes," he'd said dramatically.

"But she's gone," Peach protested.

"Not gone. *Gone*," Harry said. "She likes to know that everything is the same even though she's not here."

Peach thought it a bit unfair but respected his wishes. The idea of a little mews house in London where no Launceton had.ever set foot became more and more tempting as the months went by and Harry seemed busier and busier. He was always dashing up to London on the ten fifteen train and he almost always called to say he was being kept late at meetings and would have to stay over. Peach had gone up once or twice with him and she'd bought quite a lot of nice English country-lady clothes, which she managed to make look very French with a beautiful scarf and enormous chunks of fake jewellery and an armful of clanking gold bracelets that drove Harry crazy with the noise. He took her to Wilton's for lunch and they went to the theatre together and Peach enjoyed herself very much. It was time they had their own place in London so that she and Harry could be together much more and with Nanny in charge there was no need for her to be eternally at Launceton.

In her new little de Courmont town car Peach zapped around the estate agents, breezing into their quiet offices with all her old zest and self-assurance. She toured endless bijou-residences with mesmerised young estate agents until she found exactly what she wanted in a mews just off Belgrave Square.

Melinda came up to London with her and together they scoured the shops buying pretty things for the tiny white house on the cobblestone mews. Its front door was enamelled a glossy black and Peach bought a shiny brass doorknocker in the shape of a lion's head. It reminded her of Grand-mère's Sekhmet statue.

Harry never asked what she did when she went to London. In fact he rarely asked her anything about herself any more, not even if she were cold or if she would like more wine with her lunch. He certainly never asked her if she were happy. But Peach knew he had a new book brewing in his head and that he was worried about a delay in the publication date of his last novel, so she didn't intrude on his thoughts.

As soon as the house was finished, she planned to unveil her surprise for Harry. He had gone up to town on the usual train and she had driven up later, arranging to meet him at a quarter to seven at Claridges.

Making for Harrods she squeezed the car into a handy space in Hans Place and strolled through the Food Halls picking out smoked salmon and a game pie and salad. She chose some good French cheeses and the celery she knew Harry would like to go with it, and some enormous strawberries imported from Florida, whose sweet smell on this cold April morning made her think of sunshine and clear skies.

In a plaid skirt and a dark green sweater with a wicker basket over her arm, she felt at last that she belonged. She was Lady Launceton, aged twenty-three, mother of a three-month-old son, married to the world's ideal man whom she still loved madly. And now that she had so cleverly bought them their own little home their relationship would regain its old lustre. Without Launceton Hall and its traditions stifling her she would be his old Peach again – the same one he had had to phone six times a day just to tell her he loved her, the one he needed by his side in order to write, the one he made love to with such passion.

Peach spent the afternoon in her new house arranging the table for an intimate dinner for two. She set it up before the fireplace and draped it in a long lace cloth. She put out the new Italian dishes and the Swedish crystal glasses. She set a small exquisitely arranged basket of flowers from Constance Spry in the centre and she put the bottle of white wine – a Chassagne Montrachet chosen with the help of the nice man at Harrods – into the refrigerator to chill. She'd also bought a decent bottle of claret because it was Harry's favourite, and a superb bottle of 1900 port as her housewarming present to him.

She took a bath and spent a lot of time doing her face, the way Lais used to, and then she put on the black velvet cocktail dress that had cost her a fortune in Bond Street. She swept up her mass of bronze hair on top of her head and clipped on the diamond earrings that Harry had given her when they were married. Fastening the sapphire and diamond clasp of the heirloom Launceton three-strand pearl choker carefully she thought it looked a bit overdone, but knew Harry would like to see her wearing it. Before she left she arranged the black lace nightdress on the bed in their pretty green and white bedroom and left an album of Albinoni's quiet pretty music on the record player.

Peach waited in Claridges' bar, glancing eagerly at every new face. She had ordered a gin and tonic, a mixture she despised but which it seemed all the English drank, and it sat untouched, on the table in front of her.

"Lady Launceton?" asked the waiter.

Peach nodded in surprise.

"A telephone call for you, Madam."

"I'm going to be late, Peach," said Harry abruptly. "You'd better start back for Launceton without me."

"No, no. It's all right. I'll wait . . ."

"No use waiting, I don't know how long I'm going to be. I'm in the middle of discussions with my editor. They could go on all night. I'll probably end up sleeping at the club."

Peach replaced the receiver sadly. Her surprise was in ruins. Back at her table in the bar she sipped the gin and tonic and wondered what to do. All was not lost, she decided finally. She would stay alone in her pretty new house and she'd call Harry at his club in the morning and surprise him. He'd come over for breakfast and she'd show him their little hideaway and he'd love it. And he'd love her too for being so clever.

"Sir Harry is not in at the moment, Madam," the concierge at Harry's club said discreetly when she telephoned the next morning. "Would you care to leave a message?"

"Oh. Has he gone out for breakfast?" asked Peach.

"I dare say, Madam."

"Well, could you ask him to call Lady Launceton at Belgravia 2313 please."

Somehow it didn't seem like much fun brewing up coffee and warming croissants for one. She'd go for a walk and get some fresh air and then she'd call again. Dressing hurriedly in her old uniform of tight black trousers and big sweater she emerged into a cold blue spring morning.

Peach walked through St James's Park wishing she'd brought something to feed the ducks and watching the nannies out already with their babies in those enormous regal perambulators and she suddenly missed baby Wil like mad. She'd go back to the mews house and call Harry one more time and leave a message that she had returned home.

Waiting at the traffic light by the Ritz Hotel, she stared absently in front of her thinking about the baby. A porter in a brown uniform hurried from the hotel carrying two small overnight bags, followed by a man and a woman. The man held the woman's arm protectively and she was smiling at him as they stepped into a taxi. It was a few seconds before Peach realised that the man was Harry and the woman he was with was Augusta and by then the taxi was lost in the flurry of traffic along Piccadilly.

Melinda was in a dilemma. Peach was her best friend and she didn't want to hurt her but really Harry was such a bastard she couldn't let Peach go on thinking he was the Prince of Light.

"Maybe it wasn't Harry," said Peach, a ray of hope flickering across her miserable face.

Melinda sighed, and cut another wedge of chocolate cake. "Of course it was Harry," she said. "He's been seeing Augusta for months. Everyone knows about it."

"They do?" asked Peach astonished. "I mean – *he has?*"

"You must have known what Harry was like when you met him," Melinda went on. "After all he had an affair with you, didn't he? Augusta was quite used to it – she always took it in her stride and came back to wait for him. But this time he married you. It must have been quite a shock for her, he'd always come dashing home before, his tail, between his legs. Metaphorically speaking," she added, giggling.

"But *Augusta!*" cried Peach despairingly. "If only it were anyone but her!"

Melinda sighed. "It is," she said. "I'm sorry, Peach, but you'd

263

better know the worst. Since your marriage Harry has bedded half the women within a fifty-mile radius. Those he hasn't are either too old or not attractive or have scruples."

Peach didn't know whether to laugh or cry as she thought about Harry's infidelity. It certainly explained why he had no time for her in bed; she was surprised he could even manage a kiss! She looked at Melinda suspiciously. "What category are you?" she asked.

"The scruples," cried Melinda indignantly. "Of course!"

Peach thought of her baby innocently asleep in his linoleum nursery at Launceton Hall while his father seduced half the women in the county, and she burst into tears.

"Oh Peach," said Melinda tenderly. "You know Harry's never chased after women. He doesn't have to. It's just that they are always *there* – and he's never been able to resist a pretty face."

"What am I going to do, Melinda?" wailed Peach, frantically rocking backwards and forwards in Melinda's rocking chair. "*Tell me what to do!*"

"Oh God, I wish we were thirty-five and women of the world," sighed Melinda, "then we'd know what to do. You'd be *soignée* and brittle and not give a damn and probably just go off and have a nice comforting affair to get over it."

"I don't want an affair," cried Peach. "I don't want anything. I just want to go home." Florida and her mother had never seemed further away. She thought of her grandmother. Leonie would know how to deal with this. Leonie always knew what to do.

Harry had phoned and left a message that he was delayed in town and by a stroke of luck Nanny was taking a day off to visit her sister in Bristol. Nanny looked at Peach's blotchy face suspiciously but she said nothing and Peach listened quietly to her instructions about Master Wil's schedule. She watched from the window as Nanny was driven off down the driveway by the gardener on her way to the station and then she dragged a suitcase from the cupboard and began loading Wil's things into it. Her son lay in his cot sleeping peacefully as she clattered around dropping toys and wooden bricks in her nervous haste. She had packed her own case the night before and it was already stashed in the back of the de Courmont. Lugging Wil's things down the stairs she hurried through the front door, crunching across the gravel to the garage. Peach wedged the case on the floor in the back, wishing she had a bigger car, and then she dashed back into the house, wrapped Wil in his blue blanket and put him in his carry cot. With her bag slung over her shoulder and Wil in his carry cot in one hand and a huge bag of clean diapers and bottles and things in the other she thought she looked like a refugee. And wasn't she? She was fleeing from Harry the way other women had fled from the enemy.

She took a last look at Launceton Hall before she drove off. It looked peaceful and serene beneath the fitful April sun and a line of fast-approaching grey clouds, just the way it had for centuries.

To her surprise Peach was enjoying herself. The English Channel was as calm as a pond and she strolled the decks of the ferry with Wil in her arms, warmly wrapped against the breeze, smiling and pointing out the gulls and Dover and the departing shoreline of England to him as though he could really understand what she was saying. And maybe he did, she thought. Who could tell with a baby? Just because he didn't talk didn't mean he didn't *know*. She wondered if Wil would miss his father, but Harry had almost never held him and only ever saw him when he was clean and tidy after his bath. Harry had never given Wil his bottle or told him he loved him, the way she did. She would just have to love him more to make up for his lack of a father. Because she was quite sure she was never going back to Harry. Never.

Peach drove quickly through Calais and headed for Paris. She would stay the night at the Ile St Louis and take the train south the next day. It felt good to be back in France, speaking French again and not having to try to look and sound English so that she could belong in Harry's world. Peach's spirits rose as she drove, reading the road signs aloud in French just for the sound of it, and singing along with the songs on Radio Paris, stopping to buy a baguette and some cheese to eat while she gave Wil his bottle. She was home.

50

"It's not fair, Grand-mère," sobbed Peach. "It's just not fair of Harry to do that to me. I trusted him. I *loved* him!"

"Loved?" queried Leonie.

Peach raised her tear-stained face to her grandmother. Leonie was holding Wil on her lap and the baby was tugging on her wonderful pearls, trying to get them into his mouth, only his aim wasn't quite right and he kept putting them in his eye instead. "What do you mean?" she asked.

"You said '*loved*'. Don't you love Harry any more?"

"Yes . . . No . . . Oh, I don't know. I don't know what I feel – except miserable."

"Naturally you feel hurt," replied Leonie, removing her pearls from the baby's sticky hands and giving him a toy to play with instead. "And you feel jealous and insecure as well as feeling stupid for not knowing about it when apparently everyone else did. But ask yourself, Peach – is Harry behaving any differently now than he did before he married you? Didn't you chase after Harry when he was married to Augusta – just like these women are now he's married to you?"

Peach stared at her grandmother dumbfounded. She had come here expecting to be comforted and treated like an invalid who needed cosseting and pampering until she felt well enough to face the world again. "What are you saying, Grand-mère?" she demanded, bewildered.

"You know I never approved of you running off with Harry and I didn't approve when you married him. You've had this silly obsession about him since you were fifteen; you idolised him and now you find your idol has feet of clay. But Harry is exactly what he has always been. You were just so wrapped up in what you thought he was that you couldn't see the truth. And now it's too late."

"Too late?"

"You are married and this is Harry's child as well as yours. Harry will never let you take away his son. He's going to come after you, Peach, and if you tell him you're leaving him he'll take Wil away from you."

"He can't do that," cried Peach, horrified. "He can't take Wil from me. I'm his mother!"

"And in the English courts Harry will claim that you are too young, you are immature and a foreigner, and that you were an irresponsible mother. He'll say that the boy will be better off being brought up at Launceton Hall with his family and that he will provide a solid stable background for the child. And it's true, Peach, he *can* provide that and you were too young to marry. If there were no child involved I'd say you should divorce Harry. But now . . ." she sighed. "Oh Peach, you are still all wrapped up in dreams and romance. Now you must try and make it work, for the baby's sake."

"Everything you're saying is true," admitted Peach sadly. "Harry was my idol. And I did behave badly and very selfishly. It didn't matter to me how Augusta felt when I went off with Harry – it didn't seem to affect anyone but us. That's all there was in the world – the two of us."

"And now there are three." Leonie handed Wil to Peach and the baby laughed, kicking his legs happily. "Think carefully about what are you going to do, Peach," she warned, "because there's nothing sadder than not being able to be with your child. I know. It happened to me."

Peach clutched the baby in her arms as though he would disappear in a puff of smoke. She knew that Amelie, her mother, had been brought up by Edouard d'Aureville in Brazil but she had never known exactly why, though she suspected it was something to do with her grandfather, Gilles de Courmont.

"But that's another story," said Leonie, abruptly dismissing the past. "Now we must think of Wil and his future. And *your* happiness, Peach."

"I won't let him take Wil from me," cried Peach angrily, "and I'll never go back to Harry. Never. Never!"

"Peach," said Leonie with a sigh, "when are you going to grow up?"

Harry and Nanny Launceton arrived the following week after urgent telephone calls back and forth between Harry and Jim, as Peach refused to speak to him.

267

"I'm sorry, Peach," said Harry, looking at her with those moss-green eyes. "I didn't mean to hurt you."

"But *Augusta!*" cried Peach, full of pain.

Harry sighed. "Augusta and I have always been friends. We had to meet to talk over some financial matters. We had dinner at the Ritz and it took longer than expected. It wasn't what it seemed."

Peach stared at him suspiciously. She knew that Harry had made a financial settlement with Augusta when they were divorced and they probably did have to talk, but could she believe him?

"Look," said Harry, "let's send Nanny back to Launceton with the baby and you and I will go off for a holiday. Just the two of us. I'll take you to some tropical island and dress you in hibiscus leis and we'll start all over again. Or we could go to Venice and stay in a wonderful old *palazzo* and pretend you're a Renaissance princess. You choose."

Harry did mean it, thought Peach hopefully, she was sure he did. But what about when the next pretty girl came along – would he think of *her* then? She looked at Wil lying on his perambulator in a shady part of the terrace and she couldn't bear the thought of losing him.

Venice was as beautiful as everyone had always told her it was, even in the rain. They drifted down misty canals in wonderful high-prowed gondolas peeking into the windows of old palaces and admiring the Canaletto vistas, and they stood in St Mark's Square and watched the flood waters lapping at its corners as though they would devour it for ever, and they drank Bellinis in the bar that bore Harry's name. Harry carried his notebook everywhere, jotting down images and scenes and snatches of conversations he overheard that caught his imagination and he made love to her every afternoon in their palatial room at the Cipriani, but he never wrote about her in his notebook, the way he used to when they first met.

Lying next to Harry, Peach studied his sleeping face, remembering how she had watched him on their first night together, only now she was looking for the truth. Harry wasn't a cruel man. Behind that handsome façade he was just self-indulgent and weak. Tomorrow or next week or next month, whenever the next pretty girl smiled at him invitingly, he would forget his promises. Harry would never change.

Peach pressed her face into the cool pillows, listening to the sound of the water lapping at the jetty outside the hotel. She knew now she didn't love Harry. She had been young and silly and obsessed with a dream. But she must stay for Wil's sake. The thought of an endless succession of lonely days at Launceton stretched before her with Harry locked away in his study, remote again in his own world, and she felt the tears spring to her eyes.

"*Merde,*" she said to herself angrily. "This is no time for tears. I've cried enough for Harry and me. It's time I did something with *my* life." She remembered herself standing in front of her grandfather de Courmont's portrait, full of young ideals and ambitions, promising him she would try to put the de Courmont name back on top with Rolls-Royce and Bentley and Mercedes. Well, now was the time to do something about it.

Peach wiped her eyes on a corner of the pillow. There would be no more tears. Grand-mère was right. It was time she grew up.

51

Noel celebrated his promotion to Great Lakes Motor Corporation's youngest divisional manager by buying Scott Harrison's old apartment. He drove past the building every day on his way to work in his brand new white Great Lakes coupé with the beige velour interior and Blaupunkt radio that was a step up from the Chevrolet he'd had before, and on an impulse he stopped to take a look. The building was a touch less glossy than when he'd last been there twelve years before and there were signs of neglect in the worn grey carpet and the unpolished brass plates in the elevator, but when he heard that there were apartments for sale, he knew he wanted to live there. And one of them was Scott's. Noel walked the empty anonymous rooms with the view of Detroit's towers from their wide windows, filling them with images of his hungry, frightened fourteen-year-old self wearing Scott's soft striped cashmere robe and drinking his first Martini and almost getting himself seduced.

Smiling, he called the real estate office and checked the price, offering them $5,000 less than the $20,000 they were asking. They compromised at $18,500 and he had a deal.

Noel never had any trouble in claiming that he was thirty years old. Quite the contrary, people often took him for older. The fact that he'd added a few years in order to get his first job had carried through until now even his social security forms set his age at thirty. He wondered whether the Great Lakes Motor Corporation would have given him the job if they knew he were really only twenty-six. He was getting $30,000 a year plus profit bonuses. And in a good year that could mean an extra $40,000. And he was damned good at his job. He'd been moved up from the design studio, where he had been personally responsible for the team re-styling their low-priced model, giving it a sporty new look that offered the young market exactly what it wanted – a "sporty" car without the sports car limitations and high price. And it had meant big sales and *high* profits for the company.

It was the company's president himself who'd congratulated Noel when the mock-up car had first been displayed for top executive approval. And when the orders flowed in after the unanimous enthusiasm of the dealers at a special unveiling preview, he had summoned Noel to his office.

Paul Lawrence had been born to money and power in the automobile industry. His father had been a former president of Great Lakes Motors and, like Noel, Paul had an MIT degree in engineering. After MIT Paul had worked in a variety of departments gaining experience in production on the shop floor, and then he'd taken a job at Ford, working his way across the glittering names of the auto industry until he was president of Great Lakes Motors. Paul's own rise to the top had been meteoric and he recognised Noel's unusual talent right away. And he wasn't the sort who kept a man down just because he was considered too young.

Paul listened to Noel's carefully edited history, sizing up the man in front of him. "Obviously hard work is not your problem," he commented, "in fact it's been your whole life. Tell me, Noel, what do you do in your spare time?"

Paul had taken him by surprise and Noel stared at him blankly. "Well," said Noel finally, "I don't know that I have much spare time. I work late as often as I can – you see that's what I really like."

"Come on now," said Paul, "what about Saturday nights? And

Sundays – everybody enjoys a Sunday off – even the presidents of large companies."

"I like music," admitted Noel. "I have a good collection of records and I like to go to the symphony when I can. And the galleries. I enjoy paintings and sculpture."

"You're not married?"

"No sir."

"You haven't been standing still long enough for anyone to catch you yet according to this," said Paul indicating Noel's c.v. The young man in the badly cut dark suit and the blue button-down collar waited for what he had to say, looking like a greyhound on the leash. A very interesting face and an interesting personality. "Well, Mr Maddox," he said with a smile, "*Noel*. How'd you like to be GL Motors division manager in charge of our mid-range cars?"

Noel's face lit like a beacon on Bunker Hill.

"Let me give you a word of advice," said Paul Lawrence as they shook hands on the deal, "take a little time to enjoy yourself. A man can get too involved in the small details working day and night. Sometimes you need to be able to stand back and get things into perspective. Take up golf, Noel – you'd be surprised what a help it can be. Keeps the blood pressure down, too, take it from me."

Like a kid in a candy shop Noel wandered through the big department stores choosing carpets and furniture and lighting fixtures. He wanted instant "home" and anything that couldn't be delivered that week, he rejected and chose something else. He gave instructions and paid his money and he went to work one morning and when he came back, there it was.

Velvety smooth black carpet and two glossy black leather chesterfield sofas. A big glass coffee table and, sitting on top of it, an enormous yellow ceramic ashtray advertising a French liquor, "Ricard", that he'd bought on impulse. A pair of chrome lamps on polished black fake-marble end-tables and the Kandinsky and the Mondrian still propped up against the wall where he had left them. Noel surveyed his kingdom, feeling strange, as though he were walking through a window display. He inspected the rest of the apartment cautiously. A king-size bed, draped in a black Spanish-looking velvet quilt, dominated the bedroom. The curved brass headboard with its smiling angels, their hands and wings neatly folded, was antique, discovered on a prowl through the smart little

271

boutiques that made Noel nervous. "Of course, it wasn't originally a headboard," the effeminate young man had told him. "It's French, turn of the century, and was first used to decorate the entrance to a children's orphanage." Despite its exorbitant price Noel had felt compelled to buy it. With him it had found its true home. Unpacking a beautifully wrapped parcel bearing the logo of an expensive shop, Noel, took out the striped cashmere robe and hung it behind the bathroom door. Then with a sigh he lay down on his bed. He felt so tired, more tired than he could ever remember in his whole life. He was asleep within minutes.

Claire Anthony's husband was vice-president in charge of the car and truck division at Chrysler. That's why it was particularly galling that the damned great lump of a station wagon wouldn't start. She'd wanted a nice sporty little Jaguar, or even a little MG – something imported and with style – to suit her personality, she thought with a smile. Instead she was stuck with the company's top-of-the-line station wagon that was so long and with her near-sight it was hell to back up and even worse hell to find a parking space big enough.

Sighing, Claire climbed from the car and stared at it dolefully. Her foot shot out suddenly and she gave it a hefty kick. "Goddamn it," she said viciously.

"Having trouble?" Noel laughed as he said it and she laughed too.

"Caught in the act," she said. "My husband would never forgive me."

"Then he can't be a very understanding man," replied Noel. "After all, you only kicked the tyres. You could have driven it into a wall."

"I might have," Claire admitted, "but it won't start."

"That's probably because you left your lights on." Noel pointed to the headlamps glowing brightly in the evening sun. "It was dark and rainy this morning and when the sun came out you forgot they were on."

"Well," said Claire, folding her arms and leaning against the car, "quite the little Sherlock Holmes, aren't we?"

Noel shrugged. "An easy deduction, lady, but I'm more of the Philip Marlowe type."

"Well listen, Philip Marlowe, now that we know what's wrong, what do we do about it?"

272

He looked at her appreciatively. She was tall, five-nine or ten, with long graceful legs and small feet in pretty lizard shoes that weren't meant for kicking tyres, and she had smooth dark hair cut short and chic. She wore a red jacket and skirt and her brown eyes behind big scarlet-framed glasses were smiling at him. "We go over the road to the Pontchartrain Hotel," he replied, "we call the garage to come and charge up your battery, and I buy you the drink of your choice."

Claire sighed. "I do like efficiency in a man," she said, taking her purse from the seat and slamming the door. "Lead the way, Philip Marlowe."

She refused the drink but they had coffee instead while she told him why she was doomed to the big Chrysler wagon despite her near-sightedness and its size, making him laugh at her version of the problems of parking. She lived in a white, two storey colonial-style house in Bloomfields Hills with her husband, the Chrysler executive, and two children, Kim aged thirteen in junior high and teeth braces, and Kerry aged eleven and a beauty.

"Like her mother," suggested Noel.

"Actually, she's like her father. But thank you anyway, for the compliment."

"You must have married very young," hazarded Noel.

She eyed him quizzically. "If you want to know, I'm thirty-four," she said. "And yes, perhaps I did marry a little too young. I've often thought so myself. You mustn't take that as any sign of major miscontent," she added with a smile, "just – well, middle-aged restlessness, I suppose. And what about you?" Claire changed the subject abruptly.

"Thirty, division manager at GL Motors. I live here in Detroit – in town."

"Is that all?"

"What do you mean?"

"You know – all the rest. Where are you from, what did you do before you became divison manager . . . your wife?"

Noel reached across the table and caught hold of her hand, examining the wide gold wedding band and the large solitaire diamond engagement ring. "I can read your palm," he said. "Nice New England girl, good family, engaged at nineteen to the up-and-coming young guy from the Ivy League college, married at twenty, a baby right away . . . a life of quiet domesticity in Bloomfield Hills – ladies' lunches and literary circle meetings and dinner parties,

273

and Christmas with all the family and lots of presents for everyone."

Claire's eyes met his steadily then she turned over the hand that held hers. "And I can read your palm, Philip Marlowe," she said quietly. "I see a very lonely man."

Noel curled his fingers, gripping her hand in his. "Maybe you're right," he said lightly, "I've never stopped to think about it."

"Then maybe it's time you did." Claire stood up abruptly. "I must go. I'll get a taxi home and have someone pick up the car for me later." They walked together from the hotel.

"Wait," said Noel. "I'd like to see you again."

She eyed him carefully, bunching her red jacket under her chin with a gloved hand. "We haven't been properly introduced," she said finally, smiling.

"Noel," he said. "Noel Maddox." He scribbled his telephone number rapidly on the back of his business card. "Claire," he said, "please telephone me."

A taxi pulled into the kerb and she stepped in, tucking her skirt over her pretty knees as Noel waited anxiously, holding open the door.

"I'll call," she said, her eyes meeting his.

Noel slammed the door shut and the cab pulled away. When she turned to look at him he was watching her.

Noel couldn't think where you took a married woman who was obviously known in Detroit society to make love to her, so he took her home.

"My God," said Claire, standing in the doorway. "It's a cross between a tomb and an airport lounge." She advanced cautiously across the black carpet, eyeing the cold slippery leather sofas with horror. Her eyes travelled across the room to the two prints, still propped against the wall. "A plant," she wailed, "a touch of green, a cushion – some evidence of human life."

Noel smiled and walked to the expensive record player. Choosing an album he switched on the machine and the delicate strains of Handel's Water Music filled the room. "How's that?" he asked. "A little more human?"

"Oh thank God," breathed Claire, "I was beginning to think I'd made a terrible mistake. I thought you were cold and heartless and as sharp-edged as this room." Kicking off her expensive high-heeled shoes she wandered to the bedroom. The golden brass angels smiled serenely at her across the big black bed. She felt better. "Any man who could buy that can't be all bad," she said with a grin. Noel watched bemused as she peeked into his bathroom. "Mmm," she commented, touching the striped cashmere robe. "A man of expensive tastes." She drifted across to the compact open-plan kitchen, opening cupboards and examining their contents interestedly. "You're a very neat man, Noel Maddox," she said, opening the refrigerator. It contained a jar of olives, a slab of Camembert cheese, a small can of Beluga caviare and a bottle of Dom Perignon.

"No milk," she said wonderingly, "no juice, no eggs. A man of *sophisticated* tastes."

"I got the champagne and caviare for you," said Noel. "I figured Philip Marlowe would have done that."

Claire laughed. She liked him. "Glasses are in the top cupboard," she told him, "and where's the thin, hot toast?"

He looked at her puzzled. "For the caviare," she told him.

Noel took down a box of crackers from the cupboard. "I thought these would do."

Claire took the carton from him, putting it behind her on the counter. Taking off her glasses she slid her arms around his neck, looking at him. His face was lean and craggy and the bones seemed to crash forward beneath his taut skin. His black hair grew thickly and he wore it slightly too long for a young executive on the way up, and there was already a blueish hint of beard on his freshly shaven chin. Beneath the blue shirt Noel's body looked hard and young and very tempting.

"This is all very wrong," she whispered, "and of course I shouldn't really be here. But nevertheless here I am. Shall we have the champagne later?"

Taking her hand, Noel led her across to the bedroom. Lying on her back she raised her skirt, inching it over her hips. "I can't wait to undress," she murmured, "I can't wait for you, Philip Marlowe."

She wore cream lace underwear and black stockings and Noel couldn't wait either. Unzipping his pants he fumbled himself free, trembling as she touched him. "Now," she breathed, "now, please oh please." She cried out as he entered her, twisting her head away from his mouth into the pillows, moaning as she felt him climax. "God," she gasped. "Oh God . . . I couldn't wait for you. I've been dreaming about you. Erotic dreams, just like this." She laughed, rolling over and kissing him. "I was acting out my fantasies – using you. Isn't that terrible?"

275

"I don't know," said Noel bemused.

"Shall we have the champagne now?" Claire suggested. "Before we continue."

Noel began to laugh. "You're crazy," he said. "I thought you were a nice quiet housewife from Bloomfield Hills."

"Wait," she warned him, laughing too, "you don't know what we Bloomfield Hills housewives are really like. Just think – you'll be able to write the definitive exposé." She watched him carefully as he carried the tray with the champagne in a bucket of ice and two saucer-shaped glasses and placed it on the table beside the bed. He'd taken off his clothes in the bathroom and he wore the striped cashmere robe. His legs looked strong and muscular as he padded back again to the kitchen and returned carrying the opened can of caviare, a spoon and a box of crackers.

"Sorry," he said holding out a cracker piled with caviare. "I'll have the toast next time. I've got a lot to learn."

He was serious and Claire looked at him in surprise. "That's all right," she said gently, "I'm a good teacher."

The champagne was cold and delicious and afterwards he peeled off her black stockings and kissed her knees and her soft instep and then he kissed her breasts, lingering over them until she moaned again wanting him. And then his mouth travelled down her belly until it found what it was seeking and Claire arched her back in ecstasy to meet him. When he took her this time it was with power and control. Noel Maddox needed no teaching in making love.

52

Claire went to Noel's apartment twice a week – more when she could manage it, but with two children and a husband it wasn't easy. How much shopping could you say you needed to do in Detroit? She hadn't really intended for things to go this far – it had been a tempting anonymous impulse the first time, something that she had needed because sometimes Lance, her husband, made her feel like she was blending into the wallpaper. Of course she understood. After fourteen years of marriage familiarity became a dangerous element. Claire would bet it caused more divorces in Bloomfield Hills than adultery or drink. She loved Lance and he loved her but he also loved his job and that created a "*ménage à trois*". She was just balancing things out a little, that's all.

Noel Maddox's off-beat charm was insidious. Being with him was like being with two different people. When he talked about his work he was the steely, self-assured businessman who knew what he wanted. His ambition burned too clearly for him to hide it. But his personal life was uncharted. He'd told her only that his parents had died when he was young and that he'd had to work his way through school. There had been no time to learn about living. Just work.

Claire never went empty-handed to his apartment. She took him green growing plants – big ones in huge woven baskets to stand on the black carpet near the windows, softening the harsh view of Detroit. She bought a beautiful thick plaid rug from Scotland to throw over the cold leather sofa and yellow and scarlet and blue cushions that picked up the colours in his Mondrian and Kandinsky prints. And she gave him bright soft towels to take away the operating-theatre sterility of his white tiled bathroom. When she brought him the pair of antique silver photograph frames, Noel just stared at her. "What am I supposed to put in there?" he asked.

"You put photographs in them," Claire replied puzzled, "of people you love, your family, your friends . . ."

Noel replaced the frames in their box and gave them back to her. "I have no photographs," he said. "You keep them." Sometimes she thought Noel could be a little frightening.

But usually when she arrived his face lit up with pleasure. Taking her glasses from her nose he would kiss her and she'd kick off her shoes and cling to him. She'd be lost right away in his passion.

He bought her champagne and caviare and albums of his favourite music so that he could share it with her. And she bought him books on the history of art and biographies of composers and interesting new novels. "I feel like Scott Fitzgerald giving his lover a reading list," she said, handing him her favourite Harry Launceton book, *Nectar*. Its intriguing cover showed the half-hidden curves of a woman soft and out-of-focus in peach colour and gold. "Launceton's changed his style completely in the last few years," she said, "since he married the de Courmont girl."

277

"The de Courmont girl?"

"The French car family – you know? Peach, I think her name is. Anyhow, she certainly changed Harry Launceton for a while."

Noel was gripping the book so tightly she could see his knuckles gleaming white. Then he placed the book carefully on the coffee table and poured her a glass of champagne. Walking to the window he stared out into the night.

Claire watched him in silence. Something was wrong but whatever it was she knew he wouldn't tell her. He kept everything locked away in some secret compartment that she wasn't even sure Noel himself ever opened and looked at.

"Come here," commanded Noel roughly. He didn't undress her as much as tear the clothes off her, in a hurry. And when he made love to her this time it was almost as anonymous as with Lance.

"I'm giving a party," she told him afterwards as they sipped the champagne. "And I'd like you to come," she added, biting into the toast smeared with caviare.

Noel looked at her surprised. "Is it usual for Bloomfield Hills wives to invite their lovers to their parties?"

Claire sighed. "I wouldn't know. But it's the sort of party that *you* need. Top men in the industry will be there – chairmen, presidents, vice-presidents, influential dealers. As you know the wheels of Motor City wouldn't go round without those dealers. It's they who make the sales. And, besides, it's for charity," she added, "a garden party in aid of the orphanage society."

"Then I see I shall have to come." Noel's smile didn't reflect what she read in his eyes.

"Look," she said, exasperated, "I don't know what's wrong today, but I thought this party would be a good opportunity for you. If you're ever going to make it to the top you'll have to learn how to play the executive game."

"Teach me what to do." Noel leaned back against the plaid rug and Claire curled into the crook of his arm, tucking her bare feet under her.

"It's not just talent and hard work, Noel. There's already an excess of talent in this city. And a hell of a lot of ambition. What you have to learn is how to climb the corporate ladder. I know, I watched Lance do it."

"No doubt it came easy to him," commented Noel moodily, "the right background, the right schools . . ."

"Noel! This is a *tough town*. *Numbers* are all that matter. If you

278

went to the right schools and don't make your numbers, you're out." Claire lit a cigarette exhaling a thin spiral of blue smoke. Reaching across to the table she put on her glasses.

"Don't do that," said Noel suddenly, "it makes you look dressed. As though you're about to leave."

Claire was wrapped in his robe with nothing on underneath and she laughed. "I need to see you," she said firmly, "and you know I can't see more than six inches in front of my nose. Now, do you want to hear this or not?"

"Tell me," said Noel quietly.

"You can't be the loner, Noel Maddox," she began, "or be too 'different'. You have to become a 'team player', part of the corporate family. First, you should apply to join every professional automative and engineering society connected with the industry that you can. Use the company if you need pressure to make them let you in. Paul Lawrence gave you the promotion – he's rooting for you. Drop his name. And it's important to make social contacts with other young executives, play golf with them, get yourself invited to their homes. Buy their wives flowers when they have you to dinner, admire their homes and play with their kids. *Learn from them!*" Claire crushed out the cigarette in the yellow Ricard ashtray – the only thing in the room that she really liked. Noel was leaning back against the sofa, his eyes closed.

"I'm listening," he said.

"And you have to start thinking 'short-term'," she said.

"What do you mean?" His eyes flew open and he stared at her puzzled.

"You understand that it's all a game of *numbers*," she said. "All executives are under pressure to achieve their goals or quotas set by the top management. The men whose feet are climbing the ladder are not the ones who've planned a campaign to revolutionise the company five years from now. Success depends on *today*'s goals being achieved. And those young executives who are today's successes will be wooed by other companies offering them a better job. They're not interested in the man who just *shows promise*. You told me yourself that Paul Lawrence gave you the division manager job because of what you had achieved. Fast turn-around, quick concepts, immediate action . . . You've got to keep moving, Noel, you can't brood over being turned down on an idea even though you know it's good – and even if you are proved right. It's like Monopoly. If you pass 'Go' today you are rewarded with money

279

and another chance to go round the board. To get more you just keep on passing 'Go'."

Claire sat back and took off her glasses. "Take it or leave it," she said, watching him, "but that's the truth. That's the way it's played, Noel."

She peered at him near-sightedly. He was frowning, staring at the view of Detroit outside his windows.

"Will you come to my party?" she asked.

Noel looked at her, his grey eyes unreadable. "I'll come," he said.

"Good," Claire sat back, relieved. "At least it's a start."

Noel had driven through the pretty suburb many times, cruising slowly through its quiet streets where the spacious houses were set back from the road behind smooth green lawns. Bloomfield Hills is "Management", Claire had told him. The next step is Grosse Pointe – that's where the solid, old money lives – and, when they've really made it, the new top management. Every man on the second floor of the executive tower aspires to reach the fourteenth "power" floor, and every executive wife in Bloomfield Hills aspires to a house in Grosse Pointe. Noel had admired the homes from a distance but they had seemed no part of the life he envisaged for himself. He hadn't thought beyond the "tower". Now he looked at them with new eyes. He watched a pretty woman unloading her shopping from a large luxurious station wagon helped by a white-coated maid, and kids riding new bicycles along unlittered sidewalks. There were sleek automobiles in the two-, or even three-car garages and the windows of the big houses were open to the sunshine with their flowered curtains blowing in the breeze. These were your rewards if you played the game well.

He knew where Claire's house was, he'd driven past it several times on lonely Saturday nights, staring at its lighted windows and imagining her with Lance giving a dinner party and enjoying the company of their friends. Their two children would be upstairs in their pretty rooms – one for each child. Shelves would hold rows of stuffed animals and dolls and maybe they'd be watching television or reading, or perhaps they'd have other kids sleeping over. Claire's life looked to him like the American dream – the one every man was striving for.

A parking valet in a red jacket came towards him as he pulled into the kerb. The driveway was already packed with cars, solid top-of-the-line vehicles with personalised number plates that showed they belonged to the top brass. Other smart cars lined both sides of the wide street and the valet took Noel's GL Coupé and drove it to the far end of the street where the less expensive cars were parked.

Straightening his tie nervously, Noel strode up the driveway. The double doors stood wide open and a smiling servant directed him through to the drawing room that ran the length of the house. Beyond its open french windows lay an acre of green lawns and flower beds. There was a glint of turquoise blue from a swimming pool, sheltered behind a low white brick wall. People were standing around laughing and gossiping and sipping glasses of champagne with orange juice. The tickets had cost twenty-five dollars and had said "barbecue" and one section of the immaculate lawn had been covered with fake grass and a whole bank of barbecues were already blazing under the supervision of four white-jacketed chefs.

Noel saw at once that he was wrongly dressed. All the men wore light pants and linen jackets and their wives wore trim summery cottons. They looked casual yet chic. Feeling conspicuous in his dark business suit he lurked on the patio, looking for Claire.

"There you are," she said, pushing her spectacles – blue today – down her nose and peering at him over the top. "I thought you weren't coming."

"Perhaps I shouldn't have," muttered Noel.

Claire sighed. "I should have warned you that it would be informal, though people don't usually wear business suits for a barbecue."

"Forget it," snarled Noel, "I'm leaving."

"Noel! Noel wait. You mustn't leave." Her hand rested urgently on his arm and he turned to look at her. "Please Noel. For your own sake," she said, "stay."

"Hello there." The man walking towards them was tall, brown-haired, clean-cut. Noel knew at once that it was Lance, her husband.

"I don't think we've met." Lance held out his hand, his keen blue eyes assessing Noel. "I'm Lance Anthony."

"This is Noel Maddox," said Claire.

"Of course, of course." Lance shook Noel's hand warmly. "I've heard quite a lot about you."

Noel glanced at him warily.

"On the grapevine. All good things, Noel. Great things in fact. Everyone says you show great promise. I hear you're one of the up and coming men at GL. Now, let me get you a drink." He claimed a glass of Bucks Fizz for Noel from a passing waiter. "Sure hope you're hungry, Noel," he commented as they walked across the patio together, "there's a hell of a lot of steak cooking over there. But first let me introduce you to some people." Putting an arm around Noel's shoulder, Lance led him towards a group of men standing in the shade of a great oak tree. "I'd like you to meet Noel Maddox," he said genially, "I expect you've heard of him – news travels fast in this town. Noel this is Mort Shively, Stan Masters, Paul Lawrence, who I'm sure you know – and Dick Svenson."

Noel's gaze met those of the assembled top brass of America's motor industry – US Auto, Ford, Great Lakes Motors . . . My God, he thought, if anyone were to drop a bomb the whole industry would be in a shambles . . .

Paul Lawrence smiled at him. "Glad to see you took my advice, Noel, and are getting out and relaxing. Noel's one of our most promising division managers," he told the others, "but the man's a workaholic. Gotta get him out on the golf course more, let him relax."

The talk was of golf and cabins on the lake for fishing and Noel just listened. He couldn't think of anything to say. After five minutes Lance said, "There's someone over there you should meet, Noel. He's your opposite number at Ford." Introducing them Lance left to check on the barbecue operations and Noel smiled at the man's wife, asking where they lived and if they had children. He commented on how pleasant it was to be here on such a nice day. "And for such a good cause," the young wife added.

"Enjoying yourselves?"

Claire was at his elbow, smiling at him, and Noel smiled back, relieved.

"I must introduce Noel to my children," Claire said, pulling him away. She laughed. "Looks as though you're finding the small talk hard work," she said.

"It's not easy," admitted Noel.

"Here," said Claire. "This is Kerry and this is Kim." They were neat brown-haired preppie children in identical khaki bermuda shorts and pink polo shirts. They smiled at him nicely, the elder one showing an expanse of metal that glittered like railway tracks in the sun. Saying hello politely they skipped off in the direction of the barbecue. "And this is my father," said Claire, dragging Noel towards a table near the pool. Beneath the umbrella sat a man

282

familiar to anyone in the motor industry. Clive Sanders, former head of US Auto and, it was said, still the power behind the throne – even though he was retired.

"Noel Maddox is one of the up and coming young men in the business, Papa," said Claire.

"Used to be one of those myself," said Sanders, smiling and holding out his hand. 'Come and sit down over here and tell me all about yourself, Mr Maddox. I'm always interested to hear a new viewpoint on the same old business."

Noel spent half an hour chatting to the older man and then it was time for lunch.

"You didn't tell me you were Clive Sanders's daughter!" he said accusingly to Claire, clutching a plate with an enormous steak.

"Come and sit down over here," she replied, guiding him to one of the umbrella-shaded tables that dotted the patio and pool areas. "Why should I have told you?"

"No wonder you knew all about the business." Noel's gaze was serious.

"I learned it all from him," she said simply. "And he knows what he's talking about. My father's word still counts for a lot in this town, Noel."

Noel cut into his steak, watching as the blood followed the knife. It was too rare for his taste.

"That's why I wanted you to meet him," she said as Lance appeared with the two girls in tow.

"We need you, Mom," called Kerry. "Dad's not sure if the caterers have brought enough ice cream for the pies."

Left alone, Noel ignored his steak. People were grouped at each other's tables, talking as they ate. They all seemed to know each other, though the hierarchy was clear even in the seating arrangements. The top brass were on the patio near the house, the lesser executives near the pool. A few children had already changed in the cabana and were sitting on the edge, contemplating a swim.

Steeling himself, Noel picked up his plate and walked across to a neighbouring table. "Mind if I join you?" he asked quietly. "I seem to have been deserted."

Two hours later, driving home to his black cubic apartment, he re-ran the day's events in his head. First Claire had shown no embarrassment at all in introducing him to her husband. And Lance was a nice guy, he'd gone out of his way to see that he met influential people – and probably because Claire had asked him to.

But Noel had been uncomfortably aware of his role as the "other man"! Paul Lawrence had been genial, too, and the young couples he'd sat with at lunch had accepted him easily as one of them. When he'd left the wives had said, "Oh, but you must come to dinner, Noel, some time soon." And his talk with Clive Sanders had been interesting – the old man had wanted to know what his views were on the current state of the industry and its aims. Noel had told him, forgetting about keeping his mouth shut and keeping a low profile. Sanders had listened, nodding in agreement every now and then, or stopping him to interject a question. He'd shaken hands again, firmly, when Noel left, saying it was very good to have met him and to have talked . . . for whatever it meant.

Back in his apartment Noel took out his old portfolio of drawings and ideas, spreading them across the big new drawing board he'd placed beneath the window. Dreams! he thought staring at them, this aerodynamic concept, that clean de-chromed bumper, this revolutionary new fascia for the dashboard . . . all dreams. Dreams were easy. It was reality that was so difficult.

53

Peach divided her weeks neatly into three days at Launceton with Wil and four days at the de Courmont offices on the Avenue Kléber in Paris. At first she'd felt terribly guilty about leaving Wil and once or twice she'd even stepped off the plane in Paris and taken the very next flight back to London, driving frantically up to Launceton, afraid that Wil might be missing her or that he couldn't live without her. But of course Wil could and he was quite happy with Nanny. Harry seemed to notice she wasn't there only when it affected his own plans, though Peach had found that the four o'clock Friday flight to London got her back home just in time to greet his weekend guests. Even the boring dinners had improved since she'd taken to dashing into Fouquets on her way to the airport, picking up extra little goodies – mousses and terrines, cheeses and fruit sirops, to lighten up cook's leaden meals.

Harry had moved out of their big room into one of his own next door. He said it was because he hated being in their room when she wasn't there, but Peach wasn't sure she believed him. It didn't matter, she preferred it that way. Melinda told her that Harry was still seeing Augusta and though Peach never tried to find out, she was sure that there were other girls as well.

Harry never asked her to accompany him on his frequent travels – "It's too much to expect the lady tycoon to drop everything just to be with her husband," he'd said waspishly, but Peach knew he looked forward to being alone – without her. Of course he still made love to her but she had come to the conclusion that for Harry – now she was no longer his inspiration – making love was like exercise, something to be done every day for his physical well-being, and she hated herself for responding to him, knowing that it could have been any one of a dozen girls in his arms and he would have been equally happy.

But when Peach stepped into the de Courmont offices on Tuesday mornings she felt free to be herself. She wasn't just Wil's mother or Harry Launceton's wife. She was Peach de Courmont and she was learning her way in the complex world of the automobile industry.

Her small office was tucked away near the back of the building and it contained only a large plain desk, a filing cabinet and a black telephone. Peach had been taken aback when Jim first showed it to her. Gerard had assigned his full interest in the family company to Peach and, as the de Courmont heiress, she now owned these offices; somehow she'd expected to have a palatial suite overlooking the Avenue Kléber with walnut bookcases and Savonnerie rugs and a beautiful feminine Louis XVI table. She'd imagined herself choosing pictures for the walls and answering telephone calls from a battery of important red telephones and floating out to lunch meetings at expensive restaurants.

"If you're serious," said Jim, "and I think you are, then this is where you start. At the bottom like everyone else."

Peach sat gloomily behind her new desk on the first morning while Jim explained things to her. "De Courmont have dropped from being one of the top-class producers of automobiles in the world and are fighting a battle to stay in the industry," he told her, "and at the moment, while they're not exactly losing, they're not winning either. They're managing to hold on to their European market – but only just and of course their American market is now almost non-existent. Our automobile plants took a beating in the war and there was never enough money afterwards to rebuild and re-tool the way it should have been done. In fact de Courmont could quite easily have gone under after the war. Of course we could have sold off the real estate and still come out with a million or two. Your father left the decision to me and for your sake I wanted to try to keep it going. It was your inheritance and I felt you should have the choice when you were old enough. However, in order to go on we needed to raise capital and there were two ways to go. We could have got money by making the company public and selling its stocks and shares, but that would have meant losing complete control. Or we could have sold off the steel foundries and *some* of the real estate. I chose to do the latter because I wanted you to have the de Courmont company intact. One day it will be yours to do whatever you want with, Peach, but I'm going to make sure that when you make any decision in the future you understand what you are doing. Is that clear?"

Peach nodded, interested.

"Right," said Jim. "The first thing you'll do is learn the history of the company. There's a library on the third floor with all the old documents and letters filed since 1895. Your grandfather, 'Monsieur', kept a record of every meeting and every transaction. You'll find design drawings and blueprints of the first cars there and details of their specifications and costs. You'll even find out how he brought the rubber for the tyres all the way from the Amazon, cutting out the middle-men importers and manufacturers, making them in his own factories and saving de Courmont a fortune. You'll read about his search to find the finest leathers and the best woods, and the methods that were used to give the de Courmont cars their special depth of colour. Monsieur's cars were among the finest in the world, and one of the first cars on the roads of France. Learn its history, Peach, and then I'll take you to see de Courmont as it is today."

Peach was in her office by eight thirty every morning and for two weeks she did nothing but read. It felt strange to hold pages written by the grandfather she'd never known and she examined his severe unadorned handwriting carefully, as if expecting to find a clue to his mysterious personality. His notes were clipped to sheets of suggested designs and reading them she was amazed by the scope of his plans and his attention to detail. By the end of her two weeks she had a good working knowledge of how Monsieur had built his automotive empire from the first de Courmont to the present models being turned out from the automated shop floor. She was ready for the next phase.

Jim knew that two months alone in the industrial provinces near Valenciennes would be enough to test Peach's strength of purpose. He arranged for her to stay in a small family hotel near the plant and every morning she followed the streams of cars and men to the factory as the early shift began.

Peach spent a week touring the factories learning what each process was and exactly how a car was constructed from beginning to end. She was taken to see the tooling plants that made automotive parts for the engines and the rolling mills producing the steel. She watched deafened as giant machines stamped out cold grey car bodies and she saw them sprayed in bright new colours. She admired shiny engines being assembled and sat in on discussions about interiors, learning why some upholstery fabrics were good and others not. And she watched, awestruck, as the assembly line rolled relentlessly forward and men crawled over and under and into the skeletons of cars fitting them together bit by bit until, miraculously, at the end of the long line a complete automobile appeared.

After that Peach spent one week in each of the departments. She went to meetings, listening while problems were thrashed out on the structure of the next de Courmont model, and she learned the reasons for its design and which market it was aimed at and how it had been costed and why that price range was important. She listened to complaints in the personnel office about changes in shifts and too-short work-breaks and she met union shop-stewards and management, sitting quietly in a corner and taking in everything that went on. Peach went to work early and she stayed late. She took a train back to Paris every Friday to catch her London flight and she was back again promptly on Tuesday morning having taken the first flight out.

"Do I get a bigger office now?" she asked Jim with a grin when she returned from Valenciennes.

"You don't even rate a secretary yet," he replied. "The next thing you need to learn about is sales."

The entire ground floor of the de Courmont building on Avenue Kléber was a showroom. Enormous plate-glass windows displayed the latest model cars, their rich polished colours glowing under spotlights against a background of deep grey carpet. "This is our window to the world," said Jim. "Everyone who walks down the Avenue Kléber – the foreign businessman, the tourist, the city-dwellers, the French family in town from the provinces – will see what de Courmont has to offer. But the *real sales* are made by our dealers. Go out and meet them and find out how it's done."

Peach spent another exhausting month criss-crossing France and Italy and Germany – even England – doing exactly that, covering thousands of miles in her brand-new dark blue de Courmont – the official family colour.

After that Jim kept her hopping, learning about sales figures and studying market research surveys that showed new trends in the industry and how public opinion was reflected in the new designs. Peach juggled statistics in her head when she was sleeping and analysed colours and carpeting and interior upholstery when she was awake. After she'd stuck with her crash course for six months Jim said, "Okay, now I know you're serious, the real work begins."

Peach sank back in her chair with a groan of pure agony. "*Oh No!* What was all this then?" She waved her arm at the desk littered with papers.

Jim grinned. "That was just the beginning. Now, are you ready for the real hard grind or not?"

She glared at him sullenly. "I suppose so."

"Well then, get yourself smartened up. It's time to meet upper management."

Peach hadn't bought a new dress in ages – not since all those English country lady clothes when she was still trying to be an Augusta for Harry, and she had forgotten what fun it could be. She went to Givenchy and Balmain and Dior and indulged herself disgracefully, buying smart little suits and dresses to wear to the office and a dazzlingly pretty deep blue velvet evening dress that would startle the hell out of Harry's weekend guests' wives! And she swept, like a cyclone through the newest boutiques buying luxurious satin lingerie and beautiful high-heeled shoes and expensive handbags. Away with cashmere and shetland, she thought, away with loafers and wicker shopping baskets. I'm a businesswoman and I'm going to meet my managing directors.

As chairman, Jim had the large corner office on the first floor with a view along the Avenue. It had the wonderful carpets, the walls lined with bookcases and the paintings and banks of telephones that Peach herself had anticipated. His secretary, who had been with the company twenty-five years and probably knew almost as much about its wheelings and dealings and ups and downs as did anyone else, guarded the entrance from a huge desk that was twice as big as Peach's desk.

Chic in a business-like grey Chanel suit and a soft claret-coloured blouse, with her russet hair swept firmly back in one of Chanel's pretty velvet bows, Peach was introduced to the company's acting president and her directors. Feeling like a nervous schoolgirl she sipped a glass of sherry while they smiled at her indulgently, enquiring how she was liking her job? When they asked about her son she brought out the photographs she always carried in her bag and showed them around proudly and they smiled and said they expected she missed him, and he was such a fine, good-looking boy.

Jim took Peach to lunch afterwards at the Tour d'Argent, watching as she toyed with her food. "Well?" he asked.

"They were being kind to me," cried Peach seething, "indulging the runaway housewife pretending to be a businesswoman. And I provided them with poor little Wil's pictures. They think I'm just dropping in to see how the family business is ticking over. I proved their point, damn it. Harry's right – he calls me 'the tycoon' – laughing at me!"

"To them you are an amateur. And a woman in a man's world," replied Jim. "Can you prove their judgement wrong?"

Peach glared at him. "Traitor!" she snapped. "What have I been doing all these months? Haven't I worked hard enough? Didn't I do everything you asked!"

"You did. But that was just the beginning." Jim leaned across the table and took her reluctant hand in his. "I must admit I didn't think you'd last this far, but now I'm betting on you. It's going to be hard work and long hours and I can see how exhausted you are dashing back and forth to England. Can you take it, Peach?"

"I'll do it," said Peach stubbornly. "It's my company and one day I'm going to run it."

"Good," said Jim laughing, "then let's drink to that and to my potential retirement."

The house on the Ile St Louis was far too large and grand and Peach felt lost in it. She hadn't had time to feel lonely before but the meeting today had made her aware that she was. She soaked away her anger and the pent-up fatigue of the past months in a hot bath, wondering if she were right. Could she do it? Was this what she wanted from life? The answer stared back at her as it always had. She adored Wil but in order to keep him she had to stay married to Harry. And in order to stay *sane* while she was married to Harry, she had to have a life of her own. Being the "business tycoon" may not be exactly what she wanted from life, but it kept her so busy that she didn't have time to think how miserable she was. It would do.

Climbing from the bath tub she threw on a white terry robe and ran down the stairs into the hall. Monsieur's portrait stared back at her with her own dark blue eyes. "I'll do it," she said fiercely. "I'll show them I'm your granddaughter. But now I'm going to do it my way – and I'm going to have some fun."

54

Noel's desk in the small office on the fourteenth floor was neat. Papers lay tidily in the out tray and there was another stack neatly aligned in front of him ready for his attention. Major changes were taking place at the top of the industry. Mort Shively had left US Auto suddenly, supposedly with a contract pay-off in the millions, taking his executive vice-president with him. And Paul Lawrence was leaving Great Lakes Motors to take over Shiveley's job – at a salary and stock options reputed on the grapevine to be around $750,000 a year with a five-year contract. And now the competition was going to be hot and heavy for the position of Lawrence's second-in-command.

The hierarchy of the company from the top was the chairman, the vice-chairman and the president. Then there were the executive vice-presidents who were their right-hand men. Below that came the vice-presidents in charge of a group of whom Noel was now one at Great Lakes, and below that, the group divisional managers. It was unlikely that all of these jobs would be changed at once but Paul Lawrence was going to appoint his own executive vice-president immediately and, working on the old Machiavellian concept that those who are only ninety-nine per cent for you are basically against you, Paul Lawrence would want his own man in there. A man who would be one hundred per cent loyal to him and a man he could trust. Noel wanted that job. And, analysing his likely rivals for the position, he saw that the man who stood head and shoulders above any other was Lance Anthony.

Paul had moved Noel rapidly upwards from division manager to vice-president in charge of design, giving him as much leeway as he wanted to push forward new concepts. And Noel knew that Paul was pleased with him. The new model four-wheel-drive truck had already been given his blessing and various modifications he had suggested and designed had been made mandatory on some of their existing cars, mainly new refinements in engineering. Noel pushed his designers hard, charging them with his own energy and employing a pool of young people straight from design college for new "street" input to get a feel of the young market and ideas. It was exciting and it worked. He was happy in his job.

When Noel had moved to the fourteenth floor he had thought he had finally made it. As the youngest and newest vice-president he had an office off the green-carpeted corridor nearest to the door. As you progressed further along the corridor so the rank of importance rose, until at the far end was the executive suite – the chairman, vice-chairman and the president's office – currently empty now that Paul Lawrence had left. No one knew yet who would get that coveted job but it seemed panic buttons were being pushed and odds were it would be someone already in a similar position. A big company like Great Lakes couldn't afford to take chances on any less.

Noel's private phone rang and he picked it up quickly. It was Claire. He hadn't seen her for several weeks, the children had been ill with bad colds and coughs and then she'd had the 'flu. Last time they had spoken Claire had sounded harassed.

"Can we see each other tonight? Lance is in New York and the children are sleeping over with friends. I'm alone."

"Alone at last!" said Noel.

"Oh, Philip Marlowe – always good with a cliché," she commented but could tell he was smiling.

"Your place," she said, "seven-thirtyish."

He was late but Claire had her key and she was waiting for him. There were flowers in a blue vase on the table and tall pale candles gleamed in the twilight.

Claire had brought Chinese take-out food and a bottle of chilled Mersault. Noel realised that he had never once taken her out to dinner. They never went out together. His apartment was their entire world. Occasionally they met socially at other people's houses but naturally Claire was with her husband, and their assignations had become less frequent because of the hazards of continuing such a friendship.

"Sometimes I need you," sighed Claire hugging him.

Noel grinned. "Is life that hard for a true princess of Motor City?"

"And what did that ever do for me?" she exclaimed.

"It got you good schools and a beautiful home, ponies, houses by the sea, European travel. And all before you were eighteen! God, I was working at three jobs as well as studying then. You should count what it bought you, Claire – and count yourself lucky," said Noel angrily.

Her brown eyes behind the red glasses were cold. "It paid for my nose fixing and my teeth straightening – and a lot of pairs of spectacles," she assured him. "God, think of the mess I would have been without it. You wouldn't have looked at me twice."

"You shouldn't joke about having money, Claire," said Noel irritably. "Your father worked hard for it."

Pushing away from him she walked to the table and poured white wine into the Baccarat crystal glasses she had bought him.

"I came here tonight hoping to get away from exactly this sort of discussion," she said angrily. "I might as well be with Lance. I'm sick to death of talk of money and ambition. This whole town talks of nothing else."

Noel took the glass of wine and tasted it. It was good. "It's Motor City," he said, "we're all here to play its game. Remember, it was you who taught me the rules."

"It wasn't me who gave you that ruthless streak of ambition," she retorted.

"No. My mother gave me that."

Claire had never heard him mention his mother before and she stared at him curiously. Noel's face looked pinched in the grey twilight, but he said nothing further.

"Well," she said finally, "Lance is just as bad. But thank God it looks as though he's going to get the job he's after and then we can all sleep in peace again. He's driving us crazy – even the children can't put up with his irritability."

"You mean the executive vice-president for Paul Lawrence?" Noel asked, carefully casual.

"He deserves it," said Claire. "He's the right man for the job and my father had a word with Paul yesterday. It looks as though it'll go through." She looked at Noel worriedly. "Let's not fight," she said gently. "Come and have some Chinese food, darling. It's in the oven keeping warm."

Noel sank on to the sofa placing his glass on the coffee table in front of him. "Sorry Claire," he said, "but I don't feel much like eating. You go ahead."

Claire watched him in silence. His eyes were shut and he looked remote, as though he were on some other planet. Picking up her coat from the chair where she had thrown it as she came in, she walked over to him and kissed him. "Something tells me I've overstayed my welcome," she said softly. "It's time I left, Noel Maddox."

His eyes flew open and he reached out his hand to her but Claire was already half-way across the room. She turned at the door. "Call me when you need me," she said, managing a smile.

As the door closed behind her Noel turned his head away, burying it in the soft plaid rug she'd bought him. He'd lost her. And he'd lost the job. He wasn't about to pass "Go" and he wouldn't get another turn at the Monopoly board.

Paul Lawrence requested Noel's presence at lunch at the Pontchartrain Hotel the following week.

Smart in a well-cut grey flannel suit from Brooks Brothers, and the striped tie of the Detroit Athletic Club, Noel waited for his host at the bar.

"What can I get you, sir?" the barman asked deferentially.

"A Virgin Mary," ordered Noel. He never mixed drink and business. He liked the Pontchartrain and was beginning to feel comfortable in its tapestry-hung, soft-carpeted luxury.

Paul Lawrence greeted him affably and Noel could feel curious eyes on them as they made their way into the busy dining room. Everyone knew everyone else in Motor City and the word would soon be around that Noel Maddox was lunching with Paul Lawrence and conclusions would be drawn. Rightly? he wondered.

"Quite frankly," began Paul over excellent roast beef, "I had another man in mind for the job. A very able man. A little older than you, Noel – not that age is a detriment in your case, you've proven that. But sometimes seniority and experience count for a lot. I won't mention his name because this is kind of confidential and his father-in-law is a friend of mine. But there have been some disqueting rumours about this man's wife, that she's running around with some other guy. It's not that I'm a prude about these things, though I can't say I approve of it. But a potential domestic disaster can cause havoc with a man's work. Divorce has lost me more good executives than I'd care to think about. So, I'm afraid I had to pass on him. And his bad luck turns out to be *your* good luck, Noel. I'd like to offer you the job as executive vice-president in charge of all our divisions. You'll answer to me and where necessary the chairman and you'll have free reign for your creative concepts." Laying down his knife and fork he beamed at Noel, his eyes twinkling in his pink-cheeked jovial face like Santa Claus bestowing a gift. "I dare say we can reach agreement on the money," he added, "and it will be generous, Noel, I assure you. I know you're getting fifty thousand at Great Lakes. I think I can promise you double that, plus stock options and bonuses. We'll take care of you at US Auto. Well – what do you say?"

Pushing any thought of Claire firmly into a recess of his mind Noel held out his hand. "I'd be delighted to accept, Mr Lawrence," he said. "And thank you. You've made my day."

Paul Lawrence chortled gleefully. "My boy," he said, "I may just have made your entire life."

55

Harry Launceton slammed the newspaper down on his desk glaring angrily at the photograph of Peach. The caption over the top read, PEACH OPENS DE COURMONT'S NEW BEVERLY HILLS SHOWROOM – and there was Peach standing between two famous film actors snipping a ribbon with an oversize pair of scissors and smiling her celebrity smile, looking glossier than any fashion model.

Since Peach had become the star of de Courmont's new advertising campaign her face appeared everywhere – in the daily papers, in double-page spreads in magazines and zooming across billboards ten-times life-size – at the wheel of the latest de Courmont, with "It's a Peach of a Car", or "Take it from a de Courmont – it's the Greatest" and other such rubbishy blurbs emblazoned across the top. He rarely saw her, she was always dashing around the world promoting de Courmont cars and having her photograph taken with rock-stars and actors and hosting parties and giving press conferences.

Of course it was the row about Wil that had finally separated them. Peach had never fitted in with the English way of doing things and there was no question that Wil was to be sent off to board at a prep school when he was seven. But Peach had ranted and raved about Harry's cruelty in storms of tears and made him feel like an ogre when all he was doing was the proper thing. He'd had Augusta take Wil to Peter Jones to buy the boy his uniform because Peach refused to be party to his "barbarism" and to Augusta's credit she hadn't once said about Peach, "I told you so". After Wil had finally gone off to school Peach had spent most of her time in Paris, only coming to Launceton for Wil's holidays and then, if Harry were busy writing, she'd whisk Will off to the South of France or Florida.

Of course he should never have divorced Augusta and married Peach, but when he was writing he was like a man wearing blinkers and Peach had led him up an erotic new path that he'd been unable to resist. She'd been his inspiration for what might eventually, in his obituary in *The Times*, be called "his two greatest novels". Harry's last two books had been difficult ones to write, involving lots of research and painstaking marshalling of facts and it galled him that they hadn't been received nearly as well. And now Peach was flaunting herself around the globe, probably with a pack of men sniffing at her heels, while he was here at Launceton worrying about his next book.

Thrusting the newspaper into his waste-basket Harry picked up the phone, glancing out of his study window as he dialled Augusta's number. It was a lovely blue summer morning, perfect for young Wil's great day. "Augusta? Forget your plans for today. I want you to come with me to watch Wil's cricket match. I'll pick you up at eleven thirty and we'll have lunch on the way down. What about Peach? Yes, I suppose she will be there, Wil told me she was flying in from Paris specially . . . I don't give a damn what she thinks, Augusta. Right. See you then."

Checking his watch, Harry walked to the door, hands in his pockets, whistling. He felt like a school kid himself, now he'd made the decision. He needed someone to look after him and be a decent mother to his boy. He was going to divorce Peach and ask Augusta to marry him – again.

Peach sat up in bed sipping coffee and admiring her new room. The interior designer had done a marvellous job, though of course she'd told him exactly what she wanted. After six years of lonely nights at home on the Ile St Louis she'd realised what a waste it all was – one person and four servants and a house that was just a great gloomy relic of a past way of life. With a flash of inspiration she'd decided to make the house work for its living. The de Courmont mansion would be part of the new de Courmont *image*, the way the *châteaux* were to the wine industry. It would be the company's hospitality house, lunches would be held for visiting VIPs, for company executives and their wives, for visiting car dealers from the USA or Japan, and celebrities whose photographs could be used in publicity – anything that would sell more cars.

Peach had learned early in her new career that if you wanted a decision from a busy director you didn't go to him with an idea, you went with your total concept mapped out from beginning to end – what it would involve, how it would benefit the company and what it would cost. Then all the man had to say was yes or no. It saved his time and hers. And since she had taken over as head of publicity and made such a success of the new advertising campaign, the board took her seriously.

She had plotted and planned with the interior designer how to turn the mansion from a gloomy family museum into an elegant Parisian symbol for de Courmont. They had removed a great deal of the heavy old pieces of furniture, opening up the house into new vistas of space, so that each lovely antique was displayed at its best. They'd brought a breath of fresh bright colour into the rooms and now, when the house was filled with flowers and lit by glittering chandeliers and soft shaded lamps it glowed with a new warmth.

Peach liked her room best of all. Its long windows overlooking the river were swagged with apple-green silk taffeta tied back with great bows, and she'd chosen a beautiful needlepoint rug from Portugal in shades of green and apricot. A comfortable white sofa stood in front of the marble fireplace with a low table holding her books and papers and there were pretty lamps dotted about throwing pools of soft light. Everything was new in here, including the man in her bed.

He wasn't the first one Peach had shared her bed with in the past six years and like the others he was charming and amusing and for a while he made her feel good. Laurent Lessier's family owned a famous old champagne house in Épernay. Peach's grandmother still kept up with her old friends from the war years and returned to Épernay annually to visit them and she had met Laurent then. He was thirty-five years old, good-looking and very charming. He'd taken her to dinner and to parties at *châteaux* in Reims and Épernay and then he'd come to Paris to see her and one thing had led to another. I'm like Harry, thought Peach, sipping her coffee, I can't resist a pretty face. But that was being unfair to Laurent! He was nice and he cared about her and he made love to her beautifully. Then why did she wake up in the morning with him naked beside her and feel so insecure? Here she was, the successful businesswoman, part-time mother and occasional lover, and she felt as lonely as when she'd first left Harry.

Putting down her coffee cup with a sigh Peach got out of bed and walked across to her desk. Her engagement book was open and across the usual black scrawl of dates and times and places she had written in red ink and large letters: WIL'S CRICKET MATCH. 2 O' CLOCK. SCHOOL. She'd meant to return to London last night but Laurent had shown up unexpectedly and taken her off for dinner and then he'd come back with her and she hadn't needed much persuading to stay. The little green enamelled Fabergé clock entwined with pearl lilies of the valley that had been Grand-mère Marie-France de Courmont's showed exactly seven o'clock. Plenty of time to make the nine o'clock flight. She'd go to the mews house in Belgravia first and make sure the daily housekeeper had made up Wil's bed and that the refrigerator was stocked with milk and juice, and she'd pick up the special cake he liked from the pâtisserie in Sloane Square. She always felt better when she was seeing Wil, especially when she could whisk him out of school and have him to herself for a night or two. She and Harry had been sharing him in the holidays, more for Harry's convenience than anything else, but mostly she had him because when Harry was writing he needed to be alone. Sometimes Peach stayed at Launceton but then both she and Wil would soon get bored and she'd take him up to London or off to Paris for a few days and they'd have fun together. It was the best part of her life, being with Wil. The odd thing was that Wil wasn't in the least like Harry – except that he was good at cricket. Wil's eyes had never changed from the dark blue of babyhood and were like hers – and Monsieur's. And he had Monsieur's dark hair and strong face and mouth.

The fight with Harry over the school had been tremendous and she'd felt such a fool afterwards because Wil liked school so much. He enjoyed boarding and being with the other boys – Harry had been proven so smugly right. Peach knew that Harry took Augusta, dressed in her proper English-lady manner, to visit Wil at school. And of course when Peach went she wore the latest Courrèges or Givenchy short skirts and little flat shoes. She'd given up trying to be like Augusta for Harry. She was herself.

Peach lifted the curtain and peered out into a grey morning. The river was swathed in a soft mist. *Fog.* My God, she hoped it wouldn't delay the flights . . . she couldn't be late for Wil's big day!

Wil Launceton carried a cup of tea carefully across the grass to Aunt Augusta, managing to spill only a little bit in the saucer even though he wasn't concentrating on what he was doing. He was worried about his mother. She had promised to be here for the match and he'd been waiting for her since twelve o'clock because she was supposed to be here for lunch. The headmaster had given him a message that his mother was delayed by fog in Paris. It was expected to lift and she would take the very first available flight. But it was now tea-time and she still hadn't arrived.

He handed Aunt Augusta her cup politely and sat down on the grass beside them, still worrying about Peach.

"You'll get grass stains on those nice white cricket flannels," Augusta told him, sipping her tea.

Wil stood up obediently but he did think that his mother would never have said that. Gosh, he was looking forward to staying at the house in London! His mother was sure to take him out to dinner at the sort of restaurant he liked and not the stuffy grand ones he went to with Augusta and his father. He wished she would hurry up, though, because soon it would be his turn to show her off to his friends – they all thought she was super and not a bit like a mum and they told him all their fathers thought she was *really* pretty.

"You've got a good team there, my boy," said Harry, proud of his son. "There'll be a second Launceton name joining mine on that trophy today, I'm sure of it. Just keep your eye on the ball and your arm steady and you'll do it. Good luck, Wil."

Wil sipped his lemonade nervously while Harry and Augusta chatted with the other parents. Slipping away from the crowd he

298

circled the broad gravel drive and ran down to the gates, peering along the road to see if she were coming, but there was no sign of her. He ran all the way back again and just made it to the pavilion in time to put on his cricket cap and send his first man out to bat.

It was five-fifteen when Peach swung the car through the school gates, parking in a flurry of gravel. Running her hands hastily through her hair she leapt out and sprinted around the corner of the school buildings towards the playing fields. God it was hot – that's why they'd had the fog! She just prayed she hadn't missed Wil.

All the parents were sitting round on deck chairs watching their small white-clad offspring. Checking the scoreboard Peach saw that Wil's team was forty for three wickets. Their opponents were all out for sixty-three so Wil's team were doing well. Relieved, Peach strolled across the grass towards the pitch. She could see Wil at the wicket now. It was his turn to bat. Thank God she hadn't missed him!

Wil frowned. He'd got the sun in his eyes and he was up against a very fast bowler. The hard leather-jacketed ball came at him like a bullet and with lightning reflexes he hit it solidly, sending it flying across the field to the boundary for a four. Wil grinned, he had the bowler's measure now, he could handle it. They were going to win this match. He just wished his mother were here, she'd promised him and she'd never let him down before. His eyes searched the crowd for her as the bowler paced back along the pitch and then turned running towards him, bowling a fast spinning ball. Reaching into it Wil caught sight of Peach walking along the field towards the pavilion. She was here at last. The hard ball spun off the grass and he was just a split second too late for it. It hit him on the left side of his forehead and Wil staggered for a moment and then fell.

Peach stood frozen at the edge of the pitch as men rushed towards Wil. The group of small cricketers were clustered around anxiously and she saw Harry hurrying towards him. Then somebody brought a stretcher and they lifted Wil on to it and he lay like a stone as they carried him off the field with Harry walking next to it. With a cry of terror she ran towards them.

"Wil," she cried, "Wil." He looked pale and qute normal except for the dark bruise on his forehead. But his eyes didn't open when she spoke to him and she gazed at Harry tearfully. Augusta appeared at Harry's side and the headmaster talked about ambulances while Peach listened nervously.

She took Wil's hand in hers, holding it tightly, praying that he would be all right.

"It's probably just a concussion," someone said kindly as they waited for the ambulance. "I've seen this kind of thing happen before."

At the hospital they took Wil off for X-rays and tests and Peach sat opposite Harry and Augusta in silence, waiting. Waves of guilt swept over her, the same guilt she'd felt when Lais had been shot. And now she'd brought disaster again. If only she'd taken the flight last night as she'd intended she would have been here on time, but instead she'd spent the night with Laurent. She hadn't thought there might be fog. Peach had caught Wil's glance just as the ball swung towards him. She knew she had distracted him at the crucial moment. "It's all my fault," she blurted into the silence. "If I'd been here on time it wouldn't have happened. Oh God, this is all my fault!"

They put Wil in a white hospital bed and somehow he looked so much smaller than she remembered. Tubes ran from his arms and his throat and machines monitored heart beats and brain waves. But his eyes remained shut.

"You're just sleeping, darling," said Peach tenderly, stroking back his dark hair, "you're just resting for a while. Then you'll be all right."

Harry watched them from across the room, saying nothing, and Augusta slipped tactfully through the door, leaving them alone.

"You don't deserve to be his mother," snarled Harry finally. "If Wil comes through this, Peach, *if* he does, you can count yourself lucky. But I'll see to it that you never get near to him again."

56

Anna Rushton arrived early at her job at US Auto even though it was her birthday. She always liked to get there in good time because Mr Maddox had a habit of arriving even earlier and he'd usually opened his mail and gone through it by the time she got there. She was forty years old today and she'd worked at US Auto for fifteen of those years. The company was her life but she'd never been as happy as she had the last six years working for Mr Maddox. They could say what they wanted about him in the executive dining room – and she'd heard via the waitresses that there were quite a few grumbles about his high-handed manner – but Mr Maddox was a gem to work for. And he had a magic touch with the trade-union officials as well as the workforce. "Our man Maddox," they called him at the plant. He was one of them. He'd come from the streets just like they did, he'd worked on the assembly line and he'd endured the same grinding monotony and shared the same frustrations – and he'd made it all the way to the top. Or almost to the top. Paul Lawrence was still up there as president but Noel was next in line and Anna knew – because as his personal secretary she knew everything that went on regarding Noel – that other companies were already sending out feelers as to whether Noel might not like a change of scenery. Noel Maddox was a brilliant man and if he weren't so young – still only thirty-nine – he might have been president of one of the major automobile corporations by now.

The bouquet of pink roses was waiting on her desk, just as it had every birthday for the past six years, and there was a little parcel beside it wrapped in a nice blue paper with a silver ribbon around it. Anna smiled as she put away her bag and tidied her hair. Picking up her flowers she read the note. "Happy Birthday Anna – best wishes, Noel Maddox." In all these years he'd rarely said anything personal to her – not that she looked nice today in her new suit, or that she'd changed her hairstyle – but Mr Maddox always seemed to know when she wasn't feeling well and sent her home to bed, telling her not to come back until she was sure she was up to it. And when her mother, who was her only living relative, had been so ill, Noel had come to the hospital personally to make sure she had the best doctors. Then when her mother "passed over" he'd had the head of personnel make sure that the funeral arrangements were taken care of and asked if Anna would like a leave-of-absence for a few weeks. Of course she had preferred to work, because hard work was the only way to recover from that kind of blow, but she'd appreciated his thought – and the flowers he'd sent to the funeral.

Anna put the roses in a vase of water and arranged them on her desk. Smiling, she set the little parcel aside until later and began to sort out Mr Maddox's mail. When she'd done that she folded his newspapers – the *New York Times*, the *Washington Post*, the *Los Angeles Herald Examiner*, the *Wall Street Journal* and the London *Times* and *Financial Times* as well as the local Detroit papers – and carried them with his mail through to his office. Mr Maddox liked to keep an eye on current political and economic affairs both nationally and internationally.

His big rosewood desk was empty except for the telephones and the special box that meant Noel could talk on the phone from across the room without having to hold the receiver. Anna placed his mail in the centre of his desk and the newspapers on the left, looking around to make sure everything was tidy. A large sheet of drawing paper was clamped to the cantilevered steel drawing board by the window and she wandered over to take a look at it.

The idea for this new car was Mr Maddox's and he had been working personally on it with the company's young designers for almost two years, until it finally emerged the way he wanted. She remembered taking minutes at the very first meeting.

"This has to be the kind of car that if I were twenty-five years old, married with a kid and the price were just a little more than I could afford, I'd go into hock for it," Mr Maddox had told them. "It's got to be zappy and sporty and yet have enough room in the back to seat two adults in reasonable comfort. But that young guy has got to be able to feel like he's at the wheel of the sports car he always dreamed of having."

"Why not make it cheaper?" the design chiefs and the accountants had asked him. And Anna knew he was right when he answered, "Because everyone needs to have something to long for, something he can't *quite* afford so that it means more to him when he gets it. Give him a car he can afford and he'll compare it with a dozen others on the market. This has to be the compromise between the sports car he's wanted since he was sixteen and the car he can still take his family out in. If it's a bit more than he can afford his reasoning will be it means it's that much better a car."

The Stallion was the end result and it was already scheduled to roll off the lines early next year. She herself was going to spend her fifteen-year-bonus on one. Metallic blue, she thought. She liked blue.

Taking out a little duster Anna flicked away a speck of dust missed by the cleaners and went to make sure the coffee was brewing. Mr Maddox still drank coffee all day long, even though she'd told him it was bad for him. Then she checked his engagement calendar and noticed he was lunching at the Pontchartrain Hotel with two gentlemen from a French automobile company. He would be out between twelve forty-five and three. His morning was free for work in his office and for telephone calls and he had three meetings in the afternoon that would take him up to six o'clock. After that he was going to the studios to work on some new ideas with the latest bunch of kids he'd recruited fresh from design colleges. He probably wouldn't finish much before nine or ten and then she knew he'd grab a bite at a hamburger stand and go on home to his penthouse apartment atop one of Detroit's newest and tallest buildings. She had never seen Noel's apartment and whether he would spend tonight alone or not, she didn't know. Anna never pried into Mr Maddox's personal affairs though she'd heard it said, on the grapevine, that there was always a glamorous girl on Noel's arm when he went to public functions. She wasn't surprised because, though Mr Maddox wasn't what you might call handsome, she thought he had an odd sort of appeal. Yes, she'd say Noel Maddox was a very attractive man. But that was none of her business.

Sitting at her desk she opened the parcel, pulling off the silver string carefully and rolling it into a neat loop, saving it for another time. Beneath the wrapping paper was a little suede bag in the distinctive blue of Tiffany's the jeweller's and inside the bag was a bracelet made out of ropes of gold and silver entwined. The card with it said, "Just so you know your own value, Anna. What would I do without you!? My very best wishes for your birthday and thanks for all your help to me. Noel Maddox."

He must have bought it when he went to New York last week. He'd gone to Tiffany's specially to get *her* a present! Of course it was far too extravagant of him, she'd expected the usual bottle of perfume – large size, of course – but she really appreciated it. She'd felt lonely this morning, forty wasn't a birthday anybody relished, and now Mr Maddox and his lovely gift had made her feel that she was still wanted. It was nice to know you were appreciated. Smiling, Anna slid the bracelet on her arm, admiring it. Then, tucking the box into her drawer, she began to sort out the comparative figures Mr Maddox wanted on the sales of four-wheel-drive pick-up trucks over the past five years.

Noel waved to her as he hurried into his office. "Morning Anna," he called.

Anna smiled. "Good morning, Mr Maddox. And thank you for

the flowers. And the present. It's *wonderful* – more than I deserve."

"Never underestimate yourself, Anna. You're the world's best secretary and that's just a token to let *you* know that *I* know."

In his office Noel took off his jacket and sat at his desk in his shirt sleeves, glancing rapidly through the papers. *Wall Street Journal* first, then the American papers, the foreign ones finally. Sipping his second cup of black coffee he turned to *The Times*. He'd enjoyed reading the British paper ever since he'd first been there – four years ago? It had been his first trip abroad and he was on company business. He'd stayed at the Savoy in a small suite with a river view and his copy of *The Times* had arrived every morning with his bacon and eggs. Now he only ever ate bacon and eggs when he was in England, but he'd become addicted to *The Times* newspaper. It was on page 2 of *The Times* that he noticed the paragraph about Peach de Courmont. It said briefly, 'Wil Launceton (8), the son of Sir Harry Launceton the writer, who was struck by a cricket ball at his school six weeks ago, is now out of a coma and making progress though he won't be released from hospital for some weeks yet. Lady Launceton is better known as Peach de Courmont, of the French motor car family."

Noel stared at the bleak little statement. It wasn't easy for him to think of Peach with a son, but there it was in black and white and she had almost lost her child. Of course, he saw Peach's face everywhere – she seemed to be on every billboard on every highway across America! De Courmont were making a concerted push for the American market, but despite all their advertising and the publicity, he didn't think their new car would make it. It was too feminine, and even *women* didn't want feminine cars. It had been tried before and proven. They wanted masculine, gutsy automobiles, so that they could compete with men on the roads.

Walking across to the bookcase he pulled out the latest copy of a trade magazine, flicking through its pages until he came to the de Courmont advertisement. Peach's face smiled back at him behind the wheel of the little pale blue convertible, "The Fleur". The car door stood open showing her long legs stretched comfortably, making the point that the car had enough room even for a tall person. Noel hadn't seen her since that party in Boston ten years ago. But he hadn't forgotten her.

The dining room of the Pontchartrain was crowded but Noel's usual table had been kept for him even though he'd lingered late in the

304

bar. Everyone knew Mr Maddox at the Pontchartrain. Doors were opened for him before he reached them and the doormen greeted him by his name, as did the barmen and the waiters. Lunch with the French management team was as dull as he had expected but it was afterwards, that one of them finally said something that interested him.

"We could use more forward-thinking men like you in the industry, Mr Maddox, especially in Europe. We too need a 'Stallion' and cars like the de Courmont 'Fleur' are not the answer."

"That's exactly what I was thinking this morning," Noel commented.

"De Courmont are in trouble," added the Frenchman. "The 'Fleur' is selling – but not enough to justify an expensive production. It's been a big mistake and not even Peach de Courmont's publicity campaign can save it. That company is in financial trouble."

"Big financial trouble?" asked Noel, interested.

The man nodded. "That's what the word is. Jim Jamieson is a good businessman, one of the best. But he's never been a true automobile man. He's had to trust his management team to guide him on that. And they've let him down badly this time."

Noel remembered their conversation later that night driving home after the design meeting, and he was still thinking about it when he took the private elevator up to his penthouse.

After he'd worked as Paul Lawrence's executive vice-president for two years Noel had decided it was time to move house. He'd toured Bloomfield Hills with a real-estate agent looking at attractive houses and wondering what the hell he was going to do alone in three reception rooms, gourmet kitchen, five bedrooms and four and a half baths? "Forget it," he told the agent, "I'm a bachelor. What I need is a great apartment." The man had found the penthouse for him the very next week and Noel had contacted the interior decorator that Paul's wife had used when the Lawrences re-did their house last year. Sliding glass windows surrounding the sitting room led on to a terrace and Noel had a wonderful view all the way across the city to the trees and parklands of the suburbs and beyond. His only brief to the decorator had been to keep it simple and to avoid using black. He'd created a restful decor in pleasing earth tones, cream, sand and taupe, just adding a flash of cool colour here and there – an angular gold-yellow chair or a bitter-green rug. Furnishings had been kept to a minimum, giving a feeling of space, with a seating area by the window and another in front of the modernistic steel fireplace. The only possessions Noel had kept from his old apartment were the orphanage-angel headboard, the Ricard ashtray and the two cheap art prints – the Kandinsky and the Mondrian. Only now they hung opposite the real thing. Noel had squandered his hefty annual bonuses on the paintings. Kandinsky and Mondrian and others. He had a small Monet landscape in his bedroom and a Marie Laurencin flower painting near the dining table. He had bought strong modern abstracts and a wild Roy Lichtenstein cartoon-strip acrylic, as well as a couple of sculptures by unknowns whose work he really liked. He'd had his eye on a Seurat Breton seashore scene but the price had gone too high at auction and that's when he'd bought the cabin at the lake instead.

There was a pretty girl waiting for him on the oatmeal tweed sofa in front of the fire and he dropped a kiss on her blonde hair as he threw his coat on to a chair and headed for the bedroom.

Della Grieves stretched out on the sofa, smiling. He was late, but then Noel was always late. They were supposed to drive out to the lake tonight but what difference if they went in the morning instead? She liked it here.

Noel came back into the room in a dark blue terry robe, his hair still wet from the shower. He took off the Fleetwood Mac album she was playing and put on his favourite Mozart concerto instead. Leaning back against the cushions he looked exhausted and he still hadn't said a word to her. That was all right too. A man like Noel Maddox had a lot on his mind. He was a workaholic, Della could swear he was thinking about business sometimes when they made love.

"How's the fashion world today?" asked Noel finally as he began to unwind.

Della shrugged, smiling, "The same." She ran her own boutique in a smart area of Detroit financed by her wealthy father and she enjoyed it, but she knew better than to bother Noel with its up and downs right now.

They sat listening to the music until he fell asleep on the sofa and Della left him there and went to bed alone.

Della was used to Noel's silences but this weekend it was unnerving. He paced the apartment the next morning in silence. She fixed salad and grilled the steak she'd bought while Noel stared out of the tall windows and they ate silently. By six o'clock Della was close to tears and she thought she'd better ask him what was wrong.

Noel lingered by the windows watching the sunset over Detroit. The de Courmont situation had been brewing in his mind since yesterday and the more he thought about it the more interesting it got. It was a good company and in the right hands it could become a profitable one. His mind made up, he strode over to the phone and called Paul Lawrence at home. Paul said he'd speak to the chairman but he gave him the go-ahead to open tentative negotiations with de Courmont.

Noel scarcely saw Della as he walked back to the windows, staring at the nearly dark sky.

"Noel?" said Della, tears in her eyes. "Is anything wrong?"

Noel stared at her in surprise. Della was a lovely girl. A sweet girl too. She wasn't the only one he went out with but she was the one he was with now and he realised he was neglecting her. There were always plenty of girls to fill up the lonely corners of his life – those that were left over from his crowded business schedule. The trouble was they never lived up to his image of Peach de Courmont, the little golden girl of freedom, the exotic young girl in the scarlet dress at the party. *The dark-eyed girl killing him with her words, "You're Noel Maddox of the Maddox Charity Orphanage."*

He went into the kitchen and Della heard him open the refrigerator and take out some ice and the sound of drinks being mixed.

"Martini?" asked Noel handing her a glass and a little blue parcel. Then he smiled at her and Della knew why she put up with him. When Noel looked at her like that she melted. She opened the little blue suede bag delightedly and took out the pair of large gold hoop earings.

"I was in New York last week," said Noel. "I was passing Tiffany and I thought about you. The sales clerk told me they were fashionable. I hope he was right?"

"Of course he was. And so were you. Thank you," said Della, kissing him.

Noel stared at her pretty smiling face. "I'm going over to Europe next week on business," he said suddenly. "How'd you like to come with me?"

There were a million reasons why Della couldn't go but she knew she'd put them off. "I'd love it," she said smiling.

57

It was Leonie's opinion that Jim should have given up control of the de Courmont company before now. He was too old to be constantly hurrying up and down to Paris trying to solve its problems. That's why she had insisted that Mr Maddox came down here to talk with him.

And if she thought Jim were too old to travel what about herself? Had Paris seen the last of Leonie Bahri Jamieson? The last time she had been there was for dear Caro's funeral two years ago and with Caro gone, her old ties with the city were severed. Now she spent her time quietly pottering around her garden or simply sitting on her terrace watching the sea and thinking about the past. Even her little cat was old now and preferred a cool corner in the shade nearby or else simply to curl up on her knee, contemplating its life too.

Leonie couldn't remember the exact day she had started looking at life from this new angle but it was an odd sensation approaching the end of your allotted time and looking back instead of forward. Was it then she had begun to *feel* old? Her body just wouldn't respond the way it used to and her bones were stiff, though she still managed the walk around the headland and she still swam every day in the sea. Over the years she had watched her beloved Côte d'Azur – the beautiful blue coast – change from a simple innocent turn-of-the-century beauty to a painted bejewelled courtesan luring the summer hordes into her temptingly baited trap. Leonie and the Riviera had begun their lives together but *her* part of the coast was still green and unspoiled because Jim had bought her all those surrounding acres forty years ago. *Could it really be forty years? Where had the time flown?*

Now the highlights of her year were when the family came to visit them and she lived vicariously, enjoying their stories and sharing their experiences. Darling Amelie and Gerard had always been so happy together, and it was so pleasing to be with Lais and Ferdi, who lived at their castle in Germany and whose contentment and tenderness for each other were so touching. Of course she saw Leonore more often because she ran the Hostellerie in the summer season, returning to spend the winter months at the new mountain-top resort in Switzerland, and what a successful woman she was. It was Leonore's energy and flair that had turned the hotels into such world-renowned successes. And then, of course, there was Peach.

Leonie stroked the cat on her lap, gazing at the calm blue sea. A couple of sailboats tacked slowly across the almost windless horizon and an enormous white yacht sped purposefully in the direction of Monte Carlo, the sound of its powerful engines cutting across the quiet morning. The sight of it reminded her, as it always did, of Monsieur. Old as she was, there wasn't a day went by that she didn't think of Gilles de Courmont. There was no doubt that Peach's son resembled him, but Leonie felt sure that young Wil Launceton would not be like his evil great-grandfather in anything except looks.

The news of Wil's accident had come as a terrible blow and she had wanted to go at once to London but Jim had insisted that the journey would be too much for her. He'd gone himself and stayed with Peach until Amelie had arrived from Florida, and between them they'd comforted Peach and helped her through the terrible time.

Thank God now Wil was getting better, but it was Peach she was disturbed about. No amount of dashing about the world promoting de Courmont automobiles could replace love in her life and Leonie worried that she might have done the wrong thing in advising Peach to stay married to Harry. By doing so she might have deprived her granddaughter of her chance to find happiness with someone else. Peach was staying at Launceton now to be near the boy and perhaps this near-tragedy had brought her and Harry closer together. Leonie hoped so for Wil's sake.

Jim sat opposite Noel Maddox in the salon, a tray of untouched coffee between them. He had been pleased when Noel had called from Detroit last week saying he was going to be in Europe on other business but that he'd been following de Courmont's progress with the "Fleur" and thought there might be one or two interesting points they could discuss. Jim had imagined that the big American automobile company was interested in taking over production of the "Fleur" for the United States. Which just went to show that he was getting old because of course the young man knew exactly what de Courmont's position was. He had figures at his finger-tips that Jim couldn't even remember! And now he'd come out with an astonishing offer. US Auto would take over de Courmont, incorporating it into the public company – at a price of 75 per cent shareholding to US Auto, the remaining 25 per cent to remain in the de Courmont family.

"These are just basic opening points for our discussion, of course," said Noel unsmiling. "There are many others open to negotiation. But I think we could guarantee you, Mr Jamieson, that 25 per cent of the new de Courmont company would be worth much more to the family in a few years' time than a full holding in de Courmont as it stands now."

"That may or may not be true," replied Jim, "and I must congratulate you on your 'homework'. You know a great deal about de Courmont. But there's one detail you've overlooked. I have been chairman of the company for twenty years now, but in essence I've merely been acting as caretaker for my son-in-law, Gerard de Courmont. I'm only the power behind the throne, Mr Maddox."

"Then Gerard de Courmont is the man I should be talking to?" asked Noel, irritated that in his hurry and preoccupation with the figures he had overlooked the structure of the family company. "Along with you and the rest of the de Courmont board obviously."

"Not necessarily," said Jim, enjoying himself just enough to take away the sting of Maddox's offer. "You see, five years ago when his daughter began to take an active part in the company she was destined one day to inherit, Gerard assigned control of de Courmont to her. So you see my granddaughter, Peach de Courmont, is now the only person who could sell the company, and I doubt very much that she would want to – not even for all that promised future money. Peach is a very 'family' person, Mr Maddox. She's working hard to make de Courmont the success it used to be – as you've probably noticed in the newspapers."

Noel's face was expressionless as he put away his papers and snapped shut his briefcase. All those years of self-control had given him the anonymous expression of a poker-player with a winning – or losing – hand held close to his chest. But behind it he was angry with himself for not getting all his facts straight before he came in to make his offer. It was a grave mistake and he knew it. *Peach de Courmont, his golden girl, stood between him and what he wanted most in the world – control of de Courmont and its projected new operation in the States. And its presidency.*

"My wife and I would be happy if you would join us for lunch," invited Jim affably. He had nothing against Maddox, he was a businessman doing his job and he'd flown down from Paris that morning. The least he could do was to offer him lunch.

Noel hesitated. He didn't like feeling foolish but on the other hand Jim Jamieson was a decent man. He'd worked all these years to protect de Courmont; you couldn't expect him to be thrilled about the idea of handing it over on a plate. Besides, he was curious about Peach's family; he'd heard about the legendary Leonie from Della, whom he'd left in Paris, sight-seeing. "Thanks, Mr Jamieson," he said, smiling for the first time. "I'd like that very much."

The fact that Leonie was an old woman didn't detract from her beauty and Noel's eyes returned to her fine-boned face time and again across the lunch table in the cool green-shuttered dining room. Her skin was soft and smooth with a network of fine lines around her large tawny-coloured eyes and when she smiled that wide entrancing smile you knew why she had been considered one of the great beauties of her time. And although Peach didn't really resemble her grandmother, she had the same cat-like face and Leonie's smile. He wondered what Leonie would think if he told her that he'd been an inmate of the Maddox Charity Orphanage when she had visited it in 1945? But Noel never admitted that secret to anyone. Peach was the only one who knew his past.

Leonie had met dozens of tight, bright young executives during Jim's tenure at de Courmont but none quite like Noel Maddox. Tension rippled behind his smile like an undertow beneath the surface of a smooth-flowing river. He paid her compliments and told them easy amusing anecdotes of life in the United States today while Jim compared them with his memories of his home country, but Leonie had the feeling that Mr Maddox's mind was on other things. He seemed to her to have the ability to be two people at the same time, just as Monsieur had. Noel Maddox was a man of strange depths and for once she was at a loss to know what they were.

They had finished lunch and were having coffee in the salon when the telephone rang and Noel looked away politely as Leonie answered it.

311

It was Peach calling on a terrible crackling line. "Peach? Where are you, darling?" asked Leonie. "I can barely hear you. Where? Barcelona! But I thought you were still at Launceton with Wil?"

Noel sipped his coffee and gazed out through the arched windows across the terrace to the sea.

Leonie covered the receiver with her hand speaking to Jim. "It's Peach and she sounds distraught. I can hardly hear her, Jim." She spoke into the phone again. "Look darling, tell me what's happening quietly and calmly if you can." Leonie listened for a while and then said, "Why not come to us? At least we can talk about it and try to work things out. Harry can't just take Wil from you. He'll have to get a court order. He *has* a court order? Oh my God! I see. He's divorcing you and then he'll marry Augusta . . . But, Peach, I don't understand why you didn't come here . . . I see. Yes. All right. But please give me the telephone number of your hotel. The Hotel Recuerdo. I've never heard of it. Oh, you're not surprised. Very well, darling, but I'll call you later tonight and, Peach, when you've had enough of being alone and sorting out your thoughts, please come to us. This house has seen the family through all its disasters and it is a comfort to be where you know you are loved . . . Yes. Yes, darling. I love you too."

Forgetting Noel's presence, Leonie gazed tiredly at Jim. "I suppose you've guessed what happened," she said. "Harry has served divorce papers on Peach and forbidden her to come to Launceton. He has the boy there and has taken out a court order claiming that she is an irresponsible mother. He blames her for the accident. And, of course, Peach blames herself. She's run off to Barcelona because it was the first flight out of Heathrow that she could get a seat on. She wants to be alone to sort out her thoughts."

Jim couldn't bear to think of Peach in a strange city with no one to help her. "I'll go to her," he suggested anxiously.

"Peach knew you would say that and she asked me to tell you not to. She's calmer now. Of course she was expecting to divorce Harry some day and she's sad about the failure of the marriage but not upset. It's Wil she's frantic about, but then she keeps on saying that it's true. I don't know what to make of her."

Leonie suddenly felt her age. She was tired and very upset. Peach's life was in shreds and for the first time she had no answer.

Noel coughed, putting down his coffee cup. "If you'll excuse me," he said, "I'll be on my way."

"I'm so sorry," apologised Leonie, suddenly remembering him.

"I didn't mean to interrupt your discussions with family problems."

"Not at all, Madame. I understand. And our discussions were completed anyway – for the time being," he added, smiling at Jim.

A big white US Auto limousine with a chauffeur at the wheel waited outside to take Noel to Nice and he easily caught the four o'clock flight to Paris.

Their suite at the Crillon was empty and Noel remembered that Della had gone to visit Versailles while he was away. Picking up the phone he called the valet and a maid to come and pack his clothes and then he called the florist to order some flowers. He had the concierge telephone the airlines and book a flight and within half an hour he was on his way out again. He paused at the door to look back. The suite was filled with roses of every colour and the envelope addressed to Della waited on the desk with her return ticket next to it. He'd taken care of everything.

He just made the eight o'clock flight to Barcelona.

Part IV

Part IV

58

Peach wandered through the cloister of trees circling Barcelona's fascinating Parque Guell, not caring where she was going. She had roamed the anonymous city streets all morning escaping from a sleepless night in a tiny claustrophobic hotel room in the "Ramblas", where the upper storeys of ancient buildings leaned across the narrow alleys until they almost touched in the middle and noise and music and laughter from the cafés and bars went on until all hours.

Peach was sure now she had lost Wil for ever. Harry had told her his detectives had been following her in Paris for months – not that she'd ever tried to hide anything, she'd just never discussed it with him. After all, it was Harry's infidelities that had shattered their marriage and she had merely been picking up the threads of her own life. And now he was planning on using it all against her to make sure he got custody of Wil.

Harry had pointed out how unsympathetic the British courts would be to a woman who lived in Paris while her child lived in England – even though Peach had protested that she saw Wil every possible moment she was allowed. But Harry had been remorseless. "And a woman who is an adulteress," he'd said over-dramatically – even though Peach had pointed out again that their marriage had been non-existent for years, thanks to him. And there was no doubt that Harry's position in English society gave weight to his case. He was an Establishment figure and he would use it to his advantage – he'd be bound to get the sympathy of the courts.

Finally, Harry had told Peach that if she contested the divorce with her version of his infidelities it would mean the whole story would be splashed across the tabloids with disastrous effects on Wil. And it would all be *her* fault.

No, Harry had made it quite clear. If Peach didn't contest the divorce and the custody order he would make sure that the case went through discreetly. If she did, then it would only go further to prove what a bad mother she was. And she would still lose Wil.

Peach sat on an undulating mosaic wall designed by the art nouveau artist Gaudi, oblivious to its strange beauty. Her gaze was fixed on the small boy riding his bicycle round and round the large empty arena with solemn solitary pleasure. The lonely child symbolised all she had lost and Peach began to cry, mopping at her eyes with the last of the tissues she had bought that morning. There was no way she could win. No way at all.

From the shade of the avenue of trees, Noel watched her. He had been at the café opposite her hotel since six-thirty that morning, drinking endless cups of coffee and sharing a table with blue-overalled workmen dropping in for a breakfast of black coffee, brandy and a hunk of crusty bread dipped in pungent olive oil. When Peach had emerged at seven-thirty, looking pale and wearing dark glasses, Noel had known it was the wrong moment to speak to her. He'd tracked her solitary route to Guell Park up on the hill overlooking the city and now, watching Peach watching the child, he could see that she was crying. Noel couldn't hold back any longer. Walking towards her he held out his hand. "Peach," he said quietly, "let me help you."

Peach spun around, startled – and she was looking into the shadowy grey eyes and the lean harsh-boned face of a man she knew . . . someone she had met years before . . . "You're Noel Maddox," she said.

"Of the Maddox Charity Orphanage," added Noel with a faint smile.

With a stab of guilt, Peach remembered the party in Boston. "I thought you were going to kill me when I said that," she stammered. "And I wouldn't have blamed you – it was stupid and unforgivable. It was just that I had remembered your face suddenly from all those years before."

Noel shrugged. "That's all in the past, and right now I have a feeling we should be talking about your future." He blotted her tears with his handkerchief. "Come with me, we'll get you a cup of coffee and you can tell me all about it."

Peach didn't know why it was so easy talking to Noel. Perhaps it was that he was uninvolved – he was a person who wouldn't judge her on her past or Harry's, the way the family would, but who could offer impartial advice. He sat opposite her in the little restaurant, arms folded, listening, and he looked strong and calm as though nothing would ever be beyond his control. Noel would never make a mess of his life, the way she had. "I just don't know what to do," she said finally.

Noel looked at his watch. "It's seven in the morning in New York. I'm going to call my lawyer and find out who to contact in London. Do you have a copy of that court order?"

Peach rummaged in her bag. "Here it is."

Noel's suite at the Ritz on Avenida José Antonio was vast and luxurious and Peach wondered what he would say if he saw her odd little room at the Hotel Recuerdo. She prowled his sitting room trying not to listen to Noel's conversation, staring out of the windows at the traffic surging past and the flower-seller tucked into her kiosk amid mounds of bright carnations.

"Right," she heard Noel say, "John Marcher . . . and the number. Got it. I'll call him right away. Thanks, Bill. I'll let you know what happens. Yes. I agree. I'm sure it will. 'Bye."

Peach watched nervously, thinking of Harry's threats as Noel dialled again and asked for a London number. Noel caught her eye and smiled. "You're not going to give up Wil without a fight, are you?" he said encouragingly.

Peach couldn't bear to listen while he talked to the London solicitor and she shut herself in the bathroom, staring in the mirror. Under the harsh light she looked pale and her eyes were puffy. Noel must think her unattractive and foolish. *Why was he helping her like this? And where had he come from?* She supposed he was in Barcelona on business and had been taking time out to see the sights. Whatever . . . she couldn't be more grateful for his offer of a helping hand. He was exactly the sort of calm, logical thinking person she needed.

"Peach," called Noel, as she emerged from the bathroom, neatly combed and lipsticked. She looked about seventeen and scared. "It's all arranged," he told her. "The London lawyers agree that it's obvious Harry is trying to use intimidation to take the boy from you. Harry's romantic activities are as well known as his books and so is his affair with Augusta. There would be no problem in you sueing him for divorce – regardless of whatever you do when you are alone in Paris."

His grey eyes met hers searchingly and Peach turned away. "But Wil," she said, "I don't want Wil to be hurt by all this."

"Wil would be far more hurt losing his mother," said Noel

abruptly. "Get your head together, Peach, and start thinking straight."

Peach stared at him in surprise, he seemed suddenly so cold and hard. "What happens now?" she asked in a small voice.

"They'll be back to us tomorrow, hopefully with the news that the court order has been rescinded. They know Harry's lawyers and they'll discuss it with them in that nice polite British way and they'll arrive at a solution that will be best for you both. But I can promise you this, Peach. You won't lose Wil."

Looking into his harsh, attractive face Peach knew she could believe him. Noel Maddox wouldn't make rash promises. The fears of the past few days began to roll away and she ran to him, flinging her arms around him, relieved. "What would I have done without you? Thank you," she murmured, gratefully. "It was all so complicated and confused before. There seemed no way out."

"There's always a way out, Peach," said Noel, putting his arms around her. "You just have to look for it."

"But what were *you* doing in Guell Park?" demanded Peach. "*Why* were you here in Barcelona?"

Noel held her, looking at the face he had kept in his memories all these years, at the wide sloping cheekbones and the straight positive nose, he looked into her dark blue eyes and at her vulnerable soft mouth. It would have been so easy to kiss her.

"Were you sent by God as an angel of mercy?" asked Peach, smiling.

"It was just destiny, I guess," replied Noel.

The British Airways flight from Madrid touched down precisely on time at Heathrow Airport in London and Peach gathered together her belongings hastily. "Please remain in your seats with the seatbelts fastened until the aircraft has completed taxiing," commanded the trim red, white and blue hostess firmly and Peach sank back with a sigh. It seemed eternity instead of only a few hours since Noel had put her on the plane, waving goodbye as he headed off to catch his flight to Paris, and she was already missing his calm authoritative presence.

Noel had looked after her so well, waiting with her in Spain until the lawyers worked out her future, doing his best to divert her with sight-seeing, dinners and movies, cramming her empty days with events until she had complained she was exhausted.

"Good," Noel had said, "we've exhausted you and we've exhausted Barcelona's repertoire of attractions. Let's try Madrid." And within a couple of hours they were on a plane to Madrid.

This time they stayed in the same hotel but Noel booked a small suite for Peach and a room for himself, and in the daytime they explored the Prado, lingering over the Goya and Velasquez paintings of Spanish courtiers. They toured nearby villages and castles and paradores in a rented car – neither a de Courmont nor a US Auto – but a tiny Seat that they both just managed to fold themselves into amid much laughter. "I'm taller than you," complained Peach, hunching her knees under her chin.

"And I'm bigger than you," countered Noel, attempting to flex his elbows.

At night they wandered the city companionably, sipping tingling dry sherry at a bar in the Plaza Mayor, tasting the spicy Serrano ham, and dining on a hundred different little snacks called *tapas*.

By agreement they didn't talk about Harry or Wil, except for the daily telephone call to London. The matter was under discussion, they were told in a lawyerly way, and they would be kept informed of any progress. "But there doesn't seem to be any progress," murmured Peach nervously.

Noel said calmly, "That's the way it is with lawyers, they don't tell you anything until they have something definite to tell you."

Peach couldn't remember ever talking about herself so much. In the past four days she'd told Noel her entire life story. She told him about France in the war and about Lais and her own guilt. She'd told him about her love for her grandmother and her friendship with Melinda and about falling in love with Harry and how she'd chased him – everything. Except for some reason she didn't tell him about having polio and having to wear the steel braces on her legs. She still felt ashamed of her weakness and her ugliness. She'd told Noel about buying the tiny mews house in Belgravia and holding her hand he'd said, "I'd like to come over and see it for myself."

Peach had blushed like a silly schoolgirl and said, "Well, of course you must," wondering if he had meant something more than just that.

"You are the only person who knows what I am," Noel said to her as they walked through the bustling evening streets of Madrid.

Peach stared at him puzzled. "Don't you mean *who* you are?"

"I'm nothing," said Noel with an edge of bitterness to his voice. "I'm just the orphan-kid made good."

"Tell me how you made good," demanded Peach.

Threading her arm through his, her head bent towards him, Peach listened. Snatches of music and laughter spilled from the cafés and bars as they walked along, editing his life into patches of light and shadow the way she felt sure Noel himself was doing.

Noel told her about Luke and Mrs Grenfell and Mr Hill, the sports coach, about cleaning the cars and working at Joe's Garage and the library books on engines and engineers. He told her about the boxing trophy and about walking the streets of Detroit, cold and penniless and afraid, aged just fourteen. He confessed to lying about his age in order to get a job, so that now everyone thought he was four years older than his thirty-five years. He told her about working his way through the University of Michigan and MIT, commenting that he was still a pretty good barman and a hell of a fast hand with a power wrench from all those years on the assembly line. He told her that he'd climbed the ranks until he was second-in-command to the president of US Auto, adding that it was an odd coincidence that they were both in the same business.

"But I remember," cried Peach, "when I first saw you at the orphanage, you wanted to look inside the car. It was the *engine* you were interested in even then."

"I'm the best engineer in the business," Noel had said, "and engines are still the love of my life."

"Then there's no wife? No lover?"

His eyes had locked with hers. "No. There's no wife, Peach, and no lover," he said seriously.

She had wondered if he were going to kiss her, but he hadn't. He'd just said, "It's the first time I've ever told anyone about myself, and it'll probably be the last. It's just because in an odd sort of way you seem to have been involved in my life since we first met."

And then he'd swept her into a café for a glass of wine and they'd listened to the guitars playing plaintive Spanish folk melodies and snatches of Rodrigo and de Falla, until he'd taken her back to the hotel and said goodnight. And again he hadn't kissed her.

Peach peered out of the aircraft window at the tarmac. The plane was just being attached to its umbilical exit tube and she wondered if Noel were in Paris yet. He'd kissed her when he left, just a small light kiss on her cheek and she touched the place furtively, thinking about him.

"We are ready to de-plane now," called the smiling hostess as Peach hurried thankfully for the door. She was home again, and in

a few hours' time she would be with Wil. She was to have joint
custody of her son with Harry, and the divorce would go through
uncontested with an unnamed woman as the guilty party in Harry's
life. Noel had won her battle for her.

59

Noel liked the Crillon. It was a very civilised hotel, it was calm
and luxurious and its switchboard operators were efficient. His
telephone had been kept hot by calls back and forth to Detroit and
after a final conference call with US Auto's top management he
had the go-ahead for his plan. Tomorrow half a dozen bright young
executives from US Auto Marketing Division would be on a plane
from Detroit to Paris. Noel would brief them personally on their
approach and then he'd wine them and dine them in gay Paree
before sending them off to do their job.

On the table in front of him was a list of the de Courmont dealers
throughout Europe. The names of the largest and most important
had been underscored in red – in France, Germany, Great Britain,
Italy, Spain and Portugal. Noel was empowered to offer them
exclusive European distribution of US Auto's successful "Stallion"
at initially very favourable terms with the promise of solid advertising and promotional back-up in each country – a chance they would
jump at despite their loyalty to de Courmont. Of course Noel
didn't plan on asking them to drop the "Fleur". That wouldn't be
necessary. Presented with a choice between the "Stallion" and the
"Fleur" he knew which the customer would choose. The "Fleur"
didn't stand a chance.

It hadn't been easy to get the go-ahead from Detroit. Management were cautious, but they trusted his judgement and when he'd
told them that he had an inside edge via a personal relationship
with a member of the de Courmont family, he had finally clinched
it. Of course this was only phase one of his game-plan. He had

learned his corporate lesson well from Claire Anthony . . . results and numbers, a fast turn-around – today's success for today's rewards. He'd present US Auto with de Courmont's market and then, with the company weakened by drastic sales losses, he would have driven a wedge through its door.

The high-pitched shrill of the French telephone system splintered his thoughts and he answered it abruptly.

"Noel? Are you all right?"

"I'm fine, Peach," he said, leaning back in the chair and propping his feet on the table. "Just busy, that's all."

"Oh I'm sorry . . . shall I call you later? It wasn't anything important."

"*You* are important," said Noel quietly. "And, besides, I can't think of anything I'd rather be doing than talking to you. It's a lot more interesting than what I have on my desk at the moment."

The sound of Peach's light breathy laugh warmed the lonely hotel room. "At least this time I'm not calling with more of my problems," she promised, "I just wanted to tell you that Wil is here with me in London. Since your lawyers put pressure on him Harry is being very reasonable – I suppose it's only because he knows he had no choice but it does make it easier to have a veneer of an amiable relationship – and of course it's so much better for Wil."

"How is Wil?" asked Noel.

"He has to go to the hospital for final X-rays but then, if all is well, he'll be able to travel. I plan to bring him to France to stay with Grand-mère on the Riviera. He'll soon get back his strength there."

Noel tucked the receiver under his chin and placed his hands behind his head, waiting.

"Shall I meet you in Paris, Noel?"

"I'd like that, Peach, but I'm not sure I shall still be here. Why don't you let me know what your plans are?"

"Yes, of course I'll do that." Peach sounded disappointed. "I wanted to thank you again for your help – I don't know what I would have done without you, Noel. Yes I do know – I would have lost Wil. How do I thank a man who put the pieces of my life back together again?"

"No thanks needed, Peach," said Noel gently.

"I miss you," said Peach suddenly. "I liked being with you, Noel Maddox."

324

"Good. I miss you too, Peach. More than I should."

There was a pause and then Peach said, "I'll let you know then – when I'll be in Paris."

"Do that." Noel replaced the telephone receiver and leaned back in his chair smiling. Life was good – and on perfect course.

60

Wil Launceton was a bright child. He'd observed the tight-lipped silent clashes between his father and his mother over the years and knew that their relationship wasn't the same as those of his friends' parents. But of course his father was said to be a genius and his mother was known to be French and eccentric, as well as being quite spectacular looking. All the fathers liked her, anyhow, though Wil didn't think she was beautiful. Her mouth was too wide and she didn't have one of those nice little turned-up noses like Jake Northrup's mother, though Jake had told all the boys in his division at school – in confidence, of course – that his mother had had her real nose replaced by plastic! Wil had wondered for a long time how Mrs Northrup could breathe through a plastic nose until Peach had told him, laughing, that it had been something called "plastic surgery" that Jake had meant. Anyhow – Peach was too tall, she towered over everyone and she wore different clothes from the other mothers, but Wil had got over the stage of wishing that she looked like them and that she would use her real name – Marie or Isabelle instead of Peach – which he'd gone through for a while when he was younger – six or something – and now he was really proud of the way she looked, especially in those enormous advertisements. His mother had suddenly become a "star" and Wil's stock at school had soared.

Of course, he'd known something was up even before the accident. Aunt Augusta came to stay at Launceton more and more often, and his mother stayed in Paris or she met him in London instead of at

325

home. Aunt Augusta was all right but he couldn't imagine why his father preferred being with her to being with Peach. Augusta was too predictable to be much fun. When she was at Launceton Wil'd bet anything he could tell you exactly what they'd have for lunch each day of the week; he'd bet against himself once and he'd been one hundred per cent right. But he supposed Dad liked knowing that.

It had been a bit of a blow, though, just when he was beginning to feel better to be told that he was going to live with his father and Augusta for ever and Peach wouldn't be coming back. He'd cried every night for ages and he'd even overheard the housekeeper saying it was a shame, the boy was pining for his mother. Then suddenly it all changed again and life would go on pretty much as it had done before, sometimes with Dad and sometimes with Peach – but never again with the two of them together. And here he was in Paris with Peach. And this new man.

Wil inspected Noel suspiciously across the table on the *Bâteau Mouche*. His mother looked very pleased with herself, all sort of smiley and soft, and he could tell she wanted him to like Noel Maddox. It had been Mr Maddox's idea that they go on this boat trip down the River Seine, though personally Wil thought it a ridiculous thing to do – who wanted to eat dinner and look out of the window at a lot of old buildings, anyway, even if they were floodlit? When they'd gone to meet Mr Maddox at the Crillon and he'd told Peach that he'd booked a table on the *Bâteau Mouche* because he thought it might be fun for Wil, Peach's eyes had met Wil's in a signal that he knew had meant smile and be nice, so he had. Hadn't he said, "Thank you very much, sir, that will be very nice"? But it didn't mean he had to *enjoy* it. He'd have preferred a hamburger and chips at the "drugstore" near the Place de l'Opéra and the new James Bond movie was showing at a cinema in the Champs Elysées, but this American had thought he was a *tourist*. Why, he knew Paris just as well as he did London – and that was a lot better than Mr Maddox!

"Look, Wil," said Peach as the *Bâteau Mouche* slid beneath the Pont de Sully, emerging to the glorious view of the Ile St Louis on the right with the spires of Notre Dame on the Ile de la Cité ahead. "Look darling, you can see the house."

Wil stood up, peering through the sloping windows of the boat, and Peach turned to smile at Noel. "We've never seen it from the river before," she said.

"You live there?" asked Noel, staring at the imposing grey stone façades.

"There!" shouted Wil excitedly. "The one almost on the corner, just there!"

Other diners turned to stare and Peach said, "Ssh, darling," smiling at his excitement. "The house was built by a de Courmont in the seventeenth century and is quite famous. All the great private houses in Paris were called 'hôtels' like the 'hôtel de ville' – the town hall. I'm afraid the Hôtel de Courmont has had to go through a few changes lately. It's working for its living now – like the family. It's become part of de Courmont's identity – the company's Parisian image to the world."

Noel's face was impassive as he turned back to the table and poured more wine.

"Look, Mum, look at that," cried Wil excitedly as the stern ramparts of Notre Dame hove into view, floodlights illuminating the gargoyles and creatures that climbed its buttresses and projected from its towers.

"You see," murmured Peach, "he is enjoying himself after all."

Noel shrugged. "I've not had any practice in knowing what small boys would really like – but I guess he'd rather have grabbed a burger and seen the new James Bond movie than had a grown-up dinner like this while looking at a lot of old buildings."

Wil turned and grinned at him, eyeing him with a new respect. "That's all right, Mr Maddox," he said kindly, "I don't mind. We can see the Bond film tomorrow."

"You're on," promised Noel, smiling back.

Later Noel wandered through the splendid salons of the de Courmont mansion, while Peach said goodnight to Wil upstairs. He stared at the grand marble staircase and the frescoes of flying cherubs on the great domed ceiling, imagining Peach as a tiny girl walking up those wide steps, one step at a time, on her way to bed. He paced the squared black and white marble hall wondering if she'd played hopscotch there, and he strolled the cushioned elegance of the grand salon admiring the Helleu portrait of Marie-France de Courmont – Peach's grandmother. On the other wall hung a portrait by Sargent of Leonie, looking ethereally beautiful in a clinging golden gown, her arms outstretched and a sleeping black panther at her feet.

"That's Grand-mère," said Peach behind him.

"I know," said Noel.

"Come and see 'Monsieur'," she said, taking his hand and leading him back into the hall. The portrait was a head and shoulders view of a handsome man whose mouth held a touch of cruelty in its stern curves. His eyes had a forceful piercing stare that seemed to follow Noel even when he moved away. And Monsieur's eyes were the same blue as Peach's, dark and disquieting. The small gilt label underneath said, "Gilles, le VIme Duc de Courmont."

"I talk to him sometimes," confessed Peach, "when I'm here alone."

"What do you talk about?"

"Oh, I tell him what decisions I've made about his company, I tell him what I'm trying to do – I promise him I'll do my best to win."

"And are you?" asked Noel keenly.

"I'm trying," sighed Peach.

"Tell me," asked Noel suddenly, "when you were a kid did you ever play hopscotch on these marble tiles?"

Peach suddenly remembered the hated ugly braces and the smell of the black leather straps as though they still trapped her legs. "I never played hopscotch," she replied abruptly. Taking Noel's hand she led him along the wide corridor to the grand salon.

They sat opposite each other on the new white sofas on either side of the vast fireplace, beneath glittering Venetian chandeliers from the seventeenth century. A maid in a white lace apron placed a silver tray of coffee on the table beside Peach.

"Wil's a fine boy," commented Noel, "and bright too. He knew I'd made a mistake with the *Bâteau Mouche* but he let me off the hook."

"Don't feel badly about it. I make mistakes with him all the time – taking him to things he would have loved six months ago but are suddenly far too 'babyish'. You can't win with growing boys – they're always one step ahead of you."

"And one day all this will be his," said Noel, sipping his coffee.

"All this – and whatever's left of Monsieur's 'empire'." Peach looked at Noel hesitantly. "I hate to bother you about this when you've been so good to me already, but I'd value your opinion. I know that you are one of the most respected men in the automobile industry."

Noel watched Peach kick off her shoes – low heels, he noticed, so that she wouldn't look taller than him. She curled up on the white sofa, propping her head on her hand, meeting his eyes. In a soft coral coloured dress, with her golden skin and mane of russet hair, she had the earnest beauty of Rossetti's pre-Raphaelite girls. And her eyes were the deepest marine blue tonight, gazing anxiously into his.

"You see, Noel, the 'Fleur' isn't selling the way we had hoped," explained Peach. "It was supposed to be de Courmont's giant step into the world market, to compete with Japan's Datsun and Italy's Fiat and Germany's Volkswagen range. It's a good car, Noel, a bit expensive perhaps for the size, but it's solid and well-made. The door handles won't fall off and it starts on cold winter mornings – it's *reliable*."

"The 'Fleur' is a nice car," agreed Noel cautiously.

"But then *why*, Noel? Why isn't it doing well? All the dealers have massive stocks, they have been loyal to de Courmont for years – since before the war some of them. But the 'Fleur' is just sitting in the showroom windows instead of driving on the roads!"

"You want the truth?" asked Noel.

She looked at him. "Is it that bad?"

"The 'Fleur' is undersized and overpriced. The mistake began at the concept stage. The car was aimed at a market that doesn't exist. Then the designers took the mistake a step further. The car is neither one thing nor the other – it's too large for a compact and too small for a family car. There's no room in that back seat for a couple of kids and a dog and maybe the shopping too. The lines are wrong – it's not 'sporty' enough, it's not quite 'today'. The de Courmont 'Fleur' looks like last year's style made-over. If you'll forgive me for saying so, Peach, your design team should be fired – all of them."

Peach stared at him aghast. "But the 'Fleur' was meant to *save* de Courmont," she protested. "They've invested millions in it."

Noel shrugged. "I'm sorry, Peach. You asked for the truth. Of course you can ask other people, but I'm afraid in the US that's the consensus of opinion."

"But at first the response was so good," said Peach, "although the reviewers were unkind. Or truthful, I suppose."

"There's always a good initial response to an ad campaign like yours," said Noel, "and I congratulate you. It was the one really good thing about the 'Fleur'. Besides, you looked beautiful."

Peach managed a smile. "Noel, you realise what it means if the de Courmont doesn't sell? The company won't be able to carry on – they're too heavily into the production of the 'Fleur' financially."

"It was a mistake ever to go downmarket," said Noel. "De Courmont's competition should be Mercedes not Volkswagen! The old boy in the portrait was right – he created an expensive high-class vehicle and an image to match. Your face should be selling the high-priced, up-market answer to Mercedes and Porsche, not a little run-about to the suburban housewife, for God's sake! You need new design planners, efficient costings, and a limited production. De Courmont can't compete in the scrabble for the mass middle and bottom ranges, Peach. It's as simple as that. Aim for the top with the right team, and you'll win."

Peach sat up straight, her hands folded in her lap, her knees together like a girl at school listening to her teacher's lessons. Noel noticed the coral varnish on her toenails and the soft sheen of her bare legs. Her arms in her sleeveless dress looked smooth and soft and the light from the chandeliers shimmered on the golden curve of her breasts where the dress was cut lower. With an effort Noel looked away.

"It all seems so logical – *so simple* now you say it," said Peach dispiritedly. "I know it's all true. I believe you."

Noel smiled at her. "People pay me thousands for that kind of advice," he said. "Act on it if you wish. I guarantee it will work."

"I'll pay you," said Peach suddenly, "if you'll come and work for de Courmont, Noel Maddox, and show us how to do it!"

"Peach," he said, standing up and stretching, "I'm afraid de Courmont can't afford me."

She walked with him to the door, padding through the marble hall in her bare feet. The night was warm and the ropes of light glimmered along the Seine as they stood together at the top of the steps. "But only *you* could save de Courmont, Noel," Peach said persuasively. "No one else understands."

Noel smiled at her. "Well then," he said, "I'll have to think about it, won't I?" Leaning forward he kissed her lightly on the lips. "Goodnight, Peach."

Peach ran after him down the steps. "Noel. Goodnight."

He waved as he strode away. "I'll call you tomorrow," he said.

Peach waited for Noel alone at a table at Maxim's. She was one of only three women there – all the other tables were occupied by businessmen, talking important deals and high numbers over poached chicken and Grand Cru wines. She had invited Noel here to talk business and she was nervous, torn between remembering

330

the faint tremor of his lips as he kissed her – surely that hadn't been her imagination? – and the need to act on his advice – or see de Courmont fail. She'd stopped at Monsieur's portrait as she left this morning. "I'll do my best Grand-père," she'd promised.

There he was, coming through the tables towards her! Noel's lean dark face looked stern and composed. He looked like a man in command of any situation, a man in full control of himself and his own life. Oh God, the last time she'd felt like this was when she saw Harry for the first time at the cricket match at Launceton! But Noel Maddox would never be seduced by a woman the way Harry had. Noel was a man who would find what he wanted – and take it. His deep-set grey eyes that could look so dark and withdrawn lit up as he saw her.

"Peach," he said, holding out his hand, "I'm so sorry I'm late . . . a call from Detroit – a few problems I had to sort out."

"Nothing drastic, I hope?"

"Nothing important enough to make me late meeting you," he said lightly. "I'm truly sorry." He glanced at the champagne waiting in an ice-bucket by the side of the table. "Are we celebrating?"

"I hope so, that's why we're here."

Noel laughed as the waiter filled their glasses. "It's a celebration just being with you, Peach." He added awkwardly, "You look so beautiful in that yellow dress, like rich vanilla ice cream with butterscotch sauce."

Peach recalled Harry's exotic images of her . . . barefoot maidens robed in flower leis, a panther on England's green lawns, exotic in tropical jungles and on soft white beaches . . . "That's the nicest compliment anyone has ever paid me," she said, pleased.

"I'm not too good with compliments," admitted Noel, embarrassed, "I'm better at business."

"And that's really why we're here," said Peach. "I spoke to Jim Jamieson this morning. Noel, he told me he'd met you a few weeks ago?"

"I had a preliminary discussion with him about a possible US Auto involvement in de Courmont," admitted Noel.

"You never told me that US Auto might be interested?"

Noel shrugged. "We'd never discussed business until last night. I happened to be in Europe for US Auto and I heard about the de Courmont situation. I thought it worth while having a discussion with Jim although he probably told you I didn't even know the structure of the company."

"Anyhow," said Peach, "I told Jim our conversation last night and he had to agree that what you said was right. And he also agreed with me that de Courmont needed you, Noel. Not someone *like* you, but *you*."

Noel suppressed the smile of triumph that lurked at the corners of his mouth. He'd won. He had what he wanted – the presidency of de Courmont was within his grasp. He savoured the moment before he said, "Peach, do you realise what you are asking? You know that I'm a very highly paid executive at US Auto – in a few years I'll be in line to be its president. That's not just *any* job, Peach, it's one of the top jobs in the world, and they pay a hell of a lot of money. Why would I give up all that to try to save an ailing foreign company?"

Peach stared into her glass as if analysing the fine spiral of bubbles. "I just hoped, I suppose, because . . . because of our friendship. I realise now it was silly of me – and very unfair."

Noel took her hand. "Peach, our friendship is still there." Her eyes looked anxious. "I'll have to think about this," he said. "There may be a way – but I'm not sure de Courmont would be happy with it."

"*I'd* be happy," cried Peach, "and *I am de Courmont!*"

"There might be a way to incorporate the company into US Auto. Then we could get financial backing to put the company back on its feet and begin production again. Of course, it would mean that you would have to give up partial control of your company – but that's the only way anyone would be willing to put up the money. But I promise you, Peach, that if you decide to take this route, de Courmont will become one of the top names in the auto industry. It'll be back where it belongs – where Monsieur put it. At the top."

"It seems I don't have much choice," said Peach, torn between the bitterness of losing control of the family company, and elation at its salvation. "Either de Courmont goes under, or I surrender control." Her eyes met his. "I trust you, Noel, I'll do as you say."

Noel smiled at her, sipping his champagne. "It may take a few months," he said, "before we can get things worked out." He knew that by then de Courmont's "Fleur" would have been ousted by the "Stallion". And de Courmont would be desperate for him and for US Auto's money.

"I'll wait," promised Peach, her eyes sparkling again.

Noel lifted his glass in a toast, "Then let's celebrate," he said, smiling at his golden girl. She, too, was everything he'd ever wanted.

61

Detroit was not looking its best to welcome Peach de Courmont. The usual February crust of snow bordered its icy streets and sleet splashed against the windscreen of the vast US Auto's Premiere limousine as it pulled under the portico of the Hotel Pontchartrain. Wrapped in a sable coat that had been her grandmother's and dressed by Dior, Peach swept into the lobby followed by a slew of porters carrying a dozen pale leather suitcases and bags. No one would ever have known that she was nervous and that she was so unsure of herself, venturing into this high-powered American business-world, that she'd brought far more clothes than necessary simply because she couldn't decide what to wear. She wanted to make an impression on these hard-headed businessmen and tomorrow she would be severe and tailored in Dior or Balmain for the meetings on the fourteenth floor of the "power tower"; she would be seductive and French at night, wearing the slender gold panne-velvet dress from Valentino, or maybe the bouffant-skirted coral silk from Givenchy, or perhaps the sliver of clinging sapphire satin that she'd bought at a new little boutique in London.

Noel had made sure that the top American advertising agency who were to run the new publicity campaign would feature Peach and the de Courmont mansion as the company's classy "image" for their new car – already provisionally named the "Duke" – and her arrival at Detroit's Metropolitan airport had been carefully stage-managed for maximum publicity, with photographers and newsmen and television cameras in attendance. *But no Noel!* Just a bouquet of peach-coloured roses and a note: "It's all yours – enjoy it! I'll call you at the hotel later."

Peach closed the door of the suite behind the last of the porters, the hotel manager and the maid and the three minions from US Auto who had been sent to "make sure she had everything she wanted and to offer any assistance she might need". Kicking off her tall boots she sank thankfully on to the sofa.

The formation of the new company had taken longer than Noel had anticipated, but it hadn't come too soon for de Courmont, what with sales of the "Fleur" dropping so suddenly once the "Stallion" hit the market. But somehow Noel had been able to secure distribution rights to the "Stallion" for de Courmont and now their dealers were eager to see what the new company under Noel's presidency would come up with. The "Duke" was to be a top-range luxury car competing with the Mercedes, but with sleeker Italian styling, and the model was already at fibreglass body-shell stage. Peach was to see it tomorrow for the first time. And she would also be seeing Noel for the first time in two months.

Noel had been flying backwards and forwards to Paris bringing teams of efficiency experts and executives and designers and accountants, taking the company's structure apart, piece by piece, and reassembling it into his streamlined version of the new "de Courmont". Peach had looked forward to his visits the way she had looked forward to Christmas as a child, counting the days and waking eager and excited on the mornings she knew he would be arriving. She'd asked him to stay at the house on the Ile St Louis, but he had said it was better if he retained his old suite at the Crillon. Peach had felt disappointed; she hadn't realised how much she had wanted to have him to herself in her big old house. Just the two of them.

When Noel came to Paris it was often "just the two of them" – when he wasn't working, of course, because with Noel work always came first. They went to dinner and to concerts and Peach had taken him to Germany to meet Lais and Ferdi at their fairy-tale castle looming on a crag over the Rhine, and to Switzerland to stay for a weekend's rest at the family's mountaintop hotel. But she hadn't taken him to her grandmother's. She wouldn't take any man to see Leonie unless he were a serious part of her life. And much as she wanted Noel to be that, they remained just good friends and business partners. Noel had never done more than kiss her lightly when they met or said goodnight though she'd felt sure he wanted to, as much as she did. She had been only too right when she'd thought that Noel Maddox wouldn't be seduced by a woman: he would take what he wanted. Well, it seemed he didn't want her and she wasn't about to throw herself at him, the way she had with Harry.

The phone rang and Peach picked it up quickly.

"Welcome to Detroit."

"Thank you, Noel. I feel very welcomed," said Peach, glancing round her flower-filled suite. "The Detroit florists must have run out of roses!"

"Most of them are to apologise for my absence," said Noel. "I'm afraid I shan't be able to see you this evening. Something's come up on the new design and we need all the facts and figures ready for tomorrow's press conference."

Peach felt her elation sag into disappointment. "It doesn't matter," she said. "I'm tired from the journey anyway."

"I'll pick you up tomorrow then," said Noel crisply. "It's the big day."

Peach leaned back against the cushions. She was alone in Noel's town. She'd been hoping that once they were away from Paris things would be different. And now on her first night in Detroit Noel had deserted her, just when she could have used his reassuring presence to tell her that what she was doing tomorrow was the right thing. But it wasn't just the right thing any more – it was the *only* thing. Without Noel, de Courmont would have gone under three months ago. In fact without Noel in her life she would have lost everything.

Noel watched as Peach, seated at the desk of the president of US Auto, signed the document with a flourish, looking up to smile for the photographers. She looked wonderful in a tailored jacket and a blue buttondown silk shirt with a striped silk tie – a feminine joke on their executive uniform. Paul Lawrence added his signature and shook hands with Peach for the photographers.

It was done. De Courmont was now an autonomous division of US Auto and Noel was the youngest president of a major automobile company in the industry's history. Then why did he feel no elation? This was the day he had achieved everything he had set out for. What was wrong? He stared broodingly at Peach. He'd used her to get what he wanted, manipulated de Courmont's poor financial situation to gain his own – and US Auto's advantage. But that was only good business. Wasn't it? At the back of it all hadn't there been the memory of Peach at that Boston party, and her wide smile accompanying her lethal words as she told the world he was Noel Maddox, the charity orphan? Hadn't there been a streak of vindictiveness behind his plotting? A desire for the orphan kid to get his own back on the beautiful little rich girl?

"Noel," called Paul, "come over here and give these boys a picture of de Courmont's new president."

Noel took his place beside Peach, feeling her eyes on him. He'd forbidden her to wear low-heeled shoes when she was with him unless they suited the occasion and today she seemed especially tall and slender with her hair swept up and the high blue suede pumps.

"You look tired," Peach said to him at lunch afterwards.

"I'm all right," he replied curtly. "I just hate all these publicity jamborees." Noel glanced around the crowded dining room and the busy buffet. "I'm an engineer not a party-goer."

The smile died on her face.

"I'm sorry," he said. "I guess I'm a bit tired. It's been a long haul."

"We de Courmonts have worn you out," she commented.

"More than that," he apologised. "I think the past twenty years just caught up to me."

After lunch he sent her back to the hotel to rest, promising to pick her up at seven-thirty for the reception for the press and the dealers and the unveiling of the new de Courmont "Duke".

He was there promptly waiting in the lobby for her rather than going up to her suite and he made no comment on the Valentino gold velvet dress, hurrying her into the limousine as though they were late.

Peach gazed at his silent profile, puzzled. What could be wrong? Was he regretting becoming de Courmont's president already? Maybe he didn't want to live part of his time in France? Or maybe he didn't want to see her any more now he had the company?

The hall was decorated with French and American flags and red, white and blue flowers. Standing between Paul Lawrence and Noel with the chairman and vice-chairman of the company flanking them, Peach shook hands with US Auto executives and their wives, and with dealers and their wives, smiling at each one, greeting them by name as she read the little badges on their lapels. Then, with the photographers banked in front of her and Noel and Paul on either side, she pulled the velvet cord, drawing back the regal purple curtain and unveiling the fibreglass shell of the new car.

"My grandfather, the Duc de Courmont, would have been proud

336

to lend his title to this wonderful new car," she said, smiling charmingly.

The night that was the beginning of a new era for de Courmont seemed like an eternity and Peach was glad when Noel finally said that it was time to leave. Detroit's streets were quiet as they drove back and impulsively Peach took Noel's hand. "I'm sorry if today hasn't been what you wanted," she said quietly.

"Today was exactly what I thought it would be," he replied, turning to look at her. Her lids drooped tiredly over her blue eyes, making them look shadowy and mysterious, and in the muted light of the car her mouth looked very soft and vulnerable. He wanted very much to kiss it . . . to kiss her eyes . . . to tell her everything was all right . . . that he would look after her . . .

The limousine stopped at the canopy of a tall apartment building and as the smartly uniformed doorman helped her from the car Noel said, "I thought we might go to my apartment for a nightcap. It's a bit more private than your hotel and I feel as though we've been in the public eye enough today."

He put his arm around her as they hurried from the freezing night air through the lobby and into the elevator.

"There's only one button?" said Peach, puzzled.

Noel smiled. "It's a private elevator to the penthouse."

"Do you know something," she said as they zoomed silently upwards, "that's the first time you've smiled tonight. You didn't even smile for the photographers. You looked stern and businesslike – but I suppose it'll frighten away the competition."

"We'll be the beast and the beauty," Noel said. "Because in that column of molten light you call a dress you look very beautiful, Peach de Courmont."

The elevator bounced gently to a stop and as the doors slid back he said to her, folding her in his arms, "And would the beast turn into a prince if he kissed her?"

Her lips were cool from the freezing night air and they trembled slightly as he kissed her. He could smell her scent and feel the softness of her cheek and the smooth lines of her body as he held her close.

Their eyes met as he drew away and taking her hand he said to her, "Come with me. You showed me your world, now I want to show you mine."

Trailing her sable coat she wandered through the white airy spaces of his apartment, liking its subdued monochrome decor and

337

the subtle lighting. She stood in front of the Lichtenstein, captivated by its wit, and lingered over the Marie Laurencin, saying it made her feel at home. She admired the Kandinsky and the Mondrian and ran her hand over a smoothly carved marble sculpture. And all the time she was thinking of his mouth on hers and her body was tingling from remembered contact with his.

"Come here," called Noel, "I want you to see this."

He was standing by the long sweep of windows gazing out across the twinkling lights of the city below. "There it is," he said, "Detroit. Motor City. That's *my* territory, Peach. I fought my way up from those freezing, lonely streets – all the way up to this penthouse. And to president of the company where I once worked on the assembly line."

Peach knew she would never understand what Noel had been through. How could she? She had never known poverty or loneliness, never needed to claw her way to the top. There was a dark side to Noel that only he was permitted to view. "It's a job only you are qualified for," she said gently. "Without you there would be no de Courmont, Noel, I don't know what I'd do without you."

He looked at her with those hungry eyes, searching to see if she were speaking about the company or herself.

"I mean it, Noel," said Peach softly.

The sable coat dropped to the floor as he swept her into his arms, crushing her to him desperately. "Oh God," he said, "I've waited so long to tell you I love you. I've wanted to tell you I can't live without you, that I need you."

"Then why?" whispered Peach. "Why didn't you . . . I was just waiting."

"I couldn't have borne it if you'd rejected me," he groaned, "and besides . . ."

"Besides?" Peach held his face between her hands, smiling at him.

"Besides, I didn't want to take advantage of you," admitted Noel, "I didn't want anyone to say I'd seduced Peach de Courmont in order to gain control of her company."

"But I would have *given* it to you, Noel," Peach laughed. "I would have given it to you on a silver platter, along with myself."

His kiss crushed the words from her lips and when kissing was no longer enough, he took her hand and led her into his bedroom. Beneath the smiling eyes of the brass orphanage angels he slid the supple sheath of panne-velvet from her breasts, kissing them gently.

And then he took off her high golden slippers, waiting while she removed her stockings. Then he kissed her toes and her instep and the inside of her thigh where it was softest. Peach unbuttoned his shirt, sliding her hands inside, loving the way his hard-muscled body felt, breathing the fragrance of his skin. And then she lay back, watching and waiting as he undressed.

"There's no need for kisses to transform you," she told him quietly. "You are beautiful."

But he went on kissing her, running his tongue along her nipples, and along the curve of her breasts, down the golden groove of her belly, touching his way gently through the mound of russet hair. And she ached for his touch, moaning her pleasure, calling his name. As his body entered hers Peach wrapped herself around him, gripping him to her in a frenzy of passion.

And, as his love spilled into her, Noel cried out in triumph.

62

"I'm taking you away from all this," said Noel teasingly as she awoke.

"Don't," Peach murmured burrowing deeper into his arms, "I love it here."

"Too many people, too many telephones, too much business," he murmured between kisses. "I've got a hideaway just meant for the two of us."

"A hideaway?" Peach pushed back her hair and looked interested.

"Come on, drink up your coffee and get dressed. We'll pick up some clothes from your hotel and we're off."

Peach sipped her coffee, smiling at him.

"I can't wait for you to see this place," Noel said.

"Would a few minutes more make any difference, or half an hour – or whatever?" she asked setting down the cup and lying back naked in the tumbled sheets.

"We've been making love all night," he said laughing.

"I remember," Peach murmured holding out her hand to him.

Noel grinned as he grabbed her to him, "You're too distracting, too tempting, too delicious."

"And you are beautiful," said Peach, running her fingers along his smoothly muscled back. "Oh God you're so beautiful." She lay beneath him, feeling the power of his body on hers, her eyes locked in his deep passionate glance, and then he was kissing her again, and again, and his body was so wonderful she didn't want to let him go from her – ever.

"I love you," she cried in the heat of their passion, "oh I love you!"

And afterwards as he lay by her side, Noel said, "I love you, Peach de Courmont."

The road to the cabin by the lake had been swept clear by snow ploughs, and banks of crystalline snow as high as the car shimmered in the sunlight beneath a cloudless sky, as they sped north with Noel at the wheel.

"But where are we going?" demanded Peach, not really caring as long as she was with him.

"Wait and see," replied Noel.

Realising they had forgotten about breakfast and they'd had no dinner the night before, they stopped at a country inn and ate snacks of pancakes with fresh maple syrup, and Peach held Noel's hand, reluctant to let go of him for a minute.

Peach slept the last hour of their two hundred-mile journey, the roughness of Noel's plaid wool shirt making a small red patch on her cheek where it rested against him.

"Open up your eyes and see what God will send you," said Noel mis-quoting a childish rhyme.

The lake stretched before her, glimmering green near the shore and deep blue into the distance. Snow swept to its edges, tipping a million soaring Christmas trees with white, and the redwood A-frame house rested solidly in its folds, blue-grey smoke spiralling from its chimney.

Hand in hand they climbed the steps to the house and Noel flung open the door with a flourish. It was modern and simple and labour-saving with pale waxed wooden floors and vistas of trees and water from huge windows. There were no decorator touches here. In fact there was almost no furniture. Just an oversize couch and a couple of big chairs that Noel had thought looked comfortable. A Navajo Indian rug in front of the massive fireplace, a pine table and chairs in the dining-area and a king-size bed covered in a plaid rug in the bedroom. The Detroit penthouse in the sky had been Noel's statement to the world. But *this* was what he *was*. A man stripped of emotion by his harsh life, a man who had been afraid to love, and instead had poured his passion into music and paintings and the solitary beauty of this wonderful place.

The caretaker from the cabin at the top of the hill had stocked the refrigerator and lit the fires and the house was cosy and welcoming.

The only ornaments Peach could see were a huge pottery jar filled with dried grasses and leaves and, on the rough stone mantel, a small silvery cup. Picking it up she searched for an inscription but it was blank.

"Boxing trophy," said Noel gruffly. "I won it at the Maddox when I was fourteen."

"But then why isn't it inscribed?" Noel's eyes had that familiar remote look as they met hers.

"I didn't stick around long enough," he said. "I ran away that same night."

Peach drew in her breath sharply, "Ohh . . . I see. Then it's more than a boxing trophy, Noel, this cup marks the beginning of your new life. And it should be inscribed – with your name and the orphanage . . . the date . . . everything."

"Maybe," he said turning away. "Maybe one day I will."

They went for a walk by the lake, crunching snow underfoot in their heavy winter boots, making icy snowballs and tossing them into the freezing lake and at each other, hurrying home with numb fingers and scarlet cheeks to mugs of hot mulled wine that Noel brewed expertly on his big white stove.

And as the blue dusk fell over the steely lake they made love on the vast sofa in front of the log fire, consumed by their own heat and warmed by the flames.

Afterwards they showered together in his huge bathroom and Peach soaped his hair and licked the drops of water from his lashes and Noel lathered her body until she was dressed in white suds and slippery as an eel in his arms. And they kissed endlessly, as if they were making up for all the months of not kissing.

Warmed by the roaring fire and his love, Peach sipped chilly champagne, gazing out of the windows at the fairytale landscape, watching the first flutter of snow settle on the wooden deck while

Noel cooked supper. He emerged briskly from the kitchen bearing sizzling melted cheese sandwiches and they drank more champagne and ate enormous hot-house strawberries from California.

"Five bites," said Peach licking her lips and finishing the last strawberry. "I counted."

Noel laughed. "Why count? Why not just enjoy it?"

"I always count things like that. I counted the first time a boy kissed me. I still remember it was thirty-two seconds. And do you know who he was? Harry's brother – Tom."

"You mean I should be jealous of all the Launceton brothers?"

"Only two. Archie was too young."

Noel groaned. "Let's not talk of the Launcetons."

"And what about you? Who am I to be jealous of? You haven't told me a single thing about any women in your life. For all I know there could be a sweet little wife tucked away somewhere."

"I promise you there isn't."

Peach lay back on the sofa staring up at the soaring beamed ceiling with Noel sitting on the floor beside her.

"What's the matter?" asked Noel, taking her hand.

"I'm just feeling jealous of all those unknown women, thinking about them in your arms."

"Foolish girl," murmured Noel, kissing her fingers. "There have been no women in my life until you."

"Really, Noel?" she sat up looking at him seriously. "Has there been no one in your life you loved?"

"There have been women I cared about – but none more important to me than my work."

"Or your ambition," Peach guessed shrewdly.

"As you wish," replied Noel. "But that was before you. I want to ask you to marry me but I'm too afraid you'll say no."

Peach lay back on the sofa with a sigh, waves of pure happiness washing over her. "I warn you if you do ask, I'll say yes."

Noel knelt at her side, leaning over her as she lay there, "Will you?" he asked.

"I will," replied Peach.

63

Leonie sat at the head of her table wearing black lace and heavy diamond drop earrings, her silvery hair piled up Edwardian-style, and the ebony walking-stick – hated symbol of old age – resting against her chair. The headaches that had been troubling her for months and which Dr Mercer in Nice, who was himself almost as aged as she, told her were due to high blood pressure, had disappeared and she felt better than she had in a long time. Having all her family here at the villa for Peach's wedding made her happy and that seemed a better cure for what ailed her than all Dr Mercer's little white pills.

Her gaze rested on Peach sitting beside Noel, happiness blazing from her every glance, so in love with him she could hardly bear to let go his hand in order to eat. But the cool, tense Mr Maddox was still an enigma, only allowing them to see the part of him that was public domain. Who knew what lay beneath that calm, assured surface? When he looked at Peach as he did now, his eyes had a naked, hungry look as though he were afraid of losing her – even though he was marrying her tomorrow. Studying Noel, Leonie thought there was a vulnerability about him when he looked at Peach – it was only then that his façade slipped. But why did he need a façade? It bothered Leonie that she couldn't read Noel's character, that she couldn't get beneath his surface. And when she thought about their marriage the question that always came to mind was, did Noel truly love Peach? Or was it the de Courmont company he wanted? Remembering Noel's meeting here with Jim and the events since, she doubted his motives.

Leonie took a sip of her champagne, smiling across at Lais and Ferdi. Just look how content they were with each other, and how solicitously Ferdi looked after her without ever making it obvious! It seemed only yesterday Lais was the headstrong beautiful young girl, juggling with life and always ending up empty-handed. Still, despite everything, in the end Lais had found what she wanted.

Now Leonore was quite different. Who would have thought shy, retiring Leonore would emerge as this elegant self-possessed beauty and one of the world's best hoteliers? It was a pity, though, that she didn't seem as successful in love as in business. But Leonore had chosen her own direction and it was her very singlemindedness that made her so successful.

And then, of course, there was Amelie – fine-boned, beautiful and as strong-willed as herself. Looking at her daughter, lovely in her favourite yellow silk, Leonie saw herself as she had been years ago. Amelie's resemblance to her was strong, but her daughter's temperament was resilient and optimistic. Amelie was always the one who saw the patch of blue sky even as the rain fell. Leonie was justly proud of this fine forceful daughter who had brought her the happiness of a true family. It was sad but true that Gerard had never fully recovered from those harsh experiences of the war and his disillusionment with humanity showed in a weariness in his eyes behind the warm smile. All Gerard really cared about now was Amelie and his girls. Their happiness was his.

How different life might have been, thought Leonie, if Gilles de Courmont had been more like his gentle son! No one, not even Jim, would ever know how desperately she had loved Monsieur, and how she had longed for his love and wanted his child. Now Monsieur's great-grandson – and hers – was sitting beside her at this table. But nine-year-old Wil did not possess the de Courmont name and, though Wil looked like Monsieur, he was as open and uncomplicated as his grandfather had been devious and complex, manipulating lives to gain his own ends – even going so far as . . . murder. The memory lurked in the back of her mind, waiting with the old ghosts to come forward and remind her, again and again and again . . . forcing her to face the truth. And it was true also that even afterwards, when she'd known, she'd still been attracted by him, still felt the powerful pull of his presence.

Leonore reached out to stroke Wil's thick dark hair and he smiled up at her. She knew now there would be no more sons or daughters bearing the de Courmont name. Peach was the last. And Gilles de Courmont, founder of his great company, would become just a part of history, as she herself would, quite soon.

"You're very quiet," remarked Jim.

"I'm just watching my family, remembering when they were

small and I was young." Leonie pushed back her chair. "Let's have our coffee on the terrace." Disdaining the silver-topped stick that waited to remind her she was old, Leonie walked slowly into the warm night, tall and straight, as though she were a young girl again. Wil rushed after her, anxiously offering her his youthful arm and the walking stick.

"Thank you, Wil," Leonie said with a smile. "I don't know what I'd do without my great-grandson."

"Well maybe you'll get more great-grandsons now that Mum's marrying Noel," replied Wil. "I wouldn't mind a brother or a sister."

"Did you hear that, Peach?" called Lais, laughing, "your son is planning on having brothers and sisters."

"And why not?" Clutching Noel's arm Peach smiled up at him, but Noel's face was impassive – a look she was beginning to know. They walked to the end of the terrace to look at the view of the headland under the white glare of the full moon. "Are you upset by Wil's talk of brothers and sisters?"

Noel's eyes were hooded as he glanced at her, guarding some part of himself that she had yet to see. "Our children won't be de Courmonts, you know. Nor even Launcetons. They'll be Maddox kids – sons of a man who doesn't even know who his father was. When I see your family, the traditions, the sharing of lives and experiences – *your past*, Peach, I think that I have very little to offer you – or a child."

Looking into his bleak dark face Peach was shocked by how deep Noel's wounds went. "Did they never tell you who your parents were?" she asked gently.

"The Maddox never volunteered any information to their inmates. To them you were just another of the world's dispossessed – to be fed just enough and to be clothed in others' cast-offs, to be polite and clean and scrubbed and put on display for the governors or the local civic groups, so they could feel the warm glow of their own goodness as they bestowed their second-hand gifts on us. It's easy to drop a penny in a beggar's cup – it's not so easy to love him."

"It's a long time ago, Noel," said Peach urgently. "Look at you now! Look what you've made of yourself! You should be proud!"

"It's just that sometimes," replied Noel wearily, "I think to myself how much easier it would all have been if I didn't have to fight every step of the way."

345

"The fighting's over," whispered Peach, resting her head against his shoulder, "and you're not alone now. *Our* children will be proud to be called Maddox."

Noel smiled wryly. "Then I can promise you one thing, Peach, they'll be the first."

Despite Leonie's protests that it was still early, the family were dispersing, kissing goodnight and hoping for a fine day to bless the bride tomorrow. Jim walked with them back to the hotel and Peach, who was staying at the villa, went to say goodnight to Wil.

Leonie studied Noel as he leaned against the rail, gazing at the silver swell of the Mediterranean under the moonlight. "It's a view I never tire of," she said finally, "even though I must have looked at it every day for more than sixty years."

"I can see why," replied Noel. "There's a fascination about the sea; perhaps it's because it's different every time you look at it. When I was a kid the only waves I saw were waves of wheat rippling in the wind across the Iowa plains. You could go for mile upon mile and see nothing but wheat, never changing, never ending – into infinity."

At last, thought Leonie, the man had revealed a chink in his armour.

"It frightened me," said Noel quietly. "I used to think that there was nothing beyond it, that no matter how hard I'd try or how fast I'd run there would be just another endless expanse of wheatfield in front of me."

"You don't strike me as a young man afraid of what's in front of him. And there's nothing any of us can do about our past." Leonie pulled herself to her feet with the ebony cane. Old as she was, she was straight-backed and taller than he, and she'd always felt better facing an adversary standing. "Noel," she said, "I was here the day you came to offer Jim a deal for the de Courmont company, the same day that Peach telephoned from Spain to say she was in trouble. She told me how you found her in Barcelona and helped her. Am I right in thinking that wasn't just a coincidence?"

Noel leaned against the rail, folding his arms. "I went there to find her. To help her."

"But why Noel? Why should you have wanted to help Peach? *Unless it was so that you could gain control of de Courmont through her?*"

"I first met Peach when I was thirteen. Our paths crossed several times since. I knew her and I wanted to help her."

Leonie sighed. "I wish I could feel sure you were marrying her because she is Peach and not because she's de Courmont," she said bluntly.

Noel stared at her in silence. In the moonlight Leonie looked half her age and she had the strength of will to match. And she was determined no fortune-hunter was going to grab her granddaughter without a warning. "You are a wise woman, Leonie," he replied abruptly. "You see more than most. You must judge for yourself."

Peach hurried towards them along the terrace. "There you both are," she cried. "Now what have you been talking about, you both look so solemn? And how can anyone be serious on a night like this when there's moonlight and the sound of the sea – and tomorrow is my wedding day?" She smiled radiantly at Leonie. "Aren't you pleased, Grand-mère, that at last one of your granddaughters is having a proper wedding for you to remember?"

"I'm pleased, child," said Leonie, looking at Noel, "if that's what makes you happy."

Linking her arm in Noel's Peach beamed at them both. "I'm so very happy," she said, "I can't wait to be Mrs Noel Maddox."

Leonie went in to kiss Peach goodnight as she always had done, only this time Leonie knew it was different.

Peach's old room at the villa was still filled with the memorabilia of her girlhood – family pictures and long school photographs with a hundred tiny smiling faces, most of them now only names from the past. There was a bulletin-board pinned with layers of ageing holiday snapshots and long-ago party invitations, fading postcards of sunny resorts and white-capped ski slopes and once-important letters curling at the edges, their writing blurred. There was a pressed flower still in its silvery wrapper and a solitary pretty earring, one of a long-lost pair. Well-worn stuffed animals ranged the dresser and the window seat and stacks of books tumbled across two walls of wooden shelves. The narrow white bed and tiny red-enamelled table with the silver framed mirror that had been Peach's since she was nine years old seemed too small for the rangy young woman who sat brushing her long chestnut-bronze hair and staring contemplatively into its depths.

Peach's eyes met Leonie's in the mirror and she turned, smiling.

"I've only come to say goodnight, my darling, and to wish you happiness. Tomorrow you'll be too busy and I wanted to speak to you privately."

"Oh Grand-mère, I was just thinking how different it is this time.

It's not just the silly obsession I had for Harry. Noel loves me and I love him. Nothing can stop you from being happy when you start out with that, can it?"

Leonie sat down tiredly in the armchair under the light. "Love is such a fragile emotion, Peach, it can become obscured by all sorts of things – the difficulties of adjusting to living together, boredom, jealousy – oh, a dozen different things, and suddenly you wonder where the love went and who this stranger is you're living with."

"Like Harry."

"Not quite. Harry was a mistake, on both your parts. You are a romantic, Peach, but love goes beyond just romance. It's caring for someone more than yourself, sharing your strengths and taking from his to shore up your own weaknesses. Love is understanding his life and trying to make it easier and more pleasant and he must do the same for you. It's sharing your joy in your children, seeing them through their illnesses together, and taking pride in their achievements. Love is so complex I'm not sure anyone truly understands exactly what it is – the first feelings of appeal and romance are only the foundation. Love is a long path, Peach, and to achieve it you need understanding and compassion."

"Grand-mère, that sounds as though you are speaking from the heart," murmured Peach. "Did you love Monsieur like that?"

"I loved Monsieur more than any man in my life – I loved him more passionately than Rupert, my first love, and more intensely than Jim – my last. But there was no laughter between us, the way there is with Jim and me, and there was no innocence the way there was with Rupert. Looking back I can see now that the man I thought was so strong and invincible was as vulnerable as any of us. Every man has his Achilles heel, Peach, and perhaps if I'd understood Monsieur better, if I'd been less concerned with myself and my own feelings, if I'd have known *why* he was like he was, then maybe I would have acted differently. Monsieur needed my compassion as well as my love and I never gave him that." Sighing, Leonie smoothed her forehead with a trembling hand. "And how different our lives might have been if I had," she said.

"Oh Grand-mère," whispered Peach, not knowing whether she quite understood, but sensing Leonie's deep emotion, "I'm so sorry."

"It's in the past, child, and you are facing your future. In his own way Noel is as complex as Monsieur. He hides his feelings from the world the way Monsieur did. One day he may need your compassion and your strength. And when he does, Peach, I want you to remember, my darling, that *love* is all that matters."

Peach stared at her solemnly, a little frightened by her words. "I'll remember," she promised. As Leonie bent to kiss her, Peach put her arms around her grandmother, feeling the warmth of Leonie's lips against hers and the brittle bones under the soft skin.

"Then goodnight, my darling Peach," murmured Leonie, smiling at her tenderly, "and be happy with your Noel. You know," she added, "you've always felt more like my daughter than my granddaughter. I was so lucky, I had a double share of you."

The little brown cat was waiting outside the bedroom door and Peach watched as it followed Leonie along the shadowy corridor to her room, before returning thoughtfully to her dressing table.

If there were a lovelier sight than Peach on her wedding day then Lais had yet to see it. Peach looked beautiful in the dress of creamy silk taffeta, chosen from Leonie's vast closets and dating from the turn of the century. Her smooth golden shoulders emerged from flounces of delicate cream lace and the full backward sweep of the skirt with its tiny Edwardian bustle made her waist so small it looked breakable. With her russet hair upswept and wound with fresh blossoms, Peach looked the perfect picture of a bride. But it was the look of love darkening her blue eyes when she gazed at Noel and the sparkle of on-top-of-the-world happiness that projected her into a dazzling bridal beauty. Holding Peach's bouquet as she vowed to love and honour Noel, Lais remembered the "little sister", her constant companion, always just a foot behind her, hoping to be told it was all right, she could come along; or sitting on the white rug in her bedroom, sliding Lais's rings on to her fingers just the way Noel was sliding the gold wedding band on to Peach's hand now. Lais recalled the charming child, waiting by the side of the dance floor on the ocean liner, loath to go to bed, waiting for her big sister. She remembered the sick little girl, tossing with fever, and she felt the pain again and the shock of seeing those baby limbs encased in steel. If she had saved Peach's life by hurling herself in front of Kruger then Lais knew she would do it all over again. But that was in the past and watching Peach as she turned to kiss Noel, Lais knew that at last her little sister had grown up.

Of course the marriage to Harry Launceton had been doomed from the start but at least one good thing had come from it. Wil. Lais never envied Peach her long strong legs but she envied her her

349

son. But it was no use wishing that she and Ferdi could have had a child like Wil. They had each other and their own private world in their castle overlooking the river, and they were happy.

Dust motes hovered in the warm shafts of sunlight beaming through the windows of the tiny little white church in Nice, gilding Leonore's smooth blonde hair. She put up her hand to smooth back an errant strand, smiling at her mother as their eyes met. "She looks so happy," she whispered.

Amelie nodded. She didn't know whether to smile or to cry, Peach looked so lovely and so happy. Cheated of a ceremony and a party by Peach's first runaway romance with Harry, Amelie had insisted on this "proper" wedding – for her own sake and for Leonie's. "So that your grandmother can see at least one of her grandchildren married," she said.

Leonie sat with her back straight, chin up, looking pensive, a delightful fantasy of a hat, all veil and flowers, sweeping across her brow. Beautiful as Peach was today, looking at her mother's strong profile Amelie wondered if anyone could ever be as lovely as Leonie? Reaching across Wil she touched her mother's gloved hand. "Are you happy for her, Maman?" she whispered.

Caught between their linked hands Wil gazed from face to face.

"I was just remembering when she was a little girl," murmured Leonie, "somehow I thought Peach would never grow up. And now she's surprised me."

"She surprises me all the time," whispered Wil solemnly.

His grandmother and his great-grandmother smiled at each other over his head.

"Well, I don't suppose she'll ever change," said Leonie, as the organ pealed triumphantly.

At the reception at the Hostellerie la Rose du Cap it was Gerard, proud father of the bride, who proposed the first toast, and Paul Lawrence, President of US Auto and Noel's best man, who responded. He and Mrs Lawrence were Noel's only guests at the church, but Noel and Peach had invited top-management from the de Courmont company to the reception along with their wives as well as the new American executives that Noel had brought over from Detroit to work for de Courmont. There were a dozen or so long-service employees from de Courmont's factory, and a couple of retired old men who had known "Monsieur" and remembered him well enough to see the resemblance in his great-grandson. In tight dark blue suits they quaffed champagne and chatted about cars while their plump wives in floral Sunday silks nibbled the delicious food and asked for recipes from the chef.

Swinging round the floor in her father's arms as they danced the first waltz, Peach smiled at Gerard delightedly. "Isn't this the most perfect wedding?" she demanded. "Everyone is here who means anything to our family."

Gerard looked at her quizzically. "And what about Noel's family?"

Peach laughed. "Oh, everyone is here who means anything to Noel. His car people. And me. That's all Noel needs to make him happy."

Looking into his lovely daughter's glowing face, Gerard prayed that this time Peach was right.

64

Leonie sat up in bed wearily. The night had been warm and humid and its blackness had seemed to close around her so densely she almost felt she could touch it. She had lain awake, tense with pain, waiting for the throbbing in her head to subside and for morning to come, when she knew she would feel better. As the first pale hint of dawn split the sky outside her open window she stepped on to the terrace, feeling glad that Jim was in Paris – she would only have kept him awake with her restless tossing. And today she welcomed her solitude.

Chocolat, emerging from her warm corner of the bed, padded softly after her mistress as she slowly paced the terrace, clutching her thin robe around her while the cool early morning breeze cleaned the night from the sky. Leonie took deep breaths of the fresh scented air, sweeping the bay with a glance that knew its every different shade of blue, its every change of mood. Today it was calm and azure fading to pale crystal as it rippled lazily along the smooth shore. She thought it had never looked more beautiful.

Curling into a deep cushioned chair she tucked her bare feet beneath her, marvelling that this morning there was no sign of the lurking stiffness in her limbs. They felt as limber as an eighteen-year-old's: she could have walked miles across the hills today, just as she used to . . . but she was dreaming again. She was just an old woman, living in the past. The future was Peach and Noel and Wil, and their children.

The warmth of the sun's rays relaxed her and as the throbbing pain began to recede from behind her eyes, she dreamed against the cushions, the little cat curled in her lap. She remembered Jim saying that the only credit he gave the Sekhmet legend was that it kept her young for ever – but Leonie knew that it was just in his eyes only. Darling, wonderful Jim. She could recall when they first met as clearly as though it were yesterday, and remember the first time he made love to her in New York and how crazily, happily in love they'd been. She had run away from him and returned to France to face her responsibilities, but Jim had found her again and this time he'd given her his strength as well as his love.

Leonie dozed through the morning, waking to sip the tea that the new housekeeper, Marianne, brought her, but eating nothing. Old Madame Frénard had been dead for years now and Marianne must have been here with her for at least a dozen, but she still thought of Marianne as the "*new*" housekeeper – age played funny tricks with her concept of time, lengthening it or shortening it to suit her emotions. Now wasn't *Marianne* the name of the manageress at Serrat's lingerie shop where she had worked when she was just seventeen, the one who'd accused her of stealing the red silk stockings and had dismissed her, calling her a thief? Of course she had paid for the stockings and Marianne knew it, she'd just been jealous of her – though at the time it had been hard to understand why. She had bought those stockings to go to Caro's party, she'd been wearing them when she met Rupert . . . "I saw the longest red silk legs," he'd said to her, "disappearing up the steps in front of me and I knew I had to meet their owner!" Of course her dress had been disgracefully short – what a sight she must have been! And now that she thought about it she remembered tucking five francs into the top of her only pair of black silk stockings as insurance when she first went to the casino at Monte Carlo – just in case she lost everything. Which of course she had . . . and then she met Monsieur. He'd been watching her, knowing she was gambling for survival, knowing it was inevitable she would lose, waiting to make his move. Of course Monsieur hadn't needed to gamble – he knew he would win her. And then hadn't she worn cream silk stockings when she married Jim? They had matched her beautiful pleated silk suit and she had such a lovely sweeping-brimmed hat, piled with flowers . . . she could almost smell the flowers in the church now, she remembered it so clearly . . . or were they flowers from Peach's wedding? Yes, of course, they must be . . . her memory was playing her tricks again. Odd though, how silk stockings had played a role in her life, red for Rupert, black for Monsieur and pure cream for Jim. Leonie smiled as she dozed.

"Madame, Madame Leonie."

Leonie awoke as Marianne shook her shoulder. "Yes? What is it, Marianne?"

"You've been sleeping a long time, it's almost four o'clock. You should eat something, Madame."

Leonie sat up, stretching. She felt refreshed. "Do you know what I'd like most in the world right now, Marianne?" she asked. "I'd like a glass of champagne – and maybe one or two of those little pink biscuits the champagne house sent me. Yes, Marianne, that would be perfect."

Muttering about not eating properly, Marianne hurried off to her kitchen, and Leonie glanced down at herself in dismay. Here she was barefoot and in her robe at four in the afternoon. This would never do. Standing up she stretched again, feeling the suppleness of her spine with pleased surprise. She felt wonderful, quite her old self. She would bathe and dress in something special. This would be a celebration, the return of the new youthful Leonie.

There was a special room in the villa where Leonie's collection of clothes spanning seventy years were stored, including her favourite couture gowns and all her fabulous stage clothes. Like Caro, she had thrown nothing away and it was from here that Peach had chosen her wedding dress. *There* was the one she was looking for, the thinnest gold tissue pleated and designed by Fortuny that had clung to her body like a second skin! It was her first stage costume. Oh, how afraid she'd been that first night, and how reluctant to face the prying curious eyes of the audience who had come to see the notorious mistress of the Duc de Courmont! The young black panther at the end of the golden chain in her hand had shivered with fear too but neither of them could have had their freedom until she stepped into that spotlight and sang. She could still feel the sweat trickling down her back and hear the animal's low growl as her song ended and the spotlight closed leaving them in darkness and the endless seconds of silence before the great roar of applause. It was all so long ago . . . but this was the dress to wear today, a dress to wear to drink champagne. A celebration dress.

Cool and perfumed from her bath, barefoot and dressed in her beautiful exotic gown, Leonie sipped her champagne, smiling as she fed the rose-coloured biscuit to her cat. She felt so happy this evening, so very happy. But how quickly the hours were flying by. The sky was losing its calm blue and taking on the pearly hazy look of evening. Where had the time gone, oh where had it gone?

She watched the sun change from gold to bronze and to a smooth scarlet disc and then she walked slowly along the terrace towards the steps that led to the curve of beach below. For once the little cat didn't follow her and Leonie glanced back to smile at her.

The setting sun had laid a long golden-red track across the glittering satin sea and Leonie stood at its edge, letting the small waves wash across her feet. Then with her arms flung wide so that the sleeves of her golden robe spread like a fan she waded into its coolness, following the path to the sun. As the water deepened she turned, floating on her back in the gleaming golden-red sea. She could feel the sun's heat on her closed eyelids, she could feel its red heat consuming her . . . Sekhmet was reclaiming her and she was becoming one with the sun-god Re, as it was always meant to be. She was his mistress, his consort, his lover and she was entering the tunnels of night with her love. Leonie was floating, safe in her lover's arms, towards infinity and another new dawn.

65

Peach couldn't stop crying. They'd returned from their honeymoon in Japan to find Maman and Papa waiting with the news of Leonie's death.

"We didn't telephone you because we knew that Grand-mère

would not have wanted to spoil your happiness, and besides there was nothing you could have done. There's to be a service in her memory tomorrow at Notre Dame. Oh Peach, you can't imagine how many tributes she has received, not just for her talent and her beauty, but for her generosity and her charity, and for her courage! Newspapers around the world have written her obituary. Leonie was a remarkable woman."

"How can you talk about her so calmly," cried Peach, the pain of her loss still searing her, "when you know we'll never see her again?"

Amelie bit her lip to stop the tears from flowing and glanced helplessly at Gerard.

"Your mother is trying to adjust to her loss, Peach, just as you will. You'll cry away your pain and grief and then you must try to come to terms with it."

Noel waited silently by the fireplace as Gerard sat beside his sobbing daughter, trying to comfort her.

"But you said they never found her," said Peach. "Oh Papa, what if she's not really dead after all, what if she just went away . . .?"

'But that's all she has done, darling, she's just gone away, and you'll find her again everywhere you turn, in your memories."

"Peach darling," cried Amelie holding her in her arms, and crying too, "we must think of Jim now, and try to help him. He's desolated . . ."

Peach looked at Noel, thinking how she loved him, imagining life without him . . . and Leonie and Jim had been married for *fifty* years, how must it be for Jim?

"If there is anything I can do," offered Noel. "Perhaps Jim would like to stay here . . .?"

"Not here," said Amelie quickly. "Jim has always thought of this as Monsieur's house . . . but thank you, Noel."

"Now, Peach," said Gerard, "Lais and Ferdi are already here, at the Ritz, and Leonore is arriving tonight. Your mother has arranged for a reception here, after the service. I'll give Noel the details."

"I'm sorry we had to bring you this bad news on your first day home," said Gerard to Noel later.

"I'll take care of her, sir," promised Noel, "and although I barely knew Leonie, I can imagine how deeply you all feel her loss."

"It's a sad business. See that Peach gets some sleep, if you can."

* * *

355

The great grey cathedral was hung with embroidered silken banners and decked with flowers. The scent of Leonie's favourite jasmine hung in the air and sunlight brightened the great rose window as the pure voices of the choir boys soared in an anthem. Peach stood stiffly at Noel's side, dressed in black with a broad-brimmed hat shading her wan colourless face from curious eyes, and he clasped her hand in his comfortingly, lending her his strength. He scanned the crowded church, marvelling at the power the strange indomitable old woman commanded to summon presidents and royalty, as well as those who had simply admired and loved her, to a service in her honour. And afterwards, as they sipped Leonie's favourite champagne in the house that Leonie had once longed to call her home, he observed the faces of those who cared for her. There were the Sisters who looked after Leonie's orphan children at the Château d'Aureville and some of those children, now grown and with their own families, and there were men and women whose lives she had helped to save through her Resistance work during the war. There were theatre managers and conductors, musicians and stage-door concierges, titled families of Europe and simple families from the south who had worked for her and loved her, and those who lived in the village and had felt the quiet benefit of her generosity and kindness. Leonie commanded them all.

"She would have enjoyed this party, you know," noted Jim approvingly, "it would have pleased her to see them all here, and it comforts me to know how many lives she made just a bit brighter by her presence."

Afterwards, when the family were alone, he told Peach that the villa was hers. "Leonie wanted you to have it when we were gone," he said gently, "and I can't bring myself to live there without her – so now it's yours."

"But, Jim, where will you go?" asked Peach. "It's your home."

"Don't worry about me, it's all been arranged. I'm moving into Lais's old penthouse apartment at the Hostellerie. After all, it's no good an old man like me living alone and I'm sure to find a bit of company there when I feel like it."

Peach had never thought of Jim as being old and she looked at him, shocked by the truth. It just wasn't fair, she thought angrily, people shouldn't get old, they shouldn't have to go away and leave those who loved them . . . tears sprang to her eyes again.

"Don't cry, Peach," murmured Jim soothingly, "I shall be happy thinking of you at the villa and so, I'm sure, would your grand-mother."

Sitting between her sisters as the lawyer told them the contents of Leonie's will the following day, Peach could barely control her trembling. This was the worst part of all . . . dividing up Leonie's beautiful things, the jewellery she remembered her grandmother wearing all her life, her beautiful collection of clothes, her treasured objects . . . a terrible thought struck her suddenly and she grabbed Lais's hand, panicked. "The cat," she cried, "where is Leonie's cat?"

"Chocolat disappeared the same day as Leonie," whispered Lais. "Oh Peach, I'm so sorry."

Peach didn't want to hear any more, she didn't want to know who should have which possessions – she just wanted jt all to be the same as it was . . . never changing, always there. Sobbing, she ran for the door with Noel after her.

Closing their bedroom door behind him, he watched as Peach raged around the room, screaming her anger and hate at fate and at time and at death and then he he took her in his arms and held her close. "It'll be better, Peach," he said calmly, "it'll be better now, you'll see."

Peach sagged against him, her despair and anger spent. She felt secure in his arms, protected from the hazards of life and death. "Oh Noel," she sighed tiredly, "whatever would I do without you?"

66

Noel could never quite get used to the grandeur of the de Courmont mansion. Even after two years of living there he still felt like a guest in its lofty panelled rooms. Nodding to the concierge at the gate, he drove the new car into the courtyard as the butler hurried down the steps to open the door.

"Is my wife home?" asked Noel, standing back to admire the car.

"Madame is in her sitting room, sir."

"Then would you ask her to come down here, please. Tell her it's a surprise, Oliver."

"Of course, sir. And may I congratulate you sir, the 'Duke' is magnificent."

"Thank you, Oliver." Noel prowled around the car, checking it from every angle. Its long sleek lines, the rich gleaming dark blue paintwork and soft pale leather proclaimed it a thoroughbred. It was the car he had always longed to design, the reply to all those years of compromise. The "Duke" was the car of his dreams.

"Noel, it's wonderful," called Peach hurrying down the steps towards him.

Noel pointed to the satin bow decorating the wheel. "It's a present," he said, "the very first 'Duke' is for Monsieur's grand-daughter."

"Really? It's mine?" Peach ran her hand delightedly across its shining surface. "But this is *your* car, Noel, more than anyone's. The first should be yours."

"I reckon old Monsieur had as much to do with it as I did and as his granddaughter and chairman of his company, you get the first 'Duke' – and the numberplate."

Peach ran around to inspect it. "DUKE 1," she cried, pleased.

"And there's something special inside," added Noel, opening the door for her.

The car smelled luxuriously of new leather and flowers. Sitting in the superbly comfortable driver's seat Peach looked around her. A small wing-shaped Lalique vase, an exact copy of the one in the first de Courmont, held a single spray of jasmine.

"I had it copied especially for you," said Noel. "No other car will have one." He looked at her eagerly, hoping she was pleased.

"And there was always a spray of jasmine in the vase for Leonie," said Peach. "You think of everything, Noel Maddox!"

"Then you like it?"

"It's wonderful! Thank you, not just for the lovely car but for everything you've done for de Courmont! You've put the company back on its feet financially because of the 'Stallion'." Her hand rested on the leather steering wheel centred with the de Courmont family crest. "And with this car you've taken de Courmont back to the top – Monsieur would be proud."

Noel grinned at her, relieved. "Then do me a favour, lady," he said, climbing in next to her, "take me for a ride."

People turned to stare as the great car purred up to the Paris traffic lights, waving as they recognised Peach from the television advertisements. "You see how they like it," she cried exultantly, pressing her foot down on the accelerator and heading for the open countryside. Beethoven's Ninth Symphony blasted through quadrophonic speakers as the car ate up the miles and Noel sat back, enjoying the controlled power of the engine he knew so well, noting how the new aerodynamic shape kept wind-resistance to a minimum, making the ride virtually noise-free. A million details that he'd checked a thousand times ran through his head and he ticked them off one by one. The car was as near perfect as it could be.

Peach swung into a side road and from there along a rough country lane. A broad glassy river lay in front of them, swept by green willows and reflecting the pale evening sky. Pulling on the handbrake she leaned back against the cushions with a satisfied sigh. "Oh how perfect, how absolutely perfect!" she cried. "You deserve a medal for this, Noel."

Noel slid his arm around her and she rested her head against his shoulder, gazing out across the deserted lake. "I'd trade the medal for a kiss," he suggested.

Peach looked up at him with a quizzical smile. "Since when did you have to trade anything to get a kiss from me?"

"I'd trade *anything* for a kiss from you," he murmured, nuzzling her ear.

"Even the car?"

Noel laughed. "That's unfair, Mrs Maddox – and, besides, you just said a kiss wouldn't cost me anything."

Why was it when he kissed her the real world seemed to disappear and he was alone with her in a warm fantasy world of his own making? Her skin was as soft as petals and as smooth as marble and he felt drunk on the scent of her. Noel pulled the pins from her upswept hair and ran his fingers through its luxuriant waves, kissing her pale eyelids, running a finger along the curve of her cheek, and then down, along the curve of her breast. Her eyes locked with his as he cupped her breast in his hand and then he bent to kiss her again. "Peach, Peach," he murmured softly, "I love you so much."

The back seat of the car was wide and soft as they lay down together and there was only a slow-flying heron over the river to witness their love-making. Peach's body was warm and pliable and familiar under his. And afterwards as he held her, trembling, Noel

359

thought he had everything he could ever want – he had Peach and de Courmont and his dream car.

The following week Peach started work on the advertising campaign she'd been planning for a year and a half. She travelled through Europe with a production team, first photographing the "Duke" high in the snowy Alps and then filming it winding down breathtaking mountain curves, skis strapped to its roof. They photographed the car outside the Hostellerie with a small mountain of chic leather cases being removed from its capacious trunk and in Paris in the courtyard of the de Courmont mansion with a beautiful long-necked Afghan hound peering from the back window. They filmed it in an aircraft hangar in between a sleek little Lear jet and a powerful Concorde, and they filmed it cruising the highways of Europe.

Noel had flown off to Detroit again and Peach was kept so busy she barely had time to think of him until she fell into bed at night, alone in some hotel room. And, if she were lucky and the time difference permitted, she would call him, waiting anxiously until she heard his decisive voice as he said, "Hello, Peach." He always seemed to know when it was her even before she spoke.

After a month they took the car over to London to film there and, reunited with Wil, she had less time than ever to think about Noel. She went with the crew to a turreted castle in the highlands of Scotland where they took pictures of the car parked by a salmon-filled river, while craggy-faced gillies held rods and creels, and over to the west of Ireland where horses and hounds and pink-coated huntsmen brushed past the elegant waiting de Courmont.

When she finally got back to their house on the Ile St Louis Peach realised that it had been almost two months since she'd seen Noel – and that she must be pregnant.

"I was just wondering," she said to him over dinner that night, "if there is room in the 'Duke' for a stroller."

"A stroller! What kind of image is that for the new de Courmont? It's supposed to be fast, elegant, racy – you know for God's sake, you created its image. What on earth made you ask such a question?"

"Would it spoil its racy, macho image to be seen putting a stroller in the back of the 'Duke'? Because we may have to do that quite soon."

Noel's face went blank with shock. "Are you telling me you are pregnant?" he asked.

"Aren't you pleased?" Peach eyed him anxiously, he wasn't

smiling, he just looked stunned, as though he had had nothing to do with it.

"Of course I'm pleased. It's just that, well we hadn't planned on this just yet . . ."

"Passion and planning are not always compatible."

Noel grinned and she felt a sudden surge of relief.

"You're right," he said, getting up and kissing her, "when is it to be?"

"Seven months – in October."

"Perfect," exclaimed Noel, "the baby will be born just as we launch the 'Duke'." Noel swept her into his arms. "Of course I'm pleased, darling. It's just hard to imagine myself with a son – or a daughter. I wish . . ."

"What do you wish?"

"I wish he would have a father he could be proud of."

"Noel!" Peach stared at him, shocked. "Of course he'll be proud of you. Why shouldn't he be? Oh I know, it's the orphanage thing, isn't it? But if it bothers you so much, why have you never gone back there? Why haven't you tried to find out who your parents were?"

"No. No, I couldn't do that. I could never go back to the Maddox!"

"Well then," said Peach gently, "you'll just have to live with who you are. And if that's good enough for me, it should be good enough for you – and your child."

67

Peach drove her new car south down the highway, enjoying the notice it caused and making mental notes to tell Noel of the admiring comments when she stopped for petrol or a cup of coffee. Noel was a genius, he'd known exactly what he wanted and he'd got it and no one understood better than she did, that in a colossus of an industry like this, Noel's achievement hadn't been easy. And now the "Duke" and their baby would be born in the same month.

It had been Noel's idea that she leave Paris and escape to the calm and freshness of the coast, but at first Peach had been reluctant. It was three years since Leonie had died and though she had visited Jim and her sisters at the Hostellerie she had never returned to the villa. Lais had understood. "You'll go there when you feel ready," she'd said comfortingly. But as the car speeded up the hill Peach wondered if she were ready even now?

The familiar square white house, its green shutters open to the warm evening sunshine, looked the way it always had. The white boulders by the iron gate and the stone urns of brilliant pink and scarlet geraniums flanking the double doors, the smell of mignonette and jasmine and the flare of colour from the hibiscus and bougain- villaea took Peach back to her childhood as she walked around the side of the house to the terrace. A beautiful white yacht, sails curved to the breeze, hung on the blue horizon like a painting. Towering dark cypresses punctuated the massed umbrella pines and silvery green olive trees on the headlands curving around the little bay. Nothing had changed. Except that the long cool terracotta terrace was empty. The blue cushions on Leonie's chair were smooth and undented by the pressure of her head and no little brown cat ran to greet her, its paws skittering on the tiles.

Marianne bustled from the kitchen, beaming. "Here you are at last, Madame Peach, and I can't tell you how glad I am to see you. It's been lonely, with the mistress gone, though Monsieur Jim comes to see me every week, and your sisters come too. But it's you who should be here, Madame Peach, you and your children, to give this place a bit of life."

Peach felt sorry for the faithful old woman, guarding Leonie's house. Marianne's own family lived in the village and she could so easily have given up and gone to live with her tall, strapping sons. But Marianne would never desert Leonie.

Peach stood at the door to her old room, staring at the narrow single bed that looked so small after their American king-size model, and at the tiny red table with its silver mirror, polished to a blinding gloss by Marianne's never-idle hands. The photographs and her faded mementoes were still there, just as she'd left them on her wedding night, but this room didn't belong to her any more. This was the room of a young, foolish, romantic girl who had refused to grow up. This was her past. She realised suddenly that it was the sort of room that Noel had never had.

Picking up her bag she trailed slowly along the corridor, peering into rooms, any of which she could have made her own. But Leonie had made her mistress of this house and it was Leonie's room that should be hers.

The shutters were closed and the room seemed very still and mysterious in the grey darkness. Peach hesitated by the door – but there was nothing to be afraid of here, she'd shared many a night in Leonie's big bed when she was a child, secure in her presence. Walking to the window she flung back the shutters, letting in a stream of golden sunlight, waking the room from its long rest. The statue of Sekhmet on its marble plinth caught the beam of light and the cool white bed stretched smooth and inviting. With a sigh Peach sat on the edge, running her hand across the simple white cotton quilt, remembering. Then, slipping off her shoes, she curled up on its comforting surface and closed her eyes, letting the warm sun erase the tiredness of the long drive from her cramped muscles, breathing the freshness of the scented air. It felt so good to be back, so very good. And what better place could there be to grow a baby?

The long summer months at the villa were the most tranquil Peach could remember. Noel spent as much time with her as he could, showing up even for just a night – playing hookey, he called it, with a triumphant grin. And Wil came for his school holidays, thrilled to be back at the villa and pleased and curious about the new baby. Lais and Ferdi came to stay, and of course Jim and Leonore were at the Hostellerie. At the beginning of September Amelie and Gerard arrived from Florida to be with her when the baby was born and at last the long gloom cast by Leonie's death was dispersed.

The house was just as Leonie had left it, except now Peach's old room had become Wil's and the guest room next to hers had been converted into a new nursery.

"Why don't you change it, decorate it in your own style like you did the Paris house?" suggested Noel, lying beside her in the white bed.

But somehow Leonie's sparse, simple room needed nothing adding. It was complete. "Perhaps I will," said Peach. "Maybe – some day."

*   *   *

363

On the fifteenth of October in Paris, Charles Henry Maddox was born and in the same month the new luxury automobile the "Duke" was launched upon the world.

Noel's expression was grave and tender as he looked at his new son. "You will be the first to be proud of bearing the name Maddox," he murmured, stroking the baby's dark head with a gentle finger. "I promise you that, my son."

68

The familiar zing of excitement Detroit always gave him hit Noel as he drove from Metropolitan Airport to US Auto – or rather as he was driven to US Auto, for nowadays he rated a chauffeured limousine. He commuted the Paris/New York/Detroit route so often that he now kept a permanent suite at the Waldorf Towers in Manhattan for his frequent stop-overs. But in Detroit, the penthouse was still home. And, of course, the lakeside redwood A-frame cabin would always be his escape.

Not that he needed to escape – not now when so much was happening. It wasn't just the staggering success of the "Duke", it was the way he'd made Detroit sit up and take notice by producing a car in a mere three years instead of the usual five. Concept to sale room, the "Duke" had taken two years eleven months and nine days – a record in the industry. Of course it was a limited-production, custom-finished vehicle but, none the less, no one in the industry could match that, and it was all due to the way Noel had re-structured the company.

Noel had gone into de Courmont with the blinkers of Claire Anthony's corporate lessons removed from his eyes. Because it was a foreign company, in an odd way, he had felt the same rules didn't apply, and because of that he'd come up with some startling answers. Noel blamed de Courmont's decline on its financial officers, always over-eager to assume the benefit of short-term profits that in the long run were unrealistic. Time had run out with the failure of the "Fleur" and de Courmont had been into a sharp downswing from which there was little likelihood of return. But there had been one startling benefit, brought about by Jim's decision to raise money by getting rid of peripheral companies manufacturing and supplying parts, and selling off the real estate. Without the need to purchase from in-house parts-suppliers, Noel found himself free to shop in the market place for the best price. Even with such a specialised high-quality machine as the "Duke", the savings were a staggering thirty per cent.

Noel had looked into the structure of the company carefully, finding it tallied with that of the big auto companies in the States, in that bureaucracy ruled and mediocrity dominated. The company was stagnant in its management, its design and its technology – and he had determined to find out why. Several trips to Japan, whose auto industry was booming, had convinced him that the old methods were wrong. Noel remembered the first car he'd worked on as a new engineer at Great Lakes Motors, filled with excitement and enthusiasm for his job. It had failed from a lack of entrepreneurism and a bureaucratic eagerness to conform: the designers, the engineers and the management had been unwilling to go out on a limb and say what they really thought and the car had ended up as a carbon copy of its predecessors – unexciting and doomed to mediocrity if not failure.

With this in mind Noel rejected the current cost-cutting measure in Detroit of "badge engineering", that is of having each of the car divisions within the company produce a vehicle of the same size built on the same platform, with the resulting lookalike cars rolling off production lines and a total loss of identity. Car buyers were hard put to find any difference between purchasing a Pontiac or an Olds, a US Auto or a Buick. The only benefit was that it looked good on paper to the financial men – at least in the beginning, until sales began to decline as disillusioned customers drifted towards the foreign market, and particularly towards Japanese cars.

Noel had decided that de Courmont – a company in decline with all the classic faults – would be the guinea pig for his experiment. As an engineer he'd never seen the benefit of the old system where the designer first "designed" a car and then the engineers were expected to adapt the design to the limitations and practicalities of mass-production, even though this allowed the massive financial investment to be spread across a five-year production schedule. De Courmont had begun its new life "frontloading" – that is, spending

365

more money at the beginning of the proposed new car and having the engineer work together with the designer from the beginning. It cost more up front, but it eliminated a whole lengthy stage in production and in the long run the economy would be proven. The "Marquis", a smaller town-car version of the "Duke", was at design-planning stage. Meanwhile, de Courmont factories were churning out the popular "Stallion" and stacking up the profits. And Noel was the whiz-kid of the auto industry.

Still, he wasn't quite where he wanted to be, thought Noel as he strode into the executive dining room at US Auto. Paul Lawrence slapped him on the shoulder cheerfully as he shook his hand. "Good to see you, Noel. How's your lovely lady, and the boy?"

"Just fine," said Noel, "and now there's another one on the way."

"Another? Well, it seems you're not limiting your success just to one field," replied Paul with a grin. "Come on then, the chairman's waiting. Let's have a bite of lunch and then you can rivet us with your latest concepts for reform in the auto industry."

Noel followed Paul into the dining room, vaguely annoyed by the jocular reference to his work. He didn't think Paul was denigrating his success, but perhaps he wasn't taking it as seriously as he should.

Alone in the penthouse that evening, he poured himself a scotch, shaking it around in the glass so that the single ice cube chilled it to perfection, staring at the lights of the city from the windows. The meeting had been shorter than he'd expected and he was home early. The chairman and senior management had listened to his six-monthly progress report with rapt attention and little comment, except for praise at the end, but Noel had been left with the uneasy feeling that they had bigger things on their minds and that to them what he was achieving was just a small cog in the giant wheel of the auto industry. Striding through the corridors of power at US Auto he was greeted with nods and cheery compliments but everyone he met was en route somewhere else, busy clocking up their day's dues in order to collect their day's rewards. And what bothered him was that at the end of it all, one of these guys would be in line for the top job when it became vacant, as it inevitably would before too long. "Out of sight, out of mind" was a maxim that breathed truth. Noel was now merely a visitor at US Auto, even though he was president of one of their most successful companies.

Noel sipped his scotch gloomily. Just a year ago he'd thought he'd beaten the world. He was president of de Courmont and he was making a success of it. He hadn't made the cover of *Time* magazine yet, but there had been a lengthy article on what he'd done for de Courmont and on the successful "Duke". He'd had praiseworthy features in every financial paper and trade magazine and he'd appeared on TV in the US several times, explaining his methods and his success. Of course, the magazines and gossip columns had latched on to his marriage to Peach de Courmont and, too often these days, he encountered his own face in the papers as he drank his breakfast coffee. Star-struck Paris seemed determined to make them a celebrity couple and photographers were hard to avoid at parties and restaurants. But in achieving success he'd made himself a bit of a maverick at his home base. After all, how could all those guys go on justifying their jobs if they agreed with his stand? It would mean a total re-structuring of the entire company, and he doubted they were ready for that. King though he was of his own French domain, when it came right down to it, in anyone's eyes that mattered success meant America. It was the only place that counted. And Noel still lusted after that brass ring of power.

Goddamn it, he couldn't stand being alone! He was missing Peach and his son. Glancing at his watch he picked up the telephone and dialled the Paris number. Oliver answered and told him that Madame had left for Germany that morning. Of course, Peach was taking Charles to visit her sister for a week or two – Noel had completely forgotten. Disappointed, he put down the phone. He could call her there, but he didn't have Lais's number. Damn, he should have asked Oliver. Should he call back? Moodily he turned away from the phone and walked to the hallway, collecting his overcoat on the way. He'd have a drink at the Pontchartrain and get a bite to eat. He just didn't feel like being alone.

Sitting in the Pontchartrain dining room with a half-dozen friends, Claire Anthony saw Noel come in. She watched as the waiter placed him at a small table and the bus-boy rapidly whisked away the extra place-setting. So, Noel was dining alone. How different he looked from the sombre-eyed young man she'd fallen in love with. Noel Maddox had become a man confident of his success and his place in the world. And yet there was still that heart-breaking appeal of vulnerability about him. Excusing herself, she threaded her way through the tables towards him.

"Alone at last," she greeted him.

"Always good with the cliché, Claire," responded Noel, smiling. "How are you?"

"I'm fine. I didn't expect to see you here, though. I thought you were in Paris hobnobbing with European royalty these days?"

"Not quite. I'm a working man, just like everyone else. How's Lance?"

She looked at him, surprised. "Didn't you know? Lance had a massive heart attack last year. No, don't look like that, he's all right – more or less. A quadruple by-pass took care of his problem – for the moment anyway, so the odds are pretty fair that he will get to see his grandchildren."

"I'm sorry," said Noel, shocked.

She shrugged. "You might say he was just another auto-accident victim. The pressure of the business got him down. Things didn't ever go quite the way he'd planned – but then, that's the way it is for most of us. Except you, Noel. Word of your success precedes you – you are the talk of Detroit."

"Really?" Noel studied her, not really caring what people said. She'd swopped the brightly coloured spectacles he remembered for contact lenses and she looked different and yet the same. He always thought of her as naked, without her glasses, because that was the only time he'd ever seen her without them. And when they'd finished making love she would put them firmly back on her nose again, before lighting the inevitable cigarette.

"You haven't heard a word I'm saying," said Claire shrewdly, "you were dreaming, Noel Maddox, and missing all the good things I had to tell you about yourself."

"And who's telling you good things about *you* these days?" asked Noel as the waiter poured them both a glass of red wine.

"What do you mean?"

"I mean you're still as attractive as ever, Claire. It was a clumsy compliment, I suppose." He stared at her. "No, it wasn't. What I really wanted to say was – are you doing anything special, Claire, or can you keep a lonely man company?"

She raised an eyebrow. "Company?" Reaching across the table, he took her hand and a thrill of excitement rippled through her. "Lance is in California at the Fremont plant and I'm dining with friends from out of town. They're catching an early flight in the morning so we won't be partying late."

"Meet me in the bar?" asked Noel.

Claire smiled as she pushed back her chair and a waiter hurried forward to assist her. "Like old times," she said.

*　　　*　　　*

Naked, she was still as pretty as he remembered. She'd kept on the black lace stockings and the garter belt and she prowled his apartment in her high heels, a glass of scotch in her hand, looking like the cover of *Penthouse.* "You are a *provocatrice,*" called Noel.

"We call it 'a tease' in this country," she said, "or are you so foreign now you've forgotten?"

"I haven't forgotten your form of teasing, Claire," said Noel, "but I remember you kept your clothes on the first time."

"I've learned since then that it's better without. Tell me something, Noel Maddox," she said huskily, walking into his arms, "just why can't I resist you?"

Making love to Claire was like a well-remembered piece of music that he hadn't listened to for a long time – familiar, but better for not being heard for a while. He knew just what she liked most and how she would react; she was beautiful and passionate and, as she always had before, she took away the ache of loneliness and restlessness he'd felt earlier that evening.

Wrapped in his terrycloth robe, Claire said, "I remember when it was cashmere."

Noel smiled. "I'm a man of simple tastes now. But what about you, Claire? What's happening in your life? I don't mean Lance – I mean you. Are you happy?"

"My children make me happy. Kerry is almost through college now, and Kim's there too. I have a lovely home and Lance is a very nice man," Claire replied carefully.

Noel looked at her, saying nothing.

"I'm very lucky," she added defensively, "a lot of my friends are in the throes of divorce, but of course, I wouldn't do that . . ."

No, thought Noel, of course you wouldn't, you're not the type to kick a man when he's down. "How's Lance doing at Great Lakes Motors? I'm out of touch with things these days."

"Lance is taking early retirement next year. We plan on buying a little place in the sun somewhere – Florida perhaps – and getting a sailboat so we can tack around the islands. Maybe find some uncharted atoll where we can play Robinson Crusoe. It'll be fun – though not quite what Lance expected from life."

"And what did he expect?" Noel poured another scotch, watching as she prowled the room nervously.

"What? Oh, chairman of Great Lakes Motors, I suppose. It's ironic that just as the job's coming up for grabs Lance isn't well enough to go after it."

Noel stared at her, stunned. "I hadn't heard that," he said.

"Not many people have. My father told us months ago that things were going that way. And Masters, the president, doesn't want the job – he's too close to retirement. Of course nothing's been announced yet but the chief is moving across into politics and I know that Great Lakes Motors have their scouts out for a successor. I should have thought it would be right up your alley, Noel, even though you're a bit young, but of course, you are top dog in your own company, so why should you bother with the rat-race here?" She looked at him sadly. "I've seen pictures of your wife," she added. "She looks very beautiful, very different. I think I'd probably like her a lot."

Noel thought of Peach, probably sleeping peacefully, four thousand miles away. What was happening between him and Claire had nothing to do with reality and his relationship with Peach. It was just a moment's passionate need to stem his feeling of loneliness. More than loneliness. A sudden sense of defeat. And now once again Claire Anthony was handing him a step up the ladder – though she didn't know it.

"I have a good life, Noel, don't I?" asked Claire. "On the whole I think I'd rather play Robinson Crusoe than be the corporate wife any longer – as you can see, I was never really cut out for the job."

Noel opened his arms and as she ran into them he held her comfortingly. "It'll be all right, Claire," he murmured gently. "I'm sure it'll be all right."

"It's just with the girls growing up and going away, and now this thing with Lance – suddenly everything's changed," she cried, tears staining his robe. "But none of us has it made, do we, Noel? You always told me that."

Noel held her, saying nothing, simply stroking her hair.

"Oh dammit, I shouldn't be crying," she said. "I'll wash out my contact lenses."

"I wish you still had your red glasses," said Noel. "I liked them."

She grinned at him shakily. "I was always afraid men wouldn't make passes at me." Claire hesitated. "Noel. Could I – I mean would it be all right if I stayed the night? There's no one home and I was dreading being alone with just my thoughts."

"Be my guest," said Noel.

She fixed him some coffee and he put on some quiet music and lay back on the sofa with his head on the cushions, and an arm around her, thinking out his moves. Tomorrow, first thing, he'd make a couple of calls, one to the chairman of Great Lakes Motors and the other to the president. He barely knew the first, and was on affable greeting terms with the other, but there was no doubt that they both knew about him. And if what he'd heard about the troubles the company was having were true, and he could convince them that what he offered was what Great Lakes needed. Then he would have the prize he'd always wanted. Sure, he was president of his own company now, sure he'd got his perfect car, but chairman of Great Lakes Motors was what he'd dreamed of since he first hit the streets of Detroit nearly thirty years ago.

In bed, with Claire beside him, he lay awake for a long time, planning his approach. It was no good pretending to be a conformist – he'd already proven that he wasn't. And he knew Great Lakes Motors situation. They were in trouble, especially with the Japanese competition. But he had the answer to that – if they'd go for it. Noel tossed restlessly, only falling into a deep sleep as dawn finally broke over Motor City.

The phone was bleeping, a muted urgent sound, so that Claire felt it must have been doing it for some time. Yawning, she stretched out a hand, glancing at the clock. Jesus, it was already seven. "Hello," she said into the receiver. She looked at Noel sleeping soundly beside her. God, he was attractive, no wonder she couldn't resist him . . .! "Hello?" she asked again.

After a pause a female voice asked distantly, "Is Mr Maddox there?"

"Sorry," yawned Claire, "he's still sleeping. No, wait a minute, no he's not." Noel opened an eye and she handed him the receiver. "It's for you, sleepyhead," she said laughing.

"Hello," said Noel lazily.

"Noel?"

He sat up with a jolt. "Peach! What are you doing calling so early? Is something wrong?"

There was silence on the other end and his eyes met Claire's shocked ones worriedly. "Peach, are you there?" he called.

"Obviously I called too early for you," Peach said distantly. "Oh Noel . . . how could you . . .?" The phone echoed emptily in his hand, the connection severed.

"Oh my God, Noel! I'm sorry," said Claire. "I answered it without thinking – it's a reflex . . ."

Noel climbed from the warm, crumpled bed. "It's not your fault, Claire," he said quietly, pulling a robe over his nakedness.

371

Claire eyed him anxiously as he paced to the window, and then she headed for the bathroom and turned on the shower.

Noel paced the stretch of polished wood floor alongside the windows that framed the city he'd always longed to conquer, wondering what to do. It was almost eight o'clock – he had two hours before he would call Great Lakes Motors. Two hours in which to sort out what had just happened. But how? What should he do? Lie to Peach? Tell her it was the new housekeeper? If that would hurt her less then maybe that's what he should do – a soft lie to cover a one-off night when he'd suddenly felt he was back at the bottom of the heap. Because how could he expect Peach to understand the truth? How could anybody understand him when he wasn't even sure of his motives himself? Why was he always dissatisfied? And why did he always want to put himself on the line, push himself to the limits, strive for the next self-appointed goal? He had everything a man could wish for: acknowledged success in his field, more money than he'd ever wanted. He was married to the girl of his dreams and he had a son, a second-generation Maddox. Striding to the phone he dialled Paris. Oliver answered and gave him Lais's number in Germany. Noel dialled again, waiting impatiently as the phone buzzed faintly, sounding a million miles away.

"Noel?" asked Lais, surprised. "What on earth is going on? Peach is packing, in floods of tears. She's taking the next plane back to Paris."

"It's nothing, Lais, just tell Peach it was nothing – a mistake. Ask her to speak to me – please."

"Well, I'll try, Noel – but I get a feeling that whatever it is, for Peach it was drastic. Hold on and I'll speak to her . . . ."

Noel waited, drumming his fingers on the table impatiently. Lais came back to him almost immediately. "No go I'm afraid, Noel. She refuses to come to the phone and when I gave her your message she just burst into tears again."

"Jesus!" exclaimed Noel angrily. "What flight is she taking?"

"Whichever is the first flight out to Paris, she doesn't care," said Lais. "I don't like to see her like this, Noel. I'm telling you that if I could, I would keep her here, but she's determined to go home. You'd better get there as fast as you can."

"Right. Tell her I'll get a flight out tonight, I'll be in Paris tomorrow. And thank you, Lais. I'm sorry for all this."

"I'm not unfamiliar with the situation," commented Lais wryly.

"I can guess what it's all about, Noel, although Peach isn't saying. Of course you're a fool – but then, aren't most men?"

She rang off without saying goodbye and Noel replaced the receiver grimly. Claire emerged from the bathroom, smart in last night's black dress and lace stockings, her hair neatly brushed and fresh red lipstick gleaming on her pretty mouth. He could smell her perfume from here – it was still the same one.

"I'll be off then," she said pulling on her silver fox jacket. "I'm truly sorry, Noel."

She stood there looking dejected and he smiled ruefully. "It's not your fault, sweet Claire." He walked with her to the elevator. "Thanks for being there when I needed you."

She kissed him lightly on the lips and stepped into the elevator. "We needed each other, Noel," she said as the doors closed.

Standing under the blast of cold water in the shower Noel tried to sort out his thoughts. There was nothing he could do now about Peach except plan to get a flight out this evening. He would sort it all out when he saw her, long-distance explanations would do no good, he could see that now. And lies would only demean her further. He'd hold her in his arms, he'd confess, tell her the truth; she would judge him and forgive him and they would paper over the crack he'd created in their relationship. Meanwhile, he'd got to think out his approach to Great Lakes Motors.

Noel soaped his hard, wiry body, counting the things that would go against him – at his assumed age of forty-five, not to mention his real age, he was too young; he was an engineer first and a businessman second; he was a media "star", courted by the press as much for his marriage to a socially prominent heiress and member of one of the world's great automobile families, as for his radical and outspoken viewpoint on Detroit and the status of the auto business today. Detroit liked to close ranks and present a united face to its shareholders and the press when times were rough, and they didn't go in much for your non-conformist sharp-shooters. Unless, of course, they recognised that the trouble went so deep, only drastic reorganisation would stop the decline.

Then what were his assets? What was he selling? Comparative youth in an industry dominated by men in their sixties could be an asset presented in the right way; his media prominence could gain him an immediate tangible image to the customer, the man out there buying the car – better than some faceless corporation any one of which, like their cars, looked to Joe Public much like the other. A proven track-record, from his progress through Great Lakes Motors and US Auto, to the presidency of de Courmont; his previous sucess with the "Stallion"; his current success with a radical corporate re-structuring policy, and his outstanding success with the "Duke". And, of course, his turn-around record, concept to production, of three years over their five.

Whistling cheerfully, Noel towelled dry and faced himself in the mirror, shaving away the dark growth of beard, all thoughts of Claire Anthony and the previous night dismissed from his mind. Peach would wait. He'd explain everything when he got there and she'd be so thrilled by what he had to say she'd forgive him his small mistake.

69

Paris sparkled under the October sunshine as Peach with little Charles on her knee stared out of the window of the taxi taking her from Orly Airport to the Ile St Louis; but the dark glasses she wore were to shade her swollen eyes from the world, not to protect her from the glare of the sun.

When she had called Noel there had been a warm, half-sleeping intimacy about the woman's voice that left her in no doubt about what had happened, even if the woman hadn't said what she did about Noel being asleep and then no he wasn't. The shock had left her speechless at first, before the pain hit her. Oh God, nobody told her that it would hurt like this! It hadn't been this way with Harry – but then she'd never put all her trust in Harry the way she had with Noel. She had just known that Noel would never betray that trust and on all his many trips to the States without her it had never once occurred to her to doubt him. The soft sound of the woman's laughter rang again in her ears and Peach shook her head, gazing miserably at the engaging face of her son. He smiled, still chattering about the taxi excitedly. Charles loved being in a car – Noel always said that obviously he took after him.

Charles looked out of the window as the cab pulled into the courtyard of the Paris mansion, and he laughed with delight. "Home again, Maman," he said beaming.

"Yes, we're home, Charles," said Peach, "or at least I think we are."

She stared at the house that once had seemed so welcoming and familiar. Its lofty hallways echoed with young Charles's excited cries and a sound of voices came from behind the closed double-doors of the grand salon.

"It's the seminar for selected dealers today, Madame Maddox," explained Oliver.

Of course, she had forgotten about it! In typical fashion Noel had taken her concept of the house working for its living a step further by using it for salesmen's conferences, dealer seminars, think-tank meetings with his executives. In fact, it was one of the reasons she'd gone away this week, to avoid the businessmen, even though, of course, she and Noel had their private apartments.

"Monsieur Maddox telephoned, Madame, from Detroit. He said to tell you he would call again this evening."

And what would he say? wondered Peach. That she had got it all wrong, that the woman was a maid, she'd just brought him in his morning coffee? She could have come up with a dozen excuses for him herself – easy ways out – if she chose to believe them. But what would that achieve? Trust had been shattered and no matter what Noel said she felt as though the bottom had dropped out of her world.

She glanced at her watch. She would wait for his phone call. She wouldn't question him, and she wouldn't accuse. He was taking a flight out tonight and he would be here with her tomorrow. She'd just let him say what he had to say, because she loved him so much she still hoped it wasn't true. And there was just a chance that it wasn't.

Noel had met with Bill Masters, president of Great Lakes Motors, at eleven o'clock that morning and after a few mutually complimentary preliminaries Noel had stated his reason for being there.

"You're an off-beat candidate, Noel," said Masters, shaking his head. "The Board would take a lot of convincing – and I must say so would I. Sure, you've proven yourself in France, and you've done a terrific job, there's no denying that. But this is the States, Noel. The game-plan's different. We've got Wall Street and all those shareholders breathing down our necks. Try to tell them you're pouring money into new technology and that their dividends'll be substantially lower for the next few years and see what happens. The shudder would be felt throughout the economy of the entire country."

"It needn't be that drastic," countered Noel. "The way I see it, it could be done gradually. I'd like a chance to discuss it with you over lunch, and hopefully with the chairman?"

"Arthur's in Washington today, he'll be back late afternoon. But why don't you and I treat ourselves to a decent meal and you can tell me what you're up to?"

Noel looked at him guardedly. Masters had taken the first bite, even though he'd put down the idea. It was just a crack in the door, but it was enough.

Over lunch he told Masters, "The company's profits are plummeting again; if you're not careful they'll be back on the same steep slippery slope they were in '73. Sure, they're up one half year and down the next, but we all know that Great Lakes Motors is in trouble and no amount of creative accountancy is going to fake the real situation for long. For once this industry has to face the long term. The shareholders have had a good ride for their money, it's time for some input."

Masters watched the waiter delicately filleting his grilled Dover sole, smiling as the man placed two perfect segments on his plate. A green salad with the special lemon dressing he liked was brought to the table and he waited while Noel was served his swordfish, sipping a glass of Perrier water. "I see you are cholesterol-conscious, too," he remarked, "it's the executive disease. You heard about Lance Anthony, of course? Too bad, Lance is a good man! He might have been here in your shoes, Noel, if it weren't for that."

"It's a bad break," replied Noel cautiously.

"Lucky he's got a nice wife and a happy family situation," remarked Masters. "Early retirement is tough to face when you are that good at your job. Well then, Noel, tell me what you are planning to do to Great Lakes Motors."

"Fillet it," said Noel with a grin, "just like the Dover sole. Take out its backbone and give it a new one. Scrap the old half dozen divisions that produce their own cars and make them into just two – a big car division and a small one. Run them as self-contained companies and let them be accountable for their own cars. Get rid of the in-house engineering and manufacturing divisions, so that we can shop around the market place. Create a totally separate company to research and come up with the answer to the Japanese small car – *and* undercut its cost. Involve the workers more in their jobs: give them a labour contract with management by consensus like the Japanese do, so they don't just feel like hired hands. And frontload the production with the designer and engineer working together the way we did on the 'Duke', the aim being to turn around production in three years instead of five."

Masters stared at him. "Noel," he said, swallowing his fish, "you're in for a rough ride with the Board with those ideas."

Noel shrugged. "The Board is in for a rough ride, whether they accept my ideas or not. It's the chicken or the egg."

Ignoring his food, he went over what he had just said, point by point, explaining and expanding his theories.

"Okay, okay," said Masters finally. "Let's see if we can get a hold of Arthur this evening and you can put your ideas to him."

Noel sat back and sipped his glass of water. He was over the first hurdle.

Arthur Oranelli had an Irish mother and an Italian father and a reputation for being as pugnacious as the one nationality and as volatile as the other. He was sixty-seven years old and had climbed the executive ladder almost the same way as Noel had. Sipping scotch and water in his unostentatiously comfortable Grosse Pointe home that night, Noel felt he would get a fair hearing, without any of the biases that he had totted up in the shower that morning. Arthur Oranelli would hear him out and judge him on his proven career and his ideas for running Great Lakes Motors.

It was close to midnight by the time he'd finished explaining his concepts and answering Oranelli's pertinent questions and Noel leaned back, feeling exhausted. Sipping the neglected scotch he watched Oranelli prowl the panelled library, noting the shelves of beautifully bound books, the rarer ones behind glass. Oranelli was a collector of repute.

"I love books," said Oranelli, following his glance, "but I only *like* cars. It's different with you – cars are your passion and sometimes passion can cloud a man's judgement."

Noel watched him, saying nothing.

"What exactly is it you want from Great Lakes Motors, Noel?

The word is around that your success with the 'Duke' has gone to your head, that you like playing 'the star'."

Noel's grip tightened on the glass. "That's the media's image of me," he said, "I have no control over what they print or say on television. My own aims are more personal, Mr Oranelli. I walked these streets as a penniless boy and my passion for engines and cars has brought me to this point. Stardom is not my aim. Power is. I want the power to force changes on a company that's sinking under its own weight. I have no illusions that being chairman of the company would be an easy ride – it's the hot seat and I'm ready to accept the slings and arrows that the media who love me today will be happy to throw at me tomorrow." He shrugged. "That's their game. Now you know mine."

Oranelli nodded. "You're a truthful man – and not many are. In this business truth can make or break you. And in your case I think it'll make you. Everything you've said to me tonight makes sense, but not all of it is feasible and not all of it will work for a million different reasons. But that would be for you to sort out. Meanwhile, I'll consider your bid as my successor."

Noel took a deep breath as he stood up to shake hands. "Thank you, Mr Oranelli. I appreciate that."

Oranelli chuckled. "Makes me wish I were young again and just starting," he said. "You lose the flavour of the game a bit when you get to my age. But tell me, Noel," he said as he walked with him to the door, "what about de Courmont? It's your wife's family's company, isn't it? And it's tied in with US Auto. What will happen to de Courmont if you switch allegiance to Great Lakes Motors?"

For once Noel was lost for words. He hadn't given a thought to de Courmont since Claire had given him the inside information on Great Lakes Motors. "My wife is chairman of the company, sir," he said. "We have a pretty good management team, and of course I could hand over the control to my successor. There would be no conflict of interest with Great Lakes Motors."

"Mmm," said Oranelli thoughtfully, "but there may be a personal one. Well, goodnight, Noel. Good to have met you."

Pondering on Oranelli's words as he drove back to town Noel remembered suddenly that he had completely forgotten his promise to call Peach and that he was supposed to be on a flight to Paris. Wondering anxiously if she were all right, he decided to call her in the morning and then catch an early flight.

70

Her suitcases were already being loaded into the car and the sweet young girl who Peach, with bad memories of old Nanny Launceton, had chosen to help her with Charles and the future new baby was waiting in the hall, holding Charles by the hand. Peach thought how sweet he looked in his little scarlet woollen cap, with his solemn grey eyes – eyes just like Noel's. The sharp ring of the telephone startled her, even though it was a sound she'd stayed up all night, anticipating. Oliver was outside taking care of the cases and she walked back along the hall and picked up the receiver in the small salon.

"Peach, thank God, I've finally reached you." Noel's voice sounded tired.

"You could have reached me any time, Noel. In fact I've been waiting to hear from you. I also had a message that you were coming home," she replied coldly.

"Peach, I'm sorry, I was tied up all day yesterday and couldn't get to a phone. It was after midnight when I finally shook free and I didn't want to wake you."

"I suppose it never occurred to you that I might not be able to sleep. Or even that I might be waiting for your call – though right now I can't think why."

"Peach, there are big things going on here – I can't tell you over the phone, it's too important."

Peach held the receiver away from her, staring at it in amazement . . . not a word about what happened, not a mention of the woman. All he could talk about was business. "I suppose the long days and nights didn't include the lady who answered your telephone yesterday?" she said, her voice trembling. There was a silence on the other end. "Well, Noel?" she said. "And don't bother to think

379

up some excuse because I know she's your lover – I could hear it in her voice."

"She's not my lover, Peach . . ."

"*She was in bed with you!*" She waited, praying for him to deny it, to prove to her it wasn't true. "It's true – isn't it?" she quavered.

"Peach, what do you want me to say to you?"

"I want you to tell me the truth."

"I've never lied to you . . ."

"Then she *was* in bed with you!"

"Yes, she was . . . but it's not the way you imagine it, Peach . . ."

"Not the way I imagine it? Oh God, Noel, you must think I'm still the stupid little girl that Harry married! If he could get away with it, so could you. *And I trusted you! I loved you!*"

"Don't stop loving me, Peach," begged Noel. "This had nothing to do with us – I can explain when I see you."

"When you see me? *Why aren't you here?* My whole life is in ruins and you're thousands of miles away. You don't even bother to *telephone* me because you're too busy. Goddamn it, Noel Maddox, *I hate you!*" Slamming down the receiver, Peach fled up the stairs to her room, ignoring Charles and the bewildered girl waiting in the hall.

Trembling, she sat on the bed, holding back the tears by force of will. She had to pull herself together, gain control. She had Charles to think of. She was a responsible mother even if she were no good as a wife and not lover enough to hold her husband. Going into the bathroom she drank a glass of ice-cold water, splashing some on her face, then she walked carefully back down the wide marble staircase to her waiting son.

As they walked down the steps to the car she heard the telephone ring again. "If it's Mr Maddox, Oliver," she said, "tell him that I've already left. And that I'm not coming back."

Fog enclosed Detroit like a soft woollen blanket, cutting off the city from all air traffic, and trapping Noel in his suddenly lonely penthouse. The big windows that usually framed his personal sparkling picture of the city were now hung with a blank grey canvas, eliminating the thrusting towers and granite streets that gave him life.

With his bag packed, Noel waited by the telephone. A sombre Gregorian chant boomed from the multi-speakers in the apartment and a single bright lamp illuminated the beige surface of the telephone as though it were the only thing that mattered in the room. Every hour Noel punched out the number of Leonie's villa, waiting impatiently while the line clicked and bleeped, until finally Marianne answered.

"Madame is not taking any calls at all," she told him nervously, and yes, she would ask Peach to call him back at that number. Her voice grew more high-pitched and excitable with every call as she remitted the same message. "Oh Monsieur Maddox," she said finally, "it is no use telephoning, she will not talk to you. You must get here as soon as you can."

Goddamn it, he knew that. If he wanted to save his marriage and keep Peach, he should be on the next plane out of this bastard fog-bound city. Frustrated, Noel picked up the phone and called the airport, asking them what the hell they were doing about the situation, only to be told in the calm soothing tones airlines use to keep their passengers firmly under control, that the fog was expected to lift by early afternoon and he would be contacted immediately his flight became available.

Striding into the kitchen, Noel poured himself another cup of strong black coffee, switching his thoughts from Peach to last night's meeting. He hoped he had Arthur Oranelli in his corner because Oranelli had more clout than anyone else in the industry. Bill Masters could be expected to go along with Oranelli and their combined influence and lobbying both with the Board and Wall Street could push the job his way. Noel's nerves tingled as he contemplated the idea, the top of the tower, the holder of the throne – and the power. Charged with nervous excitement he downed another cup of black coffee, prowling the apartment, hating the blank windows that cut him off from Detroit. Finally, he flung himself on the sofa and dialled France again. This time he got the busy signal and slamming it down he waited ten minutes and dialled again. He called every ten minutes for the next two hours, getting the busy signal every time. Peach had taken the phone off the hook.

The muted ring startled him and he grabbed back the receiver eagerly. "Yes," he barked.

"Mr Maddox? This is TWA calling. I'm pleased to tell you that the fog is expected to lift by one o'clock and your flight has been rescheduled to depart at one forty-five. New York is clear and you will have no trouble with your connecting flight to Paris, though we've rescheduled you on Air France, departing six thirty. Can we confirm you on these flights, sir?"

"Great," said Noel. "I'll be there." Slamming down the receiver he sighed with relief. He'd pick up a flight from Paris to Nice and be at the villa the next morning. He remembered the way Peach had sounded on the phone, distant and cold with the tremor in her voice . . . Oh God, he hadn't meant to hurt her! He'd make it up to her, reassure her that it was all nothing . . . But he could never explain to her why he'd needed Claire Anthony that night, or why he'd sought to curb his restlessness in her arms . . . only he knew the pressure of the force that drove him ever onwards to the next pinnacle of achievement.

He glanced at his watch. It was twelve o'clock – he might as well get out to the airport now, no use waiting about – there was bound to be some fog on the freeway still.

Grabbing his coat and his bag, Noel clicked off the light and the stereo and headed for the door. The telephone rang again and he glanced at it impatiently. Damn, who could it be now? Maybe it was Peach. Dropping his case he hurried across the room.

"Noel?"

It was Bill Masters's voice and Noel snapped to attention.

"Yes, Bill?"

"Glad I caught you. Oranelli said you were leaving for France today but I guess the fog delayed you. Tell you what it is, Noel. Arthur and I have been talking over the points you made and we both like what we hear. It'll be a tough campaign, Noel, but we'd both like to see you as Great Lakes Motors' next chairman."

"Thank you, Bill. I appreciate your support," replied Noel, feeling a blast of excitement rocket through him.

"Both Arthur and myself will be lobbying for you this week but there's no doubt in either of our minds that you are your own best salesman. We'd like you available here in Detroit. Noel, do you think that French company can run itself for the next ten days or so?"

Pale yellow sun flooded the room with light as the fog rolled away, exposing Detroit to his gaze. Without a second's hesitation Noel replied, "I'll be here, sir, for as long as you need me."

71

The weather in the south was unseasonably warm. A few late vacationers dotted the pool at the Hostellerie, soaking up the October sunshine like luxurious sleepy animals. Peach wandered through the immaculate terraced gardens, turning to look at the beach where young Charles was playing happily beneath an umbrella with his nurse. She thought of the baby she had been carrying for four months, Noel s unborn child. He'd been thrilled when he heard that she was pregnant. "We'll fill that nursery with kids," he told her happily, "let them wake up this great old house. The new breed of Maddoxes will give the old de Courmonts a run for their money!"

Peach remembered laughing at his excitement, pleased that he seemed to have none of the worry that had preceded Charles's birth. But Noel couldn't blame this new situation on his unknown mother. What had happened now was his own doing – and singlehandedly he'd destroyed the love and trust that was the foundation of their relationship. It had been over a week since Marianne had given her the message that Noel had been forced to stay in Detroit for business reasons – though why he should need to be in Detroit so long when his own company was here in France was beyond her understanding. And Detroit be damned – if he loved her he would have been on the next plane out, rushing to her side to try to explain, to make amends . . . Oh God, why hadn't he done that, why, why? Instead, he'd left her alone, hurting and angry. Somehow, Harry's cheating had not affected her inner self, but with Noel she felt devastated by the fact that what she *was* had not been enough. Noel had needed more than she had to offer. Was she the failure then? Was it all her fault? Unsure of herself and unable to understand Noel, Peach wandered back to the villa.

"Monsieur Maddox called again, Madame," Marianne told her.

"Won't you please answer him next time? Nothing good can come of a silence like this."

Peach nodded. "You're right, Marianne." For Charles's sake and that of the unborn baby, it was time to sort things out.

She was lying on the bed when the phone finally rang.

"Peach, I'm at the airport in Nice," said Noel, "I'll be home in an hour."

Home. He still called it home . . . and despite her anger Peach's heart leapt when he said her name.

"Are you still there?" Noel sounded anxious.

"I'm here," said Peach.

"Then I'll see you in a little while. How's Charles?"

"He's fine."

"And you, Peach?"

"I'll see you later, Noel," she said, ringing off.

It was only when she put down the phone that Peach realised how blazingly angry she was. Noel had thought he could put her emotions on hold until he'd finished whatever it was that kept him in Detroit – either business or a love affair, she didn't know which, and what's more she didn't care. He would walk in here expecting to say sorry and then she'd fall into his arms – the way other women did, no doubt. God, she was angry, she wanted to kill him with her anger, to wound him the way he'd wounded her!

Noel had never seen Peach like this before. She'd pulled back her hair tightly and the strong bone-structure that she'd inherited from her grandmother cast gaunt shadows across her face. She was so coldly angry you could almost chip ice from her. And she was looking at him with Monsieur's dark and chilling eyes.

He held out his arms to her but she went to stand by the fireplace, ignoring him.

Noel shrugged. "Where shall I start?" he asked.

Peach eyed him icily. "How about that night two weeks ago – or do we go back further than that? How many other nights were there with her?"

"There were no other nights, Peach – at least not since I met you. She was just someone I knew a long time ago. Peach, I swear to you it's not as bad as it sounds. It wasn't planned – it was just something that happened. We met by chance . . ."

"I see – it was sort of for old times' sake?"

384

Noel sighed. "No, it wasn't for old times' sake. It was just that Claire had been having a rough time and was lonely and so was I . . ."

"And what about me?" Peach's cry was anguished. "I was as lonely as you, but I was content to wait. I didn't think of filling in my nights with another man. Why was it different for you?"

"There's no way I can explain, Peach, because I'm not sure I understand myself. It was just that on that particular night I was full of self-doubt . . . about my achievements and myself . . ."

"Self-doubt? You? I never noticed that particular quality in you, Noel. It seems to me you always know exactly what you are doing, and exactly where you're aiming in life."

"And what does that mean?" asked Noel wearily.

"A lot of people said that you only married me to get your hands on de Courmont."

"You know that's not true."

"Do I?"

"Well, if that's what other people believe, now we can prove them wrong. The reason I had to stay in Detroit wasn't because of a woman, it was because the chairman of Great Lakes Motors is resigning. There was a chance I could get the job if I presented my case properly. And I did it, Peach. I did it! It looks as though the Board will offer me the chairmanship!" Noel walked towards her, his arms open supplicatingly. "It's what I've worked for all my life. Can you imagine what it means to me?"

Peach was staring at him incredulously. "Chairman of Great Lakes Motors?" she exclaimed. "*But what about de Courmont?* What about *us*? Oh I understand it now, I see what you planned, Noel. I gave you de Courmont thinking you wanted its success for the same reasons I did. It was our company, our family, our life . . . but now I see it was only another rung in your climb up the ladder. And that's why you married me – you wanted to use de Courmont!"

"De Courmont was a dying company – I could have had it without marrying you," replied Noel coldly. "Believe it or not, Peach, I married you because I wanted you. More than that," he added, suddenly humble, "I needed you."

"Why? To give you an identity you didn't have?" Peach strode towards him, her pale face flushing with anger. "An identity you *still* don't have – because you're still the little orphan boy, aren't you, Noel? You wanted a grand name to match your grand ambitions? You are an enigma, a loner, you don't allow anyone to get

385

through to the *real* you, and do you know why? Because there's nothing there beneath the façade. Why don't you face it, Noel?" she taunted. "Your mother abandoned you when you were born because she didn't want you! And to compensate for that you want *everything*! I'll bet even when she left, all you cried for was her milk – so that you could survive and go on to better things. But life doesn't work like that, Noel – you've never learned that you have to *give* something too." She glared at him, boiling with rage, her icy façade destroyed. "I don't care how rich you become, or how successful and powerful. You can't change, Noel. You'll always be the Maddox Charity orphan!"

She searched his cool, hooded gaze for a response, but his face was stony. "You're right, Peach," Noel said at last, turning and walking to the door, "that's *exactly* who I am."

The door closed behind him with a sharp, decisive click. "Jesus," screamed Peach, 'can't you even slam the door? Why don't you lose control for once, you goddamn iron man!"

She hurled herself on to the sofa, tears raining down her face, pummelling the cushions with clenched fists. Oh God, what had she said, what had she done? Peach leaped to her feet, hating herself, hating him. "I didn't mean it, Noel," she cried flinging wide the door and running down the hall. "I didn't mean it!" But Noel had gone.

72

Noel drove slowly through the bleak urban sprawl that covered the windswept once-empty plains. The small town he remembered so clearly as just one long street scattered with cheap frame houses whose sagging porches held old refrigerators and rockers, the tacky motel, the fly-blown diner and the body-shop spattered with rusting cars had all vanished into an untidy maze of factories, workshops and supermarkets. New parking lots, shopping malls and sub-developments of tract-houses had pushed back the naked fields he recalled rippling in great waves of wheat into lonely infinity.

Noel had been driving for half an hour in what he had thought was the right direction and he still hadn't found the Maddox Charity Orphanage. Pulling the big car into the parking lot in front of a neon-lit diner with a "For Sale" sign outside, he hurried through the icy rain in search of a telephone. Flicking through the pages of the directory he ran his eye down the column of Ms. *There was no Maddox Charity Orphanage listed!* Noel looked again, disbelieving. In his mind the Maddox had always been there, waiting to reclaim its son. He'd fought against it all his life and now – *when he needed it –* it had disappeared. He glanced around the diner. Surely there must be someone around here who would remember it?

Taking a seat he waited while a scrawny-looking waitress flicked cigarette ash and a litter of wrappers from the plastic table, wiping it clean.

"Yeah?" she asked without looking at him.

"Just a cup of coffee, please," said Noel, watching as she walked back to the counter and returned with a steaming jug. She was middle-aged and looked tired and defeated. Dark roots showed in her cheaply-dyed blonde hair and her face was blank and indifferent as she poured Noel's coffee.

"Do you know the Maddox Charity Orphanage?" Noel asked.

Her head snapped up, a flicker of expression lighting her eyes. Was it fear?

"What if I do? What d'ya wanna know for?"

Noel shrugged, surprised. "I just need directions, that's all."

"What d'ya wanna go there for?" she demanded harshly.

"You know where it is?"

"It hasn't moved," she replied, her face settling back into indifference. Picking up the coffee jug she sauntered away from the table to serve another customer. The strip of fluorescent light caught the pale gleam of her bare legs and her slender ankles as she teetered across the floor in scarlet stiletto-heeled shoes in a vain attempt at youthful glamour. He listened as she chatted morosely to the burly truck-driver at the counter, serving his coffee and grumbling about the sale of the diner.

"Just wish *I* could afford to buy it," she said, slamming the pot back on the hotplate.

"Well, why don'cha?" The trucker swigged back his coffee thirstily.

"Why? Take a good look at me, Mister. Ya think the bank's gonna lend money to me? Fat chance! And that's the way it's been all my life. Nobody's ever given me a chance. I'll tell you something, though, I could run it a lot better than the old man. Yes sir, this would be the best diner in the county if I had it!"

She'd probably been quite something when she was young – seventeen or so, thought Noel. Young and wild and with a year or two playing around before a half-dozen kids and poverty claimed her. He knew the pattern, the grind down into nothingness. It was all he had been determined to escape from – and it was also what had made him the man he was.

The waitress walked back towards him and stood there, arms folded, studying his face. Noel was uncomfortably aware of the shabby diner and his own smart appearance and of his rich automobile parked outside. But he hadn't wanted to return as a Maddox orphan, he'd wanted to go back all guns blazing, everything about him proclaiming his identity, shouting for him. *I'm me – I am someone!*

"The Maddox," she said slowly, "it's all changed now. It's an old people's home." She laughed bitterly. "I guess all those Maddox orphan-kids who didn't make it can go home there to die."

"Home!" exclaimed Noel, pushing back his chair and tossing a dollar on the table for the coffee.

"Turn left at the traffic lights," she called after him as he made for the door, "about a mile and a half – make a right at Dalton's Motel, then left at the next light – you'll find it."

Noel slammed the car door shut, aware of her eyes on him behind the dull, steamy window as he switched on the ignition. For once he was indifferent to the thrill of the sound of the perfect engine as he swung the car from the small parking lot and sped off towards the light.

Noel rang the polished brass bell, glancing nervously behind him. The driveway that had always seemed so long when he was a child now looked a mere fifty yards, and the tall iron gates seemed scaled down, dragged permanently open and hanging rustily from their hinges. He heard the sound of a key being turned in the lock and fought back an impulse to turn and run.

A nice-looking young woman in a crisp white shirt and a red sweater smiled at him enquiringly. "Can I help you?" she asked.

"I hope so," replied Noel. He wondered what she would say if he told her the truth, that he needed to know *who* he was to understand *what* he was. He was a man who had everything – the chairmanship of Great Lakes Motors was his, if he wanted it. But there was no pleasure in his achievement, though he'd dreamed of it all his life. Just the way he'd dreamed of Peach – and now he'd lost her too. Life had lost its meaning. Unless he knew his past, he felt he had no future.

"I used to live here," explained Noel. Following her into the familiar hallway, he waited for its smell of polished linoleum, strong disinfectant and stale dinners to overwhelm him. But the linoleum was gone, and the drab green walls. There was a cheerful rug in the centre of the carpeted hall and bright curtains at the windows and the scent from a bowl of flowers mingled with the girl's cologne.

Hesitantly, Noel explained that he was trying to find who his parents were and that he needed to see the orphanage records.

The girl eyed him sympathetically. "I'm not sure we can help you," she said, "but I'll find out what happened to all the old files. I won't be a moment."

A pair of old ladies walked slowly through the hall, leaning on sticks and grumbling quietly to each other, and Noel watched as they vanished down the long corridor that he remembered led to the dining room. He could hear music and voices from a television somewhere upstairs and there was a new elevator behind the stairwell. Somehow he'd expected it to be unchanged, still the way it was in his memory. He paced the rug nervously.

"You're lucky," called the girl hurrying towards him, "the old files are still here. But I'm afraid I'll have to ask you to look through them yourself. It's lunchtime here and we're at our busiest. I'm sure you'll understand," she smiled.

A stack of old filing cabinets stood in the old changing rooms and there was still a faint whiff of liniment and sweat about the scarred green walls, stirring a memory of the night Noel had won the boxing trophy – the same night he'd made his bid for freedom. Walking to the cabinets, he pulled open the drawer marked "M" and began to search through the files. "Maddox Board of Governors, Maddox Financial Statements, Maddox Staff Pensions, Maddox Annual Meetings . . . Maddox Girls. Maddox Boys."

The bulky files spilled with documents and Noel pulled the one marked "Maddox Boys" from the tightly packed drawer. Carrying it under the light he began to search through it systematically. After an hour he pushed the last document wearily into the file. The papers only related to the years after the war and there were no

389

records of children before that date. Dispirited, he closed the drawer. Starting again at the top, he went through each drawer in turn, working his way through the titles of the files from "A" onwards, hoping to find something that would give him a clue as to where to look. In the very bottom drawer he came across a large black ledger, bound with red on the spine and with REGISTER printed across in gold letters. Noel knew at once that this was what he was looking for. *In here he would find who he was.*

The harsh glare from the naked lightbulb cast highlights and shadows over Noel's lean bony face as he stood beneath it, running his finger down the list of dates and names.

At an entry date 5 April 1932, he read: "11.45 p.m. Male Caucasian child abandoned on doorstep. No more than a couple of days old. In good health. No identifying documents found with him. Named NOEL MADDOX."

There it was, in two or three lines of cramped writing in a black ledger along with dozens of others. *No one knew who his mother was. No one knew his father. They didn't exist!*

Replacing the black ledger carefully in the cabinet, Noel walked to the door and switched off the light. He found the girl in the red sweater in the hall and he shook her hand and thanked her for her trouble. Then he walked through the doors and down the steps of the Maddox Charity Orphanage for the last time.

Noel drove the powerful car through the iron gates and back along the route he'd come. *The past had no more claims on him. He knew now that he was the man he himself had created.* Pushing his foot down on the pedal he sped up to the traffic light, anxious to get back to Detroit. He'd take the first plane out to New York and on to Paris. Peach would be there, and his child. They were all he loved and wanted in the world. The rest counted for nothing without them.

He slowed the car as he passed the neon-lit diner with the "For Sale" sign outside, remembering the weary blonde-haired waitress still trying for glamour in her ridiculous red stiletto shoes, and he was suddenly filled with pity for her. She was someone who had never had a chance and somehow she symbolised all he was leaving behind.

The tyres screeched as he swerved suddenly into the tiny parking lot in front of the real-estate agency.

The owner of the diner was glad to unload it for the price Noel offered, though the old boy in the real-estate agency was suspicious when Noel told him it was for the waitress at the diner and that he

should put *her* name on the documents; but he'd been too thrilled
by the commission and the extra fifty Noel put into his hand to
make a fuss. At least, thought Noel, he'd given another person a
chance in life.

73

The Indian summer had turned abruptly into chilly autumn and
gaily striped umbrellas blew across the beach caught by a gust of
wind. Huddled into a bulky sweater, Peach wandered by the water's
edge, retreating as the fierce little white-capped waves encroached
further into her territory. She'd always hated the change of season,
and those first grey skies left her with the feeling that summer's
long blue days would never return. Just as Noel would never return.

Turning, she surveyed the solitary track of footsteps along the
sand, remembering when Leonie's little cat would walk with her
along the beach and her precise track of little paw-marks. Oh
Grand-mère, Grand-mère, she thought desperately, what would
you say to me now? Shivering as the first drops of rain spattered
across the sea, she hurried back across the headland to the villa.

Charles dashed along the terrace to meet her, hurling himself
into her arms, laughing. His cheerful innocence purged her temporarily of her troubles and when she was with him she almost felt
that everything could be all right again. But being with Charles'
was only one part of her life and the long evening, when he had
gone to bed, loomed frighteningly. It was the time when she went
over and over what had happened, what *he* had done, what *she* had
said, opening up the wounds and finding them still bleeding.

Tonight it was cold and drawing the curtains Peach put a match
to the fire, watching as the flames caught the logs of olive wood.
Sitting on the rug in front of the warm red glow she felt the new
baby kicking inside her and she put a hand on her belly, smiling.
If only Noel were here, he could have felt it too . . . She glanced

longingly at the telephone, wishing he would call. But Noel hadn't called since he'd walked out a week ago. Peach checked the time on the little gilt mantelpiece clock. She knew Noel was in Detroit because the Paris office had told her so yesterday when she'd called.

The grey skies outside were already darkening into night and the wind was getting up, whistling through the trees. Peach could hear the roar of the surf as it whipped the sea into a storm and huddling closer to the fire, she wished again that Leonie were here. Leonie would know what to do. She would have been sitting opposite her, in her special chair with the little cat on her knee, watching her with amber eyes of love. What was it Leonie had said the night before her wedding? Yes, she remembered now. "Every man has his Achilles heel . . . If I'd been less concerned with myself, if I'd understood Monsieur better – then maybe I'd have acted differently. Monsieur needed my compassion as well as my love, and I never gave him that."

It was Leonie who had told her that Noel hid his feelings from the world, and Peach knew it was true. Yet she had never bothered to try to find out why. Oh, she'd known where Noel's weak spot was all right, and if there were anything left of their love, she had surely killed it with her cruel heartless words, wanting to wound Noel as he had wounded her. She would give anything to take them back, anything. It would be easy to pick up that telephone and call him, she could even catch a plane and in a matter of hours she could be with him . . .

Noel had said the woman with him that night was someone from his past – and that he had needed her. Did it mean that in some way she, as his wife, had failed Noel? Or was it his own needs he was talking about? The blind ambition that always left him feeling dissatisfied with his achievements surely stemmed from his painful search for an identity he felt he lacked. The mother who had abandoned Noel might have done it because she thought he would have a better life without her, or maybe she selfishly had no room in her life for a child. Peach glanced down at the round bulge of her pregnancy, finding it hard to imagine deserting her child. But then she was lucky, she'd never had to fight her way from poverty, she'd always had her family and comfort, and love.

"Love is all that matters," Leonie had told her, "remember that, Peach."

Reaching for the telephone, Peach dialled Noel's office number in Detroit. The secretary who had been with him for years told her that Noel was out of town. Should she ask him to call her when he returned?

"No," replied Peach. "Don't tell him. I'll call him again, tomorrow."

Curling up on the sofa she knew that Leonie was right. She loved Noel. And hadn't he said he loved her, that he needed her? Tomorrow she would call him. She prayed it wasn't too late to put things right.

74

Noel had been driving steadily through the darkness for hours watching the big car eating up the road to the south, and he peered at the signpost hoping it would say Aix but he was still fifteen kilometres away. He had stepped off the flight from New York to Paris and straight into the car, and he was desperately tired.

The small town he was approaching was already putting up its shutters for the night but the lights of a café-bar twinkled through the trees on the opposite side of the square. With the thought of a cup of strong black coffee urgently in his mind, Noel parked the car and hurried across the square. The last of the customers was just leaving as he pushed his way through the glass door. "Coffee?" he enquired hopefully.

The *patron* served him and went about his business of clearing up for the night, emptying ashtrays, wiping tables and straightening chairs while Noel sipped his coffee. God, did it taste good, scalding hot and piled with sugar just the way he liked it! He thought about his son Charles, in bed sleeping, and wondered what Peach was doing? Was she thinking of him? Or had he killed her love with his stupid selfish need to be the winner? Noel prayed it wasn't too late. He glanced at the telephone, wondering whether to call her – but what he had to say to Peach couldn't be said on the phone. He needed to hold her, he wanted to tell her that it was the memory of the first time he saw her that had coloured his whole life, that it was she who had fired his ambition. An ambition he had thought was for power, but now he knew it was also a search for love. And for her. He couldn't live without her love. He wanted her to know that she was still his golden girl, that she was his freedom – and his future.

The *patron* had put up his shutters and was waiting to lock his doors, and the lights clicked out behind him as he stepped into the deserted square.

The night was dark and windswept without a glimmer of moon or even a single star as he hurried across the street lost in his dreams of Peach. He knew how she would feel in his arms, he remembered the scent of her hair and the texture of her skin.

The car came out of nowhere, travelling fast, tossing Noel into the air as it struck him. It surged on unheeding through the little sleeping town, leaving silence.

Returning from blackness, Noel was aware of the ticking of his watch. Opening his eyes he stared into the night. He was shaking with cold, an icy freezing chill that crawled into his guts. He tried to move his arms but somehow they wouldn't move the way he wanted them to and his legs were numb. Rolling on to his stomach Noel forced himself on to his hands and knees, trying to stand. It was no good, his legs just wouldn't support him. But still he felt no pain. Was it because he was so cold? He crouched on all fours, panting in an attempt to catch his breath, but the rhythm was all wrong and somehow he couldn't get enough air into his lungs. *He had to get help!* Still on all fours, Noel crawled slowly across the empty *boules* pitch beneath the plane trees, wondering if he were bleeding. He couldn't see anything, it was so damned dark, but if he weren't bleeding then he must be all right, mustn't he? God he was cold, *so terribly cold!* Looking across the road he tried to focus on the faint glimmer of light. It was a house and the light was over its door. If he could just get himself over there someone would help him, they'd get a doctor, an ambulance. He crawled slowly towards his goal, stopping every few yards to catch a shuddering breath.

Pulling himself on to the worn scrubbed steps, Noel lifted his head and stared at the gleaming brass bellpull. The light above the door dazzled him as he forced himself on to his knees, scrabbling upwards to reach the bell . . . What was the sign by the bell there . . .? Did it say MADDOX CHARITY ORPHANAGE? The cold steel letters were cutting through his brain, tearing at him in a white heat of pain. Had he come home again?

Noel sank back on to the steps fighting the pain. If he was weak and let it control him it would take him away . . . away from the gleaming brass doorbell, away from the light. *Away from Peach for ever.* He would be back at the beginning – alone. Noel's cry of pure anger shattered the silence of the cold dark night.

75

The ringing of the telephone woke Peach and she stared blurrily at the silver clock on the bedside table. It said five o'clock! The phone shrilled again and she picked it up hastily. "Yes?" she asked.

"Madame Maddox?"

"Yes, this is she."

"Forgive me for calling so early, Madame, but I'm afraid I have some unfortunate news for you. My name is Dr Etienne Chapelle. Your husband, Monsieur Noel Maddox, has been involved in an accident and is here, in the hospital at Aix-en-Provence."

Peach snapped awake, staring in front of her at the white wall and the statue of Sekhmet. "You must be wrong," she said bewildered. "Noel is in Detroit, I know he is. This must be someone else."

"Madame, there is no mistake. Your husband was struck by a car when he was crossing the street. I'm sorry to tell you, Madame Maddox, but he is badly injured. It would be better if you came here right away."

Peach stared uncomprehendingly at the receiver, hearing his words but not wanting to believe them.

"Madame? Madame, are you there?"

"Yes," she whispered. "I'm here."

"I'm sorry this has been such a shock, but there is no other way to break this kind of news. Can we expect you at the hospital then, Madame?"

"Yes," said Peach. "Yes. Of course."

The telephone receiver purred gently as she dropped it on to the bed, pushing back the covers in a flurry of panic. The walls seemed to be closing in on her and she was stifling, choking with fear. She flung open the shutters, gasping great gulps of cold dawn air. Oh God, *Noel! Noel! It can't be true*, it *must* be some other man. Noel was safe in Detroit, dreaming up new schemes for Great Lakes Motors's future. She had planned to telephone him today. But the doctor had known who he was. He knew to call her! Then it must be Noel. Oh God! Why? Why him?

The cold grey mist rolled back in swirls of pink and oyster and gold as the first hint of sun touched the horizon. Peach thought of her son, waking to another pleasant normal day, and the new child yet to be born. Only now Noel might never come home . . . Burying her face in her hands she moaned in terror. *"Noel, Noel, don't die! You can't die! Please, oh please!"* She must get dressed, she must go to him right away.

She stared around their bedroom in panic – the room where they'd shared their love – and their anger. The room that had been Leonie's. She understood now why she had never changed it. The big white bed and the simple furnishings were all it needed. Its walls were papered with memories and Leonie's statues were its decoration.

"Oh Grand-mère," she wailed staring at the Sekhmet statue despairingly, "Grand-mère!"

The sun's first strong rays stole across the room, tipping the proud lion's head with gold and painting burnished gilt shadows across its face. The sunlit statue stared back at her with Leonie's commanding tawny eyes and Peach gazed at it transfixed. Then she ran towards it holding out her hand. "Grand-mère," she called, "Grand-mère, help us, please help us!" Gripping the statue's hand for a moment she thought it felt warm – warm as her own, and then the sun's rays shifted and Sekhmet's eyes were just blank impersonal stone and the hand only cool carved granite in hers.

The drive to Aix seemed interminable and watching the minutes ticking by on the dashboard clock Peach imagined them ticking away Noel's life. Desperately she pressed her foot harder on the accelerator, speeding through quiet early-morning country towns and villages until at last she was there.

Noel lay in a narrow hospital bed, his head shaved and bandaged. Both his legs were in traction and his right shoulder in plaster and rows and rows of large neat stitches daubed with a bright pink sterile solution criss-crossed his naked chest and abdomen. A long tube fed him blood from a dark red bottle and wires linked him to cold steel machines that blinked and bleeped, marking the beating of his heart and the processes of his brain.

The flesh seemed to have melted from Noel's face and his bones jutted sharply, making him look young and vulnerable. Stripped of his carefully invented façade, Noel looked the way he had when she had first seen him that day at the orphanage.

Peach sat by his side, holding his hand in both hers, gazing into his face. "Noel," she whispered urgently, "I don't know if you care about me or not, but I want to tell you that *I love you*. You are my life, Noel. Don't leave me now. *Think of the children, Noel*." She stared anxiously at his impassive face. He couldn't die, he just couldn't. She wouldn't let him die thinking he was unloved. "*Dammit, I love you, Noel Maddox*," she cried, her tears falling on to his hands.

Watching Noel, she wondered if he would have asked her to come to him, if he even wanted her there? Yet he was near Aix when the accident happened. He'd been driving south – to her. Peach leaned back and closed her eyes. The image of Sekhmet filled her mind, staring at her with Leonie's eyes. And she could hear Leonie reminding her again that love was all that mattered. *Noel had been coming to tell her he loved her. And Noel needed her strength now as well as her love.* Peach took Noel's hand in hers, smiling. *She was surer now than she had been of anything in her life. Noel would be all right.*

76

The villa had a festive air. Its tiled roof sparkled under the early spring sunlight and mimosa trees in the gardens spilled fluffy bright balls of yellow. Indoors bowls and baskets and heavy crystal vases were massed with lilac and iris and fragile white narcissi, and bright spears of tulips opened wide like jungle flowers in the heat, displaying flamboyant scarlet petals with soft powdery yellow and black hearts. The long table in the dining room had been covered with a fine lace cloth and a cake iced in white with delicate pale pink roses waited, exact centre. Champagne cooled in silver buckets on the marble side-table and Leonie's beautiful old Lalique glasses, treasured intact throughout the years, awaited the celebration.

The rattle of dishes and a smell of good things cooking came from the kitchen accompanied by cheerful chatter and snatches of song, and nearby two small, lithe, chocolate brown cats sprawled on the warm terrace, absorbing the sun with sensuous feline abandon.

The sea was blue and silken calm under a sky dotted with high puffed clouds and cicadas buzzed a familiar anthem, blending with the sound of church bells as the trail of cars wound its way up the hill towards the villa. Peach glanced at Noel, sitting beside her in the back of the old, chauffeur-driven dark blue de Courmont that had been Lais's for so many years. She knew he was assessing its performance as it purred smoothly up the incline, and she smiled. Not even his daughter's christening could remove Noel's thoughts completely from automobiles.

When he was finally on the mend, he'd said to her with a wry smile, "Ironic isn't it? The thing I help create almost kills me?" Then tears had rolled down his face, not tears of self-pity, but, he told her, tears for the way he'd almost destroyed them. He'd been coming to tell her that what mattered was their love, their children, their lives. He had more than any man deserved – success, love and happiness, and now with his visit to the Maddox Charity Orphanage he'd finally realised that where he came from and whatever his past was, no longer mattered.

"It's the present and our future," he'd told her, his dark grey eyes pleading for understanding.

"And what about the chairmanship of Great Lakes Motors? I know you too well, Noel. Nothing can kill your ambition."

"Ambition is part of me, it's built-in, Peach . . . but now I know where to channel it. You'll see, de Courmont will become the greatest automobile company in Europe – and one day our prestige cars will be the most sought-after on the American market. I can play my game from here, Peach – if you'll put up with me?"

As the car turned off the dusty white lane into the courtyard the baby in her arms, cool in a simple white lawn dress edged with lace, yawned and stretched sleepily and Noel and Peach smiled at each other, remembering her strong yells of protest in the church. Peach waited while Noel manoeuvred his crutches and hauled himself from the car, disdaining any help. She knew he had set this special day – the christening of his three-month-old daughter – as the day on which he would be back on his feet. No more wheel chairs, no more anger when he feared his limbs would never obey him, no more signs of invalidism.

It was in his darkest moments of pain and despair that Peach, with a shamefaced smile, had brought out the old photograph of herself wearing the dreaded callipers. "I never told you before," she'd whispered, "because I hated so much not being like everyone else that I isolated myself in my shame of those ugly steel bonds. And I thought if I told you you'd think of me as scarred and ugly . . . the way I thought of myself. But I beat it, Noel, and so will you . . . I know you will."

He'd held her in his arms, disbelieving her foolishness. "Scars and all, I'd still have loved you," he'd said, kissing her. And she thought that maybe her confession had helped him through the long days of operations to pin shattered bones, of traction and the grinding ache of physiotherapy. It would take more months of work, maybe even a year, but Noel would be his old self again. And her photograph, elegantly framed, now stood on the mantel alongside Noel's boxing trophy – with its proud inscription, 'NOEL MADDOX, Junior Boxing Champion. Maddox Charity Orphanage, 1946.

Everyone was there for the christening. Wil, sixteen and looking very grown-up, keeping young Charles under control. Jim, Gerard and Amelie, Lais and Ferdi, Leonore – even Jean-Paul had come from Brazil, and Peach couldn't help hoping that maybe this time Leonore and he might find more than friendship, they were so suited to each other. Friends and villagers crowded the terrace and the two cats perched arrogantly on the balustrade, looking like Egyptian sculptures.

It was, thought Noel, looking around as the champagne corks popped and glasses were filled, a true family celebration – and this time it was *his* family. There were no pangs of regret for that pinnacle of power in Detroit. He had his priorities right. For him, at last, his family meant everything.

Peach lifted her glass in a toast, smiling tenderly at Noel, at her family, her friends. "To Leonie," she said clearly.

"To Leonie," they called, smiling at the new infant who opened her golden amber eyes wide in surprised response to her name.

But it was the other Leonie who was in their hearts too. Never to be forgotten.